Typewriter Pub, an imprint of Blvnp Incorporated
A Nevada Corporation
1887 Whitney Mesa DR #2002
Henderson, NV 89014
www.typewriterpub.com / info@typewriterpub.com

ISBN: 978-1-64434-419-4

LIFE IN THE UNDERWORLD

BY:SAVANNAH O.

ISBN: 978-1-64434-419-4

CONTENT WARNING

The following story contains scenes that depict violence and brutality, sexual abuse of a minor, child abuse, and drug abuse.

Reader discretion is advised.

CHAPTER ONE

KALINA

Love is what scares me most in this world. Always at risk of being ruined, leaving you to suffer at the actions of someone else.

For most of my life, all I had known was struggle: the constant fear of the people around me, the worry of when I would eat my next meal, the ever-growing rage at the world, and the hatred I felt for everything in my life.

The struggle was all I had known and all I expected for my future. After years of being the girl who was beaten, I reshaped myself and became the girl who fought. It was as if that ruined child had died and I was reborn.

Everyone had scars of their own, demons that haunted them in their times of peace, enemies slithering around—all preparing for their downfall.

There was a difference between physical and mental scars, however.

Physical scars were the marks that got left on someone's body, engraved into the skin like writing on a tombstone. They marred what was once perfect smoothness into a rough, horrid past.

Mental scars, though, were far worse. They were the scars others could not see. Mental scars were wounds that had never fully healed, playing away like a piano in an orchestra for years, non-stop.

I had both.

As a child, I remembered dreaming of a knight in shining armour who would come and save me from my life. Someone who would take me away from the woman who was my mother.

Back when I believed there was a god—who was not a total arse—I would pray every night that he would send my messiah. But, like every child must learn someday, knights in shining armour were only in fairy tales.

*   *   *

The jail cell door opened with a clang, and I was guided inside by the guard. He removed the cuffs from my wrists behind my back and left the tiny room, letting the cell door slam shut behind me. Smirking to myself, I leant back on the concrete wall and stared at all the cells below. The chatter of long-term inmates drowned the cries of the newly convicted.

The new kids always suffered from homesickness during the first week. Most of them were spoiled brats who could no longer use Daddy's money or Mummy's tits to escape a sentence. Those like me, however, were grateful to be locked away in juvenile detention. At least here, we had shelter, clothing, showers, and food on a daily basis.

The government forced teachers to come and educate us, yet it rarely worked.

"What're you smirking about?" my cellmate and current best friend, Rose, asked.

Rose was the typical runaway who had nicked one too many things. She had been sentenced to two weeks in juvie during the first time she got caught. This was her third, and we had formed a very close bond.

"I nicked his cigarettes." I chuckled, pulling a brand-new pack from my navy prison clothes.

Giggling, Rose chucked me the lighter from beneath her pillowcase and hopped down from the top bunk. The two of us shared a cigarette, trying to make it last as long as possible.

The guards started their rounds an hour later, telling us it was time for bed, and then the lights went out. I lay down on the bottom bunk, staring at the photos I had tucked to the underside of Rose's bunk.

One was a photo of me, my mother, and my brother. We were huddled together under a tree in the park after playing football for hours. My hair had grown considerably since then, now curling tightly down to my waist. My feminine figure had also become more pronounced with age. Unfortunately, I hadn't grown any taller, leaving me at five-foot-one.

"Kal?" Rose's voice was quieter than usual.

"Yeah," I answered, rubbing my tired eyes.

"Do you ever miss the outside world?" she asked, leaning down to look at me from the top bunk.

I took a moment to ponder her question. After everything I'd seen beyond the barbed-wire fences and tall trees that blocked the prison from the view of the city, there were times in my life I wished I could be anywhere but the outside world.

To most people in here, this place was a prison. To me, it was a sanctuary. My sixteen-year-old self had learned that the second I stepped through the gates eight months ago.

If it weren't for this prison and the security it offered to keep us inside, I had no idea where I'd be now. But I knew one thing: there was no way in hell I'd be safe.

And I was due to be released in a month . . .

"No," I answered.

Rose fell asleep an hour later, but I remained awake. I always had struggled to sleep, especially after everything that had happened. I was used to the constant tiredness, the pull of sleep fighting against my constantly overthinking brain.

I often wondered what my life would have been like if things had been different. What if my mother had been an actual parent, someone I could look up to and aspire to be. If my brother were still around to protect and guide me. What if the family I longed for were real.

When I was little, I often heard stories about my father from my older brother. Apparently, he had been a good parent, far better than our mother, and he had custody of our other brothers. Me, being the child with abandonment issues, refused to listen any more.

Yet when you're stuck in a cell with no one to talk to for hours, you can't help but conjure fantasies in your head.

All the childhood dreams that never became a reality had their chance to break free from the cage I had locked them in.

But then, once again, I was pulled back into the real world. My mind reminded me that in a few weeks I would be released, left to survive on the streets of Manchester all alone—or, even worse—be trapped in foster care until I turned eighteen.

I would gladly live on a park bench again if it meant I wouldn't have to deal with a foster family.

CHAPTER TWO

CHRISTOPHER

The dangers of living in the underworld were not unknown to my family and me. For years, we held the highest respect and most enviable power and continued to do so. Ever since that night, though, I had always maintained strong defence around my family and myself.

Love in the life of the mafia was beyond dangerous, no matter who you were—whether a simple associate or the don, like me. As a child, my father always reminded me of the importance of having an heir when running our business. The second I married the woman I thought I would die with, I made sure there would be an heir to take over my role. But, unlike my father, I would not pressure any child of mine into this business, so we had more children.

Eventually, she started having them because the only real connection we had in our relationship was sexual. Then, one day, I found out she had betrayed me, and we divorced months later. During the battle for our children, I won full custody of all of our boys. Then, one day, while I was visiting Manchester on a business deal, I ran into her while she was working at a strip club. I hadn't seen her since that day and didn't plan to.

My eldest son, Mateo, and I were working in my office on legal business. Due to the amount of money we earned in the mafia, we needed a front to cover our illegal activities, which happened to bring in a lot more money than we had originally planned. We were the second-best mafia in the world, following closely behind the Irish Mob.

"Dad, the fashion business is losing money," Mateo said, placing documents on my desk.

Today, we were working in the Montessori Building, with large windows overlooking the business district of L.A. I took the documents from the surface of the desk and saw we were losing seven percent a month from our projected income.

"We're going to need someone to fix this," I commented, leaning back in my seat.

"Any ideas?" Mateo asked, rolling up the sleeves of his white button-up shirt, revealing his tattooed, tanned skin.

I shook my head, and Mateo placed the documents into the sorting pile. This meant we would send the work over to my secretary, who would provide options for fixing the problems.

We worked until nightfall and drove home in his matte-black Ferrari.

The drive home was short and silent. After a hard day's work, we had little to converse about. The black iron gates of our home opened as Mateo's car approached, the guards recognizing him immediately. He drove up the long driveway, past the rose bushes and across the gravel, and parked outside our garage, which was lined with an impressive collection of cars.

Mateo went to his room while I headed to the kitchen, where I found the rest of my sons. Antonio was pouring himself a glass of orange juice, his eyes snapping to mine at the sound of my footsteps on the hardwood floors. Stefano sat at the breakfast bar with his sketchbook, as usual. Tristan was at the kitchen table, copying what looked to be homework from Tommaso's chemistry book. The two of them always exchanged homeworks. Tristan was older but had been held back a year due to missing so many classes and receiving multiple suspensions.

"Evening, Dad," Antonio said, taking a sip from his glass.

Tommaso offered me one of his joyful smiles; Tristan just nodded and turned back to his copying, while Stefano didn't move at all.

"Boys." I offered a small smile—which was a lot more than I would give to others.

They all returned to what they were doing. I grabbed a crystal glass from the cupboard and filled it with some bourbon.

I took a seat next to my two youngest, glancing down at the homework Tristan was copying. I silently chuckled to myself when I saw that Tristan was copying the wrong sheet. He looked up at me, momentarily confused, and then back down at his work. Then it was as if something had clicked in his head.

"Oh, for fuck sake, you fucking piece of fucking shit chemistry!" he yelled, crumpling the piece of paper and throwing it behind his head.

"Watch your fucking language," Antonio said instantly.

All of us just gave Antonio a look, and he hung his head in regret. Then he lifted it back up and pointed at me. I only smirked happily.

"You taught us this shit," he commented, glaring at his brothers, who were laughing.

"And I'm not scolding you for it," I answered, taking a sip of my drink before placing the glass on the table.

As I was about to leave the room, Stefano called out to me.

The thing about Stefano was that he didn't talk often, but when he did, it was only a few sentences, spoken in his deep-toned voice. Whenever I got the chance to hear my boy speak, I always took it. I wanted him to emerge from that shell he had retreated into so long ago.

"Someone overseas was calling for you earlier. I left their number on the fridge."

Walking back into the kitchen, I took the number off the post-it-note and dialled it into my phone. It rang for a second before the call was answered.

I placed it on speaker, leaving the phone on the countertop as I grabbed an apple from the fruit basket. Mateo walked in, wearing black sweats and running a towel through his wet hair.

"Hello, this is Officer Roberts with the Manchester Police Department," the woman said, her British accent clear.

"This is Christopher Montessori. You called my home earlier today," I said, glancing at each of my children, who raised their hands in innocence.

In other words: *we didn't do it.*

"Oh, yes. Hello, sir. I am sorry to inform you that your ex-wife, Angelica Otto, passed away from an overdose earlier this morning," the officer continued.

It seemed the air left the kitchen at her words. Despite everything—from kicking her out of my life to banishing her from my mafia and home—she was still the mother of my children. I glanced at all of my boys; none of them seemed affected by the news. *I mean, she had left seventeen years ago.*

After she gave birth to Tommaso, she left the hospital while I was fetching our other sons from home to welcome their new brother. I hadn't seen her since, except for that night in the strip club.

"Right, well, thank you for telling us." I was about to end the call when she frantically asked me to wait.

"Sir, I also called to ask you what you wish to do about your daughter?"

All of us frowned in confusion, wondering what the officer was talking about. As far as I was aware, I had five children—all boys.

"Daughter?" I enquired, placing down my half-eaten apple.

"Yes, sir. Kalina Montessori. You're listed as her father on her birth certificate."

Antonio immediately started typing and searching on his computer.

"I'm sorry, Officer, but I'm going to have to put you on hold for a moment." Before she could respond, I put her on hold and went to stand behind Antonio, the rest of my sons gathering around us.

With technology this advanced, every detail our hardware provided was current and mostly factual—and let me just say, this girl was trouble.

Name: Kalina Montessori
Age: 17
Birth Date: November 21, 2005
Physical Description: Brunette, blue eyes, 5'1"
Mother: Angelica Otto
Father: Christopher Montessori

The file also detailed her criminal and medical records, along with a list of all the foster homes she had stayed in.

"Holy shit," Tommaso muttered. "I have a twin?"

"Seems so," Mateo said, sensing I was too shock to speak.

"How did we never know about her?" Antonio asked, glancing at me.

It was then I noticed the rest of my boys looking at me for answers.

"I was never allowed to see the scans. She refused. I wasn't allowed in the delivery room either," I said. "She must've seen this as her final revenge when she knew I was kicking her out. She took my daughter as payback."

Within seconds, Stefano had my phone in his hand. He spoke in a deadly, calm tone. "Where can we find her?"

CHAPTER THREE

KALINA

The cell door clanged open again, and we all spilled outside, lining up for the yard. Guards shepherded us through the halls. The doors at the end led to the fenced-in gardens.

Rose and I made a beeline for our spot by the gates, sitting down on the wooden bench and watching the cars roll in and out of the kids' prison. We lit up, the guards too indifferent to bother stopping us.

What caught my attention, though, was the massive limousine rolling through the gates. As the vehicle parked, three large figures emerged.

They were all well over six feet tall. The one on the left had sleeves of tattoos that continued onto his hands. His muscled arms marked him clearly as a regular at the gym. His black hair was combed back from his face, and his eyes were a dark, stormy blue.

The second man, slightly smaller and less muscular, had far fewer tattoos—none on his hands or neck. His hair was the same dark brown as my own, his eyes matching the tone of his hair.

And then the last one. Older, taller, but slightly less muscular than the other two. His hair was salt-and-pepper. The only wrinkles on his face were the crow's feet by his familiar light-blue eyes. His black beard was neatly trimmed, and his black turtleneck and trousers made the gold watch and rings gleam.

They clocked us straight away. The moment they set eyes on me, they froze. I blew out a puff of smoke, and the youngest-looking one blinked himself out of it. The other two followed, slower, still looking well shook.

"Freaks," Rose mumbled, taking the cigarette from my fingers and dragging on it herself.

"No shit." I chuckled, man-spreading on the bench as the autumn breeze of England swept cold air across the yard.

The two of us sat there, snickering, watching the little kids' eyes dart around, terrified they'd get stabbed. It wasn't until we were being herded back to the cells that a guard stopped me in the middle of the line.

He spoke to the guard leading us before beckoning me over after calling my name. When I was in front of him, he spun me around, cuffed my hands, and led me down a different corridor.

"You going to tell me where we're off to?" I asked after another turn.

"The warden wants to see you," he grumbled, gripping my arm more harder than needed.

Once we left the cell block, the desks of the office staff came into view. All of them had computers and printers, papers scattered everywhere.

He stopped at a large wooden door, knocked twice, and a soft voice told us to come in. He opened it and walked me inside.

"Take the cuffs off," a man with a deep, brooding voice said.

Turning to the back of the room, I spotted the three men who had arrived in the limousine. The oldest one was the speaker, his eyes burning into the metal around my wrists.

The guard glanced at the warden, who nodded. He removed the cuffs and left at her signal.

"Montessori, good to see you out of solitary." The warden smiled, her blonde highlights framing her pale face.

"Good to see you divorced, finally." I smiled back, noticing the white line where her wedding ring used to be.

She offered me a small smile, aware I knew of her situation. Rising from her desk, she walked around to the sofa was and patted the cushioned seat for me to join her.

Leaning back into the velvet, I took another look at the three men, all staring intensely at me. I waited for someone to speak.

"Montessori, your mother passed away two days ago," the warden began. When she realised I didn't care, she continued, "As you are seventeen, you're still in need of a legal guardian. This is your father." She nodded towards the group.

My head snapped to the men in the corner—the older one clearly the father she was talking about.

"He hired a lawyer, went to the courts, and was able to reduce your sentence. He is taking you home today."

The more I looked at him, the more I noticed our similarities. I had his nose, his eyes, and his curly hair. I had always known I got my curvy figure from my mother, along with the brown color of my hair.

"I've had your things bagged up and ready to go, so you can change into your clothes," the warden said.

I said nothing, my mind racing with questions—whys and hows—while weighing the prison's "protection" against what I might actually gain from this arrangement.

I stood up and left the office. On her secretary's desk, I found my bag of clothes. In the toilets, I changed out of my navy prison uniform and into my clothes. I wore black bicycle shorts, a long-sleeved white crop top, a black, white, and red racer jacket, and a pair of black Nike trainers.

I left the room, putting in my helix hoop and my three other ear piercings. The three men—including my father—were in the waiting room as I finished with the final piercing: a nose ring.

"Kalina, I just wanted to say—"

"Do you have any food?" I interrupted him.

Shock flashed across his face, but once he regained his composure, he replied, "We can pick up McDonald's on the way to the airport."

Nodding, I followed the guard out the front door, hearing footsteps behind me. Moments later, the three of them were walking beside me, their towering heights dwarfing my own.

The driver, dressed in a suit and tie, opened the limousine door. The two other men climbed inside, and my father nodded for me to follow. Once we were all seated on the black leather seats, the door closed, and the driver pulled away.

Through the back window, I watched the place I had called home for almost a year disappear behind the trees and bushes. I had no idea where I was going.

But as long as I wasn't going back to prison or the foster system, I would be fine.

CHAPTER FOUR

CHRISTOPHER

The brown-haired little girl had eyes identical to my own. She held a cigarette between her fingers as she stared at me and my sons. I took note of her small height—far too small compared to myself and her brothers. Even her mother had quite a bit of height. She had curly brown hair and a golden tan to her skin. She also had sticker tattoos on her left forearm, all of them—no doubt—holding their own meaning.

I also saw the scars.

One started from the left side of her forehead, slitting through her eyebrow and down to the middle of her high left cheekbone. I saw the scars littering the back of her right hand and her right bicep. There was a long knife scar that started at her collarbone and disappeared beneath her navy prison uniform.

When we saw her file, we decided to only view the basic and medical information so we could keep her safe. We didn't read her criminal history, deciding she should get to tell us herself. Her medical file held only her birth certificate and the required infant and toddler injections. Nothing more, nothing less.

There was no explanation for the scars or the loneliness in those pale blue eyes.

She walked with confidence and pride, as if anyone who tried to take her down would fail miserably. I saw straight through her fake smiles and false displays of happiness. I had no doubt Antonio and Mateo did too.

* * *

KALINA

"Kalina, what do you want to order?" the man with the tattoo sleeves asked.

"A box of twenty-piece chicken nuggets with extra-large chips and a cheeseburger with black coffee," I recited, not bothering that I didn't even know his name. I was starving.

"Mateo, I'm the oldest brother," the guy with the tattoo sleeves said.

"And I'm Antonio, the second oldest," the other unidentified man added.

There was no drive-thru, so Mateo got out of the car and ordered my food for me. A few minutes later, he came back and handed me my meal.

As I munched away, I noticed we were getting closer and closer to the airport.

"Where are we going?" I asked, glancing out the window at a plane landing on the runway.

"Home," my father answered.

"And where is your home?" I continued, growing uneasy around these people who were technically strangers.

"L.A. Our jet's waiting for us," my father said, giving me a small smile.

"What's your name?" I asked, not comfortable calling him my father.

"Christopher. You can call me that if you wish," he said, a hint of disappointment in his tone.

I just stared at him before continuing to eat my McDonald's. The drive remained quiet, the three of them glancing at me occasionally while I just ate. Eventually, we arrived at the hangar, and all four of us piled out of the car.

The private jet was completely black, with white interiors visible through the windows and open aeroplane door. A boy, maybe a little older than me, stood by the steps. He wore a white button-up shirt with a vest, paired with slacks. He greeted Christopher first, as he was the first to climb the steps.

"Good morning, Miss Montessori," the boy said.

He had light blond hair and fair brown eyes, his accent slightly broken English. He sounded Dutch.

"Goedemorgen," I replied. My Dutch was a bit rusty, but I reckoned it was understandable. *(Good morning.)*

"Spreek jij Nederlands?" he asked, a small blush forming on his cheeks. *(You speak Dutch?)*

I just nodded, sidestepped a gobsmacked Christopher, and took a seat in the corner of the plane.

Antonio started chuckling when he saw which seat I'd taken, while Mateo just grumbled under his breath. Judging by that, I guessed the chair belonged to Mateo—and that I had stolen it.

Not the only thing I've stolen.

I finished the rest of my meal and dumped the rubbish in a bin before leaning back in my seat. My feet started tapping out of sheer boredom.

It seems Antonio noticed, as he asked, "Do you have any games on your phone?"

"I don't have a phone." I chuckled, man-spreading across the fine leather seat.

"What? Your mother never gave you one?" Christopher asked, his eyebrows furrowed in confusion.

"Please." I laughed. "With her addiction to drugs, there was no money for a phone."

The three of them exchanged odd looks before Mateo pulled out his phone and handed it to me. "Download whatever you want. It's a long flight."

I gave him an appreciative smile and started downloading games to pass the time.

A few hours later, Antonio and Mateo went into the bedrooms while the sun sunk beneath the fluffy white clouds. Later, when Antonio returned, Christopher took the former's bedroom and went to sleep.

Antonio sat beside me and read a book. I just stared out the window, clouds below soft and fluffy. Some time passed before he closed the book and looked at me with a curious expression.

"Have you ever flown before?" Antonio asked, leaning back on the cushioned leather sofa.

"No, only ever travelled by motorbike, car, and boat," I answered, picking up the glass of orange juice the blushing Dutch boy had brought me earlier.

"And where have you travelled to?" Antonio continued, smiling a little as I rattled off the places.

"The Netherlands, Italy, Spain, France, Poland, Belgium, Germany, Austria, China, Monaco . . . especially Ireland and Scotland."

"So you've had your fair share of travels." Antonio chuckled, folding his large arms across his broad chest. "How did you get there if Angelica was hooked on drugs?"

"I've got certain friends, who've got certain friends, who love me to bits and convinced them to take me along." I smiled, thinking of the wonderful times I'd had with my real family.

"Do you still see them?"

My eyes snapped to the door of one of the bedrooms, where Mateo's voice had come from.

He had changed suits, and his hair was slightly messier. There was a dangerous look on his face, but also a look of curousity.

"Most of them got arrested with me. Since they weren't blood-related and are known criminals, they weren't allowed to visit." I sighed, wishing I could see their faces again.

Mateo nodded silently, while Antonio clearly bit his tongue. I leaned back and relaxed for the remainder of the flight.

Christopher returned after some time and didn't ask about the tense silence between the three of us. He did, however, give the brothers a look that said they would discuss it later.

Hiding was always a skill of mine. It started off as a simple game of hide and seek, but later, it progressed to so much more.

The sounds of heavy footsteps mixed with high heels clattering on hardwood, the smell of alcohol and cigarette smoke filling the house I lived in, the twisting of the squeaky doorknob—they all played an essential role in teaching me the art of disappearing.

Unfortunately, hiding became less of a game and more of a necessity. Without it, the places I would have ended up would have been utterly horrific.

If it weren't for those friends I made and the families I was welcomed into, I would have spent my teenage years in worse places—or in a coffin. The comfort they had brought me was unlike anything I had ever experienced, and I was not willing to lose it.

Moments later, the plane landed.

"Can I use your phone to call someone?" I asked Mateo as we made our way to the car.

He squinted. "Who are you calling?"

"Some friends of Daniel's."

At the mention of his name, all of them stiffened, guilty and remorseful expressions flashing across their faces.

"We'll wait in the car," Christopher said, and the three of them climbed into the waiting black jeep.

I typed in the number Daniel had made me memorise and waited anxiously as the phone rang. After a moment, he answered, his voice just as deep and scary as I remembered.

"Who the fuck is this?"

"That's no way to speak to a 'little girl,' Teddy," I scolded playfully, a smirk making its way onto my face.

"Kiddo?" His tone was full of hope and joy, cracking as he spoke.

"It's me." My eyes pooled with tears, the pain of hearing his voice creeping back into my heart after so many months.

"Holy shit," he muttered. "GUYS! IT'S THE KID!"

The sound of thundering footsteps echoed in the background, and I could hear it even over the phone. Cheers and shouts erupted from all my friends, along with the occasional slap for fighting over the phone. It didn't end until Teddy yelled that he'd put it on speaker if they let him talk.

"Kalina, where are you?" Teddy asked, fear seeping in his words.

When I didn't answer, he repeated my name, sharper, almost provoking me.

"L.A."

And the screams and shouts returned . . .

You'd think grown men would be a bit more mature.

"QUIET!" Teddy barked, and silence fell. "Kal, how did you get there? Who are you with?"

"Angelica's dead. The cops called my father, and he's taken custody of me," I explained, wishing I could be with them. "He's some sort of rich businessman. He brought two of my brothers to come and get me, and I think there's more."

"How are you calling us? Did they give you one of their phones?" Teddy asked, the sound of keyboards clacking and chatter buzzing in the background.

"Yeah, they're waiting in the car to take me to their house."

I heard him sigh before speaking again. "We've got people in L.A. now. I'll let them explain everything to you. Go to the L.A. Sunrise Mall as soon as you can. I'll have someone there to meet you."

"Ok. I'll find a way to get there," I said, a small smile on my face.

"Kiddo, take care of yourself," Teddy whispered, his voice cracking slightly once more.

Closing my eyes, I wiped a tear that had escaped before answering, "I always do." Then I hung up.

Once I had composed myself, I turned and saw the three of them in the car, their faces etched with worry as they peered out the windows.

I opened the door and climbed in, struggling slightly due to my short stature, and handed Mateo his phone back.

Antonio noticed the tear I had wiped away but chose not to say anything.

The driver pulled away from the tarmac, and time passed before we reached the city—traffic that lived up to every stereotype of American congestion.

Almost as bad as the bloody M25!

Eventually, we arrived at a mansion in a suburban area, where children played and rode bikes and women tended their gardens while the men washed their cars.

As if it weren't stereotypical enough, the driveway we pulled into had a guard stationed beside the massive black iron gates.

The mansion itself was grey-bricked, with white window panes, dark wooden doors, and white outdoor lights. Fancy sports cars were parked outside the garage, each costing hundreds of thousands, no doubt.

As we piled out of the tall jeep, the front door opened, and three people stepped outside.

The first man was almost entirely covered in tattoos, some curving around the sides of his head and tracing the edges of his face. Though patches of bare skin remained, it was clear he had a tattoo addiction. He stood around six-foot-five, the same height as Antonio, with the same brown eyes as my mother. His hair, shaved on the sides but long on top, was black like Mateo's. Muscles were obvious, though less pronounced than the others. His face was stoic and empty, as if nothing could shock him anymore.

The second was a glaring teenager. He looked maybe a year or two older than me. His hair was a dark brown, almost black, with the same eye colour as the first man. The muscle he had was phenomenal for his age, along with his six-foot-four height. Just a guess, but he looked an inch shorter than the first one. It was almost as if he lived in the gym. The glare on his face was not aimed at me; it was directed at the world. His nose was crooked, clearly broken multiple times.

Finally, the last boy looked like the male version of myself, with curly brown hair and light blue eyes. He was the same height as the previous boy but had less muscle on his arms, taking on a lankier form. A bright smile spread across his face as his eyes—identical to my own—landed on me. He had a silver septum piercing and a silver stud in his left ear.

The boy wasted no time running over to the four of us. What I didn't expect was him to charge at me, though. He picked me up and spun me around. Fortunately for me—and not him—my instincts kicked in.

"Kalina! Stop!" Antonio yelled frantically.

I had the boy in a chokehold, having snuck under his arm and climbed onto his back. Years of training and street fighting had taught me a trick or two.

By the time Antonio managed to drag the boy out of my hold, he had turned a steady purple, frantically fighting for oxygen in his deprived lungs.

The glaring boy was stomping forward, but he was stopped by the looks Christopher and the boy I had choked gave him.

"M-my bad." The boy coughed. "Didn't think that through."

"Kalina, this is Tommaso, your twin brother," Mateo said, shaking his head as he looked at the boy.

Of course I have a twin brother.

May as well throw in a biologically related unicorn at this point.

"You can explain that later." I sighed, already tired of this stressful day.

"Right," Christopher mumbled. "Anyway, that is Tristan—he's a year older than you both—and that's Stefano. He's twenty-three."

The one with the glare was Tristan, and Stefano was the walking tattoo art.

A yawn accidentally slipped from my lips, and Antonio, Tommaso, and Christopher chuckled. Mateo offered a small smile, Tristan stopped glaring, and Stefano didn't show any change of expression.

“I’ll show you to your room,” Antonio said and smiled, walking towards the house and beckoning me to follow.

The interior was similar to the exterior—dark oak doors, hardwood floors, and light grey walls. Photo frames lined the walls, all of them showing them as a happy-ish family. After climbing the curved staircase, I was taken down a hallway with four doors.

“Tommaso’s room is on the left.There’s a bathroom next to him, but all the rooms have an en-suite anyway. You’re next to Tristan at the end of the hall.”

Antonio opened the door for me and revealed a stunning white-walled bedroom. The carpet was light grey. The California king bed had black bedding with four plump cushions and two pillows. A vanity sat in the corner, next to a desk by the large windows.

Two doors were beside each other—one for an empty walk-in wardrobe, the other for a white marble bathroom. A grand TV was mounted on the wall opposite the bed, and a small sofa sat in the corner of the room by the balcony.

“Is this okay for you?” Antonio asked, nerves showing in his tone.

This was more than anyone had ever given me.

I’m not going to tell him that, though.

“It’s fine.”

CHAPTER FIVE

KALINA

Antonio left not long after I collapsed on the bed in a ball of exhaustion. The mattress was unlike anything I had ever felt before—as cliché as that sounded—it felt like a literal cloud.

Definitely better than the beds in juvie.

For the first time in eight months, I managed to log back into the old Netflix account my friends and I shared, and I continued my rewatch of *Friends* right where I had left off before the arrest.

Hours passed before a knock sounded at the bedroom door. After telling them to come in, Tommaso poked his head through.

"Hi!" he chirped happily.

"Hi . . ." I replied, watching him cautiously as he plopped onto the end of my bed.

"I brought these for you since you don't have any clothes at the moment."

Taking the clothes from him, I saw a pair of cycling shorts, a Marvel tee, grey joggers, a black button-up and a vest, and some socks and undies still in their packets.

"I bought the boxers last week so they haven't been worn. The rest are clothes from when I was twelve, but I think they will fit you," he explained, his face turning slightly red.

Biting back a smile, I offered a small grin and thanked him.

"Extra large," I read aloud, making him go beetroot red, "Congratulations."

A loud chuckle broke past his lips, forcing one to escape my own. Out of all of these brothers, Tommaso seemed to be the easiest-going.

"We're going to take you to the mall this weekend so you can get your own clothes," Tommaso said, shuffling back against the headboard.

"I don't have any money for clothes," I said, already thinking of ways I could nick some.

"Please, Dad's wanted a little girl his entire life. He'd buy the whole damn mall if you asked." Tommaso laughed, placing his arm behind his head.

"In that case, can we go to the Sunrise Mall tomorrow?" I asked, thinking it perfect opportunity.

"Sure, it's a pretty famous mall with fancy-ass stores," Tommaso said, totally missing the fact that I already knew the name after living half a world away my entire life.

"Phoebe and Joey are fit as fuck," he commented, unpausing the TV.

We spent the next hour watching *Friends*, laughing at the screen and sniggering whenever Matt LeBlanc appeared. It had been months since I had such a peaceful moment with someone I barely knew.

And it was rather refreshing.

When it turned six o'clock, Tommaso switched off the TV and lifted himself from the bed. I watched as he walked towards the door and turned back to me.

"It's dinner time. Let's go."

With that, I stood up and followed him out of the room. The hallways were long and empty, making our footsteps echo. Once downstairs, he guided me through a grand and luxurious living room to a pristine dining room.

Everyone else was already seated, and the food was spread across the table. Tommaso took the seat beside Tristan, leaving only two seats vacant at the ends—beside Christopher or Mateo at either head.

I took the seat beside Mateo, simply because he was closer to the meatballs.

Food first.

Once we were all seated, everyone began piling food onto their plates. I noticed Tommaso and I were the only ones who had water. Everyone else had either wine or whiskey.

As Tommaso took a sip, he instantly spat it out across the table, frantically fanning his mouth. Tristan was laughing his arse off at his reaction.

"Vodka, you fucking bastard." Tommaso reached over and took my water, chugging it down as he fought the burn of the alcohol.

While Antonio was scolding Tristan, Stefano showed no interest. Mateo and Christopher only smirked. I took the glass of vodka and drank it with ease.

Silence filled the room as they all stared at me, mouths agape, as I placed the empty glass down.

"What the fuck," Tristan muttered.

"What?" I replied. "I haven't had a drink in eight months."

"And it'll be your last one till you turn twenty-one," Antonio commented, eyes still wide as he stared at the empty glass.

"Twenty-one? What the fuck?" I said, surprised.

"This is America. Twenty-one is the legal drinking age," Mateo informed me, chuckling slightly at my expression.

"Fuck off. I've been drinking my whole life," I said, taking the glass of whisky Stefano was pushing closer. He offered me a wink as I took a sip.

"Wha-no-you're a chi-DAD!" Antonio said, fumbling his words and waving his hands around.

Christopher just sat at the head of the table, smirking as he sipped his own alcoholic beverage. "As long as she drinks at home, where we can make sure she's safe like we do Tommaso and Tristan, I don't give a shit."

"I hate all of you," Antonio sulked, stabbing his fork into his meatballs.

The rest of them chuckled at him while I just ate my food. Within minutes, I had finished my meal, not used to such wonderful food.

"Do you want any more, Kalina?" Mateo asked when he saw my empty plate.

"No thanks," I replied, sipping Stefano's whisky.

Later, once everyone had finished, Christopher rose from his seat and dismissed everyone—but not before asking me to stay behind for a moment.

The brothers went their separate ways. Christopher sat down again and motioned for me to do the same.

First, he slid an iPhone box across the table.

"I think this is well overdue."

I checked the box, and it was an iPhone 14, along with AirPods, a charger, and a screen protector.

I stared at it in shock—no one had ever bought me something so expensive before.

"Thank you," I muttered, looking up to find a soft smile on his face.

"It's only fair you receive the same things your brothers do." He stood from his seat and walked around the table to sit beside me.

"Now, I'm not going to sit here and tell you rules about relationships or say you can't have any friends who are boys, because it would be unfair and sexist of me to do so. But the crimes must stop. From what I understand, your mother was neglectful, so stealing was a way to survive, but you have support and money now. You can have friends of any gender because, frankly, I don't care. Boyfriends . . . as long as they treat you right and your brothers and I approve, that's fine.

The drinking, as long as one of us are with you so you're safe. No drugs whatsoever. Swearing? I don't care. If you're going to have sex—which I hope you don't—be safe, and please, not in the house. I can't promise you won't get shit from Antonio about those, though. And if you're going out, let us know, and if you're staying out for the night, call first."

I acknowledged Christopher's words and waited for anything else. When he didn't add anything, I nodded in understanding.

"I understand Tommaso gave you some clothes to wear for now, and he mentioned you wish to go to Sunrise Mall tomorrow? How do you know of this place?" he asked, catching what Tommaso had missed.

"There was this rich bitch in school who went on a shopping spree while on holiday. It was the first place I thought of," I answered, thinking quickly on my feet—becoming a useful skill.

"Right . . ." he muttered. "Well, we'll get you some decorations too so you can design your room. Do you have a driver's license?" His interest seemed piqued.

"Real or fake? I have both," I answered honestly.

He shook his head with a laugh before giving me a small smile. "Get to bed. I'll have some of the boys take you shopping tomorrow."

I left my seat and ran up the stairs, smirking internally as I had finally found a way to get to the mall. As I ran, I noticed multiple hidden security cameras along the walls and ceilings.

Time to see my boys again . . .

I didn't remember much of my happy years. I recalled the photo I had on my bunk bed—that was the only happy memory I had with my mother. After that, the only joy I received came from my brother and our friends.

My real family.

The day Daniel introduced me to them, I thought they would hurt me, like so many other men did. But they did the complete opposite. They healed the wounds she had left, physically and mentally. They had fixed what so many others had broken.

Even after we lost Daniel, they never turned their backs on me. In fact, they became even more protective of me. After the age of twelve, I never returned to Angelica. I would spend my night either at Teddy's house or in the bedroom they made for me in the clubhouse. That was how much they did for me—a bunch of bikers gave up a hook-up room just to give me a place to sleep.

There was nothing they wouldn't do for me, and nothing I wouldn't do for them.

Hell, I got sentenced to a year in juvie for them.

Moonlight shone through the large windows as I rose from the bed with a screeching stretch. After a shower and changing into my gym gear, I checked the clock—two o'clock. Sighing, I began exercising to pass the time. Every morning, I followed the same routine:

A hundred sit-ups, two hundred press-ups, two minutes of squats, fifty Russian twists, a ten-minute plank, fifty lunges per leg, and hour of weightlifting, and shadowboxing until dawn, throwing punches into the air since there was no punch bag. I didn't even know if they had a gym with all the equipment here.

By the time I finished, it was five o'clock, and there were already movement downstairs. I took off the joggers and Marvel T-shirt Tommaso had given me, showered again, and changed.

I wore a cami-top style vest with the black button-up tied loosely in a small knot, and the bicycle shorts. Tying my hair into a high ponytail, I left the room and made my way down the stairs.

I went through the dining room into the kitchen and Christopher, Tristan, and Mateo already there. Christopher was frying some eggs, Mateo was typing away on a computer at the side, and Tristan was gulping down what appeared to be black coffee.

"Oh, morning, sweetheart," Christopher said, looking up from the stove.

"Hi," I mumbled.

Everything about this was so domestic. Half of the family was awake whilst the rest slept. The father was cooking breakfast, the eldest was busy with something, and the younger one just sat there, looking pretty.

"You're not allergic to anything, are you?" Christopher asked, placing an egg sandwich in front of Tristan.

"Vegan food," I answered, earning a chuckle from Tristan and a deadpan look from the other two.

I sat a seat away from Tristan on the kitchen island. The bar stool was firm leather and could swivel.

A few minutes later, Christopher put an egg and bacon sandwich in front of me after stopping me from getting my own breakfast.

"Do you have any tea?" I asked, craving for a cuppa.

"Sorry," Mateo said, sipping juice from the fridge.

"Il tè è una merda," Tristan muttered, raising his coffee cup to his lips. *(Tea is shit.)*

"Tristan, *lasciala stare*," Mateo said, giving Tristan a pointed look. *(Tristan, leave her be.)*

I ate the rest of my breakfast in silence, simply enjoying the well-seasoned and well-cooked meal. Before I went to juvie, the mother of the club—Teddy's sister—would bring breakfast every day on her way to work. Waffles, scrambled eggs with toast, and tea to last us all day.

Something I dearly missed.

When I finished, I took my plate to the dishwasher. Stefano and Antonio were approaching the kitchen when I turned around in the doorway.

"A proposito, penso che preferiresti che bevessi il tè piuttosto che lo sperma," I said to Tristan, just after Mateo mentioned we would leave for the mall in an hour. *(By the way, I think you'd prefer me drinking tea than cum.)*

I didn't know why I said it. Probably just for the satisfaction of seeing his face.

Walking up the stairs back to my bedroom, I smirked at the sound of a yell and a plate smashing against the wall. Then came thundering footsteps chasing after me.

"KALINA!" Tristan screamed from the other end of the hallway.

I ignored him completely—until a firm hand gripped my shoulder, spinning me around and pinning me to the wall. It wasn't harsh or painful, just strong.

There he stood, fury burning in his eyes, face flaming red, chest heaving, glaring down at me.

"What did you say again?" His tone, by contrast, was unbelievably soft.

Tommaso ran out of his bedroom. Seeing me pinned against the wall by the seething Tristan, he was at my side in seconds, ready to drag Tristan off me.

I held my hand up to stop him, showing I wasn't hurt.

"I'm not a child. I never have been. When you deserve to know, I will tell you."

Tristan's eyes squinted slightly, almost as if in pain.

"Now, please let me go."

He did as I asked before storming into his bedroom and slamming the door. Tommaso was instantly in front of me, holding my face in his hands.

"Are you okay? He didn't hurt you, did he?" His voice was frantic, begging for answers.

"I'm fine. Are you coming to shop in an hour?" I asked, giving him a small smile.

Tommaso let me go and said he would gladly join. He went downstairs whilst I returned to my bedroom, spending the next thirty minutes setting up my phone.

I decided to call Teddy whilst I had some spare time.

"Kiddo?" I heard his intimidating yet hopeful tone.

"Hi, Teddy Bear." I grinned, and his groan at the nickname made it grow even wider.

"I told you not to call me that," he whined.

"I told you I didn't care." I laughed. "I just called so you'd have my number for the person I'm meeting."

"Okay, he can't wait to see you again." Teddy chuckled. "Where'd you get the phone?"

"My father gave me one. Said I deserved to have everything my brothers have," I informed him.

"Is he a good guy? Like, better than all the other men your mother had."

I knew straight away what Teddy meant and was quick to answer. "So far, I think he may be a bit better."

He was actually treating me equally with the guys. His words were, basically, that I was his child and there was nothing he wouldn't do for me. Also, he and the brothers just wanted to keep me safe."

Teddy chuckled through the phone. "Sounds exactly like what you deserve, but you refused to hear what Daniel had to say about your father. Everything I know, however, proves he treats everyone differently."

"So you're saying I should be careful," I summed up.

"Yes," he replied. "The person you're meeting has already prepared the spare room for you, so you'll always have somewhere to go. And some of the guys and I are flying in for a business deal at the end of the month."

A giant smile broke out on my face. Not only would I see the mystery friend once again, but I would see Teddy and the guys also.

"How's things been so far?" Teddy asked, worry evident in his tone.

I hesitated for a second, wondering if it was worth bothering him, but I had never lied to Teddy before. "There was an incident half an hour ago."

"What happened?" He wasn't asking. He was demanding.

Gone was his joyful and kind tone. Now, he was horrifyingly authoritative, the gang-leader edge shining through.

"I said something that pissed off one of the brothers. He pinned me to the wall and questioned me until I told him to let me go."

I heard a crash, then a course of profanities that even I didn't want to repeat.

"Teddy! Calm down." He was about to speak again, but I interrupted him. "He didn't hurt me, just confronted me. I'm perfectly fine. Another brother was ready to kill him, but I'm not hurt, not scared. No panic attacks or horrifying flashbacks."

I heard Teddy sigh into the phone before a mumbled, "Okay," escaped his lips.

I was about to speak again when I heard somebody call my name from downstairs. That was when I realised it was time to leave.

"I have to go. I'm heading to the mall."

"Be careful, kiddo."

CHAPTER SIX

STEFANO

Silence was how I spent most of my time. I learned at a young age that having a voice didn't always produce the effect you wished. Not everyone would listen to your words, and even fewer would truly acknowledge them.

Instead, I expressed myself through art and tattoos. Every single tattoo on my body told a story or represented something I never had the courage to say aloud. That confidence had been ripped from me at a young age, and I had never fully recovered.

We all watched as Tristan ran out of the kitchen and up the stairs. Then we turned to Dad, who paid him no mind at all.

"Are you not going to go after him?" Mateo questioned. "He may kill her!"

Shaking his head, Dad took a seat at the circular kitchen table, sipping his coffee casually. "He won't hurt her."

"How do you know that?!" Antonio yelled, panic in his voice, though he froze in shock at Dad's dismissal.

We all were.

"How many girls has Tristan ever hurt?" Dad asked.

That was when everyone calmed down, returning to what they were doing.

Tristan was many things. His anger could skyrocket at the single wrong word, and his violence was unmanageable and ferocious at times. There had even been occasions when the police had been called to the high school to stop him from killing students he was fighting.

But not once had he ever hurt a girl. In fact, the only one in the family who had was Antonio. That was because that girl bullied Tommaso for not having a Mommy and for having a stupid accent. The most he did was break her nose.

Tristan would never hurt a girl, let alone his little sister.

Father had raised us not to hit women, but if we had to, it would have been for the family. After everything we went through with our own mother, hitting women was a sore subject for us all. However, it was not so sore that we were vulnerable to others.

I always remembered seeing that girl at school the next day, screaming that Antonio had attacked her after she refused to sleep with him.

He did it in the cafeteria after he saw her throw Tommaso's food all over him. Also, Antonio was gay and not afraid to show it.

He broke her nose, then pulled his boyfriend onto his lap.

For the day, it was decided that Tommaso, Antonio, and I would go shopping with Kalina. Tommaso would be there to offer her fashion advice; Antonio to make sure the clothing was appropriate; and I was there to stop them from killing each other in a disagreement they were bound to have.

* * *

KALINA

I was at the bottom of the stairs when Tommaso, Antonio, and Stefano told me they would be the ones to take me shopping. They were all dressed and ready to leave.

"Why didn't you just button up your shirt like normal?" Antonio asked, glaring slightly at my belly-button piercing.

"It's massive on me. Plus, the weather is hot as fuck," I replied, not used to the hot American weather.

Rolling his eyes, he left ahead of us and got into a black Jeep parked outside. Stefano followed wordlessly, Tommaso and I doing the same.

The car journey was eerily quiet. Even Tommaso, who I had learned liked to talk a fair amount, said nothing. It took me a moment to realise they were watching me as I stared out of the window.

We were passing sandy beaches filled with laughing children, sunbathing women, and surfing men. It was typical for a Los Angeles beach, and it was beautiful. The Pacific was a crystal-clear shimmering blue.

They were all smiling at the amazement on my face. Even Stefano had a hint of a smile.

"You want to learn how to do that?" Antonio asked, pointing to the surfers as his other hand steered the car.

"No, it just looks cool."

There's no way I'm telling them the real reason I don't want to learn how to surf.

After ten minutes, we pulled up outside a huge shopping centre, with car parks stretching all the way to the beach. It must have been at least two miles. There were mountains upon mountains of shoppers.

Getting away might not be that difficult.

I followed behind them as they walked into the shopping centre. Stefano slowed down since I couldn't keep up with their tall frames and longer strides.

Whilst he stared ahead, Stefano didn't notice the notification that lit up my phone.

> *"Three hours, lady's bathroom, north side of the mall, fourth floor."*

It was an unknown number. I quickly put my phone away, making sure none of them saw the text, and quickened my pace. The doors of the mall automatically opened, and we strode inside.

"I was thinking we start here at the south entrance, do a big loop, and leave here by lunch," Antonio stated as he checked his Rolex.

"Can we start at the north side first?" I asked, wanting to find the toilets straight away.

"Why?" Tommaso questioned, his eyebrows scrunched together.

"British thing."

They didn't question my lame excuse further, and we made our way to the north side.

A thirty-minute-long walk!

We started shopping in Gucci, where Tommaso stacked clothes upon clothes onto Antonio's arms. Stefano flat-out refused to hold any.

When I offered to take some off Antonio's hands, Tommaso threw a fit about how he couldn't see what suited me if I was already holding another outfit.

We then spent another two hours trying on clothes and leaving Tommaso to decide if they should be bought or not. They then got into an argument about what was fashionable and provocative clothing. This led to Stefano smacking the both of them on the head, leading me to realise why he was really there.

It's a common occurrence whilst shopping.

"I'm hungry!" Tommaso whined as we finally left another store with far too many bags of clothing.

"You're always hungry," Antonio said in a growl, still pissed off at his younger brother—my twin.

Fuck. It was still weird to think that I had a brother, let alone a twin.

"To the food court," Tommaso yelled after we paid for another batch of clothes and charged off into the distance.

Antonio chased after him as best as he could with all the bags in hand, whining as he did about feeding children, leaving just Stefano and myself.

"I need the loo. I'll meet you at the food court," I said, pointing to the toilets in sight from where we were standing.

"I'll wait."

It was the first time I heard him speak. His tone was soft and kind, his demeanour the complete opposite. It was as deep as Teddy's and as deadly as Mateo's.

The look on his face held no room for argument. Begrudgingly, I went to the loo whilst Stefano waited by the archway leading to the toilets.

Once inside the ladies' room, I checked if any women were in there. There were none. Instead, there was another door on the other side, probably for people coming in from the other wing so they no longer needed to walk five minutes around.

As I was about to check the last cubicle, a lock clicked.

Spinning around, I saw a tall man. He was wearing a black hoodie that covered his face. His height was roughly six foot five. The beginning of a large tattoo showed on his hand. His skin was somewhat pale, with a fresh tan from the California sun showing in some areas.

He lifted his hood, revealing his face.

He had a crooked nose and a recently stitched cut on his cheek. His hair was a dark blond—longer than I remembered—shaved on the sides and combed back from his dark brown eyes. The same stupid grin was plastered on his face as always.

"Ace?" I whispered.

"Hey, Kal."

CHAPTER SEVEN

KALINA

When I was eleven, Daniel introduced me to the motorcycle gang he had joined, and they became my family.

Everyone knew and loved each other, no matter what happened. The bond of family and brotherhood was constant and unwavering, as strong as the stitched insignia on the leather of the biker jacket.

I remembered Daniel taking me to the bar they owned—a night of abuse and torment riding on my back. It was a day when lots of men from out of town stopped by for business proposals.

I remembered staring into those disgusting eyes. The moment Teddy and Daniel saw the fear on my face, they knew something was wrong. They refused to let the cowardly man leave until they were sure of what had happened.

The moment I confirmed what they feared most, all hell broke loose. I crawled into the corner of the bar, the trauma I had fought so hard to keep at bay flowing like a river. The screams and punches and smashed bottles scared me more than anything that man had ever done.

Simply because I trusted the guys, and I had no idea how far their rage would go.

On the verge of a panic attack, I was swept up into a pair of warm arms. The scent of smoke and alcohol was strong, mingling with—what I discovered later—Dior cologne. Had it not been for that particular scent, God knew what sort of panic I would have had.

But I recognised him straight away. Few people had brought me the kind of comfort he had, and it was exactly what I needed. He was always there. If it weren't for him, I would have been dead by now.

"Ace." Within seconds, I had tackled him to the—not surprisingly—unclean mall toilet floor.

The muscles beneath his hoodie were firmer than when I last saw him, but his embrace was as warm as it had ever been. His arms wrapped tightly around my waist as he pressed his head at the side of mine, kissing my cheek as tears streamed down his face.

"I've missed you," he mumbled against my skin.

"What are you doing here?" I cried, pulling back to look at his face once again. "And what's this?" I added with a chuckle, running my fingers along his slight stubble.

"Teddy sent me here when I got out of prison. He is making a deal with some high-powered individuals in L.A. and need someone he trusts to run things for him here." His Scottish accent remained strong and thick.

"When did you get out?" I asked as I stood up and pulled him with me.

"Two years ago, on parole. A college in L.A was still willing to give me a scholarship, so I used that as an excuse to come here," he explained, pushing my brown curls out of my face.

We spent the next ten minutes catching up. I told him every single detail of my life.

He wasn't too pleased about my smoking.

"It's not good for you," he said whilst leaning against the wall.

"Neither is emotional, physical, and mental trauma, but I still got that shit."

The two of us burst into a fit of laughter, almost collapsing into tears.

It wasn't until a sharp bang sounded on the toilet door that I realised Stefano was still outside.

"Shit." We both spoke in unison.

"I'm gonna go," he said, heading toward the door on the other side. He quickly kissed the crown of my head before saying, "I'll send you my address."

I stared at the door for a solid minute. I was simply thankful I got to see Ace again. I had spent four years without him in my life, and it was the loneliest I had ever felt.

"KALINA!" Stefano yelled.

Quickly, I darted into a cubicle and locked the door. Stefano finally broke the lock on the ladies' toilet door and stormed through.

"Kalina?" His voice wavered, almost painfully.

"Yeah?" I answered casually.

"It's been twenty minutes! I thought you were hurt." His voice was quiet this time, filled with relief.

"I needed a tampon. A woman just came in through the other door and gave me one," I answered, lying though my teeth.

"Why was the door locked?" he pressed further.

"She said there was some strange-looking guy outside, so she must have locked it just in case," I said, proud of myself for coming up with these excuses so quickly.

"Are you almost done?" He sighed, clearly tired after his little panic.

I lifted the lid of the bin beside me and let it drop after a few seconds before answering yes. I flushed the toilet and left the cubicle.

Stefano was standing outside the stalls with his cold look once again, watching me as I washed my hands and walked out of the toilets first.

He guided me to the food court, where Tommaso was stuffing his face and Antonio was shaking his head in disappointment.

"What took you guys so long?" Tommaso asked through a mouthful of food.

"Toilet," I replied, smirking as he recoiled and continued eating with a disgusted face.

Chuckling, I took the chips and burger Antonio offered me, and several minutes later, I accepted the milkshake Stefano handed me after getting one for himself.

I ate silently whilst Tommaso listed off the remaining stores we still needed to visit, which was a fuckload. Antonio told him to calm down, and Stefano played on his phone.

"You're related to Stefano Montessori?"

Looking up from my phone, I scanned the food court and spotted Ace hiding behind a doughnut stand, his hood pulled low over his eyes again.

"Yeah, he was the one banging on the door."

"Be careful around him Kal, he's fucked up"

"What do you mean?"

"Went to a street fight one night, knockouts and subs only. Stefano killed his opponent . . . pulled out the guy's tongue and didn't let anyone stop him while he was choking in his own blood"

I glanced up from my phone and met Ace's gaze, shrugging my shoulders like it was nothing. Truth be told, after everything we had seen, it was just whatever it was.

"It was his best friend from childhood Kal."

"Okay . . . That's actually bad."

Putting my phone away, I looked cautiously towards Stefano, whose face remained devoid of any emotion.

What the fuck have I gotten myself into?

CHAPTER EIGHT

ANTONIO

The first time I saw Kalina, I was shocked, to say the least. She smoked a cigarette with complete nonchalance.

Up close, meeting her for the first time, she seemed just as unfazed by the knife and burn scars on her hand and the faint marks on her bicep.

It was clear she was comfortable with them, which meant the scars were from when she was younger. She reminded me so much of our mother and Tommaso that it was actually a bit scary. She was a smaller version of her and a female version of him. In that moment, I knew she was my sister.

But the loneliness in her eyes was what scared me the most—the idea that after Daniel, she had been alone. That we had spent the past seventeen years happy together, but she was alone. With no one to hold her hand when she cried, no one to teach her how to fight or pull pranks on her siblings. That we hadn't had the chance to teach her how to ride a bike or swim.

Those ideas were unbelievable to me. Being the second-oldest, I always had my brothers.

Working in the mafia as the underboss, there had been numerous times when I had to leave home for business trips. With Mateo training to become Don in the near future, he had to travel a lot too. Even just a night away from home was agonizing.

There were no yells for silence from Mateo, no grunts and middle fingers from Stefano. I had to survive without Tristan's outbursts of anger and frustration. I couldn't hear Tommaso sprinting downstairs for a midnight snack.

The poor guy had always thought he was so slick with it when, in truth, we had all heard him do it since he was four years old. We simply didn't have the heart to tell him.

The first time he did it, he entered the kitchen the next morning with dried chocolate around his lips, and we had already wiped the hot chocolate powder off the counter. For the sake of his young mind, we said nothing.

He smiled the whole day.

Once Tommaso decided that we had shopped to our heart's content, we headed home. Since Kalina and Stefano had joined us at the food court, she was practically mute—only simple sentences or single-word answers.

"Do you need help bringing the bags inside?" She was struggling to lift the three bags on her arms, so I offered some assistance.

"Um . . . sure," was all she said.

Throwing her ponytail behind her, she turned around and went inside the house.

I followed her to her bedroom with eight bags in hand, walking with ease.

She just rolled her eyes at the bags as she opened her bedroom door and put them on the bed. After another two trips downstairs, and with the help of a guard, we had all the bags in her room.

As she began organizing the clothes, I took out some storage boxes for the accessories she bought.

"What are you doing?" Kalina questioned, eyebrows furrowed in confusion.

"Helping," I replied.

I organized her hair bobbles, hair styling products (electrical stuff), cotton buds, cotton pads, makeup brushes, makeup, skincare, and other related items. I handed her the bags of underwear, unsure if she would be comfortable with me sorting them.

I ended up organizing the majority of her bathroom items, jewelry, and shoes while she handled the clothes. Thanks to Tommaso and his need to spend Dad's money, it took us two hours to sort everything.

"What do you want to do with the decoration crap?" I asked.

While at the mall, we had bought bedding, blankets, paint, and posters. She just put them in the corner, leaving out the electronics bag.

I insisted she buy a MacBook Pro, whatever phone case she wished, an Apple Watch, and some charging stations and chargers. When we were finally finished, I left her alone in her bedroom.

I headed downstairs to the offices, where I found Mateo working. I took a seat on the sofa after taking a pile of paperwork from his desk and began reading through documents and contracts.

"How was shopping?" Mateo asked after a decent amount of time.

Leaning back, I took the glass of scotch he offered me and let out a small smile, remembering our time.

"She came out of her shell for a bit. She smiled and was on the verge of laughing." I grinned. "But when she and Stefano returned, she was her quiet self again."

"Why?" Mateo sounded concerned, as he easily does regarding all our siblings.

But now we have a sister.

"I don't know. Stefano seemed just as confused as I did," I informed him. "All I know is they were gone for twenty minutes. She was in the toilet while he waited outside. When she took too long, he freaked out and broke the door down."

"And the guards said this?" Mateo pressed.

Without Kalina knowing, we had guards following us all day. Before, they were simply for our usual protection, but now that the underworld was aware we had a mafia princess, security was more important than ever.

"Yes," I answered.

"And she was alone?"

"As far as I know," I told him, sipping my beverage.

Mateo nodded and returned to his work. I did the same, but my mind kept trying to figure out why Kalina was being secretive again.

A few hours passed, and we had completed all the paperwork for the day. The head housekeeper, Marcy, had stopped by a few minutes earlier to inform us that dinner would be served soon. We told her to let them begin without us.

The two of us left Mateo's office, suit jackets in hand. When we got to the dining room, everyone was seated in their usual spots, munching away. Kalina had not changed out of the clothes Tommaso gave her.

"They're comfy," she replied when I questioned her.

Chuckling, I took my seat beside Stefano and Dad. I ate my food peacefully, as did everyone else. However, I could tell something was bothering Dad. His shoulders were tense, and his eyes were fixed solely on his food.

Once all the younger ones were finished, Dad dismissed them to their bedrooms. He asked Mateo, Stefano, and I to remain seated.

The three of us turned to him, curious why he needed to talk. Sighing, he finished his almost-full glass of bourbon before speaking.

"Anthony Vecoli was spotted in the mall today," Dad said, eyes glaring hard at the table.

Anthony Vecoli was underboss to our biggest and strongest enemy, Aidan Rossi, the Irish-Italian don. The man was a monster who destroyed anything and everything. He had no mercy, no forgiveness. Nothing and no one could survive him.

"Were we at risk?" I asked Dad.

The idea that an accomplice of that man was near my sister was beyond horrifying. While we may not be at war, the tension was as high as it had ever been.

"Not that we know of, but . . ." He rubbed his hand across his face. "The guard said Kalina was in the bathroom for over twenty minutes, apparently waiting for a . . ."

"What?" Stefano prodded.

"Anthony was in the bathroom with her," Dad finally said.

It felt like my breath got caught in my throat, and all the air sucked from my lungs. Anthony worked for a monster. That could very well mean he was one himself.

And he was locked in a lady's bathroom with my sister—my sister who barely said two words after returning with Stefano.

I thought Stefano had told her off for making him worry or something, but what if it was something worse.

"What if Anthony Vecoli hurt her?"

CHAPTER NINE

KALINA

In life, we are always racing.

Racing against family for achievements. Racing against friends for boyfriends and girlfriends. Who can get drunk the fastest. Racing against society. Racing against time.

Because, after everything, time is what will fuck you over the most.

I hadn't realised how much time had passed until I saw Ace again. He had matured so much in the space of three years.

When he left, he was a young adult, his teenage attitude and youthful appearance still evident. His hair was longer, and his frame had once been extremely lanky. Now, he had filled out and was far more muscular.

The moment I saw him, I wondered how much everyone else had changed.

"What if Anthony Vecoli hurt her?"

Whilst Tommaso and Tristan went to their bedrooms, I realised I had left my phone in the dining room. I went back down, but just as I was nearly there, they mentioned Ace's full name, stopping me dead in my tracks.

How do they know Ace?

I actually had to stop myself from breathing so I wouldn't laugh at Antonio's question. Ace had never—and would never—hurt me.

When they remained silent for over two minutes, I moved, making my footsteps loud and deliberate. Every eye turned to me as I stepped through the dining room door.

"Everything okay?" I asked, seeing all their nervous faces.

"Of course, *tesoro*." Christopher smiled. He looked a little pale sitting at the head of the table. (*Darling*)

There was anxiety in Mateo's eyes, fear in Antonio's, horror in Stefano's, and worry in Christopher's.

"How was the mall today?" Mateo asked cautiously.

Everyone seemed unusually interested in my answer.

"It was good. I had loads of fun," I replied, picking up my phone. I gave them a tight-lipped smile before leaving. On the the stairs, a notification appeared on my phone.

"456 Chester Avenue, stop by whenever you like."

I replied:

"Very soon."

Smiling, I placed my phone on my bedside table and reached into the drawer. I took out my bottles of medicine, took one each of the sleeping pills, anti-anxiety meds, muscle relaxers, and other, and swallowed them all.

All of the bottles were nearly empty and were in desperate need of a refill. Sighing, I put them all away again. As I was about to settle in and let the sleeping pills take effect, there was a knock on my bedroom door.

"Come in," I mumbled, sinking beneath the covers.

Christopher poked his head through the door and took a seat at the foot of my bed. He gave me a confused look before speaking. "You tire down fast."

"Long day," I quickly replied, muffling a yawn behind my hand.

"Right. Well, I just came to tell you that you'll be starting school on Tuesday. The enrollment was held back a day."

I rolled my eyes, hating that I was already being thrown back into a mini hell so soon.

"Relax. You'll be in classes with Tommaso and Tristan. I'm not going to be a *stronzo* and tell you that you have to spend time with them, but don't wander too far." *(Asshole)*

I just nodded in response, lying back on the bed. "By the way, I'm going out tomorrow."

"Where?" Christopher asked quickly.

"Some of my friends moved over here. I'm meeting up with them."

"Who are these friends?"

"People who kept me alive when no one else did," I snapped, tired of all the questions.

Christopher got the message and rose from the bed. "Keep your phone on you and be back by dinner."

The need for sleep had been overpwhelming, but Christopher's presence kept me awake, nightmares of the past jolting me into semi-consciousness. The moment he left, though, I was out cold.

* * *

TRISTAN

Sleeping had never been my friend. When I was a child, I would always cry and complain about being sent to bed at night. It got so bad that Dad would lie with me until I drifted off, only for me to wake up hours later in the dead of night to crawl into bed with him.

After everyone had settled, I quietly played on my phone, letting the silence of the night drown out my thoughts. It was not until I heard a quiet scream that my attention sharpened.

Within seconds, I was out of bed and bolting down the corridor. This hall only had Tommaso's, mine, and Kalina's bedrooms. The others would not have heard the scream that came from the room of my *sorellina*, and Tommaso would sleep through anything. *(little sister)*

I flung open her bedroom door, only to see Kalina quivering on her bed, her eyes closed. She was shaking as she let out small whimpers of either fear or pain.

Running forward, I wrapped my arms around her tiny figure and held her to my chest. Rocking her gently, she calmed down in her sleep before opening her soft blue eyes. She stared up at me in panic and desperation.

"Tristan?" she whispered, shocked at my presence.

"Are you okay?" was all I asked, wiping the running sweat from her forehead.

She gave me a timid nod, avoiding eye contact as she did so. It wasn't until I forced her to look at me that she completely broke down. Shaking and crying in my arms, she held on to me, and I held her close, letting her do whatever she needed. Eventually, she calmed down, but the need to question her was becoming overwhelming.

"Do you want to talk about it?" I offered, leaning back against the headboard as she rested on my chest.

"No," she mumbled, still tense in my arms and gripping my shirt tightly.

"Do you want me to leave?" I asked, feeling her tension persist.

"No."

I let her relax in my arms, lying there as I contemplated what could have scared her so much.

Kalina was a brave girl. Zombies and thunderstorms couldn't possibly be the content of her nightmares.

I could only wonder what frightened her.

Because I would never force her to tell me.

I stayed awake the entire night until around the hour I knew Dad would leave his room and Antonio would go to the gym. I knew Kalina spent most of the night awake. She only drifted off for an hour or so after three o'clock.

When I moved, she did too, then stood and walked straight into the bathroom without a word. After that, I took my leave, returning to my bedroom and dressing in a fresh outfit—black jeans and a black shirt. I headed downstairs to find everyone eating in the kitchen except for Tommaso and Kalina.

I sat down on a barstool and took the cereal Dad had poured for me upon my arrival. Giving him a nod in thanks, I began eating whilst my brothers—except Stefano—talked aimlessly amongst themselves. Mateo and Antonio were talking about mafia business, whilst the others chatted about mundane stuff.

Moments later, Kalina arrived downstairs and poured herself an iced coffee from the fridge. She wore black ankle boots with heels, black jeans, a white tank top, and black-and-red leather racer jacket. Her hair was down and flowing freely, making me smile at how much she resembled our aunt, our adoptive mother.

"What time are you leaving?" Dad asked her, anxiety in his tone.

"Now," Kalina replied, walking back around the counter.

"Be safe," he said, staring at her as if it might be the last time.

She ended up standing in front of me. For a moment, she did nothing, then she gave me a small hug. It was a silent thank you.

A thank you for not telling anyone about her nightmare.

CHAPTER TEN

KALINA

Starting my way into the city, I passed through the large iron gate that the guards opened for me with farewells. I had refused the offer of being dropped off by Antonio, who had been hovering anxiously whilst I was still at the house. He tried to get me to take an umbrella.

The lively morning of Los Angeles buzzed with traffic that piled up in no time.

No idea where they're going on a Sunday.

Wandering aimlessly, I slowly made my way to the address Ace had sent me. It wasn't long before I entered a questionable part of the city. Drunk people were still strolling around as they recovered from a night of heavy partying. I saw at least three different gangs before I took out my pocket knife for easy access.

Three men, clearly high and drunk, emerged from the ally I needed to pass through. All of them towered over me, staring me down with lustful eyes.

"What's a pretty little thing like you doing here?" The obvious ringleader smirked.

By now, I had walked so far that it was well past noon, and the sun had begun to set in the sky. After getting lost repeatedly, this was my only way to Ace.

"Walking," I bluntly replied.

"Ooh, a feisty one," his friend commented, smirking down at me as he and the other friend backed me into a corner.

"Just fuck off, will you," I shouted, trying to push past them.

My attempts failed, however, as the final man shoved me by the shoulder, pushing me against the wall. I stared up at the three of them, figuring out who I had to take down first. We were interrupted, though, by three gunshots echoing through the alleyway.

Blood splattered all over my face, the three of them dropping to the ground in quick succession.

Wiping the blood from my face, I was ready to see the person responsible emerge from the shadows.

But he or she didn't.

Sighing, I continued my way through the alley, picking up my pace in case the police showed up—which I doubted. The sky had had darkened a little by now, the sun still hanging just above the downtown skyscrapers, yet the temperature remained unbelievably warm, as always.

I think I actually miss British weather.

As I was about to cross the street, I had to practically fling myself backwards as a swarm of motorcycles flew past.

"KALINA!" one of the bikers up front yelled, shock lacing his tone.

All motorcycles halted to a stop, and three people hopped off in an instant. As they turned around, and their faces became visible, I recognised each and every one of them.

Caleb—curly, blue-haired, and twenty-one years old. We met when I was fourteen and he was eighteen. He hadn't grown since I last saw him, being six-foot-one with a lanky build. His eyes matched his hair, and they are filled with tears at my presence.

Maddie—brunette with purple tips, thirty years old, shimmering brown eyes, and a pale complexion. She was five-foot-eleven and became my first female role model at age thirteen. She was Teddy's older sister and, just as much, mine.

Jamie—blond, green-eyed, and nineteen years old. He was Daniel's best friend in secondary school. Jamie actually introduced Daniel to the gang. Without him, we wouldn't have had our family. He was six feet tall with a fair bit of muscle and the brightest smile in the world.

All three of them swept me up in a tight hug, passing me around like pass-the-parcel. Jamie gripped me tightly in his arms and spun around, holding my head to his shoulder as if I were a toddler. I hugged him back just as tightly, embracing the warmth and love I had not felt from him for so long.

"Hi, kid." He smiled, tears welling in his eyes as he stared at me.

"Hi, Jamie," I muttered, holding him close and refusing to release him from my grip.

He set me back down on the ground, only for me to be scooped up again. Squealing, I clung desperately as my ass was smacked playfully, again and again.

"WHERE DID THIS BUNDA COME FROM!" Maddie screamed in laughter.

"MADDIE!" I giggled, flailing my arms around as I tried to get down.

She placed me back on the ground.

Caleb gave me a small hug and a kiss on the head. He was less affectionate, so his reaction was far more reserved compared to Jamie's.

"Holy shit! I missed you." Maddie sighed as she stroked my hair away from my face.

"Ace told us you were stopping by, so we headed back to the club straight away." Jamie smiled from ear to ear.

"Mind giving me a lift then?" I smirked, watching the three of them instantly begin fighting over who I should ride with.

Getting tired of standing, I climbed onto the back of Jamie's motorcycle. He immediately started dancing around in joy whilst Maddie and Caleb grumbled under their breaths.

I scooted back for Jamie and wrapped my arms around his waist once he sat down. Resting my chin on his shoulder, I took note of the journey to the clubhouse for future reference.

After the final turn down the street, we pulled to a stop inside a motorcycle-filled car park. The building was a garage, packed with motorcycles and sport cars commonly used in street racing.

Ace was in his overalls, talking to a guy working beneath a car. He turned his head in my direction, and his once serious face broke into his usual playful grin. He waved me over, and I jogged across the car park.

Maddie called out to Killian, another friend from back home. "KILL! SHE HAS A BUNDA!"

Ace embraced me once I got to him. However, my attention was on the car behind him: a new Nissan GT-R with white paint and black leather seats. The bonnet was up, the engine removed for—what I assumed were—modifications.

A tall figure lay under the car.

"Kal, this is Aidan, my best friend," Ace said, introducing the guy beneath the car.

Without looking at me, Aidan gave a small wave. I didn't care, though, because I was too fascinated by the vehicle before me.

"Oh, I forgot you were already racing before you got locked up." Ace chuckled at the pure awe on my face.

"You forget a lot of things," I commented.

Ace was about to argue, but one look from me made him give up the futile attempt.

Jamie strode into the garage and ruffled my hair, giving me a small grin as I slapped his hand away.

"We need to get you a car," Jamie commented, wrapping his arm around my shoulders.

"Or a motorcycle," I countered, a cheeky grin on my face.

The two of them gave me a pointed look, instantly shutting down the idea. Before I got arrested,

I had begged the guys to get me a motorcycle. Teddy refused, saying I was the most probable target for enemies, as everyone adored me so much. On a motorcycle, I was most vulnerable.

"Worth a shot," I muttered.

"We'll get you a sports car," Ace promised with a grin.

After listing off the cars I could get, Maddie called us all in for beers. We sat and sang and played pool in the modernised clubhouse with bars and sofas. There were rooms and bathrooms just like in the UK, and everyone was dancing to the blasting music.

This was the Los Angeles clubhouse for the Chained Angels.

But I never got to properly meet Aidan.

CHAPTER ELEVEN

KALINA

When I met the members of the club for the first time, I was scared shitless. All of them were smoking, drinking, and getting high, just like all the monsters I had met before. Every one of them was intimidating and ruthless.

The second they saw me, though, all drinks were set down and cigarettes stubbed out, each and every one of them curious about the child brought before them by a member. When Daniel explained the situation of our home—or what he knew of it—they practically adopted me.

Everyday after school, Daniel would take me to the clubhouse, where they all smoked and drank happily, occasionally doing business. There was always someone there to make me feel safe and ready to protect me.

Sitting on the arm of the couch, I shared a cigarette with Maggie, who was seated on the couch, each of us holding a Corona in hand.

Men surrounded the room, wearing their leather Chained Angels biker jackets. Several women, desperate for a man in the deadliest gang in the city, flirted shamelessly.

"I've missed this." I laughed, puffing out a breath of smoke.

"We've missed you," Caleb replied, sitting on the couch adjacent to mine.

The music blared through the room as the party continued, celebrating a new business deal that had gone through. Maddie and Ace had closed a deal with another gang to sell military-grade weapons.

The Chained Angels dealt in just about anything, but we were the biggest suppliers of drugs. That way, we could control who the drugs were sold to. Kids would not get drugs from us.

"Kal!" Jamie shouted from across the room.

I heeded his call, skipping happily towards him. I stopped in front of him as he held a pool cue in his hand, a baffled look on his face. He was playing against Ace, who stood there with a smug grin on his face.

"Yes," I said, fully aware of his situation but wanting him to confess himself.

"I . . . I can't get the shot."

In our family, Teddy and Daniel were the best pool players. They could make a shot from anywhere and won every game they played.

And I had been taught by both of them.

Taking the cue from his hand, I aligned it with the ball and potted the black ball that Jamie couldn't sink. He started cheering along with all the bystanders who were watching, whilst Ace sulked in his corner.

Sitting on the pool table, Jamie and I laughed and talked about his time in America and my time in juvie. Story after story flowed between us as we drank and smoked the night away.

My phone buzzed continuously, so I checked the messages. All of them were from Christopher:

"Kalina, where are you?"

"Kalina I'm getting worried"

"I'm serious"

"Call me now"

"I'm sending the boys to come and find you if you don't call"

"Kalina, this is important!"

Sighing, I jumped off the pool table and left the music-filled clubhouse. I called Christopher; the phone hadn't even started to ring before I heard his scream echo through the empty car park.

"KALINA, ARE YOU OKAY?"

"Yeah, I'm fine," I answered honestly, leaning against the garage wall as I spoke.

"You scared the shit out of me," he said, then relayed that I was fine to—I assumed—the brothers.

"Why? It's not like you cared before," I snapped, tired of his loving-father charade.

I had grown up on stories of how Christopher was never a true father to his children; how he never cared about any of them. How he just wanted the power offsprings could bring.

That it had always been our mother who raised his children. After all the torture and abuse she endured with our father, drugs and alcohol were her only escape.

"What?" he blurted. "Kalina, that's not true."

"The fuck it isn't," I snarled, pissed that he wouldn't leave me alone.

"Are you drunk?"

I could hear the smashing of what sounded like glass in the background and muffled shouting.

"Why don't you tend to the children you wanted whilst I spend time with my family."

Before he could answer, I hung up the phone. For the last two days, everything my mother told me had been surfacing, and the whole act Christopher was putting on about being a great and loving father was exhausting to watch. Even Daniel had said he wasn't a good father.

My bet was that he would try and play happy family for the public eye as a businessman, but once I turned eighteen, I would be out on my ass.

"Problem?"

Spinning around, I saw the outline of a figure sitting on the bonnet of the Nissan GTR. He was tall—giant, even. He rose from his seat, revealing his six-foot-five frame. The muscles of his body were insane. He held a beer in his hand, bringing it to his lips, though I couldn't make out any of his facial features in the darkness.

"What's it to you?" I retorted.

"Nothing, but you sound pissed off." His voice was deep, brooding, every syllable enunciated a rich Italian accent mixed with Irish.

"I'm always pissed." Not a lie.

"And why's that?" he asked, folding his tatted arms across his solid chest.

The muscles in his arms flexed, visible even through the white vest he wore. He had paired it with black joggers and boots.

"Shitty childhood, shitty teenage years, and being forced to live with a biological family that never wanted me," I answered, a bit too bluntly.

"Sounds dreadful," he said sarcastically, ending with a small chuckle.

"Believe me, it is." I chuckled back.

"Who are you anyway? Another lass wanting to get fucked by an Angel?" He lit a cigarette and took a drag, standing there nonchalantly as he did so.

"I doubt anyone who raised me would want to fuck me." I laughed at the thought.

One time, when I was fifteen, Jamie walked in on me getting changed. Half an hour later I found him with a haunted look on his face and tears streaming down his cheeks. The poor guy just said that he had walked in on his little sister.

"You're the kid?" His tone was thick with shock.

"Kalina," I corrected, shooting him a small glare before taking another sip from my bottle of Corona.

"When Ace told me about you, I imagined a little kid," he said, then chuckled. "I got the 'little' part right."

"Fuck off, you giant-ass twat," I shot back instantly, flipping him off for good measure.

"A little girl like you shouldn't have such a foul mouth," he commented, taking a step forward.

Moonlight carved across his face. His crooked nose was pierced with a silver stud on the left nostril—just like mine. His skin was more tanned than my own, beautifully complementing his hazel eyes. His jawline was sharp as broken glass, dusted with short brown stubble. His hair was slicked back, revealing a scar that started on his forehead and ran down to the right side of his face. Those soft lips curved into a smirk as he met the glare burning on my face.

"I'm not a little girl," I responded, stepping forward until almost no space remained between us.

I had to crane my neck to look up at him. He raised the beer to his lips again. Ring-clad, tattooed fingers. His Adam's apple bobbed as he swallowed. His thick neck was covered in an assortment of ink.

"To those guys, you'll always be a little girl," he replied, staring down at me with deadly brown eyes.

"Maybe so, but they don't treat me like one," I answered, taking the cigarette from his fingers and placing it between my lips.

"Little girl." He laughed.

"Who are you, anyway? You don't have an Angel jacket."

He was about to respond when a shout from Ace took his attention from me.

"Aidan! You still out there? Is Kalina with you?" His tone was frantic and hurried.

"Yeah!" the man, Aidan, called back. "She's here."

Ace jogged over and let out a sigh of relief upon seeing me. Then he whacked me lightly across the back of my head.

"Don't wander off," he scolded, a parental glare on his face for a moment before his grin returned.

"Don't worry so much," I replied, giving him a little grin of my own.

Ace took the cigarette from my hand and gave it back to Aidan, muttering about how I was not supposed to smoke.

"What time do you need to get home?" Ace questioned.

Aidan let out a chuckle, making Ace give him a slightly stunned look. Then he glanced back down at me.

"Not anytime, really, since I just told Christopher to go fuck himself," I answered.

Ace let out a hearty laugh, ruffling my hair. He guided me back inside, Aidan following behind.

"Give me your phone," Ace said, holding out his hand.

I had always trusted Ace completely, so I gave it to him without any hesitation. Ace handed the phone to Aidan, who sat down at a table and took a toolkit of sorts out of a drawer beside him.

I watched carefully as he took the phone apart, bit by bit. Ace handed Aidan what looked liked a chip after the latter pulled out an identical one from my phone and dropped it in an open beer. Aidan put the new chip in the phone and put it back together.

Aidan handed it back to me and made his way outside with another cigarette. I gave Ace a curious look, waiting for him to explain.

"He took out the tracker your father put in your phone. Now, you have one of our trackers, like all members."

He was tracking me . . .

And he told me I would have my privacy.

The beer was stone-cold, and the blaring music swallowed the crowd whole. An entire gang had gathered to party the night away—simply because they could.

At some point during the long hours, I had flung my hair back into a ponytail, letting my sculpted jawline and tan skin catch the low light. It wasn't until four in the morning that people began fucking in every available space.

Leaning against the bar, I flirted with a member of a different gang. He had a black buzz cut and dark brown eyes. As my head began spinning, I felt a hand on the small of my back guiding me towards the back rooms.

A pounding in my head started, the dizzying sensation increasing with every step I took. The guy was practically carrying me there himself.

Once we were down the back corridor, he opened the door to a bedroom. Before I could take a step inside, he was flung backwards with an alarmingly powerful force.

Swaying side to side, I could not make out the true extent of what was happening. All I was aware were the blood staining the soft grey carpet and the harsh grunts of pain and sharp intake of breath.

Leaning heavily against the far wall, I tried to focus my sight on anything close by.

The scent of expensive cologne, mixed with surprisingly delightful-smelling cigarettes, engulfed me all of a sudden. I was then lifted from my spot, feeling extremely tall in the broad and muscular arms.

"Rilassati, amore. Ti ho preso." I heard the recognisable but unusually soft voice in a whisper. *(Relax, love. I've got you.)*

With that, I allowed my head to fall, and the sound of heavy footsteps lulled me to sleep.

CHAPTER TWELVE

CHRISTOPHER

"Kalina! KALINA!"

My shouting into the phone was futile, as she had ended the call. She had spoken of how I had not wanted her, only my other children . . .

The lot of us were sitting in the kitchen, none of us having heard from her since she left at beginning of the day. We had grown worried.

Antonio was already at the computer, tracking her phone. It wasn't until there was a shake of his head that I realized she was more informed than we believed.

All of the boys set out to find her, two in each car. Mateo ordered more men to join the search as he strapped in his seatbelt.

I remained at the house, trying to track her from here and waiting for her return. Sitting at the kitchen computer, a glass of bourbon in my hand and a cigar in the other, I typed away hopefully.

I managed to access some information on the tracker, which had located her to the south side of the city. Had it not been destroyed or tampered with, there would have been an exact location.

I called the boys, who had an open line on walkie-talkies, and told them the last area where the tracker pinged. They all answered that they would be there soon.

Knowing there was nothing else I could do, I leaned back in my chair and continued to call her phone. She must have turned it off as the phone wouldn't even ring anymore.

The worry and frustration grew minute by minute as I waited for any sign of my daughter.

But all I could think of was: why did she not consider herself one of my children?

She had spent her entire life under the influence of her mother—a cruel, vile woman with nothing to show for her life but her addiction and fertility.

Never had I thought she would be such a monster. When we met, she was sweet and kind, the type of person who was liked by all. Then we got married, and everything changed.

She stopped being joyful and became rude and nasty. Every word she said, every breath she took, venom oozed from her.

I had often wondered if it was my own doing that caused such a downfall, but then I reminded myself that, while I did try, she didn't.

At the end of the day, she made her bed, and the moment she had to lie on it, she came crawling back. I couldn't understand why. While I may not have been the best husband, she certainly didn't make it any easier.

My phone rang, breaking me out of my trance. Within seconds, I had it up to my ear and was ready to talk.

"Dad," Tommaso said.

"Sì?" I answered, willing to hear any news he had. *(Yes?)*

"The area on the south side she was last spotted is filled with gangs."

I could feel my heart stop for a moment.

"Most are minor criminals out on the piss, but there is a major gang residing here."

"Who?" I questioned.

As a powerful mafia, there were many other groups who wished to overthrow us. If they were to learn I had a daughter, she would be in danger. If they were to learn she was vulnerable and alone, God only knew what would happen.

"The Chained Angels." Tommaso sighed.

The Chained Angels were led in L.A. by Anthony Vecoli and worldwide by Teddy Stevens. They were more powerful than some minor mafias. We had often had problems with them in the past, to the point where war was on the verge of breaking out.

Our main issue was simply that their strongest ally and closest friend was Aidan Rossi.

I once tried to make peace with the boy when he first came to power, but he refused.

Too much damage had been done to both our families—his more than my own. Sadly, there had been constant tension since, just waiting to explode.

"Tom, you find her. Whatever it takes. She's not safe out there," I ordered.

While I may no longer be the don, I was still very much in charge. Even Mateo still listened to me. It came with the respect earned from leading for thirty years. Now, I was an adviser to my son, guiding him and showing him the ropes of the mafia world on a new level. I had been the don for thirty years, catching liars and thieves every which way, yet I couldn't catch my wife. And when I did, she had the final say.

I should've noticed how suspicious she had been during the pregnancy—how she was much rounder and bigger at the time—but I only assumed that the baby would be bigger.

The only reason we stayed together in those final months was the knowedge that she had my baby. Before I caught her, she was already pregnant, but we did a prenatal paternity test to prove the baby was mine.

I assumed that once she found out that not only was she having twins, as I had always wanted, but also my only daughter, she would take her final revenge. She managed to wound me one last time by taking my daughter for the first seventeen years of her life.

I guessed that after everything, she was not the person I thought she was.

It had been two hours since I sent the boys out, and not a word had come back to me since Tommaso. Grabbing my phone, I called Antonio.

"Dad, I can't find her! Fuck! How could we have lost her already! It's been three fucking days! Dad! I'm so fucking worried! What do I do!?"

The thing with Antonio was that he had always taken the motherly role. Even after I stepped back and started becoming more of a family man, Antonio was always the mother they needed.

And when one of the kids was hurt, even Mateo, Antonio would be the one to panic.

"Calmati, figliolo. Ricorda che dobbiamo rimanere concentrati per Kalina," I told him in a soothing tone. *(Calm down, son. Remember, we have to stay focused for Kalina.)*

He took a deep breath before he spoke again. *"Si."*

"Now, where are you?" I asked, hearing loud bangs and glass smashing in the background.

"At the side of East a—SHIT!"

"Tony? Antonio!"

There was no response.

"Dad," he said after a few minutes of silence.

"What happened?" I questioned, my own worry now extending to my son.

"Aidan Rossi just drove past," Antonio said, a fierceness in his tone.

"Fuck!" I muttered.

"Tony, get Kalina home. She can't be near that monster," I told him.

If Aidan Rossi got a hold of Kalina, he was guaranteed to kill her and torture her in some way.

CHAPTER THIRTEEN

KALINA

"Thirty pounds for the hour; sixty for two and so forth," my mother said.

Her long brown hair was tied in a bun, a joint between her lips as she counted the money the man handed to her.

This was one of many men. His hair a fair blond, skin pale and slightly wrinkled. Those predatory eyes stared down at my small figure.

"How old is she?" he grumbled, eyes furrowing at my size.

"Ten," she said, a villainous smirk on her chapped lips.

"You couldn't get anyone older?" He sighed.

"You've paid. Use your time or leave," my mother snarled.

The man turned to me, gesturing for me to lead the way. Sighing quietly, I opened the bedroom door and guided him inside.

He took a seat on the bed, eyes lingering all over my body as he waited patiently. I untied the robe on my body and let it fall to the floor.

The man bit his lip and leaned back.

I walked forward as he took off his shoes and socks. Once he stood up, I began unbuttoning his shirt.

Just as I had done for so many men before . . .

* * *

A loud bang snapped me out of my slumber. Opening my crystal-blue eyes, I didn't recognise the room I was in. I was lying across a large bed, black sheets pooling around my waist. I was wearing the same clothes as the night before. A pile of fresh clothes lay at the foot of the bed.

Rising, I looked out of the window at the L.A. skyline. The room was painted white, with grey carpets covering the floor. The windows were black-framed, floor-length, and led onto a balcony.

Walking towards it, I realised I was in a room perched on a cliff's edge. Stepping out onto the balcony, I looked down and saw I was in a three-story house. The surrounding area was silent and peaceful, with no one else in sight.

I walked across the room, past the TV mounted on the wall, and picked up the pile of clothes. I opened the door next to the TV, revealing a bathroom of black-and-white marble. The bath was large enough for three, and the shower could accommodate four. There was a double sink and a porcelain toilet with stainless-steel fittings.

After locking the door and stripping off my clothes, I stepped into the shower. I washed my body with what was available—men's body wash. I shampooed and conditioned my hair with another man's products, then I rinsed thoroughly with water.

Once finished, I jumped out of the shower and dried myself with a towel draped over a radiator. I put on the clothes, which were—unsurprisingly by now—also men's clothes.

There were a pair of boxers, shorts, and a baggy Marvel tee. The shorts stopped just above my knees, and the shirt did the same. I tucked it into the shorts and left the bathroom, leaving the towel on the radiator.

I opened the bedroom door and poked my head outside to see who was there. When I saw no one, I began down the hall. The lights were white, matching the walls, whilst the carpet remained the same grey.

A few rooms ran along the hallway, each indicated by a door. An archway led to a luxurious living room. A modern fireplace had a television mounted above it. Two black leather sofas framed the large space, with a fluffy grey rug in the middle atop the white marble floor.

Large doors opened onto a balcony with grey wood floors, overlooking the L.A. skyline, just as the bedroom windows had.

Looking further inside, there was a dining room with a modern white table and fancy grey dining chairs. The kitchen was new, with white cabinets, black marble counters, and pristine white walls.

There was a kitchen island with bar stools and a TV remote on top. Walking further in, I noticed a note on the stainless-steel fridge:

There's iced coffee and breakfast in the fridge; the pills are on the side.
-AR

AR.

I still had no idea whose house I was in, and I was beginning to grow slightly worried. But whoever brought me here did not seemed to harbour any ill intent.

So far . . .

I took the coffee out of the fridge and swallowed the aspirin on the counter. The "breakfast" was uncooked bacon, suitable for a sandwich.

I can't cook.

Sighing, I sat at the counter and took a slice of bread from the bread bin and put it in the toaster. Once it was done, I spread some jam I had found in a cabinet and sat down by the island.

I angled the chair so I could look over the city, munching on the toast as I relaxed in the seat.

The sound of footsteps broke me out of my trance, and my eyes snapped to the hallway in the living room near the one I had come from.

Aidan walked in—the man from last night—his wet brown hair falling across his tan face. He wore black joggers and a white vest, just like the night before. The ink on his body was in full display, but what caught my attention most were the burn marks on his arms. They were all covered in tattoos. If one looked closely, they were noticeable.

"You're up," he commented when he saw me.

"And I'm where exactly?" I asked, cocking an eyebrow in his direction.

"My house. In Malibu," Aidan said, ruffling his wet hair.

"Why?" I asked, slightly uncomfortable around a man I barely knew.

"Last night, a guy from another club drugged you and tried to take advantage of you. I got to him before anything could happen and brought you here." He walked behind the counter and placed a frying pan on the electric stove.

"Why didn't you just leave me there?" I pressed.

Sighing, he looked up at me through long black lashes. "Everyone else was drunk, and I wanted to make sure you'd be okay. I brought you here and put you in my bed. I stayed in the guest bedroom."

The seriousness on his face told me the conversation was over. The situation was too dangerous for him to ignore. The fierceness in his hazel eyes left no room for discussion.

"I called Ace. He's going to come and get you at noon," Aidan said, cracking an egg in the pan.

I looked at the clock on the microwave. It was just past eleven. I sat silently, watching him fry his egg and make a sandwich out of it.

"Did you use the bacon?" he asked, leaning against the island and eating.

"No," I answered.

He stopped chewing at my response, his hazel eyes darting to my blue ones. He stood up straight and opened the fridge. Without a sound, he turned the stove on again and began frying the bacon.

"I've had toast," I told him.

He either didn't care or ignored me altogether. He continued to fry the bacon until it was crispy. He buttered some bread, placed the bacon on it, topped it with another slice, and put the plate down in front of me.

"Eat."

"I said I already ate," I said, pushing the plate towards him.

"A single slice of toast is not enough. Eat the fucking food."

Grumbling, I snatched the sandwich from the plate and ate it, glaring at him intensely. He waited until every last crumb was gone before turning away and washing his dish and mine.

"You know you're a real dick," I mutter.

"You're welcome," he said in a growl.

"Thank you. And fuck you," I said, turning away and storming to the bedroom I had just been in.

An hour later, Ace was knocking on the bedroom door, a tired look on his face as he stared down at me with red eyes.

"Move your arse," was all he said.

Chuckling quietly to myself, I picked up my bundled clothes and followed him out of the bedroom. After countless times of seeing Ace hungover, I had learned to leave him be whilst he was in this state.

We walked to the living room—correction, I walked; Ace stumbled—where Aidan was seated on the sofa. His hair was now dry, and a steady glare was set on his cold face.

When we came into view, his eyes softened slightly before returning to their pissed-off expression.

"Thanks for last night," I told him, to which he responded with a stiff nod.

Ace lazily waved goodbye, leaving Aidan to smirk momentarily before turning his gaze back to the basketball he was watching.

Ace opened the door of his grey Subaru WRX, his favoured street-racing car. I sat down in the passenger seat, relaxing into the soft leather. Ace only ever drove his car when he was hungover or when other people were joining him. The rest of the time, he rode his motorbike.

I turned on the heated seats and glanced out of the window. The front of Aidan's house was fairly modern—white walls with the occassional splash of grey and black-pained floor-length windows. The stairs outside his front door led to the smooth driveway where Ace had parked. On the other side, gates marked the end of the property, with a small guard station. The grass was fake and appeared rarely used.

I then noticed that the floor beneath the one I had been on was the garage. I couldn't tell what the remaining lower floor contained, but I assumed it was a gym and swimming pool, given this was America and the house seemed incredibly expensive.

Ace pulled out of the driveway; the guards opened the gates and gave us a little nod as we passed. We turned down the street, and I realised the beach was just opposite the entrance to Aidan's house.

Children were already playing in the sea, and parents were sunbathing on the sand. We passed a few oceanside shops, which were expected for this area, especially since Malibu was known for its beaches. We continued along the road by the Pacific. Almost thirty minutes later, I recognised the area where Christopher's house was located.

"Why are you taking me back?" I asked, my brows furrowed as I turned to Ace.

"Because our gang and your family are enemies. If they find out you were with us, things could get extremely bad," Ace said, offering me a sympathetic glance.

"Enemies?"

"They haven't told you?" Ace said. He chuckled quietly to himself, shaking his head. "Of course they haven't."

"Well?" I pressed, tired of him ignoring my curiosity.

"Your brother, Mateo, is the don of the Montessori empire—or 'family,' as it is usually referred to." Ace showed no hint of a joke in his tone or expression.

I sat in silence, taking in what he just said.

In all fairness, it did make sense. The guards, the guns, the riches and luxuries. They knew who Ace was and seemed to be concerned about him being near me.

"They know about you and me in the shopping centre that day," I told him.

"I know. If I had wanted them to not see me, they wouldn't have." He grinned, changing gears as he slowed down the road.

"Why did you?" I asked.

"I wanted to see if they'd protect you," he answered simply. "And they did. The second the guards saw me, I was practically chased out of the mall."

I let out a humourless chuckle, shaking my head. "Now they care."

Sighing, Ace parked the car a street down from the house. He turned towards me, all seriousness and sternness.

"Kal, they do care about you," he told me. "Last night, they sent out a whole search party."

I rolled my eyes, but Ace ignored that and continued, "Think about it. All the stories you heard were from your mother and Daniel. They both hated Christopher. While he may not have lied, Daniel only knew the old Christopher. You'll always have a place with us, Kalina, but give them a chance. We are enemies, yes, but if they can give you a chance at life—without the guns and the violence—give them a chance."

I waited a second, contemplating his words. Then, I gave him a small nod.

Ace smiled at this. After placing a kiss on my forehead, he ushered me out of the car.

He drove alongside me as I walked along the pavement, right up until I reached the gates of the mansion. As they opened, he sped off.

The guards gave me wary glances, eyeing my clothes with apprehension. I made my way up the driveway, when the front door was flung open with such force it nearly came off its hinges.

Out came Antonio and Tommaso. Tommaso flung himself onto me, stroking my hair and pressing kisses to the top of my head. Antonio quickly pulled him back, checking every inch of me for injuries. Once he was satisfied that I was unharmed, he stepped aside.

By now, all the others had left the house and gathered around me. Mateo looked relieved, smiling slightly. Stefano remained his usual self, though his usual moodiness had softened. Tristan had a small smile, barely noticeable, which quickly vanished when his eyes fell on the clothes I wore.

The agony etched across Christopher's expression was nothing but heartbreaking. It was as if everything had been taken from him, only for him to watch it returned, piece by piece.

"Boys, inside," he said in a near whisper.

Obediently, all the brothers did as they were told, leaving just the two of us outside. Neither of us moved or spoke, just stared at each other.

Knowing someone had to break the silence, I started, "I'm sorry for what I said."

Christopher took a step forward, the fabric of his suit jacket creasing as he folded his arms. "Why did you say it?" he asked, sadness evident in his tone.

Sighing, I looked down at the ground before staring into eyes identical to my own.

"All my life, my mother told me that I wasn't wanted by my father. Daniel always told me that you favoured your other sons. The only reason we lived with my mother was simply because you didn't care about us."

A fire slowly lit his eyes. The fury Christopher felt was laid out plain as day before me.

"Kalina, it's not true," he said. "The reason you lived with your mother was that I never knew of your existence."

My eyes snapped to his, confusion spreading across my face.

"But . . . Tommaso is my twin."

"Yes, I know," Christopher muttered. "I never saw any scan or ultrasound. I wasn't allowed in the birthing room, as we were already separated at that time.

When I left the hospital to fetch your older brothers to see Tommaso, I thought he was the only child. Your mother took you from the hospital and fled to England with Daniel. I never knew of your existence."

Shock was all I felt at the news. How could my mother be so evil? Then again, after everything, this seemed pretty minor.

"Why didn't you keep Daniel?" I asked further.

"Because Daniel wasn't my son, but my nephew. The reason your mother and I split was because she cheated on me with my brother."

CHAPTER FOURTEEN

KALINA

Christopher guided me inside and told me everything that had happened. Everything I had believed was a lie. The reality wasn't that my father didn't want me, but that he never known about me. Daniel was wrong when he said Christopher wasn't a father, because to him he wasn't.

I stayed silent as Christopher recounted the past. Every word he said grew more clearly true as he spoke.

Now, we sat silently at the dining-room table. Neither of us said anything since Christopher had finished his explanation.

"Kalina . . . please say something," Christopher begged.

"What do you expect me to say?" I retorted, feeling empty.

"Anything." He had a desperate look on his face.

"Is there anything else you need to tell me?" I asked, waiting for him to reveal the truth about his mafia family.

He didn't say anything for a moment before shaking his head.

With that, I rose from my seat and headed to the kitchen, already knowing Christopher was following me. I took an apple out of the fruit bowl and stared at him.

"Where were you last night?" he asked.

"Why? Did you not use the tracker?" I said, taking a bite of the apple.

Regretfully, he hung his head in shame, knowing I had caught him betraying his word. He said I would have to follow the same rules as the boys, but not once did he mention a tracker in the phone he had bought for me.

"For that, I apologize. I know I broke the little trust you have in me, and that is my own responsibility," he said sincerely. "I guess, after knowing I spent so long unaware of where you were, I didn't want that to happen again."

I leaned on the countertop, not having forgiven him just yet. "I was with friends. I was safe, and that's all I'm willing to say."

He nodded in understanding. "I'll take what I can get."

With that, I stood up straight and began leaving the room. But when he called out to me, I turned around.

"You'll start school tomorrow with Tommaso and Tristan," he said. "And, Kalina, I am sorry."

Then I left him alone in the kitchen.

I went upstairs to my bedroom and stripped off the clothes Aidan had given me to wear. I put on my own underwear and changed into a pair of black ripped jeans and a white Arctic Monkeys shirt.

Once I put on the remainder of my piercings I hadn't worn the night before, I lay down on my bed and let myself sink into the softness of the mattress. It was as if the weight of all my problems were crashing down around me.

The tears could no longer be held back, a way of showing the pain I was truly feeling. For years, all I had longed for was a mother to love me, to hold me when I fell down, to tuck me into bed after a long day at school. All I had wanted was a mother's love, and it had never been given to me.

It was as if a knife had been stabbed into my already wounded heart as I heard of the life I could had had—that the family I had dreamed of so desperately existed all along. Every scratch and tear on the delicate layer of my soul was torn once again, and all I could do was cry, catching every piece in my trembling hands.

I felt my throat tighten, warning me, and the need for oxygen increased as the air became thin and unreachable. With my hands over my mouth, I did everything I could to both catch my breath and silence the sounds of my heart-wrenching sobs. I didn't trust anyone here enough to see me in such a vulnerable state.

My entire body shook as the dizziness formed in my head, the tears continuously rolling down my red cheeks from my puffy eyes. The agony of every memory I held was as strong as the experience itself. With every inhale, I felt less and less oxygen entering my exhausted body.

When the panting and struggle for breath became all too much, the churning in my stomach had my mind reeling with reality. Turning on my side, I prepared for the sickness to barrel through my stomach. But as I did so, everything physical settled within me. The need to vomit subsided.

For a moment . . .

Feeling the bile rising in my throat once again, I bolted for the bathroom and hung my head over the toilet bowl. Reaching blindly for the phone in my pocket, I quickly searched through the contacts until my blurry vision landed on his name.

By the second ring, the phone was answered, and Ace's tired voice sounded through the line.

"A-A-Ace . . ." I could barely get his name out.

This wasn't the first time I had called Ace in a moment of weakness, and he knew exactly what to do.

"Count, Kalina. Count with me. One, two . . ."

I did as he said, counting step by step with him. He waited patiently as I caught my breath enough to utter the next number.

" . . . eight, nine, ten."

We repeated this method three times until my breathing had evened out and the shakiness from the sobs had subsided. My back was now against the marble wall, my head leaning back against it.

"Kalina?" Ace spoke after a few minutes, the phone, on speaker mode, resting at my feet.

"Thank you," I whispered.

My throat was drier than a nun's vagina at this point from all the panting I had done. My lips were chapped and bleeding from all the biting I had done in my state of panic. Thank God my nails were cut down this time. Before, I had dug them so deep into my palm that they bled.

"Anytime, darling," Ace replied. "Are you okay now?"

Ace could always tell when to back away and when to stay put. So, after a moment, when I muttered a small yes, that was all he needed to know that I was truly fine. After all, he could read me like an open book.

He hung up the phone, leaving me to sigh as I was alone once again. Looking at the clock, it told me it was just before noon. Soon, someone would likely come and see if I was willing to talk.

That was if Christopher had not already called them all to discuss what I thought, which I was sure he had.

Rising from my crouched position on the floor—already certain the feeling of nausea and sickness had passed—I splashed cold water from the tap onto my face, careful not to use too much in case I triggered myself again.

After I cleaned away the salty tears from my cheeks, I guided myself back into the bedroom and collapsed onto the bed, wishing I could change everything bad that had ever happened to me.

CHAPTER FIFTEEN

KALINA

No one spoke last night at dinner. The constant silence was like a drug that muted all emotion and tension.

I knew they had all spoken about Christopher's and my discussion, as they were all visibly nervous. Once the meal was over, I did not waste a second going back to my bedroom. Tommaso and Tristan were outside my room for some time, thinking I could not hear them arguing quietly about whether they should knock or not. I ignored them until they left a few minutes later.

Once again, I awoke in the middle of the night, bathed in a pool of my own sweat and horror, unable to move until I caught my breath. Tristan must have heard me wake again, as he poked his head through the door to check on me. But with a single shake of my head, he left me alone without any fuss.

I hadn't moved from my spot on the bed for three hours now, and it was currently six in the morning. Knowing I had to leave for my first day at school in two hours, I rose from the bed and shuffled to the bathroom.

Hesitantly, I turned on the shower. A flash of panic went through me. Sighing, I snapped myself out of that state before stripping out of my damp pyjamas and stepping in the shower. Holding tightly onto the marble wall, my body momentarily seized up at the feel of the water on my skin.

Reaching down, I pressed a point on my knee and held on tight before the state of anxiety passed and I could stand easily. Quickly, I washed my hair and body, shaved, and jumped out of the shower. Once dried and moisturised, I began drying my thick hair.

Half-an-hour later, it was still slightly damp but dry enough for me to leave the bathroom. I did Dutch plaits on my black curls, which ended up just below my elbow. Personally, I did not wear makeup that often, so all that was left was to get changed.

After deciding on a simple white lace bra and panties, I picked out my outfit for the day. I went for a knitted black sweater over a white cami top, a pair of black shorts, and my Adidas trainers. The black-inked tattoos on my tan skin were brought out by the clothing of choice, as well as the wide range of piercings, each of which I had decided to adorn with jewellery.

As I walked out of the bedroom door, Tommaso came barrelling down the hallway in his skintight boxers. Tristan was standing a few feet in front of him, laughing his arse off.

"Oh. Sorry, Kalina. Did Tommaso's childish screams wake you?" Tristan mused, a smirk stretching across his face.

"KALINA!" Tommaso gasped.

He turned around to face me, and instantly, a hand was in front of his boxers and his toned chest.

"Why are you hiding your tits?" I laughed at the embarrassment coating his cheeks.

"TRISTAN! Give me my fucking clothes!" Tommaso whined, irritation in his tone.

"Fine. Put your boobies away." Tristan chuckled, throwing Tommaso his shirt.

Scurrying back into his room, he grumbled about idiotic older brothers before slamming the door shut.

Tristan gave me a cautious glance, to which I just responded with a nod, answering his silent question of whether I was okay or not. With a neutral expression now on his face after causing his morning drama, he turned around and made his way down the hall.

Tristan waited at the top of the stairs when he realised I was following him. When I reached his side, he began walking again, a faint ghost of a smile on his face.

"Stop smiling. People might actually think you care." I grinned.

"Would that be so bad?" he asked, a seriousness I had never heard from him noticeable in his voice.

I contemplated his words, wondering simply if he was right. I had longed for a family for so long, and now that I had one, all I needed to do was accept them.

"Don't get soft on me now," I replied.

I'm not ready to make that decision.

Upon entering the kitchen, Christopher and Stefano were there. The latter was seated behind the kitchen island, a sketchbook on the counter, a pencil in hand, and a mug of coffee at his side. Christopher was behind the stove, making scrambled eggs in a giant pan. After he saw Tristan and me take a seat, he served us a plate each, a bright morning smile on his face.

"What's got you in a good mood?" Tristan asked, fork in hand.

"You and Tommaso are fucking off back to school!" Christopher grinned. "Summer is finally fucking over!"

Giggling in my seat, I watched as Tristan flicked a piece of scrambled egg off his fork and directed it towards Christopher. In return, Christopher took Tristan's slice of toast.

"Kalina, are you ready for your first day?" Christopher asked.

"Fuck no," I answered.

Sighing, Christopher then asked, "Do you even have any school supplies?"

As I was about to answer no again, Stefano reached down the side and picked up a black backpack. He placed it down in front of me.

"I don't have anything to go in—"

Cutting me off, Stefano unzipped the bag to reveal anything and everything I would need for school, from pens and pencils to a scientific calculator and hand sanitiser.

"Um, thanks," I said, a little taken aback.

In response, he lifted his mug towards me before bringing it to his lips for a drink.

It wasn't long until Tommaso came downstairs for his breakfast. His hair was still a messy bunch of brown curls. Both he and Tristan were dressed in simple shirts and jeans—already bored of school, and we hadn't even left the house yet.

"Dad, where's Tony and Mateo?" Tommaso asked as he placed his plate in the sink.

"They left late last night for a work emergency. Antonio said not to let you guys leave until he sees Kalina," Christopher answered, a grin on his face at my audible groan.

As we all headed out the door towards the black-and-red Ford Mustang—which I later learned belonged to Tristan—a matte black Ferrari came barrelling through the gates and pulled up next to our ride. Before it had completely stopped, Antonio flung the door open and bolted out.

"Thank fuck we weren't late!" he cheered. "Right, I want a senior year photo! Cuddle up!"

Reluctantly, I let Tristan and Tommaso wrap their arms around my shoulders as I stood between the two. Antonio then turned the next five minutes into a full-blown photo shoot, trying every angle and lighting.

He's such a mother.

Eventually, he let us go, and the three of us piled into the car. As Tristan drove out of the gates, a notification dinged on Tommaso's phone. Laughing, he showed the photos to the two of us.

"Kal, I never noticed how small you are compared to us," he commented, a grin on his face.

I blame childhood starvation.

"Add her to the group," Tristan said, unamused by Tommaso's remark.

I hope he doesn't read too much into it

Tommaso did as asked, and a second later, I got a notification on my phone:

Tommaso added Kalina to the group "Italian Stallions".
Tommaso changed the group name to "Italian Stallions and the
Princess Unicorn ⊠"

"Really, Tom?"
- Antonio

"Yes, she is too magnificent to be just a stallion!"
- Tommaso

I looked up from my phone screen and gave Tommaso a *WTF* look. He just smirked in return.

I sat listening to Tristan's rap music as we drove through early-morning L.A. It was not long before we pulled into a large car park. He parked a few lanes away from the school entrance, which was modern and fancy.

UK schools look really shit right now.

As I was about to open the car door, Tommaso locked it from the front console. Giving him a baffled look, I waited for an explanation.

"While Dad may not expect you to stay with us, we at least want to know where to find you and be within eyesight if possible," Tommaso said in a kind tone.

"But—" Tristan cut in. "We would prefer it if you made friends with our friends. Because one, we—" At the look Tommaso gave him, he corrected himself. "I want to keep you around. And two, I think you'll actually like them."

Sighing, I lay back in my seat, considering his request.

"You can't get overprotective no matter who I'm friends with," I told them. "But I'd like to spend more time with you guys."

Maybe a bit more family time won't be too bad.

The three of us piled out of the car, and the two insisted on taking me to reception to collect my timetable. The lady at the desk was quite pleasant and seemed to enjoy batting her eyelashes at Tristan.

Whilst Tommaso dragged him away from the desk, I glanced down at my classes for the day: History, Maths, English, Engineering, free period, and Biology.

Tristan peered at the paper over my shoulder, and a smirk spread across his face. "We have the same classes. All day!"

FML.

"Brilliant," I muttered under my breath.

"I've got nothing but Engineering and Biology with you both," Tommaso said, his usual smile shifting into a smirk.

Then suddenly, neither he nor Tristan was smiling. It was as if the loving atmosphere Tommaso usually gave off and the care Tristan exuded had vanished. Now, they were both overprotective bodyguards.

They guided me through the halls until we arrived at some lockers. On the back of my timetable was my locker number and code. It just happened to be sandwich between my brothers'.

How curious. Note the sarcasm.

The bell rang, and I went with Tristan to History class. Inside, groups of people were already scattered, either seated at tables or huddled away in the corners.

"Tris!" someone yelled.

Tristan made his way to the back of the classroom, where two people were standing. The girl had long black dreadlocks with dark brown skin. Her eyes were a light brown, and her eyelashes were long and thick. She wore a short-sleeved, sweetheart-neckline top and a dark blue jeans. She was fairly tall, around five-foot-nine, with a figure just as curvy as mine.

Next to her stood a boy of insane height, around six-foot-six, with a fair amount of muscle. His brown hair was cropped down to a few centimetres, and his eyes were a dark green. He wore a black leather jacket over a grey shirt and jeans.

"Who's the pretty little lady?" He grinned cheekily, walking towards me after bro-hugging Tristan.

"Call me 'little' or 'lady' again, and will I cut your tongue out and make you eat it." I glared at him, a sadistic smile on my face.

He froze, stunned, whilst the girl looked clearly taken aback. Tristan chuckled, reaching out to pull me closer with a proud grin.

"This is the little sister I've been telling you all about," he said.

"Kalina," I said, shaking the girl's outstretched hand.

"Well, that explains the threat." The girl brought me into a hug. "I'm Hailey, and you are way too gorgeous to be related to that . . . thing."

She gestured to Tristan, who was glaring freely at her.

"That's Charlie. We tend to ignore him."

Now it was the other boy's turn to glare at her.

Within seconds, Hailey had me take a seat and was grilling me for information—how my stomach and arms were so toned, amongst other things.

"Just a fuck load of gym back in juvie," I answered, a smirk on my face.

She stared at me with wide eyes for a moment. Charlie did too, whilst Tristan sat silently in his chair.

"Why were you in juvie?" Hailey asked cautiously.

She was obviously tense at the thought of being in prison as a kid.

And she's friends with a member of the mafia.

"Got busted during a drug deal." I shrugged, leaning back in my seat.

"What?!" Tristan gritted out.

"Talk about it later," was all I told him.

He seemed to be having a mental argument with himself before deciding to comply and remain silent.

A few minutes later, the teacher came into the classroom, and everyone fell into their seats. She began writing on the board about World War Two as it was the topic for the next few weeks. I sat, eager to learn history—it had always been a passion of mine.

"Copy down what's on the board," she said, before typing away on her computer.

I was seated beside Tristan and Hailey. The latter was copying down the notes in fancy handwriting. When he noticed I wasn't doing the work after lifting his gaze from his phone, Tristan nudged my side.

"Christopher expects good grades from us," he whispered through the almost-silent classroom.

"What about you?" I asked, noticing he wasn't working.

"Photographic memory. Now, write down the shit," he practically ordered.

"I can't," I whispered, hanging my head.

"Can't what?" he asked, annoyance in his tone.

"Write," I mumbled.

He gave me a baffled look before taking my book and writing down what was on the board. He wrote in block letters, but I still couldn't make sense of them.

"Can you read?" he quietly asked, a caring tone in his voice.

Silently, I shook my head, avoiding eye contact. Tristan didn't say anything—he simply wrote down what I needed to know.

It continued this way for the entire lesson. Tristan didn't question me again; he just wrote down the relevant information.

He did the same in both Maths and English. When we got to Engineering, though, I happily went off on my own.

He still kept an eye on me, though.

Since I had gathered this school was heavily funded by parent donations, I was surprised to see a garage-like classroom. We were all given a small part of an engine to assemble. I finished it within seconds.

It took Charlie by surprise as he sat next to me whilst we worked. From what I had gathered, this school's main sport was lacrosse, and Charlie was on the team like Tommaso. Apparently, Tristan had been on the team last year but was no longer allowed due to his constant fighting. Besides the whole playboy act, Charlie was actually a pretty decent guy.

I had also met another one of their friends, Alessio. He was the typical bad boy with tattoos. He wore a leather jacket and would leave class to smoke. The second I was introduced to him, he was told I was off-limits.

As Biology came to an end, Tristan passed me my book once again and told Tommaso to shut up as he went to ask why he had it. Putting my book and pen away in my bag, I waited for my brothers to get sorted, and then we left the classroom.

"Kal?" Tommaso said as Tristan went to say goodbye to Alessio.

"Yeah." I sighed, expecting some questions.

"Why was Tristan doing your work for you?" he asked, his brows furrowed in confusion.

"Because I like her more than I like you," Tristan said, glaring as he approached the two of us.

Tommaso flipped him off, to which Tristan responded by putting him in a headlock. The two wrestled for a few minutes whilst I took the car keys out of Tristan's back pocket.

As I sat in the passenger seat of the car, I chuckled to myself as I saw two panicked brothers bolting out of the entrance.

Both their shoulders sagged in relief when they saw me sitting in the car. As Tristan got in the driver's seat and Tommaso in the back, the look they gave me said they were impressed and shocked.

"You were taking too long." I shrugged.

CHAPTER SIXTEEN

TRISTAN

As we pulled into the gates of the estate, I told Tommaso to go inside, and we would follow him in. Kalina didn't hear anything because of her headphones. He might have already realized it was about the writing thing, but he said nothing.

Tommaso left the car, and as Kalina was about to go as well, I gently grabbed her hand to stop her. Hesitantly, she sat back down, took out her headphones, and turned towards me.

"You know we need to talk about the writing and reading," I told her, offering a soft smile.

Sighing, she simply nodded.

"Kalina, it's either you talk to me or Christopher and Mateo about it," I explained.

I would gladly help my sister with this. It was obvious she was self-conscious about it, but it needed to be addressed. Christopher would more than be happy to give her all the tutors she needed.

That's not what her self-esteem needs.

"I just . . . I try and I try and I try. But I can't do it," she mumbled.

For the first time since I met her, I saw a part of that confident façade crack. A single tear rolled down her cheek as she stared at the floor.

"Is it a disability or you just weren't taught?" I asked cautiously.

She just shrugged. "I don't even know."

Sighing, I reached across the console of the car and pulled her into a hug. Instantly, she latched onto me, hiding her head in my chest.

We stayed there for a few minutes. Once again, she accepted the comfort I offered.

To everyone, they only saw the outside. I was a brooding asshole who fought and hurt people for fun, then flunked school for the bad-boy act. Society says I would be dead, an addict, or in prison by twenty. In the underworld, I was probably one of the most powerful and deadly people there was. To my family, I was the hot-headed, overprotective brother and son who caused trouble and scandal for the sake of it.

But, deep down, behind the anger issues and violence, all I wanted was for my family to be happy.

I messed around with Tommaso because he loved pranks and banter. I would sit beside Stefano as he drew in his sketchbook as a way to relax. I let Antonio mother me and teach me, mafia or otherwise, because it brought him comfort to know he tried. Mateo and I cooked meals together, and we had late-night drives. It grounded him in reality, making sure he wasn't devoured by the mafia world. Then, I simply let Dad be a parent, taking his advice and bonding with him. As a child, I relied on him to help me fall asleep at night, and as I got older, I relied on him to teach me the ways of the mafia.

I never had a little sister, though.

I never had someone so clearly troubled and confused in my life. And Kalina was adamant on not letting anyone else know that she struggled. Why? I did not know, but I wouldn't go against her wishes unless it put her in danger. All I could do was offer her help.

"Did Daniel teach you how to read?" I asked after a moment.

I felt her tense in my arms at the mention of his name, but she just mumbled a small, "He tried."

As I was about to ask her if she thought an evaluation was necessary, she pulled away and whispered, "Can we leave it for now?"

I gave her a small smile and nodded before getting out of the car. She did the same, carrying her school bag inside.

The second we were through the door, Antonio was in front of us, swinging her around in a hug. As he pulled away and saw the redness in her eyes, his smile dropped slightly.

Behind her, I made a hand signal for him to ease up. He did, and straight away asked her about school.

"Let's have a look at your work!" Antonio said, the joy returning to his tone.

Kalina didn't protest as she opened her bag. She handed him her history book, and he opened it with an expectant expression.

Although he hid it well, especially from Kalina, he knew it was my handwriting.

When I was younger, he would sit me down at a table for hours and make me practice my letters and cursive writing. Most of the time, I wrote mini paragraphs about how much I hated being forced to practice my writing.

He gave her her book back and told her dinner would be ready in two hours. Within seconds, she was at the top of the stairs, running down the hallway to her bedroom.

Antonio turned toward me with a waiting glance. Sighing, I knew there wasn't a clear way to get out of this, but I didn't want him to know from me.

"Well?"

"I . . . she couldn't read the board, so I just wrote for her so she didn't get in trouble for talking or not doing her work," I explained. "I think she has shit long-distance vision or something. She may need glasses."

It's all I could think of.

Her eyesight may be the best explanation for why she couldn't read or write. I actually noticed that her left eye was weak, vision-wise. When I was seated to her left in class and Charlie threw a rubber at me, my hand nearly touched her face as I caught it. But she didn't even notice.

That scar at the side of her face ran straight through her eyebrow and down to her cheek. Perhaps her eyesight was damaged after that wound was inflicted.

I was desperate to ask her how it happened. To ask who hurt my *sorellina.* But I had only known her less than a week. I couldn't ask her that.

That scar and her nightmares had something in common. I just hoped I was wrong and she was simply just adjusting to a new home—but I knew that was not true. The scars on her right arm, beneath the tattoos and tan skin, were wounds that never really healed.

My blood boiled at the thought of someone hurting a member of my family. But I would never let her see how much I wanted to hurt them, because God knew that would trigger her.

I'll never hurt her.

"Should we get her eyes tested?" Antonio proposed.

"It's up to her." I shrugged.

"I'll speak to Dad about it. See what he thinks," Antonio said, giving me a slight pat on the back before walking away.

Sighing, I made my way up the stairs, only to find Kalina standing around the corner.

She didn't say anything. All she did was give me a small hug, then she went to her room. The relief in her eyes was bold and loud as she stared up at me.

She knew that, at some point, we would need to know about her scars and why she couldn't read or write.

But I would keep her secret to the grave until she was comfortable talking about it.

CHAPTER SEVENTEEN

KALINA

When I got to my room, I went to the bathroom and dabbed water on my face, removing the remaining tears from my cheeks. As I left the bathroom, I looked up and found Tommaso sprawled out on my bed.

He was wearing a hoodie and a pair of Nike shorts. He also had a bag of sweets in one hand. In his other hand, he held another one of his grey hoodies, a pair of my own shorts, and some fluffy socks.

"Movie night?"

Smiling, I nodded and took the clothes from his hand. I changed inside my wardrobe and brought out a giant knitted blanket.

"Fucking hell. That's huge," Tommaso commented as he watched me heave it out the door. He made no move to help.

"Don't get up. I've got it," I said sarcastically, giving him a deadpan glare.

"Okay," he chirped happily.

"Tommy!" I whined, still struggling.

"Tommy?" he questioned, an amused expression on his face.

"You could be a Peaky Blinder, by the way you walk," I responded.

It was true. He had the whole "fuck-you" vibe at school as he walked—strutted—the halls. But the second he was with family or friends, he was beyond playful.

"A whaty what the fuck?" Tommaso's face was one of pure bewilderment.

"You don't know what *Peaky Blinders* is!" I yelled, my heart ripping in two.

"No," Tommaso answered, his voice quivering slightly.

"Forget fucking movie night. It's time for basic British education."

By the second episode, Tommaso was completely engrossed. He had already declared Tommy and Freddie his favourites. Poor boy.

His eyes were transfixed on the screen, staring deep into the soul of the Shelby clan. He might have shit himself a little when they started cutting up the Lee boys with their hats. I also suspected he developed a little crush on the original Tommy during that scene.

I mean . . . Thomas Shelby is just chef's kiss.

Tommaso's growing semi, however, was put on hold by dinner.

The two of us went downstairs, only to find Mateo and Christopher missing from table. Antonio was barking orders at Stefano, who was sipping his coffee and completely ignoring him.

"Ahh. Finally. There's been an issue at work, so Dad, Mateo, and I need to go. You three"—he pointed at Tristan, Tommaso, and me—"be in bed by ten."

"That's a bit early, don't you think, son?" Christopher said, walking through the doorway.

He was buttoning up his trench coat, talking to Antonio. His gaze swept the room until it landed on me at the table. His eyes were analysing as he smiled at me.

So, he's talked with Antonio.

"Give the kids a reasonable time," he continued, a cheeky grin on his face.

"Two in the morning is not a reasonable time, Dad," Antonio deadpanned.

"You and Mateo turned out fine." Christopher smirked at his son's annoyance.

"Bed by ten-thirty."

Rolling his eyes, Christopher kissed the top of Stefano's, Tristan's, and Tommaso's heads. When he got to me, he hesitate, offering me a little shoulder squeeze instead.

Antonio followed him out, but Mateo waited till they had left.

"Kalina, tomorrow after school, Stefano is going to pick you up. Tommaso and Tristan have a job to do."

"I can have someone else pick me up—"

"You will go with Stefano." Mateo ended the conversation and marched off.

Rolling my eyes, I began eating the risotto in front of me. No one really spoke during dinner; we just ate our food.

When we finished, Tommaso and I went back to my bedroom and watched the rest of the first season of *Peaky Blinders*. By midnight, Tommaso was asleep on my bed.

So, I can either not sleep at all or sleep on his bed, surrounded by men—well, boys—room smells and other . . . interesting aromas.

Sighing, I rose from the mattress and went downstairs. The house was dead and dark, with nothing and no one in sight. I went to the kitchen and grabbed some orange juice from the fridge.

"Why are you still up?"

A loud scream left my lips. I spun around and saw Stefano sitting at his usual bar stool. Before I could answer, the sound of footsteps bolting down the stairs interrupted me.

"Kalina!"

"I'm fine, Tristan!" I called out.

"Are you sure?"

He was standing by the stairs, hands behind his back, and Stefano just out of his sight.

Probably a gun.

"Yeah, just scared myself," I answered.

Nodding, Tristan trudged tiredly back up the stairs and to his room. Once I heard the door shut, I turned back towards Stefano.

"Can't sleep," I replied to his earlier question.

"Because Tommaso is on your bed." It wasn't a question, but a statement.

His eyes scrutinised me as he stared from across the kitchen island.

"Yes."

Stefano didn't say anything else. He simply rose from his seat, walked past me, and went to the cabinet well above my reach. He pulled out a kettle and filled it with water.

He pointed to a cupboard by my feet. Inside, in front of all the bread and the abundance of food, was a giant pack of tea bags.

Smiling quietly, I opened the pack and passed him a tea bag.

He finished making my tea and handed me the mug. With a small smile, he returned to the bar stool and sat down.

Deciding to stay with him, since I wouldn't be getting any sleep in my room, I took the seat on a bar stool beside him. From where I was sitting, I could see his sketchbook and the drawings inside.

He was almost finished with the current one: a lion with flowers for a mane, scars coating its face as the petals fell to the ground beneath its paws. The eyes were shaded perfectly to show the shadows of doubt the creature held. While the mane was beautiful, proof of the animal's exoticness, the scars and claws showed damage visible only to those who looked for the pain.

"It's beautiful," I commented. "Where did you get inspiration for it?"

He didn't say anything, just lifted his brown gaze to mine.

"I'm a tattoo artist. I sketch possible designs in my spare time." He spoke quietly, flicking through the book covered in lead and art.

"You're very good. Could you do a tattoo for me?"

He simply gave me a deadpan look.

"I will if you tell me where you got the other tattoos from," he replied, lifting his coffee to his lips.

Knowing I would have to out my relationship with Ace and the gang, and there was no way Stefano would simply accept "friends" as an answer, so I remained silent.

Whilst Ace had told me to give them a chance, I had no idea how much the Chained Angels and the Italian Mafia hated each other. And I refused to be the cause of a war between the two.

"Go to bed. Tomorrow, after school, I'll take you to my shop and you can sneak out the back, away from the guards."

Smirking, I got up from my seat and headed out of the kitchen, tea in hand.

"Kalina, I'm trusting you to stay safe and return home by dinner."

Trust.

* * *

The school day came and went in a flash. It mostly consisted of Tristan writing down my work for me, and Tommaso doing the same whenever Tristan wasn't around. Charlie, Hailey, and Alessio spent more time getting to know me. Despite being popular, they were genuinely lovely people.

Charlie took the time to explain lacrosse when I asked what it was. Alessio and I playfully fought each other during most of our lessons, and Hailey introduced me to some of her girlfriends.

I prefer boys, though. They're less bitchy.

As planned, Stefano picked me up from school, whilst Tristan and Tommaso headed in the opposite direction towards the house.

Stefano was driving a black Mercedes, taking us further into the south side of the city. Just as we approached the border that led to the poorer part of town, Stefano pulled into a car park behind a row of buildings.

I followed him out of the car, and he held open a door at the back of one particular building. Inside was a well-laid-out tattoo parlour, painted grey and red. A few people were already inside, either tattooing, piercing, or getting work done on themselves.

Stefano took a seat in a chair at the back, surrounded by ink and tattoo guns. He nodded to a chair in the corner, and I took a seat in the middle of the booth-like area.

An hour passed. Stefano had already started on a back piece for a woman in her twenties. He glanced up at the bored expression on my face.

"Go," he told me. "You can come back here in an hour or so."

I gave him a small smile in thanks, jumped up, and made my way through the shop until I left through the front door. I recognised the area from when I first went to the clubhouse.

Deciding it was time to see my boys again, I continued down the pavement. After about a mile or so, the clubhouse came into view. Picking up the pace, I started jogging towards the building.

There were people working in the garage. Ace and Jamie were spraying each other with the jet washes, and Maddie and Aidan inside, apparently fixing a car someone brought in for repair.

"Kal!" Maddie shouted as she saw me approaching.

I ran up to her and hugged her tightly, and she returned it just as fiercely. She set aside the beer she had been drinking and gave me a quick, assessing look.

She's just checking.

"I'm good. You can keep going," I told her, offering a small grin.

After staring at me with analysing eyes for another moment, she picked her drink back up. Aidan stared with curious eyes, but one look from Maddie told him to drop it.

"Kalina!" Ace cheered once he put the jet wash away.

He and Jamie were soaking wet, water dripping down their foreheads and white shirts, which were now see-through. I ran up to them and hugged them both, not bothered about getting my clothes wet. The two hugged me back, kissing the top of my head before letting me go.

"What are you doing here?" Jamie asked, slinging his arm over my shoulder.

"What? I can't visit my family?" I fake-pouted.

"Of course you can." Jamie smirked, pulling me in for another hug.

He started guiding me inside the clubhouse. Ace, Aidan, and Maddie had already gone in. I took a seat at a bar stool as everyone spread themselves out, and Aidan moved behind the bar.

"I'll take a rum and coke," I said, turning towards him.

"How about just a coke," Aidan retorted, taking a glass out of the cupboard.

"Since when do you tell me if I can drink or not?" I said, reaching over the counter for a bottle of rum.

Instantly, he slapped my hand away, shaking his head. "Since I found out you weren't eighteen."

Rolling my eyes, I took the coke from the counter and swivelled around. I watched as everyone talked and played pool, happy and at peace.

Until it wasn't.

A loud bang cracked through the windows, and the main doors were kicked open. Small shards of glass flew towards me, cutting my skin.

Before I could even comprehend what was happening, I was being pulled over the bar and onto the floor. Looking up, I realised it was Aidan on top of me, covering my head, gun in hand.

"Move!" he yelled over the shouting, pointing towards the back door to the garage.

I did as he said, crawling to the end of the bar before running for the door. He was only a step behind me when a grunt fell from his lips.

Turning around, I saw blood pooling from his stomach and upper thigh. Grabbing ahold of his firm bicep, I dragged him through the door and took the keys from his hands.

I flung him into the passenger seat and hopped into the driver's. Thankfully, the garage door was already open, and, within seconds, I was speeding out in the white Nissan GT-R.

I swerved between the motorbikes and cars owned by other members. The attackers must have been on foot.

"We need to go back," I whispered as we drove further into the city. "I need to go back!"

I started turning the car around to head back to the clubhouse, but a blood-soaked hand grabbed my forearm tightly. I slammed on the brakes and met Aidan's stern glare.

"We can't go back. Drive to my house," he practically ordered.

"But what about Ace?! Jamie! Maddie!"

He tightened his grip on my arm—not to hurt me, but to stop me from talking.

"They can hold their own. However, if you're there, they'll spend their time worrying about you and could put themselves in danger," Aidan explained, his expression softening. "The most you can do is stay away."

Sighing, I pressed my foot on the accelerator and continue towards the road to Aidan's house. Every few seconds, I glanced at him as he pressed his hands to his wounds. The worry on my face must have been obvious, because Aidan simply said, "I'm fine. Don't worry."

"Where are you shot?" I asked, taking another glance at him.

"Just focus on driving," Aidan grunted, shifting in his seat.

"Just answer the fucking question!" I yelled, swerving between vehicles.

"Lower left abdomen; upper left thigh," he begrudgingly answered.

Sighing, I pulled into the driveway of his house. I rolled down the window, and Aidan leaned over the console.

The guards opened the gates, and I sped inside. I skidded to a stop on the driveway and ran to the passenger side. Aidan had already tried to get out but fell back miserably into his seat.

I helped him stand up, flinging his left arm over my shoulder so his weight rested on me and not his leg. The two of us shuffled into the house, and I dragged him towards the lift instead of the stairs. I hauled him further through the house and into the kitchen, then left him seated on a bar stool.

"Is there anyone I can call?" I asked.

"No, I can handle this. Can you grab the first-aid kit from under the sink?"

I did as he asked. Instead of a simple first-aid kit, it was actually a full-blown suitcase of medical equipment. I brought it back to him, only to find him stripped down to his boxers, his wounds still bleeding.

CHAPTER EIGHTEEN

KALINA

Throughout my life, I had seen my fair share of men—even when I didn't want to. I had seen variations of toned abs, tattoo designs, strong muscles, and sizes of dicks.

However, they were all nothing compared to Aidan's.

His figure was beyond drool-worthy. His *eight*-pack was decorated in colourful ink. His biceps were the size of my thick thighs, except his were all muscle. Aidan's locks of brown hair fell over his hazel eyes.

For a moment—only a moment—I swore my gaze dropped lower.

I visibly gulped. It was like nothing I had ever seen. The girth was impressive, the length even more so. And from what I could tell, the boxers did not do him justice.

I felt heat coating my cheeks, my eyes darting to the floor. He took the first-aid kit and tried to wipe his wounds, but it was all a struggle.

Aidan looked up at me with a pleading gaze.

Nodding slightly, I took the antiseptic wipes from his hand and began on the wound on his abdomen. I wiped it, then he passed me the tweezers.

Before I started, I grabbed him some whiskey and a tea towel. After taking a few mouthfuls of the liquor, he shoved the tea towel into his mouth. When he was ready, I took the new tweezers out the packets and wiped them down with clean wipes. I then began searching for the bullet.

It was fairly easy to find, as the wound wasn't too deep. Besides a grunt here and there, it didn't seem extremely bad for Aidan. I stitched and dressed the wound and decided to move on.

But once I repeated the process on his thigh, things got a bit more complicated. The bullet had lodged deep, to the point where my chin was practically resting on his leg to get close. After a good few minutes, I finally found the bullet and pulled it out.

Once again, I cleaned, stitched, and dressed the wound.

Then I realised the position I was in.

My face was directly in front of his crotch, and he was staring down at me with hooded eyes. Instantly, I moved from my position, giving him space to get up.

"I'm gonna go wash the blood off," he mumbled and headed towards his bedroom.

As he left, I decided to check for my own injuries. I pulled off the black long-sleeved T-shirt and grimaced at the rips—shards of glass had cut through the fabric and embedded themselves in my skin.

After sterilising the tweezers, I began picking out the shards of glass from my flesh. Once I had removed all the ones at the front, I tried to get the ones at the back. Unfortunately, I couldn't reach them.

Before I could do anything, a pair of rough yet soft hands gently took hold of the tweezers.

I winced slightly as a shard bigger than anticipated was pulled from my back. I felt him rub soothing circles with his thumb over the wounded area. As the glass was dropped into a bowl, I turned back around.

Aidan stood there in only a black pair of joggers. His eyes raked down my front, lingering on the contents of my bra.

After a moment, he seemed to snap himself out of his trance-like state and stepped back. He moved to the other side of the kitchen island and took a bottle of water from the fridge.

Once I finished dressing the wounds and put my shirt back on, I took the bottle he offered. I sat on the bar stool whilst he leant against the counter. The silence was deadly, hanging heavy in the room.

"Have you heard anything?" I mumbled after a few minutes.

Aidan simply shook his head, indicating no one had called. Sighing, I turned my gaze to the counter as a yawn slipped past my lips.

"Shit!" I said as realisation dawned. "What time is it?"

"Just past six," Aidan answered.

"Shit! I need to get back," I said, standing from the bar stool and heading for the door.

Before I could even take three steps, Aidan's firm arm wrapped around my waist. He spun me back around, and my hands instinctively shook as they landed on his chest.

Concern was etched across his face, just as fear was no doubt clear on mine. Slowly, he took my hands in his, enveloping me in his warmth. He rubbed his hand on my back in the same soothing manner as he had moments before. When I stopped shaking, he lifted my head from his chest and stared down into my blue eyes.

"You can't leave, Kalina," he said intently.

I opened my mouth to protest, but he continued, "We have no idea why the club was attacked or who did it. For all we know, they could be after you."

Sighing, I nodded. Slowly, he let me go, allowing me to take a seat on the sofa in the living room. He sat in the armchair in the corner, slumped in the seat with his usual stern glare in place.

My phone began buzzing moments later. I pulled it out of my pocket, the screen lighting up with Christopher's usual "Where are you?" rant.

"Who is it?" Aidan asked, his expression demanding.

"My biological father. He's wondering where I am," I told him. "He's quite insistent on knowing my whereabouts at all times."

"I don't blame him," Aidan said, legs spreading as he leaned back in his seat.

"Why?" I pressed, confusion boiling within me.

"Your father is Christopher Montessori, ex-don of the Montessori Mafia. And you're his only daughter. If I were him, I'd want to know where you were at all times."

Shock was clearly etched across my face at his explanation. "How do you know that—"

"That he's your father? Ace told me. He thought it better that I knew you were my enemy's daughter than finding out some other way," Aidan explained, his expression nonchalant.

"And why haven't you killed me yet?" I pressed.

"Your family isn't the Montessoris; it's the Chained Angels. Besides, kids shouldn't have to pay for their parents' mistakes."

"What makes you think I'm not just a spy?"

Chuckling a humourless chuckle, Aidan stood up from his seat and took one next to me.

"We both know you have no loyalty to that family." With that, Aidan stood and headed towards the bedroom hallway. "You can stay in the same room as last time."

And he left.

Maybe if things were different, maybe if life didn't fuck me over, maybe if I had the childhood of peace and love I had longed for, I wouldn't be so broken.

I had spent years coping with the fact that I was hated by my mother, desired by unwanted men, and abandoned by my brother.

I had learned to deal with the injuries of abuse and torture that I endured throughout what was meant to be my happiest years. I had learned to put a fake smile on my face to pretend everything was okay for the few who cared. I had developed a phenomenal skill with makeup to hide the bruises of my soul.

The small bedside clock rattled in alarm, signalling the hour was up.

"Time to go," I mumbled as the man lay on top of me.

"I'm not finished yet," he responded, trailing sloppy kisses along my neck.

I tried shoving him off me, but it was futile. He simply wouldn't budge.

Struggling beneath his weight, I screamed and cried for help, aware no one truly would come.

As he began shuffling back into the position he had been in moments before the alarm went off, the bedroom door slammed open.

"Kalina!"

In walked my mother, a sadistic grin on her face as usual.

"Kalina, wake up!"

"It'll cost you ten pounds for another hour," she told the man.

Instead of answering, he groped and attacked my body as he took twenty pounds out of his wallet and chucked it at her.

"Enjoy!" she said.

"KALINA!"

I woke up, suddenly no longer in the stinking room with the equally stinking man. I shivered beneath the sheets, sweat coating my forehead as fear swept me. I could tell it was still night outside from the darkness of the room, but what stood out was Aidan's face above mine.

A look of confusion and worry was all I could see in his expression. His giant hands rested on my small shoulders. He sat there shirtless, his chest heaving.

The moment my eyes met Aidan's, relief washed over his features and he dropped his head slightly. I gave him a look of permission when he silently asked to stay with me. I shuffled further into the middle of the bed. He took the space I had vacated, climbing beneath the blankets.

I leaned into Aidan's open arms, relaxing in his hold. He simply sat there in silence, letting me calm down in his embrace.

"What happened?" Aidan asked after God knew how long.

"Just a nightmare," I mumbled.

"A nightmare or memory?" Aidan said. The tone of his voice made it clear there was no way I could get out of this.

Not unless I really wanted to.

Am I ready though?

"Memory." My voice was barely a whisper.

Aidan didn't speak, letting my answer hang in the air, waiting to see if there was more I wanted to say.

I considered remaining silent, allowing that world of hell to swallow me whole once more and destroy everything I held dear.

"My mother . . . was a despicable woman," I began, sounding as stupid as she had. It was the only way I could describe her. "She would whore herself around the city to make money to feed her alcohol and drug addiction. If it weren't for my brother, Daniel, I would've starved from her negligence by the time I was a month old.

But when men stopped taking an interest in her as she got older, she used me instead. On nights when Daniel was out with the guys, or when I was supposed to be at school, she would take me to her regular bar. No one there protested, as I looked sixteen and they were high off their arses.

I was just ten. I missed 792 days of school in total. It wasn't until Daniel walked in on one of the "sessions" that he realised what was happening and killed the man. That was when he introduced me to the club. I moved in with them two days later with Daniel."

Aidan's grip tightened significantly on my body, an expression of horror spreading across his face. There was nothing but fury burning in his eyes as he stared at the wall opposite us.

Is he mad at me?

"Please say something," I practically begged, my voice cracking as I held back tears.

His gaze snapped from the wall to mine, his eyes softening slightly as he looked down at me. His murderous stare made me sink further into the pillows, the fear of his anger being aimed at me utterly crippling.

"You deserve the world," he began, wiping away the first tear that fell with the pad of his thumb. "These nightmares and memories are in the past. You'll never experience something so painful again."

"You can't guarantee that." The tears continued to flow down my cheeks as I leaned closer into his hold.

"I can," Aidan replied, "because I'll spend the rest of my life making sure you're safe."

That night, I fell asleep peacefully beside Aidan, who promised he would stay all night as I had asked. I didn't know why, but I felt so safe beside him. Being in his presence was comforting, like nothing and no one could hurt me again.

There were very few people I felt that way with, and the moment I met them and felt that sense of security, I knew they would be in my life forever. I had felt it with Teddy, Ace, and Jamie. I felt it it when Maddie embraced me for the first time. I had felt it when Daniel rocked me to sleep in his arms.

I had felt it with Tristan the first night he ran into my bedroom.

I just hoped I hadn't made him worry by staying out all night.

CHAPTER NINETEEN

CHRISTOPHER

I liked to believe I was not an overly strict parent. I grew up being controlled by my father and overcoddled by my mother. I just simply couldn't win in either of their eyes.

I never wanted to be anything like them. I wanted my children to feel comfortable enough to talk to me. I wanted them to experience the freedom that was stolen from me.

It was going so well—until I met Kalina.

That was not to say I wished she weren't here, because I was overjoyed at the presence of my daughter, and so were her brothers. But I just wished I knew how to bond with her and keep her safe at the same time. She refused to talk about her past or even begin a conversation about it..

I respected that, but she was beyond difficult. The fact that my own daughter was uncomfortable talking to me was agonizing. Though I was thankful that she had been having conversations with Tommaso and Tristan. I had learned that she shared information with them, like not being able to read or write. It was a mystery to me how she could not do those things, but I would help her when she asked for it. My main priority was getting her some glasses, as Tristan thought that might be the issue.

However, I was thankful she wasn't at home tonight.

"For fuck's sake!" Antonio yelled.

Tristan was dragging Tommaso inside the house, blood dripping from the latter's shoulder onto the floor. The younger one groaned as his brother left him sitting against the dining room table.

"What happened?" Mateo questioned as he inspected Tommaso's wound.

"Jamie Andrews shot me." Tommaso groaned as Mateo ripped his T-shirt.

Jamie Andrews, son of Melissa Andrews. His mother was a world-renowned underground fighter. We had had our fair share of run-ins, and I had a decent amount of scars to prove it. Jamie grew up with Anthony Vecoli in Aberdeen. The two had been the cause of some of our biggest problems.

"Bastard," I said, seething.

"In all fairness, you did take his title from him." Tristan chuckled.

Like his mother, Jamie was an underground fighter as well. So was Tommaso. They had fought six weeks ago, and Tommaso had taken his title as reigning champion of the lightweight division for fifteen months.

"Not the fucking point." Tommaso glared.

"Come on, lad. You know what we have to do," I said, taking the bottle of vodka.

Sighing, Tommaso took the bottle from my hand and drank half of it. He undid his belt and pulled it straight before drinking some more. Giving a stiff nod, he passed the bottle back.

I poured the vodka over the bullet wound in his shoulder, tuning out his groans and muffled screams.

I don't want to hear my child in pain.

Antonio passed me the sterilized scissors, and I began searching his shoulder for the bullet. After a few tugs—and no doubt searing pain for the boy—I removed the bullet from Tommaso's shoulder. He sighed in relief and only winced slightly as Mateo stitched the wound back up, closing the hole in his flesh.

Once that was done, Mateo wrapped his arm and shoulder in bandage and gave him the remaining vodka. "Drink up, To. That's gonna hurt for some time."

Kissing the top of his youngest brother's head, Mateo left for the warehouse to check on personnel.

"Besides Tom getting shot, how did things go?" I asked, taking a seat at the table.

The rest of them did the same, leaning back in their seats as they looked at the two youngest for answers. Tonight, we had sent Tristan, Tommaso, and a team to the Chained Angels' main residence in the city. That was why Stefano had been the one to collect

Kalina from school. The main reason for the attack was to show that we were not weak now that there was a girl in the family—a mafia princess. It was a message to all our enemies: no one posed a threat to us, and we had the soldiers and the guns to defend and attack. After Anthony Vecoli saw Kalina in the mall, news about the Montessori Princess had spread like wildfire throughout the mafia world.

And we would do anything to keep Kalina safe.

God knows what she's already gone through.

"We didn't kill anyone like Mateo ordered, but there were quite a few injured, including the president's sister and Anthony Vecoli," Tristan answered. "They should keep their distance for the time being."

"Good. Hopefully, word will get around and our enemies will—"

"There's something else," Tommaso interrupted me.

All eyes turned to my youngest son, who was slightly pale from the pain even after swallowing the pain killers Antonio had given him. Tristan gave him a certain look, as if warning him of the consequences of what he might say.

"Aidan Rossi was there."

Tension immediately filled the room. The idea that our biggest enemy was conspiring with another one of our enemies was a huge threat. Maybe they were forming an alliance. God only knew the shitstorm the Rossi Mafia and Chained Angels could bring.

"There's more." Tristan broke through the silence.

"What could be worse?" Antonio groaned, already clearly annoyed by the situation.

"He was with a girl. She had the Angel tattoo on her back. We saw it under the back of her shirt when he pulled her over the bar," Tristan continued.

If Aidan Rossi was sitting in the Chained Angels' bar with a girl tattooed with the Chained Angels' symbol, that meant trouble for us. Only members of the gang received the Angel tattoo. It was done by the tattoo artist in the charter there and signed by the president of the charter. The Angel was specific: an angel with a handgun in one hand, a rose in the other, and chains around both wrists and ankles, binding it to the floor.

And if Aidan Rossi was there and willing to protect a member, she must have meant something to him. Perhaps she was in a relationship with him, and, if so, we had just attacked them. So not only would the Chained Angels be angered by our actions, Aidan Rossi would be infuriated as well. Alone, the Angels posed no threat—but with a whole-ass mafia behind them . . .

"Did you hit the girl? Did you hit her?!" I yelled, rising from my seat.

"No, she and Rossi escaped, but we shot him twice," Tommaso answered with a sigh.

Groaning, I wiped my hand across my face, pissed off at the entire sequence of events. The plan had been simple: show our strength and keep Kalina safe.

But now . . . she might be in more danger than before.

Just as I was about to speak again, the front door opened, and Stefano walked in. Alone.

"Why the fuck isn't Kalina with you?" Tristan seethed at the sight of just his brother.

"I told her to take a break while she waited for me to finish with a client. She didn't come back," Stefano replied, worry etched across his face.

The already heavy anxiety in the room intensified a millionfold.

"Where is my fucking daughter!"

CHAPTER TWENTY

KALINA

From a younger age, I had learned to survive without sleep. Whether it was the agony of the abuse my dear mother put me through, the depression and nightmares haunting my soul, or being busy 'working' for her, I never slept.

One way or another, sleep was a rare gift for me.

And, once again, I failed to sleep. The worry in the pit of my stomach churned as I thought about those I loved. How many of them had died? Who had tried to kill them? Why were we attacked?

Sighing, I lifted my head from the fluffy pillow of Aidan's bed. Again, he had let me sleep in his bedroom, claiming it to be better and warmer than the one down the hall. I got out of the bed. The hallway was pitch-black, a little spooky, but I carried on nonetheless.

As I got closer to the living room, light was shining from the kitchen. From the archway between the hall and the living room, Aidan stood by the kitchen island, gun in hand, weapons were laid out across the counter. He wore a black shirt, the burns on his arms visible under the light.

"Why are you not asleep?" he questioned without turning around.

"Where are you going?" I countered, walking closer to examine all the weapons.

"Nowhere, just taking precautions." Aidan turned around, a stone-cold look on his face as he stared at me. "Why are you not asleep?"

I didn't answer, just stared at the floor. In my peripheral vision, Aidan stepped towards me and stopped just inches away. His rough hand gently cupped my chin, lifting my gaze to his. His hazel eyes stared down into my blue ones, softening at the look of apprehension on my face.

"Was it another nightmare?" he whispered.

Shaking my head, I mumbled a small answer, "Just thinking."

"About?" Aidan pressed.

"Everything," I mumbled.

Slowly, Aidan's hand fell from my face. When I thought he was going to leave, he gently wrapped his arms around my waist, pulling me into a hug. Instinctively, I laid my hands on his chest as he held me close, enjoying the warmth of his body. His chin rested on my head while his hand rubbed soothing circles on my back.

"Kalina," Aidan began. "I know you've been through a lot." A small sob left my mouth at his words, tears flowing freely from my eyes. "I understand it's hard to talk about and even harder to overcome. I think you're more than a match for a few dickheads who decide to play with guns and attack the biggest gang in the world."

Smiling through my tears, I looked up into his hazel eyes, only to find him returning a soft version of his own smile. Gently, he walked us over to the sofa. Aidan pulled me down beside him, my head resting on his chest as his arm remained wrapped around me.

"Go to sleep, Kalina," Aidan muttered. "I'll keep you safe."

For the first time in my life, I trusted a man I barely knew. Relaxing in his arms, I felt my body unwind and calm at the rise and fall of his solid, toned chest. My eyes felt heavy as sleep took over my body.

It was not until hours later that I woke once again, only to find myself sprawled across Aidan. He had moved us to lie down. My body lay over his, my head resting beneath his chin, all the way down to my toes draped over him.

He was still awake, his hands resting on my waist, not lower or higher than they should be. At my movement, Aidan lowered his gaze towards me, concern on his face.

"Everything okay?" Aidan asked, moving a strand of hair behind my ear, away from my eyes.

"Yeah," I croakily replied, offering a tight-lipped smile. "Has anyone called yet?"

Nodding, Aidan sat up, letting my body slide down his until I rested on his lap. His warmth was perfect for my icy body, so as he moved me, I held on tighter and snuggled closer.

Chucking quietly, Aidan told me, "Maddie called. Everyone is relatively okay. Ace, Jamie, Killian, and Oscar got shot, but just flesh wounds. Apparently, it was more of an attack to show power than to kill."

His tone was cold, but his features were calm. It was as if something was grounding him to reality. I simply nodded at his words, wondering who would attack the clubhouse. As I looked up at him, I couldn't help but notice some of the more subtle features of his face—the faint freckles across his upper cheeks and his long dark eyelashes that I was already jealous of.

The ringing of a phone broke me out of my trance. When I realised it was mine, I picked it up from the coffee table where I had left it earlier in the night. It showed the photo I had sneakily taken of Mateo in the kitchen. He was drinking a foamy coffee early in the morning, wearing a white vest and some black shorts. The foam had formed a moustache across his top lip, and I had managed to capture it before he wiped it away.

Reluctantly, I accepted the call.

"Kalina? Where are you?"

Mateo didn't question; he demanded. I silently asked Aidan what to say, already knowing he could hear the conversation. Aidan nodded, signalling for me to answer.

"I met up with a friend from back home. Why? Is something wrong?"

"No, everything is fine. Just please tell us next time if you're staying out for the night." The relief in

Mateo's voice was apparent. "Do you have a way home in the morning?"

Aidan caught my attention and, once again, nodded. "Yeah, I got a ride."

"You're not going to school tomorrow, but be back by eleven o'clock," was the final thing Mateo said before hanging up.

I placed the phone on the sofa beside me and leaned my head back on Aidan's chest. Resting peacefully, I drifted off quietly into a calm and nightmare-free slumber.

When I woke up the next morning, I was once again lying on Aidan's bed as the sun crept through the curtains, which covered the view of the Pacific. It seemed he had brought me back here in the early hours.

Getting up, I took a quick shower, making sure the water stayed clear of my face. I used Aidan's body wash, leaving me smelling like him without the—surprisingly nice—smoke and cologne. Knowing I had no clean clothes, I raided his wardrobe and found a pair of grey joggers, which I tied as tightly as I could around my waist, and one of his white vests, which just covered my boobs.

Tying my black curls into a messy bun, I went to the kitchen again and found a plate of food sitting in the microwave, the kettle simmering, and a tea bag in a mug.

Eat it all – A

I put down the note I found on the counter and began munching away on the food, which was glorious, but I would not tell him that.

I have a feeling his ego is big enough as it is.

When I finished, I played games on my phone, ignoring the world around me until the front door slammed open and then shut.

Due to the events of last night, I did not waste a second in scurrying behind the kitchen island. As I hid beneath the counter, I found a Glock strapped to the underside of the worktop.

This should be fun.

Carefully taking the gun, I cocked it just before the sound of footsteps echoed down the hall. A moment of silence followed, then the heavy footsteps quickened in pace.

Further into the house, the bedroom doors opening echoed throughout.

"Kalina!" Ace's frantic scream pierced the air.

"Ace?" I questioned, popping up from my spot behind the counter.

"Oh, thank the holy fuck," Ace said, panting.

His hair was dishevelled, and his eyes were wide with panic. He was wearing a black vest, revealing the obvious bandages on his shoulder.

Running to him, I gently pulled him into a hug and held him close. It seemed he needed this hug just as much as I did, as he audibly let out a sigh of relief.

In my peripheral vision, I saw Aidan watching us, a certain emotion in his eyes I could not recognise.

As I pulled away from Ace, I inspected the wound on his shoulder.

"It's just a flesh wound," he told me before I unravelled the bandages.

"Do either of you know who attacked us?" I asked.

They shared a not-so-subtle look before Aidan replied, "An enemy."

Liars.

"Which enemy?" I pressed, hoping to see their resolve crack.

"You don't need to know," Ace replied with a smile, rubbing circles on my back with his hand.

"I am a member of the Chained Angels. I have been sworn in by Teddy, the man who controls every chapter worldwide. I have just as much right to know as you do."

The sound of chuckling tore my gaze away from Ace to Aidan.

"Shit. She's gonna kill the bastard," Ace muttered beneath his breath, then let out a sigh.

"What the fuck is so funny? Well! I am sick to death of people trying to 'protect me' by keeping me in the dark! Everything bad that's ever happened to me was because I had no idea what was going on! So, please, for the love of fucking god, tell me what is so fucking funny!"

Aidan, with a sloppy grin on his face, pointed at Ace over my head. "I told you."

"Told him fucking what?" I said, seething.

I was so done with not knowing information. Knowing kept me safe.

I was at risk last night just as much as everyone else. I was a member of the gang and deserved the respect that came with it.

"I said," Aidan began, "that it's only fair, you know."

"Shit. Sorry," I instantly replied, realising I had gone off on him for no reason.

He just stiffly nodded, juxtaposing the grin on his face.

"Right!" Spinning on my heel, I turned to Ace. "Who the fuck attacked us last night?"

Sighing, Ace briefly dropped his gaze before bringing it back up. It was as if all the air had been sucked out of my lungs, and the world emptied of oxygen around me when he said, "Tristan and Tommaso."

Hanging my head, I processed his words as he stared at me with a waiting expression.

"What's the plan?" I asked.

"That depends," Aidan answered for Ace, who wore a look of anxiousness.

"On?"

"On how far you're willing to go."

* * *

ANTONIO

Night had come and gone after the attack on the Chained Angels, and Tommaso had stopped bleeding and begun healing.

For once, I was thankful that Kalina stayed out all night, as it prevented a lot of uncomfortable questions. Yet we all became increasingly aware last night of how important Kalina was to us and how unaware she was of the threat against her life because of our name.

Our actions were meant to display an act of dominance in the underworld, a way of shielding Kalina from the horrors as long as possible. But what we didn't anticipate was Aidan Rossi being in the building, let alone with a female Angel.

As everyone knew, Aidan Rossi had a new fuck buddy every once in a while, and if this girl was the new one . . .

I was thankful she wasn't shot, as I couldn't imagine the carnage that the war between our two mafias would unleash on the underworld.

As I walked into the living room, a loud bang was the first thing I heard.

Then I felt my body falling forward and connecting with the hardwood floor beneath me. The sound of bricks crumbling and glass shattering was the last sound I heard before my ears rang and my vision blurred.

"Good morning."

With ears buzzing and eyes squinting, I could just make out the voice of Kalina. Her figure was beside me as she stared me down.

"What the fuck happened?" I asked, rubbing the back of my head.

"It seems the front door was blown up." She shrugged, offering me her hand and pulling me up off the floor.

Once I was back on my feet, swaying in place, Kalina headed to the kitchen as Tommaso, Tristan, and Dad all came barreling into the room.

"Tony? You, okay? Where's our door gone?" Tommaso rambled, eyes wide as he surveyed the room.

"I'm fine," I answered.

Dad went behind me and checked the back of my head.

"You've got a concussion," Tristan said, pointing to my eyes.

It was then that I noticed the red splotches in my vision—no doubt a blood vessel that had burst as I hit the floor.

"Get upstairs and in bed, but don't sleep. Tommaso, watch him," Dad said, giving me another once-over before concluding I was semi-okay.

Doing as he said, Tommaso guided me up the stairs and toward my bedroom. I laid myself down on the black silk sheets. Tommaso sat on the chair by the window, trying to sync his phone to my speaker.

"Tony?" Tommaso said after a few moments.

"Yes," I groaned, feeling sleepy.

"Do you ever wonder where Kalina goes?"

I lifted my head to face my little brother and understood the worry written across his face like a poem.

"With her friends from when she was younger. Why?"

Sighing, Tommaso rose from his seat and moved next to me on the bed. Opening my arms, I let him cuddle into my side just as he had when he was a child. Being his mother figure of sorts, I was the person he would come to with his problems.

"What if these friends are more dangerous than she let's on?" he whispered.

I pondered his question, and the more I did so, the more I understood his reasoning. Kalina seemed very at ease with the way life had been so far, with guards everywhere and mass security teams. Her being unable to read and write was the only thing we had actually been able to pull out of her.

But when that bomb went off . . .

She seemed completely unfazed, as if this type of thing was familiar to her. Tristan had told us she was in juvie for possession of illegal drugs, which she obviously got from somewhere.

"She's hiding something."

CHAPTER TWENTY-ONE

KALINA

After discussing the correct form of attack on my biological family, without killing them—since God knew what sort of foster family I would be sent to—we came to an agreement.

The foster family is definitely the reason, because I'm not starting to like anyone.

After Aidan received a delivery at his home from some small Irish bloke, Ace drove me home and dropped me a street away from our house. As I passed the gates, I greeted the guards and acted nonchalant. When I reached the front door, I subtly opened my bag and dropped the small box beside the door, just behind the snake plants, where it would not be seen should they review the cameras.

Minutes later, the small device blew up.

The C4 was message enough. It wasn't part of the plan to kill anyone; therefore Antonio should be fine.

Not that I give a shit.

I was just thankful no one saw me in the clubhouse.

Tommaso and Tristan did not go to school, which meant one of them was injured. This confirmed they executed the attack.

I understood the pain they must have felt when they realised a member of their family had been missing for seventeen years. They would do anything to make sure the sweet and innocent little girl they hoped for stayed protected.

Sadly, I was not that lucky. My life was filled with horror and violence. I could never escape the past. All I could do was deal with it.

Embrace it.

A world of pain and anguish was all I ever knew. Unfortunately, there was nothing I could do to change that. Had I been raised by loving parent(s), able to live and not just survive, things would have been so much different.

A few minutes later, Tristan and Christopher entered the kitchen, distressed expressions across their faces.

Standing behind the counter, I drank the tea in my hand as the two sat down at the kitchen island. They waited for me to speak with expectant gazes, yet I remained silent.

"Why didn't you come home yesterday?" Christopher finally asked.

Placing down my mug, I said, "I met up with some friends. I ended up staying at their place."

"And which friends are these exactly? The ones who got you thrown in juvie?" Tristan snarled, fury exploding across his facial expression.

"The ones that were there for me when no one else was," I replied, the same amount of venom laced in my tone.

"Your friends that aban—"

"Tristan." Christopher cut him off. "Go cool off somewhere."

Grumbling in Italian beneath his breath, Tristan rose from the barstool and left the room. Christopher's gaze turned back to mine, a sense of sadness in them.

"Kalina," Christopher began. "I understand that these people are family to you. They were there for you when we weren't, and for that I am grateful. And I would like to thank these people. They are invited to dinner Saturday evening. Please inform them."

"Actually—"

"I expect them here on Saturday, Kalina. Otherwise, you will not be allowed to see them again."

This bitch had not just cut me off from my friends, dictated to me, and given me an ultimatum.

* * *

I remembered that, as a child, panic wasn't such a rare occurrence for me. In fact, panic had become more common than love or warmth.

It had been a good few months since I felt real, true, terrorising panic. Ever since I took those steps inside the gates of juvie, panic had become a stranger once again.

Now, though . . .

"Breathe! Just breathe! Everything will be fine! Everything will be just . . . fine!"

"Or it won't."

My crystal-blue eyes instantly snapped to Maddie's, who had interrupted my pep talk. She held her pale hands up in surrender, a little smirk on her face.

"She's got a point, Kal," Jamie said. He chucked a sourball into his mouth and chewed.

"Can we not point out the bloody obvious for one night!" I groaned. "I don't need the extra stress."

"Hey, at least they won't shoot you." Ace grinned. "They've already shot all of us."

"Not the time, Ace," Killian muttered, as the glare on my face only worsened.

Sighing, I dived onto the sofa and screamed as I face-planted on the pillow. After telling Ace and the others about Christopher wanting to meet them, they jumped at the opportunity.

Why? I had no idea.

As far as I was aware, they would kill each other the second the opportunity presented itself. Being arch-enemies meant that they had no reason to meet and be civil, especially given the recent events.

I had no idea how the biological family would react when they found out exactly who I valued over them—who had been there for me and Daniel when they weren't.

I couldn't see how this would play out with everyone leaving with limbs intact.

And life unscathed.

*   *   *

Fixing my makeup in the mirror, I straightened the skirt of the all-black dress with a plunging neckline. It ended mid-thigh, covering a holster wrapped around my upper thigh, concealing my daggers just in case something happened tonight.

And there most likely would.

Tonight, Maddie, Ace, Jamie, Killian, and Luke—the silent but supportive one—were all coming to the Montessori mansion. In two groups, we piled into the cars parked outside the clubhouse.

I went with Luke in his car, along with Jamie and Maddie. Ace and Killian drove behind us. Luke was the weapons guy of us all. He was like our own Q in the gang.

As Ace drove behind in his Subaru and Luke drove his Ford Mustang, I stared out the window as dread pooled in the pit of my stomach.

Two of my habits when feeling anxious were fiddling with my fingers and bouncing my knee, which Luke noticed almost immediately. He placed his rough, scarred hand in mine, interlacing our fingers before resting them on my bouncing knee. His touch helped soothe me, making me relax in the leather of the racing car.

My overthinking mind couldn't help but explore the possibilities that awaited me through the doors of my new home.

How would the Montessoris react when they found out I had been raised and cared for by the very same people they had attacked days beforehand? What would they do to the ones I loved?

Was their hatred for the Chained Angels so strong that they would hurt me to get to them? Was I simply just a means to an end in a war in the underworld?

From what I had witnessed and experienced in my short month and a half here, family was what they held most dear. Christopher was a devoted father, despite what Daniel had told me, and he cared deeply for all his children. I couldn't help but wonder if that love extended to me.

After all, he barely knew me. He had no idea of the baggage I was bringing and the traumas I carried. He had no idea of the danger I was bringing to his home.

If push came to shove, I would choose the Chained Angels over the Montessoris. They had built me up from mere ruin, shaped me into the strong woman I was today. Without them, I would still be that broken little girl, drowning beneath the waves life had crushed down on her.

It was just last year they had saved me from perhaps my biggest challenge yet. The danger that had threatened my life and survival. What had kept me away from those I loved and made me fear for them all the same. The monster who haunted my nightmares.

God only knew what he was doing now. Had he found someone else to torment, or was he simply lurking in the shadows, ready to pounce on his prey?

The cars slowed and stopped at the guardhouse of the mansion. I poked my head out of the window to show the guards that it was me.

"Buonasera, signorina Montessori," the guard said as he opened the electric gate. (*Good evening, Miss Montessori.*)

Luke drove through, the stoic look still remaining on his face. As he parked the car, he turned towards me, waiting to see if I was ready to go.

It was one of the things I loved about Luke. He knew actions spoke louder than words, and he understood that this was a tough moment for me. If I were to ask him to speed all the way back to England right now, he would jump on every ferry and road to get me there as fast as possible.

I gave him a slight nod, and he unlocked the car doors. Killian helped me out, offering his hand. I held on to it for support as we made our way to the front door.

Ace and Maddie were already there, soft smiles on their faces. Jamie and Luke went behind Killian and me, forming a sort of security team for me. I opened the door, and Maddie and Ace walked through first.

The hall was empty, making me realise we were a few minutes early. The sound of a horde of footsteps echoed through the hall from the kitchen.

Standing with my adoptive family, I watched apprehensively as Antonio, Mateo, Tristan, Tommaso, Stefano, and Christopher all stood in the middle of the room, frozen.

And within seconds, all guns were drawn.

CHAPTER TWENTY-TWO

STEFANO

Out of all the people in the fucking world—universe, the galaxy, far fucking away—I never would have expected to see five Chained Angels standing before me in my home.

I knew the people who raised Kalina would likely have an underworld connection—perhaps low-level drug dealers or street racers or the occasional underground fighter or two.

I got that and more . . .

Each and every one of them had their own individual vendetta against our family, whether it be a simple drug deal gone wrong or the killing of someone close. We all had our differences and our hatred toward each other.

But . . . everything must change now.

With Kalina in the picture, everything was different. If one of us injured the other, we would indirectly hurt the young girl we all cared about. And I was no idiot. I could see the love they held for her.

I could see the way Anthony Vecoli stared down at her with pride, watching as she defended him and his family. How Maddie Anderson placed a protective hand on her shoulder, offering reassurance I had no doubt she needed. How Jamie Andrews already had his gun drawn and pointed at my oldest brother, his aim slightly above Kalina and Anthony. The way Killian and Luke stood by her side, ready to pull her behind them should gunfire start.

What they didn't know was that none of us would risk the life of our little sister over a mafia feud.

"Kalina, perché cazzo sono questi bastardi a casa mia?" Mateo growled, his deadly brown gaze fixed on the five guests in our home. (*Kalina, why the fuck are these bastards in my house?*)

"Tuo padre ci ha invitato, idiota," Anthony said, rolling his entrancing brown eyes. (*Your father invited us, dumbass.*)

I leaned against the marble pillar by the stairs, examining each of their the movements.

Anthony stood tall and proud, a gleaming smirk resting on his well-sculpted face, which was covered with a slight stubble. The blond fringe that fell in front of his eyes gave him a darker edge. The others surrounded him as if he were some sort of king. Then again, he was the president of the California chapter.

"We didn't realize it was you who was with Kalina," Dad said, a crease forming on his forehead from his furrowed brows. "Boys, put the guns away."

"What!" Tristan growled, the gun still firmly pointed at Killian, who was smirking at the hothead of the family.

"Ora," Dad demanded. (*Now.*)

Begrudgingly, Tristan holstered his gun, but his usual glare only intensified as it remained fixed on the Angels.

"Kalina, they are your . . . adoptive family?" Dad asked, his tone calm despite his facial expression being anything but.

"Yes," she replied, an anxious look evident on her face.

"Very well then," Dad said.

He took a step forward, his suit still sharp, as Anthony stepped in front of Kalina. Dad probably thought of it as more protective than defiant, so he halted and held out his hand. Dad waited as Anthony stared at him with a scrutinizing gaze. Slowly, Anthony shook his hand, and Dad looked pleased no one had died . . . yet.

"Thank you for being there for my daughter," Dad said, honesty in his words.

"Of course. She's an Angel, after all." Whether it was an intentional jab at the fact we weren't there for her, or that she became one of them before she became one of us, I could only guess.

From beside me, Tristan rolled his eyes, but I ignored him. I was more focused on Tommaso, who hadn't moved from my side since entering the hall. The shock might have gotten to him, and by the look on his face, he felt guilty for the attack the other night. Unknowingly, he attacked his twin's protectors.

"How about we eat and resolve some of our . . . problems," Dad suggested.

"Problems being your mafia attacking them?" Kalina finally spoke up.

All of our eyes snapped to her as she stood there, a glare on her face. She was clearly displeased by our actions.

"You know about our mafia?" Antonio said in a whisper, agony flashing across his face.

When we were discussing bringing Kalina home, Antonio made it clear that we would try our best to hide her from the mafia life. Sadly, it seemed his hopes of having a sweet, innocent sister were crushed when we first saw her—and even more so after this.

"Yeah." She shrugged, heading to the dining room where the table was set.

The five of them followed her and took seats on her side of the table. Antonio, Tommaso, Tristan, and I sat opposite them. Mateo and Dad sat at the heads of the table.

The food was already plated, and the wine was already poured—except for Tristan, who definitely didn't need alcohol tonight.

No one made a move until Kalina took the first bite of her food. After that, everyone started eating. Everyone ate in complete silence. Not a word was spoken, not even a heavy breath.

"So . . ." Tommaso broke the silence. "I'm sorry about shooting you guys."

Chuckling in his chair, Jamie cut up another piece of his steak. "I'm not."

Tristan rolled his eyes, scoffing from his seat. However, a stern glare from Kalina shut him up.

"Mr. Montessori, there is an important matter that needs to be discussed after dinner," Maddie Anderson said to Dad.

"We will talk in my office," Dad replied, signifying to Mateo that he, too, will be joining the conversation.

Once again, no one said anything, just quietly finishing their food. When we were all finished, Anthony, Maddie, Dad, and Mateo went to the office. Antonio began cleaning up, leaving the rest of us to head to the living room.

"Is there any footy on?" Killian asked, taking a seat beside Kalina on the sofa.

"Footy?" Tommaso questioned.

"Football—soccer," Kalina clarified, turning on the television.

As Killian and Luke watched soccer on TV, Jamie and Kalina sat awkwardly across Tommaso, Tristan, and me.

"How long have you been a member of the gang?" Tommaso decided to ask.

"Six years."

"Seven years."

Jamie and Kalina answered in sync, causing all of us to snap our gazes back to Kalina.

Kid was just full of surprises.

"You let a ten-year-old join a gang?! One that focuses on drugs and guns!" Tristan sprang from his seat, his face steaming with fury and his hands clenched into fists.

"She didn't get properly involved till she was fifteen." Jamie shrugged, wrapping an arm around her in a protective hug.

"Fourteen, actually," she corrected.

That might have made Tristan even angrier. He stormed forward, swinging his fist at Jamie. Jamie stood, ready to defend himself, but Kalina stepped into his path.

Tristan's fist struck her cheek, and she fell back into Luke's arms, who was already on his feet to catch her.

Tristan's mouth fell open in shock, horror plastered on his face. Jamie was on him within seconds, tackling him to the floor and raining blows on his face. Blood was already pooling from the cuts Jamie had caused. Tommaso and I tried to pull him off.

Once he was free, Tommaso rushed in front of Kalina in an instant. He checked her face, but Killian shoved him aside, standing protectively in front of our sister.

"Kalina," Tristan began, tears pooling in his eyes at the sight of our sister's cheek swelling.

She stood there in Luke's and Killian's arms, a deadly look set across her face, replacing the horror that had been originally there.

No one else saw it, but I did. Before she fell into Luke's arms, it was as if her life had passed before her eyes, and panic had taken hold. She was trembling in his arms until she calmed.

"Tristan!"

All eyes snapped to the door, where Anthony and Maddie had just appeared. Dad and Mateo remained by the door.

I don't think I've ever seen them so pissed off.

CHAPTER TWENTY-THREE

KALINA

I had been hit many times in my life. Often, it was by people I thought cared for me. Other times, it was by those who had simply paid for my services for an hour or two. Then there were the bruises from street fights.

Unfortunately, with a background and childhood like mine, the abuse was expected to start at some point. Whether it came from someone close, like Tristan, or distant, like Mateo, the blows were always bound to start sooner or later.

"Kalina . . . I didn't . . . I-I'm so sorry."

Tristan tried to step forward during his apology, but a sharp shove from Ace forced him back once again. Tristan was ready to start another brawl when Mateo stormed across the room and stood in front of him.

"Get out of my sight," Mateo snarled, seething, glaring down at his little brother.

With a defeated sigh, Tristan grabbed his keys from the table in the foyer and left through the front door.

The moment Tristan was gone, Mateo spun around to face me. Despite Ace standing protectively in front of me, Mateo looked at me with nothing but care and concern. It was probably the most emotion I have ever seen from him.

Ace slowly stepped back, letting Mateo through. When he was finally in front of me, Mateo gently took my face in his hands, examining my already swelling cheek.

I flinched from the touch, but my unease settled under the trusting look Mateo held in his gaze. He tilted my head to the side, inspected the injury his brother had caused.

Moments later, without me even noticing he had left, Stefano passed Mateo a bag of ice. Antonio was now at my side as well, stroking his hand up and down my back in a comforting manner.

How it didn't make me uncomfortable, I didn't understand, but I liked the feeling of warmth he provided. All of their actions were drawing me away from my state of panic.

"Keep this on your cheek," Mateo instructed.

I jumped slightly from the bitter cold of the ice, but the soothing numbness it brought moments later drowned out the chill.

An arm wrapped around my shoulder, pulling me into a warm embrace. From the softness of the touch, I knew it was Maddie. Killian joined a moment later, pressing a kiss to the top of my head.

Ace and Mateo stood opposite each other, as if in some Western standoff.

"All acts committed by your crew against our family are now in the past. I am willing to put an end to this war once and for all. For the sake of my sister, I am willing to let everything go." Mateo held out his hand, his expressionless face betraying nothing but sincerity.

"On behalf of the Chained Angels, I forgive and apologise for actions of the past," Ace replied, shaking Mateo's outstretched hand.

But what about Aidan's mafia?

"And the Irish-Italian mafia? What about your alliances to them?" Antonio voiced my thoughts, catching everyone's attention.

"Your issues with the Irish-Italians are between you and them only. Whatever comes, the Chained Angels of California will have no role in their actions against you," Maddie responded.

"How are we supposed to trust that you won't pass information to Aidan Rossi? After all, you are his underboss, Anthony," Antonio said.

"Aidan knows the value of family. He'd never put me in a position where I must choose between Kalina and him," Ace said.

"And we're just supposed to believe this?" Antonio had always been fiercely protective of his family, but now he was just pushing it further than ever.

"Kalina means more to me than any alliance or friendship," Ace snapped. "I'd gladly give up everything I have for my baby sister."

The use of "baby sister" created a brief tension in the room, but it eased quickly. To doubt Ace's love and devotion for me would be like doubting themselves.

They should just fucking shut up.

"I am thankful that this whole ordeal is over. However, have you got any more intel on the matter you shared with my sons and me earlier?" Christopher asked.

"Aidan Rossi, despite his justified hatred for your family, has agreed to assist with the situation. He has requested to arrange a meeting to share all the information gathered on the subject," Ace said, giving nothing away about what the "situation" actually entailed.

What the fuck is happening?

After a brief silence, Mateo nodded. "A public building under the Montessori name with no weapons or security in the room."

"I'm sure Aidan will accept that," Jamie said, smoothing the hair running down my back.

"And why would the vicious bastard be so willing to help?" Tommaso growled.

Tommy did not just swear! And why is he so angry?

"Because he cares more than you think. He has his own reasons for wanting to help," Killian said.

I was utterly confused as to why no one was telling me what was happening. Ace and the others had never once kept a secret from me, no matter how big and destructive it might be. I was always informed of the issue at hand.

This seemed like probably the biggest problem of all. Well, nothing compared to *him*.

The fact that three enemy groups had come together to overthrow what I could only assume was some higher form of evil demonstrated just how much danger was coming. I had no idea what had happened between the Montessoris, Adian Rossi, and the Chained Angels, but it must have been horrific.

Two hours later, the Chained Angels left the house, heading home for the night, whilst I remained in the mansion. My brothers checked my face multiple times, and Christopher brought in some ice cream for me to eat.

Tristan didn't return until the early hours of the morning. I heard him pause briefly outside my bedroom door, as he usually did, but he didn't come in.

I knew it was my fault that I had been hit—I stepped in front of his punch—but no one was allowed to hurt my family on my watch.

No one hurt the man who had saved me the most.

For the first time in my life, when I woke that morning, I didn't bother hiding the bruises on my face with makeup. I had no doubt everyone could see them. The evidence of last night's events was etched across my slightly swollen cheek, so there was no point in deploying my insane makeup skills.

Once my usual morning exercises were complete, I got dressed in a grey cropped Eminem T-shirt, a pair of black shorts, and some grey trainers.

With my long black curls tied into a messy bun, I made my way to the kitchen.

I looked at the cupboards, not sure what to eat.

Moments later, I heard the clatter of silverware. Turning around, I saw Tommaso at the kitchen table, his mouth hanging open and eyes wide in shock.

"What?" I ask, brows furrowed as my hand dropped to my side.

"Th-that . . . You have an Angel tattoo?!" Gobsmacked, Tommaso stared at my waist, where the Angel tattoo was inked.

"Yeah. I'm a member," I said slowly, as if explaining something to a child.

"I-it's pretty," Tommaso replied after a slight pause.

I shrugged and carried on. I made myself a cup of tea. Knowing Antonio was bound to pester me about breakfast, I grabbed a small bowl of granola.

Later, everyone began filing into the kitchen for the usual morning meals. Tristan was the last to enter, the bags under his eyes large enough to hold the weekly shopping. As his gaze met mine, all I saw was a pool of sorrow.

Hesitantly, he approached me. Reaching out gently, he moved the stray curls from my cheek. A grimace formed on his face at the sight of the bruise covering the side of my face.

"Mi dispiace tanto, tesoro. Non volevo farti del male," he whispered, resting his chin on my head and wrapping his arms around my shoulders in a hug. (*I'm so sorry, darling. I didn't mean to hurt you.*)

"Lo so. Va bene, ti perdono." I smiled back, relaxing into his hold. *"Ma se mi metti di nuovo le mani*

addosso, sarà l'ultima volta che avrai le mani." (*I know. It's okay. I forgive you. But if you put your hands on me again, it'll be the last time you have hands.*)

Giving me a small smile, Tristan took a seat on the kitchen barstool beside Tommaso.

For the rest of breakfast, everyone chatted whilst eating. The boys and I left for school at our usual time and arrived just before the bell for first period.

I was wearing a North Face jacket, covering the tattoo on my back that had startled Tommaso earlier.

Don't need the school knowing I'm in a gang.

"We've got to get to the gym for a team meeting. Will you be okay alone?" Tommaso asked, staring down at me with concern.

"Yep. Bye." I laughed as the two of them ran off.

Wandering down the halls, I stared at the message I had received moments ago from Jamie, asking if my face was healing nicely or if plastic surgery was necessary.

I was so busy shaking my head at his mischief that I didn't notice the massive, solid body standing in front of me.

As I began to stumble back, a hand wrapped around my waist and steaded me.

"Shit. Are you okay?"

I looked up at a blue-eyed redhead staring down at me. He was about five-foot-ten, curls falling onto his pale forehead. As my head subconsciously rested against his chest, I could feel the muscles beneath his shirt.

"Um . . . yeah, thanks," I replied, stepping out of his grasp.

"Are you new?" he asked. He had noticed the bruise on my face but wisely chose not to comment.

"Yeah, I'm Kalina," I said, offering a small smile.

"Jayden," he replied, returning my smile.

It turned out Jayden and I shared the same classes. He had not been in school the previous week due to suspension, so we spent the lessons talking and getting to know each other.

"Do you want to have lunch with my friends and me?" Jayden asked as the bell rang for lunch.

"Sure," I answered. I followed him to his locker to dump my bag in there for the time being.

We made our way to the lunch hall, grabbed our food, and then headed to a table outside, where two people were already sitting.

The first one was a guy in a leather jacket like Jayden's, though slightly taller—roughly Tommaso's height. His hair was soft blond and cropped short, and his eyes were a striking jade green. His skin was slightly pale, but not unhealthily so.

The second one was another boy, wearing a body warmer with a grey hoodie pulled over his head. Only the tips of his brown hair peeked out. His head was angled downward, but I could hear his laughter, which was filled with happiness. His was short—I would say he was five foot five, maybe five foot six.

"Guys, this is Kalina," Jayden said as we approached the two.

The blond-haired guy smiled and shook my hand. "I'm Maxim." His accent was thick and strong—unmistakably European.

German, I'm guessing.

The hooded boy stood and shook my hand as well, though I still couldn't see his face. "I'm Carter."

The four of us ate together, taking the time to get to know each other.

Maxim was indeed German, having moved here with his sister, who had been his legal guardian since he was eight. He was a street fighter, specialising in boxing.

Jayden was the classic bookworm of the group, even reading a little during lunch. He was also very cuddly, surprisingly comforting as he draped his arm over Carter's and my shoulders every now and then. It did not bother me—having a personal radiator was rather nice.

Carter kept his hood up throughout lunch. It was obvious he was hiding something, but I chose not to question it. He could do as he pleased. He was fairly chatty, though, which I found quite entertaining. He spoke about cars, street racing, and—unexpectedly—Disney movies.

Like I said, entertaining.

Tommaso and Tristan found me later on. They usually ate inside. They seemed a little on edge about who my new friends were, but they didn't say anything.

The four of us spent the rest of the day together. Maxim sneaked into our classes since we were in a lower grade than him.

The minute they realised I couldn't read or write, they each took turns writing down my notes for me in big block letters so I could make them out more easily later on.

It was the little things that made a true friend. That was the main thing I learned in school today.

It turned out Maxim lived on the south side of the city and offered to walk with me. Tonight, I was staying at the garage.

We spent the entire walk talking, laughing, pushing and shoving each other as we joked along the way. As we neared the same alleyway from my first visit to the club, where those two men were killed, I noticed Maxim smirking.

"What's got you smirking?" I questioned.

His jade eyes turned to me, a little promise hidden in them.

"You know those dicks who hang around that door." He nodded to the same place where those men died. "I'm just . . . so glad they're not here anymore."

Within seconds, I got the silent message. I knew exactly what he was talking about.

Maybe he's a bit more dangerous than I originally thought.

The two of us continued to chat as we carried on walking. He looked at me pointedly when we arrived at the garage.

"You're aware this place is owned by the Chained Angels, right?" Maxim said as he saw me heading through the gates.

"Yeah, why?"

He just shook his head with a smirk before following me inside. Curious, I let him.

"Also, I forgot to ask, but how come you got held back a year? You know, since you're nineteen," I asked as we neared the building.

"I had to learn English after I first moved here from Germany, which is why I fell behind," he explained.

As I went beneath the semi-open garage door, I expected him to leave. Instead, he stripped off his leather jacket and replaced it with a grey overall shirt with a name tag that said "Max." I watched as he picked up a wrench and began working on a dirt bike.

"You work here?" I blurted in shock.

"Nice to finally meet 'the kid' everyone's been raving about." Maxim smirked before turning back to the bike.

Shaking my head in disbelief, I chuckled quietly before turning and making my way inside the bar. Ace and Aidan in the corner, discussing something in hushed whispers. Maddie was wearing her own work shirt, like Maxim, no doubt on a shift, and Killian was sitting on the sofa with Jamie and Oliver.

Deciding to leave Ace be for the time being, I offered him a small wave before joining Oliver on his sofa.

"How was school?" Oliver asked with a small smile.

Oliver and I had met a year before I went to juvie. We didn't have a close connection, but I loved him all the same. He was like that cousin you see every few weeks.

"Good, I made some friends of my own," I answered with a grin.

"Who are they?" Jamie asked as he took a sip of his beer.

"Jayden Turner, Carter O'Farrell, and Maxim Arnold, who works in the garage," I told him, noting the surprised reaction from everyone.

"They're boys?" Killian growled.

"Are they fit?" Maddie asked, wiggling her eyebrows.

"As long as they're nice," Oliver said.

"Max who works outside?" Jamie questioned.

The reactions that surprised me the most came from Aidan and Ace. Their heads snapped up at the sound of my new friends' names, and they were immediately drawn into our conversation.

"Yes, get over it, Killian. Yes, they are, Maddie, but I'm not interested. Very nice people, Oliver. Yes, he works in the garage, as I said," I answered all of their questions in one go.

"You're friends with Carter?" Aidan broke the momentary silence.

"Yeah, why?"

"Kalina, Carter is Aidan's brother," Ace replied, a small smile on his face.

"Is that a good thing or . . . ?" I asked, unsure why my news had caused such a reaction.

"I'm just happy he's getting more comfortable with people." Aidan smiled. It was a real, genuine smile. He usually had a smirk or a grin, so it was very rare to see him smile like this.

From his statement, I could tell he was referring to the hood thing and the fact that I hadn't actually seen Carter's full face. I wouldn't pressure him, though.

I myself have things I prefer to hide, such as the true thickness of my thighs that I have been conscious of since day one, the stretch marks on my thighs and hips that have faded but are still noticeable if you look closely, the wideness of said hips, the fact I do not have toned abs and only a flat stomach from the amount of exercise I do and years of starvation, and the scars that litter my body.

There was nothing wrong with being self-conscious, but you should never let those insecurities hold you back. There were so many others who felt the same way about their own bodies; they just didn't have the confidence to express it.

All you could do was embrace the little things that took a jab at your confidence because that was all they really are: little things. If someone judged you by the marks on your body, they had never felt what it was like to truly be human, because everyone had something they wished to change about themselves.

That was what made us all so unique.

"How come you have different last names?" I asked Aidan. He was a Rossi, but Carter was an O'Farrell.

The others cleared out of the room, heading off to do various other things. Ace tensed, probably anticipating the information I would be filled in on soon.

Then it was just me and Aidan.

"Different fathers. Mine was the don of the Italian Mafia; his, a member of the Irish mob our mother fell for as a teenager. My grandfather used her as a bargaining chip to solidify a deal between the Rossi Mafia and the Irish Mob. He sold her off when she was fifteen."

My eyes grew wide at his confession, and my heart ached for his mother.

"My father was three years older than her and completely in love with her, which was why he agreed to the deal so easily. There was also the added bonus of being able to control the Irish mob too, as my mother was an only child. After learning how he treated her growing up, he helped my mother kill my grandfather."

"Why are you telling me this?" I asked, after Aidan remained silent for a minute.

He ignored my question. "My father loved her enough to let her go and be with Carter's father when I was a child. In the end, she loved them both and couldn't choose, so Carter's father ended up living with us and becoming best friends with my father. It was a beautiful polyamorous relationship, and I grew up with three parents instead of two—until they were killed by an enemy of ours."

"Who was it?" I could already tell Aidan was going to answer this question whether I asked it or not, but I could tell he needed me to ask to build up his courage to answer.

"A monster worse than myself, Kalina. What the underworld thinks of me . . . I am nothing compared to this man. Mafias fear him so much that some refrain from speaking his name. He attacked my home when I was sixteen, Carter just a young child himself, and burnt it to the ground after butchering our parents. That's why I have the burns beneath my tattoos—from carrying Carter out."

He drew in a slow, deliberate breath, as if bracing for the storm to come.

"It was Spencer Gatwick."

All the air was sucked out of my lungs, and all the light left the world. It was as if everything turned dark and deadly in an instant.

Now I know why Ace had been acting so weird.

He was back.

CHAPTER TWENTY-FOUR

ACE

The day I met Kalina, I was horrified of the girl who stood before me. She was a mousy little thing, hiding behind the safety of her older brother—a girl traumatised by men and society for years, undeserving of the abuse she had endured.

I watched her grow into a confident, beautiful woman. Sadly, there were others who noticed her beauty as well. For months, we fought tooth and nail to keep away the idiots and dickheads who tried to form any kind of relationship with our girl.

Until she demanded we allow her to make her own decisions.

"Spencer Gatwick."

As I returned to the lounge of the bar, I heard Aidan confess the secret I had hoped Kalina would never learn. I knew that the second she would hear of his return, all the confidence, strength, and new character she had built would crumble. All the progress she made over the years would be threatened.

"W-what?"

Her voice quaked, her eyes glazing over with tears as she looked up at me.

"Ace."

I wrapped my arms around her within seconds, drawing her into one of the few embraces that calms her in moments of panic. It took some time, but I managed to soothe her trembling frame. Her body eventually settled into small quivers, easing her back into reality.

"He's back?" Her timid voice cut through the silence.

All I could do was nod as her crystal eyes fixed on me. I couldn't speak the words she so desperately feared. I couldn't bear to be the one to drag her back into a world of pain and misery.

"I want to know everything," Kalina said after a pregnant pause.

The thing one need to know about Kalina is that, in a serious situation, she doesn't ask. She simply demands. We've all learned over time that she will get the answers she wants one way or another, and it's far better to give her the information than let her find out alone.

Aidan rose from the booth, went behind the bar, and retrieved the files from the safe concealed there. Kalina and I sat together, waiting, and he returned a few moments later, passing her the thin stack of papers.

*   *   *

KALINA

"He was last seen in Chicago, talking with the Dutch mafia. As for what, we do not know," Aidan began. "Have you met or seen anyone you can confirm is Dutch in the recent months?"

I thought back over all my time since being arrested and sentenced, when I had been secure and protected from Spencer Gatwick. Then it hit me.

"On Christopher's jet from England. The flight attendant was a young Dutch boy," I told him.

Ace grabbed the laptop on the table beside him and inserted a USB stick, beginning to load it whilst Aidan carried on talking.

"We've had our guys trailing him for the past few weeks, but we lost him at a private airstrip. Six flights left that day. We have no idea which one he was on. However, our people are scanning the areas where those planes landed. Thankfully, none arrived directly here in L.A."

"And when was this?" I asked, staring blankly at the photograph of the man.

His dark blond hair was brushed back from his dark empty eyes. His tattooed, tanned skin was flawless, as it had always been, with a slight stubble growing on his sharp jaw. He stood six foot one. In the photo, he wore a tight-fitting black T-shirt and black jeans, his biceps bulging beneath the material.

To any ordinary woman, he was a dreamy man who was beyond gorgeous. To those who know him, he was their greatest nightmare.

I knew him.

The torment I had to endure was indescribable. And thanks to my fucked-up upbringing and my despicable mother, I had thought it was love. The narcissism and manipulation were mistaken for care and compassion. The obsession and violence were misunderstood as protectiveness and teaching.

I thought I had finally found someone who would love me for me. I was not just a body to fuck but a person with feelings and a personality. And my knowledge of the club's protectiveness over me dating a known criminal prevented me from telling them I knew him.

It wasn't until they saved me that I realised what kind of man Spencer Gatwick was. It wasn't until Spencer took the person who meant the most to me in this world that I realised what I had loved was a lie.

"Two days ago," Aidan answered.

It was as if Ace knew my next question, and he answered it instantly, "No, Kalina. He wasn't with him."

I felt the tears leave my eyes as I tried not to have a full breakdown. Aidan seemed confused by Ace's statement but said nothing.

I spent the next half hour looking at photos on the USB of Dutch boys under twenty-five, trying to figure out which one I had met on the plane. Once we identified the boy, we now knew who to torture for information on Spencer.

"You told Christopher everything, didn't you?" I asked Ace once I had identified the boy.

"No, Kalina, not everything. Just what he immediately needed to know," Ace answered, a solemn look on his face. "It's not my place to tell your family about him."

Ace brought me into his arms once again, letting my head rest on his chest. As I stood in the comfort of my protector's arms—my brother's arms—I broke down.

"I miss *him,* Ace," I said, sobbing.

"I miss *him* too." Ace sighed, his own tears falling down his cheeks.

CHAPTER TWENTY-FIVE

KALINA

Jamie dropped me off at the Montessori mansion at ten o'clock the next morning. Not surprisingly, everyone was up and waiting for me.

They tried talking to me, but I just brushed them off—not in the mood. Judging by the expression on their faces, they realised I must know the secret by now.

I went upstairs to my bedroom, lay myself down, and stared at the ceiling, reminiscing about my past life. All I could do was breathe as I thought about all the traumatising memories that had already taken over this week.

A small knock on the bedroom door disturbed my laziness and anxiety.

"Come in."

I was expecting Tommaso or Tristan. Maybe even Antonio. Who I wasn't expecting, however, was Mateo.

His face was no longer emotionless; it now held a frown. Unlike Tristan and Tommaso, he didn't take a seat on my bed. Instead, he pulled over my desk chair, rolling it closer before sitting down.

"So, Anthony told you what's going on?" Mateo said, a solemn look on his face.

"No, Aidan did," I corrected.

"Aidan Rossi?" I could hear the anger in his tone, but he didn't say anything else about him. "What exactly do you want to do about this Spencer Gatwick?"

"He has something of mine. I want it back," I began. "After that, as long as he suffers, I really don't care."

One thing I liked about Mateo was that family came first with him, and he would do anything in his power to grant my wish.

"Can I ask what he took from you?" Mateo asked. "And how you know him?"

"You'll find out eventually," was all I said.

"Kalina, it would help us immensely if we knew what to get from him," Mateo said, urging me to give him the answers I had tried to keep secret for so long.

I considered Mateo's words and realised something terrible could happen to *him* if they were unaware he was Spencer. So I confessed everything—absolutely everything—to my oldest, deadliest, and most powerful brother. The boss of the Italian Mafia.

I could literally feel the fury radiating off him as I laid my life bare before him. I was scared for a moment, but then I realised he wasn't mad at me, but at the people who had harmed me.

When I thought he would leave me in a pool of tears and snot from crying during my confession, he didn't. Instead, he put the chair back under the desk and lifted the quilt on my bed.

Understanding what he was doing, I shuffled over and let him embrace me. Despite his neatly steamed three-piece suit, I could feel the warmth radiating off his body. For the first time in my life, I cuddled with my big bad mafia boss brother.

Who was actually a giant teddy bear.

He rested his stubbly chin on top of my head, my own resting on his chest. His giant hand stroked my hair, holding me close to him.

"Kalina—"

"You don't have to give me sympathy or some shit."

"Kalina." Mateo shut me up with his silencing tone. "I'm not going to give you my sympathy because I know it won't change anything. What I am going to say is, I'm so proud of you."

My eyes snapped up to his, confusion undoubtedly written on my face.

"Everything you've just told me—no one should have to go through that, especially not a seventeen-year-old. You're so strong, tesoro, and you don't even notice it. You brush all this shit off your shoulder like it's simply a hiccup in your life, but it's not. It's horrible what you suffered. The fact that you can overcome this with a . . . semi-sane state—" I laughed at his words, noting how honest he was being. "—is beyond impressive."

That night, I stayed cuddled up to Mateo as he held me close.

I knew why he was being so sweet and caring compared to the gruff and emotionless person he usually was. One, because I was his traumatised baby sister; and two, it was likely to be our final moment of peace for a long while.

The moment Spencer or our people struck, an all-out underworld war would erupt: the Italians, the Irish, and biggest gang in the world against the most ruthless, psychotic cunt and his mafia.

And, apparently, the Dutch mafia too.

So I savoured this few calming hours with Mateo. While Christopher may have been the consigliere—advisor to the Don—Mateo held the ultimate power in our mafia. If anyone could protect me, it was him.

And if Spencer came for me again, I would need all the protection available.

It was what I remembered most about him, the image haunting the majority of my nightmares.

The night sky had already risen over the city of Birmingham. I had told Ace I was going to be with Spencer that evening, and, with extreme reluctance, he had agreed, on the condition that I checked in.

Laid out on the silk sheets, I sucked on the lollipop between my lips. My tanned, naked body sprawled across the bed as I stared through the floor-to-ceiling windows of the penthouse.

The bathroom door opened, steam spilling our behind his tall, lean figure. A red towel was wrapped around his waist, and he brushed his blond hair from his face.

He collapsed onto the bed beside me, eyes roaming over my naked frame.

"Always so sexy," he murmured, hands raking up and down my body. As his lips covered every inch of my skin, I suddenyly felt a coldness around my wrists.

"You'll stay here, naked, forever," he said in a growl, a look in his eyes that awakened every fear within my soul.

Because I had seen that look countless times before. With every man who had bought time with me from my mother. The worst ones, who had tormented me for years.

"Because you, Kalina, are mine. I don't want anyone else to catch a glimpse of what's mine."

Slowly, he undid his towel, and the man I had thought loved me, vanished. And I was confronted with the true monster that was Spencer Gatwick.

No matter how loud I screamed or how hard I cried, no one dared intervene.

Until him . . .

For days and nights. So many days and nights. I hadn't realised how long it had been until he saved me.

Lorenzo.

I woke up this morning alone in my room. Mateo must have left in the early hours. After completing my usual routine and getting dressed in a pair of black jeans, a knitted white sweater, and black sneakers, I headed downstairs.

However, I was stopped on my way to the kitchen by a notification on my phone:

Kalina, can you come to my office

It was Christopher. I turned and redirected myself to the office hallway, a part of the house I had yet to explore. Like much of the rest of the house, the walls were adorned with simple modern art, rather than family photographs.

At the end of the hall, I knocked on the door and heard Christopher on the other side. When he called me in, he was buttoning up his Peaky Blinder-style coat and lighting a cigarette.

"You're dressed. Perfect. Let's go," he said, a smile on his cheery morning face.

Confused, I followed him all the way outside, where a car was already waiting. He opened the passenger door for me and got into the driver's seat himself. Two SUVs followed behind us as we left the estate.

"Where are we going?" I finally asked after a few minutes.

"To the doctors," Christopher answered.

Seeing the worried look on my face, he clarified, "To figure out what is preventing you from being able to read or write."

"Who told you?"

"Antonio."

Nodding, I recalled the time Tristan had covered for me with Antonio, saying I might need glasses. It was only a matter of time before I was taken for testing.

We drove a little further into the city and parked inside a warehouse on the edge of town. It was a large, simple brick building with a few broken windows here and there.

A few guards stood by the now-open garage door. All of them nodded respectfully as we passed. Inside, it was almost entirely bare concrete, with a few hanging lights and shelves full of crates. What caught my attention most, however, were the multiple matte-black Lamborghini 4x4s parked along one side of the wall.

"This is your warehouse?" I couldn't hide the disappointment in my tone as I looked around.

"This . . . is our main warehouse." Christopher smirked.

As I went to say something, the floor beneath me shook. Then our car—the one we had just ridden in—began to descend.

"It's a lift," Christopher explained. "We own ten square miles of storage, safe rooms, cars, drugs, medical rooms, and everything else. We run our dirty money through every supermarket, corner shop, nightclub, restaurant, and any sort of public establishment within those ten square miles."

"Holy shit."

"Yes, tesoro, holy shit." Christopher laughed at the shocked expression on my face.

What had once been a stinky, wrecked warehouse was now a modernised bunker with grey walls accented by white marble. It looked like a fancy hotel, minus the luxurious windows.

I could already see a bunch of suited men and women dressed in black, wandering down what looked almost like underground streets. It was as if there was a little marble city down here.

Christopher drove forwards a little and pulled into a small car park. As we left the car, a little golf cart pulled next to us.

A fucking golf cart.

How rich are these fuckers?!?

"Let's go." Christopher grinned and got into the passenger seat of the cart.

Hopping on the back, I faced the same direction as Christopher. I noticed the bodyguard following him every time he went out in public.

"Who are you?" I asked the bodyguard, a small smile on my face.

"Altiero, Signorina Montessori. È bello conoscerti finalmente," the bodyguard replied with a polite smile. *(Altiero, Miss Montessori. It's nice to finally meet you.)*

Looking at him properly, I would say he was in his late forties to early fifties. His hair was salt-and-pepper, and his eyes were dark brown, with crows' feet at the corners.

It only took us five minutes to arrive at our destination. Christopher helped me down from the golf cart, and I realised we were in a medical street, with a clinic, a pharmacy, an optician, and a mini hospital.

"I understand you may be nervous for this, Kalina, but I simply want to help you," Christopher said, opening the door to the optician's office.

Inside, a woman was waiting for us, a bright smile on her face.

"Hello, Kalina." Brushing a strand of her blonde hair from her face, she came forwards and shook mine and Christopher's hands. "I'm Dr Shire, and I'll be giving you a check-up today."

For the next two hours, I took test after test, from eye examination to mental quizzes. Christopher waited outside per my request, though he was clearly unhappy that I didn't want him there. Once we were finished, she confirmed what I had already suspected.

"Kalina, you are dyslexic, and due to an injury, your vision in your right eye is slightly blurry, your left eye significantly worse—extremely damaged, to be exact," she said in a gentle way. "In fact, I'm surprised you can see at all."

"So, how do I sort this?" I asked.

"You'll need a strong prescription, more for your left eye than your right. There are also special lenses to help with reading. They only work for certain people, but it's worth a try," Dr Shire explained with a smile.

After several trials with the new glasses and tinted lenses, we discovered that the dyslexia-specific lenses helped me read more comfortably, and we finally settled on the perfect prescription for my regular glasses.

So now, I have three pairs of glasses: my everyday ones, the dyslexic ones, and a backup pair.

"Holy shit. How terrible was my eyesight before?" I said, peering through the black-framed glasses now perched on my nose.

"Extremely terrible, by the looks of it." Dr Shire chuckled.

"Kalina, since I have been assigned as your personal doctor, I would like to have a look at those scars."

Instantly, I tensed at her words.

"Hey, it's just a request. You can always say no," she added upon noticing my reaction.

"No. I had them looked at years ago. It's all in my file. You don't need to see them."

"Then how come no one did anything about your eyesight?" Dr Shire asked.

"I never told anyone my eyes were blurry because I thought it was just how everything looked. I guess the scar on my eye actually affected my vision, and I never knew." I shrugged.

That evening, Christopher drove us home, and everything was so much clearer to see.

And life was far more beautiful than I had realised.

CHAPTER TWENTY-SIX

TRISTAN

It was the early hours of the morning as Tommaso and I sat awake in my bedroom. We had spent most of the night collecting all the information we needed for the inevitable war.

Fury surged through my body at the news of Kalina being told about Spencer Gatwick by Aidan Rossi. However, I had managed to control my anger eventually.

I was sitting on a dining chair from downstairs, as my desk chair was now just a pile of rubble in the corner.

Maybe I should have controlled my emotions more.

Just minutes before, I had hacked into the Dutch embassy's database.

"Tom, learn these names and faces," I said to Tommaso, who was sitting on my bed behind me.

While I did most of the hacking in our family, Tommaso was the spy type. We didn't actively send him into gunfights or anything like that, but the guy could talk anyone's ass off—a very useful skill in the field.

We got him to learn the names and faces of every person we were observing or sent him in to play spy or kidnap enemies. He was very good at that.

"He's one ugly fucker," Tommaso said, looking at his next target.

I nodded, not even looking at the screen. All I wanted was to kill this bastard who had hurt Kalina. While Anthony didn't tell us exactly what he had done to her, it didn't take a genius to figure out it was bad. And unlike my other siblings, I had seen how much it had affected her. I had seen it through the numerous nightmares she suffered from—the ones that had me sprinting to her room in the middle of the night. I could still remember the pain and terror in those suffering blue eyes.

"What are we going to do with the Dutch if they are working for Gatwick?" Tommaso asked, having finished learning everything he needed.

"Destroy them." I shrugged, looking up at my little brother.

"Tris . . . what did he do to Kalina?" Tommaso sighed, desperate for answers.

Since he was under eighteen and had yet to be sworn in, he wasn't allowed in the big meetings. But since I was an official member, Mateo had filled me in on what happened—after a long-ass lecture.

"You know I can't say." I sighed. "You'll have to ask Kalina."

A knock sounded at my bedroom door, and Dad's head poked through the gap.

"It's time."

The two of us rose from our seats, buttoned up our suits, and followed our dad down the stairs. We were dressed for a formal dinner with the Chained Angels and Aidan Rossi. It was a meal to discuss how to move forward with the fast-forming war and to seal the new alliance among the three of us.

"Kalina! Hurry up!" Antonio yelled up the stairs, checking his watch continuously.

"You can't rush beauty, Antonio," Kalina said as she rounded the corner at the top of the stairs.

She was wearing a black floor-length dress with a thigh-high slit and a deep sweetheart neckline. Her hair hung in tight curls, framing her tanned face with light makeup. She looked adorable with the black-framed glasses on her face, making her seem more innocent and childlike, in my opinion.

"What the fuck is that?" I asked.

"A dress." Kalina rolled her eyes, taking my outstretched hand as she stepped off the final step.

I may not like her dress, but I'm still a gentleman.

"More like a piece of cloth," I sneered.

"Shut up, Tristan." Kalina laughed.

She was lucky she was my sister. No one else could tell me to shut up and get away with it.

"You look gorgeous, tesoro," Dad said, offering her a wide smile. "Now, let's go."

All of us piled into the awaiting cars outside. We had chosen a restaurant owned by Aidan Rossi, as a sign of good faith. That, and the fact that we knew he and the Chained Angels wouldn't risk Kalina getting hurt should they change their minds.

We arrived at the elegant Italian restaurant to find multiple motorcycles already parked outside the front door. After walking in, a waitress immediately led us to our table. She had long blonde hair and a fair complexion, emphasizing her brown doe eyes. Her figure was petite and thin, the blouse she was wearing accentuating her slightly wide hips and small breasts.

I offered her a wink, instantly making her blush and smile timidly. A smirk spread across my face.

"Good to see you, Montessoris."

My attention was drawn away from the beautiful waitress and toward Aidan Rossi.

He was already seated, wearing an all-black suit, an irritating grin on his face as he welcomed us to his restaurant. Kalina and my dad were the only ones who offered him a smile, replying to his greeting.

Anthony Vecoli, Jamie Andrews, and Maddie—the president's sister, Caleb Smith, and the two men I had learned to be Killian and Luke were all seated on the same side as Aidan Rossi.

With a clenched jaw and tightened fists, I watched as Kalina embraced all of them. It was far more open and comfortable than she had ever been with my brothers or me.

It hurt watching the girl everyone in the family had come to love treat complete strangers with even more warmth. While we may not have known about her until just over a month ago, we had all come to love and adore our sister.

But we would always be second.

Kalina had to explain the glasses to her other *family*, all of whom were angered by the fact that she had never told them about her issues with her eyesight. Her reasoning was that they had done enough for her, to which Maddie smacked the back of her head, stating that they would always have time for her.

As I observed the way they acted toward my sorellina during dinner, I realized just how much she meant to them. Luke and Killian were constantly on guard, ready to defend her. Maddie doted on her, sharing her dessert and drinks with a kind smile. Jamie Andrews was annoying her with stupid remarks and jokes—the same I did with Tommaso. Anthony Vecoli glared at anyone in the restaurant whose eyes lingered on Kalina too long.

She was the princess of their gang.

Slowly, I began to accept that while Kalina had us, she would also have them. They cared for her when no one else did. And for that . . . I was grateful.

For that, they had my respect.

"Well, I say it's time to sign the alliance agreement," Dad said as the dessert plates were carried away.

Bored out of my mind, I let my eyes wander around the restaurant until they landed on the waitress. She removed her apron and let her hair down, strands of blonde locks framing her porcelain face.

"Excuse me," I said to no one in particular as the three powerful underworld leaders signed numerous papers. Rising from my seat, I followed the girl as she went outside into the back alley.

"Hello." She smiled timidly at my presence.

"Hello, gorgeous."

"What's your name?" she asked as I approached.

"Tristan? What about you?" I answered.

"Naomi. I've noticed you staring at me, Tristan. All night." Her brown eyes looked up at mine. She took a step closer, my tall frame towering over hers.

"And what do you think about that?" I retorted, my usual smirk finding its way to my face.

"This is what I think." She wrapped her hands around my neck and pressed her soft pink lips to mine.

CHAPTER TWENTY-SEVEN

KALINA

As a child, it always confused me how others my age were scared of such minor things—a strike of thunder, the monster under the bed, being told off, the dark.

For me, the strike was a fist, the monster was on top of the bed, being told off meant degradation and neglect, and the dark was the uncertainty of surviving the next day.

Between the mafias and the gang, it was decided that I would spend an equal but staggered amount of time with each, keeping Spencer Gatwick guessing about my whereabouts.

Today was my day with Aidan.

He had picked me up from Christopher's mansion. He was wearing black slacks and a black button-up, the top few buttons undone to reveal his smooth, hairless, tanned, tattooed chest. A silver chain hung around his neck, matching the silver watch on his wrist. The sleeves of his shirt were rolled up to his elbows, showing off more tattoos. With his brown hair combed back from his face, I tried my hardest not to stare.

"I need to head to the warehouse today," Aidan said as he closed the passenger door for me.

"Fine by me."

Aidan just chuckled at my response, knowing I understood he wasn't asking.

Listening to Arctic Monkeys on the journey, I sang along, and Aidan smiled as I did. For once, it felt relatively peaceful despite the circumstances.

In other words, we are relatively calm—at least for now—even though my crazy, manipulative ex is still out there, trying to kidnap and possibly kill me.

It wasn't long before we arrived at the warehouse, located on the outskirts of the city. Passing by all the parked cars, we headed to a garage where Aidan parked his matte Ferrari.

He walked around to my side of the car, opened the door, and offered me his hand, helping me out.

As I followed him through the building, his hand left mine and moved to the small of my back, guiding me gently. For some reason, I felt comfortable in his arms, neither tense nor unsure.

Men and women training in the main area halted their movements at the sight of Aidan. Questioning looks covered their faces at the sight of me. I received lustful looks from men, glares from women, and an few gave me a warm smile.

"Carry on!" Aidan shouted as we continued to a set of stairs.

They did as they were told. Aidan opened a door and revealed an office predominantly painted black. Most of the wooden furniture was dark oak. There was an array of bookshelves and sofas, a fireplace, and a bar. Aidan took a seat at the grand desk at the far side of the room, opened a file, and began writing.

"Need any help?" I asked, taking a seat on the edge of his desk.

Crossing my legs, I tracked Aidan's eyes lingering momentarily on my thighs. They later met my gaze, and he shook his head.

"No, all these just need some signatures," he replied, turning back to the slightly thick pile on his desk.

A knock sounded at the office door, and three people barged in. One had a brown buzz cut, blue eyes, and a slightly muscular frame. He was about a few inches shorter than Aidan. He sat on the chair in front of Aidan's desk, threw his feet up, and unbuttoned his black blazer.

The other had a colder expression and opted to lean against the wall. With combed-back blond hair, brown eyes, and tattoos crawling up his forearms—visible where the rolled-up sleeves of his navy turtleneck ended—he stared at me with an analysing gaze.

And the last man, I recognised straight away.

"Carter!" I smiled, embracing my friend.

"Hi, Kalina." Carter chuckled, hugging me back. "I thought I'd come down since you're here."

"How'd you know I was here?"

Carter nodded towards Aidan, who now had a small grin on his face.

"I didn't want you to get bored." Aidan shrugged. "Ben, get your manky-ass feet off my desk."

"Who's the hot lass?" Ben, as Aidan referred to him, complied whilst his eyes scanned me from head to toe.

"No," Carter, Aidan, and I said all at once.

"Well, the answer's always no until you ask." Ben shrugged, offering me a kind smile.

"Kalina, this is Ben, the underboss of the Irish mafia. That is Alonzo, underboss of the Italian Mafia," Aidan said, nodding towards the blond standing in the corner.

I offered him a small wave, which he returned with a simple nod.

"Come on. Let's go." Carter led me out of the office, and we headed to the car park outside.

"I'm meant to stay with Aidan today," I pointed out as we piled into the Porsche.

"Technically, you're meant to stay under the protection of his mafia, not specifically with him. Some guards are assigned to me anyway, so you'll be fine." Carter sped out of the car park, exclaiming it was time for food.

We drove to a McDonald's and made our way inside, laughing and joking as we did so. His hood remained up as always, hiding most of his face.

When it was time to collect our food, only Carter went and I waited at the table. As I casually glanced around, my eyes caught sight of a heartbreaking view.

He looked slightly taller than when I last saw him. His black hair had grown a little longer. His eyes were as brown as the day he was born, his frame a little longer than before. The same tanned skin he inherited from his father gleamed under the sunlight, and the smile gifted from his dad lit up his chubby little face.

And behind him stood Spencer Gatwick, a sadistic grin on his face.

I rushed up from my seat and made it outside to the car park, only to see the wheels of an SUV speeding away.

Bile rose in my throat. I clutched my shirt as I watched the car disappear into the distance. Tears streamed freely down my cheeks.

"Kalina!" Distantly, I heard Carter shouting, his footsteps pounding closer. "Kalina, are you okay?"

"He took him," I croaked, trembling in the arms of my friend.

"Who? Gatwick?"

"He took him," I cried, desperate to see his tiny face again.

"Who did he take?" Carter pressed.

"Lorenzo."

* * *

As a child, the fears of others my age used to baffle me. Not because I was unaware of the stories told to scare children, or the imagination of a child frightened of the cruel, cruel world. I simply knew there was far worse to be afraid of.

There was the fear of watching someone take what you hold dearest and tear them from your arms as if they had always belonged to them. The agony of seeing the change that followed such loss.

I never wanted to miss any part of Lorenzo's life. I wanted to be there for him, as his father had been there for me. I wanted the boy I adored to have the love of a parent he so deeply deserved. I wanted the young boy to smile as he remembered his youth.

But thanks to the man who made me suffer, I had failed.

Still, I would do everything in my power to redeem myself, for I had promised his father I would search for Lorenzo until my dying breath.

I had always welcomed silence. It was reassuring to know I was truly alone. No one hiding in the shadows, no enemy lurking in the corner, no danger waiting to approach. I embraced the quiet, knowing there was nothing to fear.

Silence was always a peaceful feeling, whether in my bedroom or in the cells of prison. Silence was envied and rarely received.

I had hoped to be silent as I slipped out of Carter's bedroom. Aidan had taken the two of us back to his house after I had seen Spencer. Whilst Aidan prepared for an attack, strengthening the defences and security around us, Carter and I had succumed to a sugar rush, followed swiftly by a food coma.

Once I heard the door shut and footsteps fade, I crawled out of Carter's bed, tiptoeing towards the door.

Then I had another idea.

Turning back, I looked at Carter, his cheek pressed against the bed and his hood slipping slightly as he lay with his back to me. Reaching forwards, I gently grasped the edge of the hood with my fingertips.

I had always wondered why Carter hid his face so much. What scared him so badly that no one was allowed to see him properly. After all the time we had spent together since we met a month ago, I already considered him one of my closest—dare I say, best—friends.

But then I realised what I was doing.

So I let go of his hood and turned away.

If Carter was so insecure about what he was hiding, I had no right to expose him whilst he was vulnerable in his sleep. I would kill the person who did that to me. When and if Carter was ready to show me his insecurities, that would be his decision.

Quietly, I opened the bedroom door and crept down the hallway. Peeking my head around the corners, I tiptoed my way through the mansion, all the way down to Aidan's garage. Searching the key rack, I grabbed the Tesla car key and opened the—thankfully—silent garage door.

Approaching the car, I noticed a bench against the wall holding Chinese ring daggers and two guns. Grabbing the lot, I put the daggers in my boots, the gun in my waistband, and the other on the passenger seat. I got in the car and drove out of the garage through the heavily guarded front gate. The guards insisted that I must return inside, but I explained to them that I was perfectly safe with my weapons and that I was meeting my brothers on the way. Thankfully, they believed me and let me go.

Speeding down the road, I typed into the tracking system on my phone. Whilst I might not be able to read clearly enough, even with my new glasses, I knew the licence plates.

And I remembered the one on the SUV.

Within a few minutes, the car had been tracked, and I was given directions as to where it was. Speeding down the quiet streets, I had one thing in mind:

Murder.

I had no plan, I had no way in, I had no assurances I would survive. All I had was determination.

I refused to miss any more of Lorenzo's life. I refused to watch the boy grow from a distance.

I remembered the day like it was yesterday—the day I held my dying brother in my arms and promised what I was going to do.

It had been three months since Spencer had shown his true colours, the monster he truly was. The raw narcissism and madness he possessed were evident now, and I wanted nothing more than to kill him and return home to Daniel and Lorenzo.

Lorenzo was only three, but he was a smart boy. Where he got that from, I didn't know, since his dad was—well—Daniel, and his mother was a D-student who had abandoned him at the first chance she got.

A bang had woken me from my sleep, the sound echoing through the halls of Spencer's manor. Turning on my side, I groaned in pain from the open cuts on my arm, burns on my hand, the healing slash on my collarbone, and my bruised ribs. I stared at the door.

Spencer called it tough love. I called it manipulation and abuse.

It was as if he would go into some sort of trance. He would be loving and caring, and within seconds, I would be on the floor, bleeding. No matter what we were doing—cuddling, talking, fucking—he was like a ticking time bomb.

The sounds of doors and gunfire grew louder and louder until I heard them right outside my door. Suddenly, the wooden barrier was broken, and in charged a blood-soaked Daniel.

"Kalina," he said in pants as he laid eyes on me.

Letting out a cry, I ran painfully from my bed and threw myself into Daniel's arms.

"I'm sorry. I'm so sorry. I didn't mean to—"

Daniel cut me off with a soothing shush, holding me close and resting my head on his chest.

"You have nothing to apologise for."

My legs moved with his, but I did not pay attention to where we were going. All I did was enjoy being back in my brother's arms. Looking up a few minutes later, I realised we were in the main hallway downstairs.

Then, suddenly, a gunshot rang through the halls once again.

Daniel stopped, and I heard the coughs escape his throat as he became deadweight in my arms. The two of us collapsed to the floor. Daniel lifted a weak arm and shot the guard who had fired.

"Daniel," I sobbed, trying to put pressure on the wound in his chest.

"Don't cry, piccolo uno." (little one.)

"I should've listened to you when you said he was trouble," I confessed, still trying to stop the bleeding.

Gently—or weakly—Daniel removed my hands from his chest and held them in his. He had a soft smile on his face, blood coating his teeth.

"You're worth so much more than you've been given. Never give up. Don't mourn me, Kalina. I'm dying a peaceful death."

I cried at his words but nodded, urging him to continue.

"I got to see my baby sister one last time, and I know my little boy will be safe with her."

I watched as the life drained from his eyes. He took his final breath, the brown eyes that had given me comfort all my life closing for the last time.

"I promise."

Minutes later, I was speeding down the motorway, heading straight to the clubhouse, blood covering my clothes and my mind focused solely on Lorenzo.

Then Daniel's phone began ringing.

"Daniel! Gatwick attacked the clubhouse. He's got Lorenzo. We're following him now. He's on the A688!" The voice I recognised as Teddy's bellowed through the phone.

"I'm on my way," I answered, swinging the car around into a U-turn.

"Kalina! Where's Daniel!" Teddy exclaimed.

"Daniel's dead. I'm going after my nephew," I answered with determination, going faster than I had ever driven in my life.

I almost crashed three times, but when I saw Spencer turn onto the slip road to a helicopter hangar, fear coursed through my bones.

I almost had him. He had just exited the car with little Lorenzo in his arms, bolting to the helicopter, engines already running.

I had never run so fast in my life.

The sound of approaching motorbikes reached my ears as I sprinted.

But I was too late . . .

Spencer was away in the sky, my nephew with him.

Pulling up outside the compound, I once again checked my weapons before exiting the car. I had one plan and one plan only.

Kill every fucker I see.

Just as I was about to make the mile-long walk to the fence, the sound of a car stopping caught my attention.

Piling out of the vehicle were Carter, Ace, Jamie, and Aidan. All four were carrying weapons fit for an army. I just knew they were fully trained too.

"What are you doing here?" I snapped as the four approached me.

"Hello, boys. Nice to see you. Hello there, Kalina. You're welcome for the help," Jamie said sarcastically, rolling his eyes as he cocked his gun.

"Fuck off, all of you." The demand in my tone was not missed, just ignored.

"You're not going in on a suicide mission by yourself," Aidan said, stepping closer until we were almost chest-to-chest.

Staring up into his emerald eyes, I saw the truth and determination in his tone. Even if all the others had left, as I had said, he would be by my side until the end.

"Let's go."

And the first shot was fired . . .

CHAPTER TWENTY-EIGHT

KALINA

Storming the warehouse, the five of us shot down anyone in our way. The boys subconsciously formed a protective barrier around me, shielding me from the swarm of bullets in the air.

Pushing past Ace and Carter, I took the lead, shooting my way through the guards and moving further into the building.

"For fuck's sake." I heard Aidan grumble over the gunfire, following behind us with his gun raised.

Glass shattered, bangs echoed, bodies fell, and blood spilled.

When an army of guards came barrelling through the large metal doors, Aidan wrapped his arm around my waist and pulled me behind him, firing as he did so.

Pushing me towards a door to the side, Aidan shouted, "Go."

The look in his eyes was fearful, but he knew I would not turn back. He knew I needed to do this, so he made sure I had the chance.

Bursting through the door, a silent corridor lay before me. There was not a guard in sight, only dim lights brightening the way.

Jogging cautiously through the corridor, I saw a door at the end secured with a large padlock.

Breaking the lock with the butt of my gun, I threw the door open and charged through. It was a bedroom decorated in blue paint, Spider-Man artwork, and toys.

"Mama?"

The voice I had longed to hear for so many months. The little angel I had missed since the day he was taken. It felt like a knife had been stabbed into my heart, blood oozing through the wound in my chest.

While I may have been his aunt biologically, I was his mother. He had only ever seen me as such and refused to call me anything else.

"Hey, trouble." I smiled softly at him.

Standing by the open floor-to-ceiling window was Spencer Gatwick, Lorenzo in his arms as tears stained his chubby little cheeks. One wrong move, and my nephew could fall to his death.

"Hello, baby. Missed me?"

Glaring, I turned my gaze to Spencer, who stood there with his menacing smirk. He didn't want to frighten Lorenzo—I had always known he loved him like a little brother—so there was no gun in hand. But I knew Spencer. He would do anything to get me trapped again.

Even if it meant killing a child he cared for.

"Can't say I have," I snarled, taking a slow step forwards.

"I wouldn't move if I were you, Kalina," he replied, casting a quick glance at the pavement three floors below.

"What do you want?" I asked, placing my gun on the floor as an act of compliance.

"What I have always wanted. You."

"Why? What's your obsession with me?" I had been wanting to ask this question for almost a year now.

Why me? What was so special about an abused Italian girl from England. Why was I so important to Spencer that he couldn't let me go.

"I love you, Kalina," Spencer said, a genuine smile on his face. "I always have. You're the first girl I've ever loved. All you need to do is accept that you love me back."

The softness of his features, the genuineness of his tone—it was like the first time we had been together. Before he went crazy, possessive, and obsessive.

Spencer had once been a kind and caring man, much like Aidan in a way, yet, surprisingly, I didn't have with him the sense of security I had around Aidan. It was almost as if I had had so much bad luck that my heart convinced my mind I was safe around Aidan.

At some point, maybe I had loved Spencer. I had loved the pseudo-security he offered, the warmth I felt in his embrace, and the privileged life he granted me. However, I would not go back to it, because with it came abuse and manipulation.

Everything happened so fast. In a flash, the door of the room burst open once again. Jamie tumbled inside with his gun raised, Carter not far behind.

Shocked, Spencer turned and aimed his weapon at the two, but he tripped. Stumbling on the ledge, his grip loosened, and my heart stopped.

All I could do was watch as Lorenzo's tiny feet slipped over the edge, listening to the screams and pleas for help as he fell.

Red was all I could see. I bolted at a startled Spencer and dragged him back into the room. Punch after punch landed on his face.

A faint buzzing was all I could hear as I cried and screamed, attacking Spencer with everything I had. Somebody grabbed my shoulders, desperately trying to pull me away.

But nothing could stop me.

There was no bringing me back.

They said insanity was something no one wished to experience—the dreaded feeling of realising you have truly lost your mind, the uncertainty of the voice in your head.

I had always wanted to know what truly made a person go mad.

Now I knew.

It was the pain, the agony that swarmed your heart and mind, clawing at your insides to escape. It was not the loss of happiness that brought insanity, but the loss of hope.

The second I watched my little nephew—my baby boy—fall from that window, I lost all hope. He may have been Daniel's son, but he was my little boy. I was the mother he needed when his biological one had left him. I was the aunty he needed to spoil him. I was the sister he needed to play with at any time.

I thought I could take it, take the risk of never seeing Lorenzo again. What I didn't anticipate was that it would be him who would turn up dead, not myself.

CHAPTER TWENTY-NINE

AIDAN

When my guards reported that Kalina was attempting to leave the estate during the night, I told them to let her to go. I knew where she was headed—she was going to find Lorenzo.

I knew she loved him as her own. That was obvious. Carter had told me how she had collapsed outside McDonald's as the boy was taken from her once more. I would not stop her from trying. It was not my place to do so.

When I received word that she had left, I called for my brother, Ace, and Jamie. We met her at the warehouse we had tracked down the previous day.

Originally, we had been planning an attack, together with her family, but there was no convincing Kalina. We sent word to her family, but they were on the other side of the city.

As Ace and I fought our way through the army-filled corridor, I subconsciously kept glancing back at the double doors I had sent Kalina through. Even while fighting, I was worried for her.

I had tried to deny it—that I felt this way, that it was wrong to feel this way—but I couldn't. I had never met someone quite like her. She wore her pain and scars like a badge of armour. After everything she had been through, she was still strong. Her consideration and care for others was admirable. Her intelligence shone from deep within, beautifully.

The cute scrunch of her button nose when she did not like something, the shininess of her pale blue eyes, the small symbolic tattoos littering her tan skin, the glasses tangled in her long curly hair. Her I-don't-give-a-fuck attitude and her stubbornness—I found adorably frustrating.

I knew I could not try anything with her. There were so many reasons not to. She was a Montessori, my enemy's daughter. She was the closest thing Ace had to a sister. She was my brother's best friend. She was still seventeen.

But I was infatuated with her.

"Carter!" I shouted as I sliced the throat of a man charging at me.

"Where's Kalina?" he replied, punching a woman who tried to stab him.

"I sent her down the hall. You and Jamie go after her," I ordered, fighting off men and women in my path.

The two did as I said, turning and running towards Kalina with haste. After some time, both Ace and I had killed every one of Spencer's men, leaving a pile of dead bodies strewn across the corridor.

"Let's go around the back, in case they need us," Ace said.

I followed Ace down the stairs, our daggers still in hand in case of any surprises. We made it three floors down, just above the garages. There was a large balcony. The doors were open, the wind blowing the curtains.

"Let's keep an eye out for backup," I said to Ace as the two of us made our way onto the balcony.

The view was of the fence and gate we had broken through to enter the property. Leaning against the railing, I watched as Ace stood beside me.

Then a harsh punch landed on my cheek.

"What the fuck!" I stood back up and faced Ace with his nonchalant expression.

"That's for looking at Kalina," Ace replied, a small smile breaking across his face. "Don't act like you don't know. Not even Carter could carve such a deep place in your stone heart."

"So . . . are you mad, or . . ." I asked, confused as to where this conversation was going.

"I was at first. I mean, you're practically noncing on my little sister." I frowned at his words. "You wait till she's eighteen, and you'll have my full support."

I took a moment to absorb his words. After all, perhaps my future depended on them. My plan had been to fuck my hookups every night—apart from when Kalina was at my house—to try and get over her. But it hadn't been working.

I was addicted to her like a junkie on cocaine. There was just so much more I wanted to know about her. I wanted to care for her, hold her in my arms, and protect her from all the shit she had to put up with.

I wanted to love her the way she deserved to be loved.

"I've tried to get over her—"

"But you can't," Ace finished, a cheeky smile on his face. "Imagine the day Aidan Rossi admitted he was falling in love."

"I never said—"

Once again, I was cut off, but this time by a scream from above. Looking up, I saw a tiny frame falling, plummeting towards us.

I reached over the balcony, almost falling myself, but Ace grabbed hold of my legs. I caught the small figure in my arms. As I adjusted him, he wrapped his arms around my neck while I cradled him against my chest.

"Enzo . . ." Ace whispered, a tear slipping from his eye.

Then I realised I was holding Lorenzo Montessori in my arms. The boy we had been fighting to save was safe in my hold. I was not letting him go until I handed him over to Kalina.

"Enzo, was your mama up there with you?" Ace asked, catching on to my train of thought.

"She was with the bad man." Lorenzo sobbed and trembled, clutching my shirt in his small hand.

Realisation crossed both of our faces, and within seconds, we were bolting up the stairs at an intense, almost inhuman pace. Ace surged through the open doors, where groans and screams of desperation and fury echoed through the room.

Carefully, I followed, keeping Lorenzo pressed to my chest so his eyes wouldn't catch the worst of the scene.

Kalina was on top of Spencer, whose face had become almost unrecognisable in the sea of blood and swelling. Teeth had been knocked out, scattered across the floor, and knife marks lined his body.

"Kalina!" I shouted as she raised her fist for another punch.

Her eyes snapped to mine. There was only one word to describe the look on her face: broken. Mascara stained her cheeks as tears streamed down, little splatters of blood marring her face and neck, but buckets soaked her body.

Then her gaze drifted to the figure in my arms. Slowly, she rose and took hesitant steps forward, until she stood right in front of me.

Lorenzo turned towards her, probably sensing her presence. A chubby-cheeked smile spread across his face. Ignoring the blood covering her body, he reached out to her.

Gently, she took him from my arms and held him tightly to her chest, as if he might disappear. I watched her body shake as she cried silently, relief washing over her features.

Looking up at me, she took a step closer and allowed me to wrap my arms around her. She rested her head on my chest while still staring down at the toddler in her arms.

"Thank you," she whispered, reaching up to kiss my cheek.

Maybe things would finally start to look up, now that Spencer Gatwick was as good as dead.

CHAPTER THIRTY

KALINA

The moment I had been waiting for, for countless months, was finally here. In my arms, I held the little toddler that my heart ached to think of. The day he was taken had been the day my world crashed and burned around me. I had spent his entire life being the mother he never had, helping my brother raise the child I thought of as my own.

No one spoke during the car journey home, but we all wore small smiles. Lorenzo slept, curled into my chest. Aidan and Carter were on either side of me. Ace was driving, and Jamie sat next to him. Before we left, Aidan had called his cleanup crew to get rid of anything in the warehouse. Spencer had been taken to one of Aidan's properties to suffer.

"Kalina, we're here," Carter whispered, careful not to wake Lorenzo.

We were parked outside the Montessori mansion, the lights from the foyer and living room still on.

Climbing out of the car, I followed the guys into the house, where everyone began to ask questions.

"Shut up," I snapped, feeling Lorenzo stir in my arms.

But it was too late.

Yawning, Lorenzo turned to see everyone—my brothers, my father, Jamie, Ace, Carter, and Aidan—all looking towards the two of us.

His grip on my shirt tightened, but he still gave them a sloppy grin. "'Ello."

The responses he received varied: soft smiles, grins of relief, slight waves . . .

Chuckling, I turned to Christopher, who nodded for me to go upstairs. Gladly, I carried Lorenzo to my bedroom. I laid him down on the mattress and climbed in beside him, holding him close.

Hours passed as I held the toddler peacefully. It had been months since I had hugged him, and I was not planning on letting him go any time soon. The agony I felt without him in my life was crippling.

Especially since it was my psychotic boyfriend who had kidnapped him.

A knock sounded at the bedroom door, and Aidan popped his head inside.

"He's still asleep?" Aidan asked quietly as he stood at the side of the bed.

"Yeah," I mumbled, a soft smile resting on my face.

Reaching out, Aidan offered me his hand. Hesitantly, I took it, allowing him to guide me out onto the balcony. The sky was an orangey-yellow, the sun beginning to rise after the long eventful night. A soft breeze drifted past.

"It was stupid of you to go there by yourself," Aidan scolded, his emerald eyes staring down at me, his face stern and his jaw clenched.

"We all do stupid things for what means the world to us."

Staring back at him, I watched as his muscles shifted as he folded his arms, his tight V-neck shirt not doing him enough justice. He looked angry but understanding at the same time, as if he understood why I had done it but was pissed off that I had gone alone.

"Why did you follow me? That was stupid of you." Cocking my brow, I waited for an answer.

It was obvious he already had an answer, but he still seemed hesitant to say it. Sighing, Aidan uncrossed his arms and ran a hand through his hair.

"I do stupid things for those who mean the world to me."

Before I could react, Aidan cupped my face in the palm of his hands and pressed his lips softly against mine. Reacting the only way I wanted to, I kissed him back, wrapping my arms around his neck as his moved to my waist. It was as if all the tension of the previous weeks had disappeared, and it was just us.

Eventually, we had to pull away for air and rested our foreheads against each other. I stared up at his closed eyes.

"Wow," he said, causing me to chuckle.

Gently taking his hand, I guided Aidan back inside the bedroom, the two of us sitting on the sofa in the corner by the window. We sat at opposite ends, an awkward silence filling the room.

"This shouldn't have happened," Aidan said suddenly.

My heart ached, rejection stinging as my gaze met his. His expression was angry. He jaw twitched, and his fists were clenched.

"What?"

"This was wrong," Aidan said, his face shifting to a stoic expression. "I don't like you like that."

"It was all bullshit?"

Aidan simply nodded in response, his eyes not meeting mine.

I didn't say a word. I simply got up and opened the bedroom door. "You needn't be here anymore then."

"Kalina . . . that's not what I—"

"Goodnight," I interrupted.

Nodding in acceptance, Aidan got up and made his way out of the room, his tall figure almost reaching the top of the door frame, his muscular build filling the space.

He stopped momentarily, and a flicker of hope sparked in my chest . . . until he carried on walking.

Sighing, I closed the door, leaning my back against it as I shut my eyes. All this tension between Aidan and me . . .

It seemed only I was willing to go further with it.

"Mama?"

I opened my eyes. Lorenzo sitting up on the bed, rubbing his tired eyes.

Smiling, I walked over to him and sat down, letting him cuddle up to my side.

"Yeah, Enzo?" I replied with a smile.

"Did you and your friend fight?" he asked, referring to Aidan, who had just left the room.

"I was fighting too hard, apparently, and he wasn't fighting at all."

The moment I had been waiting for had arrived. Then the man I had developed a liking for—possibly even feelings for_had kissed me. It was nothing like I had expected: amazing, beautiful, and peaceful.

I had no idea why he had changed his mind so quickly, why he didn't want what I thought he did. I supposed that was to be expected when you trust someone you barely know.

CHAPTER THIRTY-ONE

KALINA

A month later

Music blasted through my ears, the tequila swimming through my system, adding to the effects of the cocaine.

Maxim and I were standing on a table, dancing to the music, my arms wrapped around his neck and his around my hips. Over the past month, I had grown closer to him and the boys, loving every minute I spent with them.

"Let's go find the guys!" Maxim yelled over the music and jumped off the table.

He offered me his hand, helping me down. As the bottom of my black heels touched the floor, Maxim's hands landed on my waist to steady me as I wobbled slightly. Since living with my biological family and actually getting properly fed, I had grown. Most girls stop growing when puberty ends, but apparently, my body changed its mind. I was still tiny, though, but I was now five-foot-three-and-a-half.

Yes, the 0.5 is important.

A month had passed since we rescued Lorenzo, who was currently sleeping at home in the care of Christopher, who had gladly taken up the role of step-grandfather.

Maxim guided me through the crowd until we returned to Jayden and Carter. Jayden had his tongue shoved down a girl's throat. Carter had his hood up, smoking a joint as he danced to the music.

At the sight of my approach, Carter reached his arms out and wrapped them around my waist. Lifting the joint to my lips, the two of us continued to smoke and dance the night away.

It wasn't until three o'clock in the morning that the four of us left. Driving back to Carter's (and, unfortunately, Aidan's) house, Jayden and I sat inthe back of the car with the roof down, music from Spotify playing.

Minutes later, we pulled into Carter's driveway, the guards giving us a sympathetic glance as they let us through, knowing we would be in trouble.

"Kal! You're eighteen next week!" Carter yelled drunkenly, slinging his arm over my shoulder.

The two of us stumbled through the front door of his house, with a wrestling Maxim and Jayden following.

"Really?" I fake-gasped. "I hadn't noticed!"

"Piss off," Carter mumbled. "Anyway! What are we going to do?"

"I say we go on a group holiday!" Jayden said, pushing himself between Carter and me with a large grin on his face.

"Oh yeah? And where'd we go?" Maxim laughed, flopping onto the couch in the living room.

I seated myself beside him. Jayden rested his head on my lap. Carter leaned against the coffee table in front of us.

"Cuba? Jamaica? Australia?" Jayden began to list countries, waving his hands around as though he had discovered these countries in his drunken haze.

"What about Tommy?" I said, pouting at the thought of my brother.

This would be my first birthday knowing I had a twin, and I was intent on spending it with him. We had spent the last month bonding, mainly watching *Peaky Blinders.*

And the rest of my family—I would like to spend my birthday with them as well, after seventeen years.

"We can bring everyone!" Carter chuckled. "Christopher can pay for everything while the rest of us get drunk off our arses!"

"And Enzo?" I said.

"The boy could use a holiday." Jayden shrugged.

Whilst Carter was heir to the Italian-Irish mob, Maxim was an Angel like me. Jayden said he worked with Carter for Aidan, mainly hacking into systems and other handling forms of software deemed necessary.

Carter and Jayden actually met because the latter stole from Aidan's legal company, and Carter had been sent to kill him. Jayden proved himself worth more alive than dead and had been with them ever since.

"You three!"

All four of our heads snapped to the archway leading to the bedroom, where a barely clothed Aidan stood in the gap. His tattoos were on full display, his defined abs and sculpted muscles proudly on show. He wore nothing but a pair of black shorts. His hair was messy, and his brown eyes glared harshly.

"Carter, get your ass to bed. Jayden, Maxim, you two can stay in your usual room."

I glared with my mouth agape as my three best friends quickly abandoned me, scurrying off to their bedrooms in fear of the man before me.

I hadn't seen nor spoken to Aidan since I kicked him out of my bedroom—the day he rejected me. I watched as his eyes raked my body from head to toe, lingering particularly hard at the V-neckline of my dress, which showcased my boobs.

"Do you need something?" I snapped, annoyed at the goosebumps on my skin and butterflies in my stomach as he stared at me.

"You're in my house," Aidan simply stated, stepping closer.

I could now see the burns on his arms more clearly, hiding beneath the tattoos, each scar a story of agony etched into his flesh.

"We're enemies now, remember?" Aidan said, glaring sharply into my eyes. "Our families only had an alliance to kill Gatwick. Now we're back to hating each other."

"Weren't you the one who said I had no loyalty to my family?" For a split second, I saw Aidan smirk at my rhetorical question.

"Besides the point." He shrugged.

"So you rejected me because of my family? Or is there another reason you're not willing to share?"

Aidan tensed at my words before he looked at me with a surprisingly soft gaze. "It wasn't because of your family."

"Well? What was it then?" I pressed.

Standing up, I walked towards him until we were almost touching. Craning my neck to stare up at him, I watched as his jaw clenched whilst he looked over my head.

"You're seventeen," he simply stated. "It's wrong for someone my age to be with a seventeen-year-old."

That was when I realised why he wanted to keep me safe. He didn't want my family accusing him of grooming me. He wanted me to avoid the consequences of our actions.

"I've been with guys twice my age before, and my mother was glad to have the money. Why would the two of us together be an issue?" I snapped.

I didn't care why he had rejected me, even if it was to keep me safe. I wanted him, and he wanted me.

"Kalina, your mother was a cunt." Aidan humourlessly chuckled. "I'm willing to bet you haven't told your family what you've told me."

I remained silent, knowing he was right. I hadn't told my brothers why being in the presence of a stranger scared the daylights out of me. I hadn't told them that their shouting and aggression could sometimes trigger memories I wished to forget. I hadn't told them where the scars on my right arm came from, nor the ones hidden beneath the Angel tattoo on my back, not even the one in my eye. Only Matteo knew what my mother did, but he only believed I had been starved and beaten—nothing more.

"There's nothing to say," I muttered.

"We both know that's not true," Aidan said, a heavy glare resting on his face.

"Why talk about what's in the past?" I shrugged, desperate for the conversation to end.

"Why? Why!" Aidan snapped, his tone forcing me to take a few steps back. "Maybe because your mother sold you to have sex with men since you were ten years old! Maybe because the woman who was supposed to protect you tore away your childhood and innocence. Maybe because she allowed you to be beaten and raped by the men who bought time with you. Maybe because you're still so traumatised that you can't have a peaceful night's sleep or be in the presence of a stranger without that fear appearing in your eyes."

As he spoke, his tone became softer and softer, comforting almost. I wrapped my arms around myself protectively, and the tears flowed freely, rolling down my cheeks.

Everything he said was true, and I hated myself for it. I hated myself for not fighting harder, for lacking the confidence to run away from my mother, for losing hope that life could get better.

For not having the ability to move on.

My cries were soon muffled by Aidan wrapping his arms around my waist, pulling me to cry into his chest. His touch was soothing and warm, almost a reassurance that I was safe.

"You need to move on, Kalina, and the only way to do that is to disclose to your family know what you endured so they can help you," Aidan mumbled as he placed his chin on top of my head.

I nodded. I knew what he was saying was true. I knew I needed to tell my brothers and Christopher what my childhood had really been like.

A few minutes passed before Aidan picked me up. I wrapped my legs around his waist as my arms did the same around his neck. He carried me towards his bedroom and laid me down on his bed, pulling the blankets over my body.

"Stay . . . please," I muttered as he went to leave.

It looked as if he were having an internal battle before he slowly slid into the bed beside me. Snuggling up into his chest, I let the tears dry before drifting off to sleep.

When I woke up later, I was still lying in Aidan's arms. I stared up at the ceiling, my mind filled with uncertainties and fear. After talking with Aidan last night, I knew what I had to do and how to move on.

Today, I would tell my family about my childhood.

Fear was eating away at me, as if everything would crumble around me and swallow me whole. The apprehension regarding my family's reactions was strong, for I had an idea of what they would do, and I was afraid it would drag me back to the past.

Mateo knew some of my mistreatment, but nowhere near how terrible it truly had been. I was afraid he would feel betrayed that I had lied to him when he asked if that was all that happened. Antonio—he would probably break down; the mother in him would be in agony at the thought of what I endured. Stefano—I had no idea. It was very rare for him to show any emotion at all, and when he did, it was usually to show he didn't care. Tristan—God only knew what he would do. I wouldn't be surprised if he blew up all of England to make sure every one of my abusers was dead. Tommaso would likely hold me as I—no doubt—cried when I told them what happened.

Christopher—I already knew he would be heartbroken. He may have not known me well, but I could tell that he would blame himself for not being there for me. I didn't understand why he felt that way sometimes, as he didn't know of my existence.

I just hoped I wouldn't break them.

Feeling the large pair of arms around my waist pull me closer, I turned to see Aidan sleepily open his eyes.

"What's wrong?" he mumbled, his voice deep and groggy.

"I'm just thinking," I replied with a small smile, nuzzling closer to his warmth.

"About what? It can't be good if it's keeping you awake." Aidan placed a kiss on the crown of my head.

"I'm going to tell my father and brothers tomorrow."

Aidan finally fully opened his eyes, sitting up slightly to look down at me, his silver nose ring glistening in the moonlight. "Do you want me there?"

"They'd probably shoot you before you got through the front door." I chuckled, placing my palm on his cheek.

"I don't care," Aidan said. "If you want my support, I'll be there."

"No. I need to do this alone," I said with a small smile. Reaching up, I pecked his lips. "But thank you."

He lay back, pulling me close so my body moulded into his side, his bicep proving to be a firm pillow. "Never thank me for being by your side."

But you're not by my side . . .

You're not mine.

* * *

When morning arrived, the nerves had increased considerably. My knee bounced up and down, and I subconsciously picked at the skin of my thumb.

Aidan had to leave early but told me to call him if I needed him. Jayden left with him, heading off to do something—probably something illegal. Maxim left too, having a shift at the shop and needing to talk to Maddie.

I sat in darkness at the kitchen island, the sun only just starting to rise. I turned at the sound of footsteps to see Carter tiredly stumbling into the main area.

Wearing only boxers . . .

I couldn't help the shock that was—no doubt—on my face at the sight of Carter, but I quickly forced it away.

His mangled, beautifully scarred face looked up, his eyes instantly meeting mine. His fluffy, messy bed hair was ruffled by his hand, causing the muscles in his bicep and well-sculpted abs to flex. His eyes were the same hazel-brown as Aidan's, but at the moment, they held only one thing: fear.

I had thought the scar on my face was bad, but it was nothing compared to his. A large badly healed knife scar that started at his forehead, cutting down his face—skimming his nose, gashing his cheek, and ending as a nasty swirl on his chin. I could see the burns on his muscular arm continuing onto his back, not hidden by tattoos like Aidan's.

"Morning." I smiled.

The shock on his face did not go unnoticed. It was as if he hadn't expected such a casual reaction.

"Um . . . m-morning." He was clearly self-conscious.

"Can you cook?" I asked, hungry but unable to do anything more than make a toast.

"Yes," he said, an anxious look still lingering on his face. "I'll just go throw something on—"

"Carter," I said. "Only cover your scars if you are uncomfortable. Don't do it for me."

The relief that washed over his rough face was clear. He took a small step back before changing his mind, then entered the kitchen, pulling out a frying pan.

"Bacon and sausage sandwich?" Carter suggested, a comfortable smile appearing on his face.

Nodding, I returned his smile. He turned to get the meat out of the fridge, allowing me to see the burns travel around his entire back.

I kept quiet, not knowing if he was comfortable talking about them despite letting me to see them. Whilst he may not have known I was still here when he came into the room, I was glad to know he trusted me enough not to leave.

Carter broke the tense silence, looking up at me as tears began to form in his pained eyes.

"Spencer Gatwick attacked my home when I was twelve; Aidan was sixteen. He killed Aidan's father over a rivalry that had started from the time of Spencer's father. He was meant to climb through the window of Aidan's bedroom, go through there, and go to our mother's bedroom, where both our fathers were.

Aidan had gone out with friends that night, so his bedroom window was locked, unlike usual. So, instead, he climbed in through my window after sneaking past the guards. Deciding to have fun before he killed my mother, father, and stepfather, Spencer took his knife and butchered my face for his own satisfaction.

While I was on the floor screaming, crying, and bleeding, he barricaded their bedroom shut after having another man nail all the windows shut. Then he set the house on fire and left us all to die.

One of the guards managed to call Aidan before he died, and Aidan raced home, catching the attention of the police and creating a car chase that lasted twenty miles. He drove twenty miles in ten minutes and brought police there with him. While the firefighters tried to put out the fire to see if anyone was alive, Aidan didn't wait.

He ran inside the house as it began to collapse and carried me out of my bedroom. That's how I got this disgusting scar. That's how I got the burns on my back, and how Aidan got the burns on his arms."

Not saying a word, I got off the bar stool and made my way to the other side of the kitchen island. Placing my hand on the right side of Carter's face, I reached up and placed a kiss on the scar on his forehead, on his nose, and on the lower left side of his face. Walking behind him, I placed a kiss on the burns on his arm and the ones on his back.

"I don't think your scar is disgusting," I said. "While my scars are not as bad as yours, I understand that it takes time to accept them. But know you're beautiful with your scars, because they show just how strong and brave you are."

I felt Carter's shoulders shake, and I heard a sniffle echo through the room. Moving to face him again, I wrapped my arms around his torso as he tightly wrapped his around mine.

I let him cry on my shoulder as he released all of his pain and insecurities.

After all, we should never let scars limit our lives, for all scars are beautiful and show the power of strength and courage. No matter where they come from or how old or new they are, they show that we can heal.

CHAPTER THIRTY-TWO

KALINA

Carter dropped me off at home ten minutes ago. Sadly, since we left the house, he returned to wearing his hood over his face. But this time, he didn't try and hide from me, allowing me to see beneath the hood.

I was standing in the living room, surrounded by my brothers and dad, as they stared at me with an awaiting gaze. I messaged everyone on the group chat that I had something important I needed to discuss. Tristan looked annoyed and ready to leave, while Tommaso was sipping on a coke, carefree as usual. Stefano looked neither interested nor uninterested. He was just Stefano. Antonio seemed slightly concerned but allowed me space as he sat on the sofa with the brothers. Mateo was manspreading on the armchair by the window, no emotion on his face. Christopher was patient, a calm expression on his face.

Now that it was actually time to tell them, I couldn't find the words.

"Kalina? Why are we here?" Tristan sighed, looking clearly bored.

"I . . . I, erm, I need to tell you all something." I managed to say as I fiddled with the rings on my fingers.

"Well, can it wait? I have somewhere I need to be," Tristan said, standing up and taking his car keys out of his pocket.

"Sit your ass down," Mateo ordered.

Looking up at him, I knew he could see the fear in my eyes. He could tell what this was about. He was expecting me to tell the others about how my mother beat me and starved me throughout my childhood.

What he didn't know was that I would be telling them that and so much more.

"When I was six," I began.

I had everyone's attention tightly in my grasp, as most of them had never heard of my childhood.

"My mother began drinking—really heavily. She'd whore herself around to feed her habit, and she did it more once she was hooked on drugs.

Every boyfriend she got would either deal or use her themselves, all hating both Daniel and me as we were always in the way—an extra two mouths to feed. They used to beat both of us, me more than Daniel, as he fought back. He was a few years older than I was. When I was kept from school because I was beaten so badly and used as a drug mule, he never realised it. I also never told him. At some point, I was rushed to the hospital by Daniel. I was sick, and it turned out I had internal bleeding. I was nearly taken away by social services if it weren't for the fact that my mother staged a break-in and made it look like I had been attacked. Then she decided on new forms of punishment for even the smallest mistakes.

She'd fill the bathtub up and hold me under till I passed out, wait for me to wake up, and do it again, and again, and again—until she grew bored."

Looking up, I could see the fury and sorrow building on each and every one of their faces. Christopher was shaking, staring at me with an anguished gaze. Slowly, he walked over. He gently wrapped an arm around my shoulder before guiding me to sit beside him.

"Is that everything?" His voice shook with anger and fear.

He was scared of my answer, scared that his daughter was even more damaged than he already knew.

"When she got older, and fewer men wanted her because her addictions had taken their toll, she earned less money from prostitution. By then, Daniel had met the Chained Angels and was working day and night to save money so he could get me out of there and give me a stable home.

Mother soon realised I was maturing and was ready to 'earn my keep,' as she said. So she'd take me down to the red-light districts and sell me to anyone willing to pay. I was ten when it began."

The smashing of glass caught my attention. Looking up, I saw Tommaso out of his seat, the glass in his hand now shattered across the floor. He turned to me, tears forming in his eyes. Walking towards me, he collapsed at my feet and laid his head on my lap, crying softly and wrapping his arms around my waist.

Tristan had a hard glare fixed on the floor, but I could see the twitch in his jaw. Stefano once again remained expressionless. Antonio was raking his hand repeatedly through his hair, gripping it tightly. Mateo looked hurt, either by the fact I hadn't told him everything and had lied, or because he hadn't realised how badly I had actually been treated.

"I met Spencer when I was fifteen; he was twenty. He found me passed out on the bathroom floor as he came to kill Mother's boyfriend at the time for betraying his mafia. He took me to his house and cleaned me up. Me believing I couldn't be loved and in need of some comfort, I grew attached, and he took advantage of that. After he kidnapped me, he treated me the same as every man in my life had before—something pretty to fuck. He killed Daniel when Daniel rescued me, and he took Enzo to punish me for betraying him."

I felt Christopher's grip on me tighten. He reached down and placed a kiss on my head, offering some type of comfort.

"To keep me 'desirable,' Mother often starved me so I remained thin. One night, she decided to give me away to a gang she owed for drug money. When I tried to fight them off, they slashed my arm so I couldn't fight, which is why I have the scars on my arm and hand.

When I was returned home the next day, they beat her because I hadn't allowed them to fuck me as they pleased. So while I was curled up in a ball on the floor, injuries from my countless rapes still hurting, she cut me from my collarbone to my right rib and across the right side of my face.

She said it was as a constant reminder of how I failed to please those who depended on me, and how I'd always be a worthless whore, incapable of being loved.

When Daniel came to check on me the next day, he took me straight to the club and refused to let me return home. From that night, I lived in the clubhouse with Ace and Teddy, who led the attacks on every man that ever laid a hand on me."

Stefano got up from his seat and took slow steps towards me. I tilted my head up to look at him. Tears were flowing down both our cheeks. He stroked my baby hairs back as he stared down at me.

"You're not worthless. You're not a whore. You're not incapable of being loved." Stefano sighed. "You're the strongest, bravest girl I know. And I can't describe how much I love you, or how sorry I am we weren't there to protect you. But we're here now, and no one will ever hurt you again."

Pulling me up, Stefano wrapped his arms around me and held me tight. One by one, each brother took me in turn and hugged me to them.

"Remember, Kalina, we're here for you," Antonio said, wiping his eyes. "We suffer together, as a family. You're not alone anymore."

"I don't care that you lied," Mateo told me when he saw the apprehension on my face. "I will never force you to tell me anything, *bambina. Ti amo principessa.*" *(Baby/little girl; I love you, princess.)*

"Ti amo." I grinned up at him through teary eyes.

"Non devi mai aver paura di dirmi qualcosa, sorellina. Non ti giudicherò mai. Sarò il conforto di cui hai bisogno e il supporto che meriti. Tu significhi così tanto per me, angelo. Non dimenticare mai che hai persone che ti amano e si prendono cura di te," Tommaso told me as he pressed our foreheads together before kissing the crown of my head. *(You don't ever have to be afraid to tell me anything, little sister. I'll never judge you. I'll be the comfort you need and the support you deserve. You mean so much to me, angel. Never forget you have people who love you and care for you.)*

When I got to Tristan, he didn't say anything. He only offered an apologetic look before storming out of the house.

Christopher turned me away from the door. "I love you, Kalina," he whispered in my ear.

"I love you too, Dad." I smiled.

Later that night, everyone retreated to their bedrooms after spending the evening with me, all of us neither acknowledging nor dismissing what I had told them.

I spent all night thinking about Tristan. The look on his face was something I would never forget—the agony and disappointment I saw before he walked out the door. I knew one of them would likely be disgusted; I just didn't think it would be Tristan.

As I lay awake in bed, someone knocked on my bedroom door. After telling whoever it was to come in, Tristan opened the door. With an anxious look on his face, he closed the door behind him and crawled into my bed, bringing me into a hug.

"Kalina," he choked out a pained sob. "I just . . . I didn't leave out of disgust, if that's what you think. I was angry—so unbelievably furious—that I didn't want to lash out in front of you." I felt Tristan's tears falling and landing on my bare arms. "Know that I'm the proudest brother in the world. I'm so proud that you survived all that agony and are still such a gorgeous, loving, and strong girl."

That night, I fell asleep in the arms of my brother, safe from all the dangers of the world, in my past, and, hopefully, in my future.

CHAPTER THIRTY-THREE

STEFANO

When I was little, my mother used to beat me. It started small—a slap here and there. But then, one day, I was brought home early from school by one of the guards while I was sick and saw her cheating on my father.

I was only four when Daniel was born, but right from the beginning, I knew he was not my father's son. It was obvious in the slight differences in his features. Father didn't notice, however, since he looked so similar to his brother. I only noticed because I had seen my mother and uncle having sex whenever Father left the house. Having Mateo explain where babies came from also helped me realize.

Both my mother and uncle would always slap, punch, and kick me until I was so broken that I didn't have the will to tell my father. Father, at the time Don, had entrusted his wife to care for his children when he couldn't. He never saw the bruises because Mother would cover them up, and the ones he did see—Mother came up with the perfect excuses.

After Father found out about the affair—and that Daniel wasn't his son but his nephew—he was still blindly in love and was willing to make the marriage work. So I told him about all the abuse I had suffered at her hands. He filed for divorce the next day.

Compared to what Kalina revealed to us last night, I got merely a scratch. If I had just kept my mouth shut, Father wouldn't have divorced Mother, and he would have known that she was pregnant with Kalina and not just Tommaso.

"Stop it," the muffled voice said.

Turning my head, I saw his slightly tanned cheek resting on the pillow. Strands of blond hair flopped forward, falling into his dark eyes that stared up at me with a kindness I was rarely shown.

"I'm not doing anything," I replied, turning on my side to look at him properly.

"You're blaming yourself for Kalina." He reached out and placed a hand on my cheek, a small smile on his face.

"Because it's my fault. If I'd just kept my mouth shut—"

"Stop," he demanded, sternness in his tone. "You were right to tell Christopher what happened. And, besides, I prefer your mouth open."

I chuckled at the cheeky grin that formed on his face, watching his eyes dance with mischief and lust.

Rolling so I was on top of him, I ran my hands through his hair before gripping it tightly.

Leaning down, I met his lips with my own, roughly kissing him as he tried to take control. When our tongues fought for dominance—and I won, as always—a smirk made its way onto my face.

"Dick," he mumbled as our lips parted, the two of us greedily inhaling as much oxygen as possible.

"Dick." I chuckled, mocking his accent. "Is that you asking, or . . . ?" I laughed as he smacked my chest.

He rolled us over and leaned down, a grin on his face as he began stroking my dick, his own visibly hard beneath the material of his boxers.

"Maybe."

*   *   *

KALINA

I was wearing a pair of black leather jeans, a leather jacket, and a red-laced cami top that made my diamond navel stud peek out. My knee-high boots clicked on the floor, my black curls bouncing as I walked.

Last night, I had told my brothers and Christopher everything. This morning, when I came downstairs for breakfast, no one said a word as I ate, the small amount finally understandable to them all. There was no criticism of how little I was eating. Antonio made seconds just in case I wanted them, but he didn't pressure me.

Those small acts of kindness were why I loved them.

Stefano wasn't at the house when I woke. Mateo said he had gone out to see his friend. He also mentioned that his underboss and crew would be at the house today.

So now I was on my way to the clubhouse.

I really can't be arsed to meet people today.

When I got to the garage, I saw Maddie and Aidan once again working on a car, the two of them drinking beers as they laughed.

At the sound of my footsteps, Maddie and Aidan looked up to see me approaching. Maddie swallowed the last of her beer before putting the bottle in the bin.

"You don't have to do that." I sighed as I hugged her.

"I was done with it anyway." Maddie smiled down at me, kissing my forehead before going inside the clubhouse.

Feeling eyes on me—or more particularly, on my arse—I turned to see Aidan.

In all fairness, these jeans make my arss look amazing.

Aidan's eyes met mine, a cheeky grin forming on his face. *"Ciao, bella." (Hello, beautiful.)*

"Any reason you're staring at my arse?" I grinned, staring up into those beautiful hazel-brown eyes.

"Because I could." He shrugged, taking a step forwards and wrapping his arms around my waist.

"Oh, can you now?" I smirked, placing my hands on his chest.

"Yeah, I can." I felt his large, rough hands begin to wander south, a grin on his face.

Reaching back and grabbing his hands, I gave his pouting lips a little peck before smirking. "Well, as you keep reminding me, this arse is seventeen. You'll have to wait a few more days."

Aidan groaned, flinging his head back dramatically. He smiled down at me as I laughed, an adorable little glint evident in his eyes.

"Why does Maddie always get rid of her drink around you? Aidan asked, a curious expression now gracing his gorgeous face.

"My mother was an alcoholic. When I first met Maddie, I was terrified of her because I thought all women who drink were abusers. I guess it just became a habit for her to get rid of it when I was around," I replied. "Now, if you'll excuse me, I need to go see someone." I broke free from Aidan's grasp.

Aidan turned around and began working on the car again. His tattoos were emphasised by the light above the engine, his muscles flexing as he worked.

"Who?" he asked.

"Ace," I replied, and went inside the clubhouse.

What confused me, however, was that Aidan began laughing his arse off as I went inside. Ignoring his strange behaviour, I went back to the spare room, where all the members either slept, hid from their wives, or fucked one of the slags who would do anything for Angel dick.

Walking down the hallway to Ace's room, I could hear music blasting from inside, confirming he was in there. I flung the door open, and the sight before me was not what I was expecting.

Ace was riding Stefano, whilst my older brother gave him a hand job, thrusting his hips so that Stefano's cock pumped into Ace's arse.

"Shit."

"Shit."

"Shit."

The curses were coming from all three of us. Stefano was quick to throw the blanket over the two of them, shielding my traumatised eyes.

"I'll just . . . wait out . . . here." I managed to say before stumbling out of the bedroom.

Making my way back to the main area of the clubhouse, I saw Maddie behind the bar, talking to Jamie, Killian, Oliver, Luke, and Marcus. Aidan was standing by the doorway, arms crossed over his buff chest, fighting the smile forming on his face.

"I see you've found out." Aidan laughed.

"I need to bleach my eyes," I practically cried.

Aidan laughed loudly as he approached me, wrapping me in his arms. He sat down on the leather sofa, placing me on his lap as he stroked my hair.

"It can't have been that bad," Jamie said, a smirk on his face.

Turning around, I glared harshly at him. "I've just seen the man who raised me—the one who was practically my father—riding and getting a hand job from my older brother. What part of that is not traumatic?!"

Everyone in the room laughed at my protest.

Sighing, I turned back to Aidan and buried my face in his neck.

"I'd rather my mother drown me again." I chuckled.

I could feel Aidan's chest vibrating as he laughed at me. I just held on to him, quite enjoying this current position.

Those fuckers are taking their time. They fucking stayed to finish!

A few minutes later, Ace and Stefano came into the room. Both were wearing joggers, Ace's hair slightly damp from sweat.

Stefano glared intensely at Aidan when he saw me sitting on his lap and holding me close. But one look from Ace kept him quiet.

"Kalina! I am so sorry you found out this way," Ace said, taking my face in his hands. "Believe me, it's not what it looks like."

"It looks like my main father figure is fucking my older brother," I bluntly replied.

"Okay, it's sort of what it looks like," Stefano said, a nonchalant look on his face.

Everyone laughed. Even Aidan chuckled a bit.

"Stop making jokes," Ace said, a smile on his face. "Seriously, Stefano and I really love each other. This has been going on even before he knew about you."

"But when you met my family, you didn't say anything. And you really didn't make it obvious." I said, slightly confused.

"Our mafia is enemies with Aidan and the Chained Angels," Stefano answered. "We had to keep our relationship a secret. We're waiting for the right time to tell Mateo and everyone in the family."

Nodding, I took in everything they said, still feeling Aidan run his hand up and down my back.

"But we won't carry on with this relationship if you're uncomfortable. Your permission means everything to us," Ace said, Stefano nodding behind him.

Permission? Why the fuck do they need my permission?

"You don't need my permission." I grinned. "But you have it."

"Thank you, tesoro." Stefano nodded. "That, however, doesn't apply to whatever this is." He pointed to Aidan and me.

"Unlike you, I won't ask for my family's permission to be with the one I love." I smirked.

"Love?"

CHAPTER THIRTY-FOUR

KALINA

All my life, I had never considered the possibility that I could love someone other than Daniel, Lorenzo, and the club. I thought the love of a family was all I would ever know.

I had accepted the words of my mother: "You are unworthy of love." I grew up believing I was just an object, a source of income for her and a warm body for the men who paid.

Over the past few months , I have slowly come to the realisation that I can love others. Aidan has crept his way into my life, making me feel as no one else ever has: safe, comforted, and appreciated.

"You said you love him!" Carter, Maxim, and Jayden all yelled.

Meekly, I nodded. All of them sat there, shocked. Carter's face pulled into a grin. "Did he say it back?"

Shrugging, I mumbled, "I don't know."

"What do you mean you don't know?" Jayden asked, scrutinising me.

"I sort of ran away."

"You ran!" the three of them yelled again.

"How has your love life come this far without us." Maxim sighed, dragging his hand over his face.

"What happened next?" Carter asked, wincing at the thought of what I might have done.

"I . . . might've run across the street, nearly got hit by three cars and a bus, and hid in an alley until I could run home."

Looking back on it now, I realised how stupid that was. I had nearly died five times yesterday: four times from moving vehicles, and once from pure embarrassment.

I was just thankful there was school today, so Aidan couldn't kidnap me and take me to his house for the day—something he would definitely do.

"For fuck's sake." They all sighed.

By the end of the day, I had been lectured numerous times by Jayden, Maxim, and Carter—on separate occasions.

Tristan and Tommaso nearly overheard our conversation until I smacked all three of them over the head. I didn't need my insanely overprotective brothers to hear about my older . . . Aidan.

On the way home, the two of them were acting oddly suspicious. It wasn't until we got to the house, and they remained in the car, that I realised why.

Waiting in the driveway were the rest of my brothers and Christopher, all dressed in black suits, sunglasses hiding their eyes.

"Kalina, your brothers and I need to go on a job tonight. Lorenzo is with Ace. There'll be guards here. We won't be back till late. Don't cause any trouble, please."

I almost laughed at the thought of a brooding mob boss was pleading with a teenage girl.

"I'll be fine," I replied, a mischievous grin on my face.

"I should just call the fucking fire department now." Christopher sighed, walking towards the car where Tristan and Tommaso sat.

I waved goodbye to the cars as they drove away, a smirk on my face as I caught the worry on most of their expressions.

Chuckling to myself, I closed the front door behind me, practically skipping into the living room and plopping on the couch. The next two hours were spent contemplating life and watching *Friends*.

Night eventually overtook the day, and my stomach began to rumble with hunger. I ordered a pizza, then waited in the kitchen and poured myself a glass of coke.

Since I had the house to myself, I concluded that snooping was the best way to pass time.

Going into Mateo's office, I began rifling through the drawers. One after another, I found meaningless documents, nothing worthy of my attention. That was until my gaze landed on a black file. Inside was a single sheet of paper.

Name: Bianca Rossi
DOB: 15/5/2001
DOD: 15/5/2013
Ethnicity: Italian-Irish
Hair: brown
Eyes: brown
Cause of death: Car accident

My brows furrowed in confusion as I read the limited information in the document. Why would Mateo have a file on Aidan's sister? Why hadn't Aidan or Carter mentioned her? Why had she died so young?

All these thoughts swarmed my mind as I held the single piece of paper in my hand. Answers I had never even thought to ask now crowded my brain.

Sneaking into Tristan's bedroom, I decided to see what I could use to blackmail him for cupcakes later. Shuffling through the drawers and cabinets, I ended up at his bedside table. Pulling open the top drawer, I found an almost empty bottle of lube and a butt plug, all piled on top of multicoloured XL condoms.

"Ew. Ew. Ew."

Quickly slamming the drawer shut, I ran out of the bedroom and sprinted to the kitchen, washing my hands with every product I could find.

Sighing, I drank my coke until I heard the doorbell ring. Getting up, I quickly answered the door. One of the guards, Samuele, was holding my pepperoni pizza and garlic bread.

"Thanks, Sam." I grinned, taking the delicious-smelling box from his hands.

I only got a stiff nod in return. It was usual for the guards around the estate. Closing the door with my foot, I held the pizza box with one hand and my glass with the other.

Spinning back around to head to the living room, a scream left my lips as the glass and boxes fell from my hands and hit the floor.

CHAPTER THIRTY-FIVE

KALINA

As a child, you tend to have dreams of fairytale princesses or superheroes who save the world. In my limited time at school, I learned that, at a young age, most children wanted to be doctors or teachers. As they got older, they wanted to be lawyers or professional footballers. Then they reached my age and had no clue what they wanted in life.

I just wanted freedom of the mind.

Fear made up a large part of my childhood. Every waking and sleeping moment, fear swarmed my mind. Even in moments of joy, fear lingered at the back of my mind.

When I met Ace and the others, that fear would disappear for some time. But when I returned home and was forced to make my mother money, that fear returned twice as strong.

Ironically, the only time I ever felt calm and safe before this year was when I was in juvenile detention. Locked behind bars, it was secure inside and out, with extreme force needed to break through the stone walls and iron fences.

But then I came here, to America, and met the family I had been stolen from. And for the first time in my life, I trusted what were practically strangers.

One by one, I built a trusting relationship with all of them. One by one, I was given a reason to feel comfortable and safe.

And my dream came true.

For the first time in my life, I felt undeniably safe. Whether it was in the Tristan's arms, in the laughing company of Tommaso, in the presence of Mateo, Antonio, and Stefano, or under Christopher's loving gaze, I felt safe.

However, seeing the outline of a huge man in my home, hidden in the shadows, I did not feel safe.

"Shit," the man said, stepping into the light to reveal Aidan in black joggers and a form-fitting T-shirt. He quickly scooped me up into his arms, lifting me away from the broken glass.

"Are you okay? Did any glass cut you?" Aidan asked as he placed me on the kitchen counter, brushing a strand of hair back from my face.

"What the fuck are you doing here?" I finally managed to speak, recovering from my initial shock. "If the guards see you, they'll kill you! What about the cameras! Shit! There's cameras in the house!"

Aidan's lips suddenly pressed firmly against my own, effectively silencing me. Kissing him back, I felt one of his rough but warm hands snake around my waist and rest on my back. The other was pressed against the back of my head, fingers weaving through my hair. Naturally, my arms wrapped around his neck, pulling him closer.

Eventually, he pulled away, resting his forehead against mine. A smile lingered on both our faces as we stared into each other's eyes.

"Aidan, why are you here?" I asked after regaining my breath.

"You love me?" Aidan grinned.

His hands remained at the back of my head, keeping our foreheads pressed together.

"You didn't answer my question," I stated, doing what I could to dodge it.

"I asked you first. Yesterday, you know, before you ran off into oncoming traffic like an idiot and nearly got yourself killed," Aidan deadpanned, a glare forming on his face.

"And your point is . . ." I sighed, hoping he would just drop the subject.

But, as I had learned in life, my hopes and dreams didn't tend to come true.

"Do you love me, Kalina?" Aidan asked, his hazel eyes staring deeply into my blue ones.

I stayed quiet for a moment, looking down at my fumbling hands. "Do you want some pizza?"

Fucked up fucking commitment issues.

Whilst his expression didn't change, I could tell he was disappointed. "I'm getting first pick of the slices." He grinned.

On the way to the living room, Aidan picked up the pizza box, not letting me touch it because of the glass on the floor.

I should probably clean that up.

The two of us sat down on the sofa. Aidan picked up the remote and put on *Spider-Man.* As I sit beside him, Aidan pulled me to his side until I smacked his hand away.

He gave me a confused and hurt expression until I kissed his cheek and nodded at the pizza. "Food first, cuddles later."

Ignoring the chuckle that Aidan let out, I grabbed a slice of garlic bread and munched away. Aidan followed suit, and soon, both the garlic bread and pizza were gone.

I curled up against Aidan's side and let him wrap his arm around me. The night passed slowly, just like the movement of his hand going higher on my thigh.

When they crept past the waistband of my sweats, reaching beyond my thongs, I finally turned my attention to Aidan. He was staring down at me with lustful eyes, a smirk on his lips.

"What happened to waiting until I turn eighteen?" I asked.

"Two days? Who said there was anything wrong with an early birthday present?" Aidan shrugged.

"Upstairs?"

Instead of answering, he sprang up from the sofa and threw me over his shoulder. He climbed the stairs two at a time, my face pressed against his back. When he turned the wrong way, I couldn't help myself.

"You did not just smack my ass."

"You're going the wrong way." A giggle left my lips as he halted.

That giggle was quickly turned into a gasp as harsh, loud slaps landed repeatedly on my bottom.

It wasn't until he got to my bedroom and flung me onto the bed that he stopped slapping my arse. Aidan reached behind and pulled his top off, revealing his chiseled chest once again. He stared down at me with a smug grin, challenging me to do the same.

Returning his gaze, and taking it a step further, I removed my top, lifting it slowly over my head to reveal my red lace bra. Aidan's eyes immediately landed on my boobs, and he practically drooled at the sight. With a blank stare, he reached back and undid the straps of my bra. Slowly, I let the straps slip from my shoulders until I discarded the material onto the floor.

That was when Aidan pounced.

*   *   *

STEFANO

I left the job early, telling Dad I was worried about Kalina being home alone when we were on the brink of war.

I pulled into the driveway, locked the car, and opened the front door. The sound of glass crunching beneath my feet spiked my worry.

The scream from upstairs confirmed it.

Bolting up the stairs, I reached back for my gun, only to realize I left it in the car.

Fuck it!

Within seconds, I was bursting into Kalina's bedroom, only to wish I hadn't. Kalina was on all fours, her hair being pulled so hard that she was practically a semi-circle. Fucking her from behind with one hand tangled into her hair and on her hip was Aidan Rossi.

Before I could think about what I was doing, I sprang across the room and pulled him away from her. Aidan was quick to rise from the floor, not bothering to hide his dick, glistening with wetness in the light.

I guess this is my karma.

"Stefano, no!" Kalina yelled as I moved to punch Aidan.

I didn't listen.

Repeatedly, I pounded my fist into his face without mercy. I may have said I had slowly grown to accept this relationship, but I wasn't prepared to find a twenty-two-year-old fucking my seventeen-year-old sister in our home.

What surprised me was that Aidan didn't fight back.

Kalina pulled me away, a robe thankfully tied around her already. Aidan's face was covered in blood, but an angry grimace rested there as Kalina stood between the two of us.

"You said you'd try to understand!" she yelled, tears streaming down her cheeks.

I glanced back at Aidan, who had thankfully covered his dick with a pillow from the sofa. His hand was on her calf, rubbing it in soothing circles.

"I didn't expect to find him fucking you," I replied, a glare on my face.

"Stefano, it's my life," she calmly told me. "I respected your decision with Ace; why can't you respect my decision with Aidan?"

"I just . . ."

"Say it." Kalina could tell what I was going to say. I could see it in her eyes.

"After what you told us about what Angelica made you do, I don't want you to ever get hurt again. Especially that way."

I could feel the tears building in my eyes, reminding me of the night she told us of her childhood. The pain on her face when she told us . . . I cried myself to sleep in Ace's arms that night.

"And I love you for that. You're my big brother. You're always going to want to protect me. Don't you want me to be happy too?"

Sighing, I reached out and pulled her into a hug. She hugged me back. "Of course I do. I won't tell anyone about this."

When Kalina pulled away, Aidan stood up and wrapped his arm around her waist from behind. He was now wearing his boxers.

"Sorry about—" I nodded to his face "—that."

"I won't hurt her. I'd die before I hurt her," Aidan promised.

"I'll hold you to that promise." I nodded, leaving the room and closing the door behind me.

CHAPTER THIRTY-SIX

TRISTAN

I had never been one to admit my fear.

All my life, I had believed that an acceptance of fear was an acceptance of weakness, something I was not prepared to do.

I found alternative ways to handle my fears without expressing them. My fear turned to anger, and anger developed into rage. And when someone became as furious as I was, violence was the last remaining solution.

Each punch sent the heavy bag swinging in a different direction, every strike releasing the rage-filled energy from my body.

In the distance, I could hear the reception door opening and closing. Assuming it was just another random person coming to train, I ignored it.

"Kalina punches better than you."

Turning towards the source of the voice, I discovered it was Aidan Rossi. He was standing there with a smug smirk on his face, arms crossed over his chest. Glaring, I pulled off the hand wrap and took a step toward him.

"Yeah, well, my sister is a great person. Far too good for you," I added the last bit with a grin of my own.

Shaking his head with a chuckle, he said, "I can't argue with that."

"Then why do you keep seeing her? She's too young for you, too good for you, and, in case you've forgotten, our families aren't exactly friends," I snapped, hating the smile that formed on his face at the mention of my little sister.

I watched as Aidan walked toward the ring before climbing under the ropes. He indicated with his head for me to join him. Refusing to back down, I followed and climbed under the ropes.

"If I win, you have to accept that I am a part of Kalina's life and that I don't plan on leaving anytime soon," Aidan said, wrapping his hands before putting on a pair of gloves at the side of the ring.

"And if I win?" I questioned, watching with anticipation.

"You can tell your family about Kalina and me, which will likely end up in my death," Aidan replied, shrugging.

Nodding with a grin, I put on my own boxing gloves. Moments later, we had mouth guards in and were standing in our corners of the cage.

At the five-minute mark of the first round, we were already bleeding. I didn't hold back, throwing the hardest and most technical punches I could. His nose was dripping blood, and a cut had already formed on his temple, blood freely flowing down the rest of his face.

I had a cut on my lip too, and I could already feel my eye swelling. Each punch landed harder than the next. He landed a blow so hard that I felt my ribs crack beneath the skin.

When the timer finished, I was panting like a dog, struggling to breathe with a likely broken rib.

"That doesn't look nice." Aidan grinned. "Do you want to stop?"

"Not a fucking chance," I snapped.

As the timer for the second round began, I put my mouth guard back in and threw the first punch. It was halfway through the second round when Aidan landed a solid left hook to my injured rib, causing me to drop to the ground in agony.

As I knelt on the floor, I could hear the timer turning off and footsteps approaching, stopping right before me.

"I win."

Looking up with a glare, I saw a smug-looking Aidan standing above me. He was holding his hand out to me. Still glaring, I took it and let him pull me up. He held his hand in a fist, waiting to see if I would respectfully admit defeat.

I touched knuckles with him and stared him in the eye as I said, "You hurt her and I'll kill you."

"I hurt her and I'll let you."

"Until Kalina is ready to tell our family about you, I'll keep it a secret," I told him with a sigh.

"Well, Stefano already knows, so we're slowly getting there." Aidan laughed, as if he were remembering something.

"What do you mean?" I questioned.

"Well . . ." Aidan chuckled. "He kind of walked in on us fucking."

Before I could even register what I was doing, my fist hit him square on the jaw. His head snapped to the side, but the grin never left his face.

"Suppose I deserved that."

"You're too old for her," I simply stated.

"I know, but she doesn't care, and I love her too much to let her go."

Before I could say anything else, my phone began ringing on the other side of the room. I went to my gym bag and picked it up.

"Yeah, Dad?" I answered, turning to face Aidan, who was staring intently.

"What do you mean Kalina's missing?" I yelled.

Within seconds, Aidan was by my side, listening to the conversation.

"Kalina's gone. She left a note on the kitchen island saying she'll be back in a few days. Get home now!"

As I hung up the phone, I could see Aidan tearing the gym apart. The veins in his neck bulged as he threw weights across the room, destroying everything in sight.

"Stop!" I shouted, catching his attention despite his rage.

"You're going to come home with me, and we're going to find my sister."

With a single nod, Aidan followed me out the gym door and toward the car.

* * *

KALINA

"This is a terrible idea," Ace said as he held his passport in his hand.

"This is an amazing idea," I corrected, a shit-eating grin on my face as we boarded the plane.

The entire ride from my house to the airport, Ace complained about how Stefano was going to kill him and Aidan was going to skin him alive.

Sitting down in the coach-class seats—Ace demanding the window seat as always—the two of us got comfortable for the eleven-hour flight.

* * *

Sitting on the wall by the car park, I swung my feet back and forth. Ace leaned against the wall beside me, the two of us staring up at the Eiffel Tower.

"There's the kid!"

Spinning around, I saw the tall, lanky man dressed in a grey suit with a black turtleneck underneath. His silver watch gleamed in the moonlight. There was a bright smile on his bearded face. His black hair was combed back.

"There's the Teddy!" I yelled, jumped from my seat, and ran into his awaiting arms. Quickly, I wrapped my arms around his neck and my legs around his waist. Immediately, he held me tightly as he spun us around.

"It's good to see you, kid."

Snow drifted down from the sky and scattered in the curls of my dark hair. Standing frozen in my skin-tight white snowsuit and ankle-length boots, I watched through the sights of my sniper. I listened through the radio headset; the exchange going our way so far.

In prone position, I was 1.76 miles away from the meet. Staring down my sights, I focused on the warmth my snowsuit provided.

The meet was for Teddy, Madison, and Killian, all of them at the drug-buy location that had been raided by coppers three weeks ago.

The same raid that got Ace locked up. Thank God he wasn't tried as an adult.

We were making a deal with the French, who had connections with the Colombians. This deal would help us cover a wider range of drug distribution across the U.K., giving us the stock we needed to run all the other dealers out of business, especially the ones who sold to children.

"Kid, you in place?" Teddy asked through the radio.

"Freezing my tits off sitting still like this," I answered, loading an extra magazine just in case.

I could hear the chuckling through the other end, knowing we were all on the same channel. I kept my eye on my guys through the sights. While this may have been a deal on good terms, we didn't trust these arseholes.

We had already lost Ace due to their lack of security, and I was prepared to kill them—and any form of law enforcement that tried to take more of my family.

Teddy drove Ace and me back to his hotel, the nightlife of Paris fresh and exciting. Restaurants were lit up, and a wide range of couples and families were seated, enjoying their meals. The happiness on their faces was oddly annoying.

What about their lives was so safe and comfortable that they could be so carefree.

The daggers in my bra and pocket felt heavier than usual, reminding me that in this life, there would always be danger.

Once we got to the hotel room, Ace was quick to kick off his boots and manspread on the sofa. Teddy took off his blazer and poured us all some whisky. There was a grin on his face that had been there since he saw us.

"So, how's life with the mafia?"

He always had a way with words.

Chuckling, I sipped on my drink before replying, "It's been . . . odd."

"What do you mean odd? Do we have to kill anyone?" Teddy's face instantly turned stern, his voice dropping an octave in worry.

"No, nothing like that. They've been great. That's what makes it all so odd," I reassured him.

"That's good." Teddy nodded, running his hand through his light hair and then over his neatly trimmed beard. "Now, Ace tells me you and Aidan Rossi are a thing."

After a long catch-up with Teddy, we went to sleep. Ace passed out on the floor, surrounded by open packets of spilled crisps.

Rubbing my eyes tiredly, I couldn't help but chuckle at the sound of Teddy peacefully snoring and the sight of drool dribbling from Ace's mouth.

Stumbling into the kitchen, I poured myself a cup of tea and ran my fingers through my hair.

A sudden bang snapped me out of my daydream. Without thinking, I grabbed the pistol from the top of the kitchen counter where Ace had left it that morning. Sprinting into the living room, my eyes immediately latched on to Teddy being held up against the wall, a knife at his throat. The figure behind him was unknown, his back facing me.

Seeing blood trickle down Teddy's neck, I fired.

"KALINA, NO!"

CHAPTER THIRTY-SEVEN

AIDAN

The stitches above my eye still held a faint sting, but I ignored it completely. If I weren't so worried and nervous right now, I would be smirking at the sight of Tristan with an ice pack on his ribs, trying to soothe the pain. The jet was silent. I was seated opposite Kalina's entire family, all eyes heavily glaring at me, their faces hard as stone.

After going to Kalina's house with Tristan, I had to explain my relationship with Kalina to the rest of her family. Then, after almost getting shot, I told them about the tracker in Ace's phone and how I knew they were in Paris.

So here we were, sitting in intense silence, halfway to France.

"Why?"

Turning my gaze to Christopher, I raised an eyebrow, indicating for him to continue.

"Why Kalina? There are millions of women in this world and you went after my daughter—your enemy's daughter. Why?"

Sighing, I answered the only way I could. "She makes me happy."

"Couldn't you find that with someone else . . . your own age?" Antonio grumbled, though his disapproval was not surprising; he was the one who had tried to shoot me.

"I tried to stop the two of us. I rejected her," I replied, my face emotionless. "But I couldn't stay away. Everything I do, I do for her. I've taken care of her, protected her, killed for her—"

"We know, but that was to get Lorenzo back," Mateo interrupted, rolling his eyes.

"I wasn't talking about that." I smirked. "The day we met, three men cornered her in an alley. I shot them with my sniper and then started fixing up my car. I don't regret it one bit."

They all sat in silence, pondering my words. I turned to look at Tristan and Stefano, seated in the corner. The two of them offered me a thumbs-up, signalling that it was going somewhat well.

This was quite an improvement after being nearly stabbed multiple times in their home, having a priceless vase thrown at me, and being pushed down a flight of stairs.

What can I say? Her family is very protective.

"And what happens when we find her?" Tommaso finally asked the question they were all thinking. "We're still enemies, but you're dating my twin."

Shrugging, I offered only what I was willing to give. "I'm up for an alliance if you are."

Antonio scoffed from the corner, rolling his eyes. "And let me guess—you want to finalise the alliance by marrying Kalina."

Instinctively, my hands clenched into fists, and my teeth gritted in seething anger. "Kalina's life is not some bargaining chip to me. When we marry, it will be because we love each other, not for some fucking business arrangement."

"When?"

*   *   *

KALINA

In my life, there had been a great deal of carnage and chaos. But amongst all of that, I had never truly lost someone I loved, aside from Daniel.

There had been many close calls; that was a given in my line of work. I remembered when I was fourteen—Jamie had been sent out on a job with Ace and another Angel, Peter. On the way, they were attacked by a rival gang, and their bikes crashed on the motorway. I could still see the colour drain from Teddy's face when he found out. I remembered the panic Liam and Killian tried—and failed—to mask. Every single one of us feared the worst and wasted no time in heading to the hospital.

Peter had a few broken bones. Jamie suffered a crushed leg, collapsed lung, and a brain bleed. Ace had to undergo surgery after a piece of his motorbike punctured his heart.

So yes, there had been many times when I had nearly lost someone I loved.

Today was another to add to the list.

"Fuck!"

No one said a word as the man turned around, revealing himself to be Aidan. His glare was harsh at first, but when his eyes landed on me, he let out a breath of relief, and a smile graced his lips. Without thinking, he crossed the room and wrapped me up in his arms.

As he got closer, I could hear what I assumed were protests. Once I freed my face from Aidan's chest, I saw my father and brothers standing to the side. Stefano was glaring silently at Ace, who looked rather forlorn.

"Aidan, I'm so sorry. I didn't—"

Aidan kissed my forehead and pulled me closer.

"Next time you decide to leave the country, a text would be appreciated."

Letting out a little laugh, I wrapped my arms around his neck, wary of the bullet hole in his shoulder.

"Or you could just not leave the country at all."

Turning my attention to my family, I saw Christopher staring at me, whilst Mateo and Antonio did the same, relief on their faces.

"I had something to do." I shrugged, letting go of Aidan as Stefano approached with a first-aid kit, Ace trailing behind him.

"You could've told us," Mateo said.

"And say what? I need to go to Paris to see my adoptive gangster father who's there on a drug deal because I want to see him before he meets my biological family for the first time so we can catch up," I replie sarcastically.

"I mean, not exactly like that." Christopher shrugged. "But you know, some insight would've been helpful."

Two hours later, we were all on Christopher's private jet back to L.A. My family sat one side of the plane, Stefano excepted, who was sitting with Ace. The latter explained how I had forced him into this, and he was sorry. I could tell Stefano wasn't overly bothered about what had happened; he knew I was with Ace and would be safe. The sadistic arsehole probably just enjoyed watching his boyfriend grovel.

And yes, on the way to France, Stefano had, apparently, finally told Mateo about his relationship with Ace. Mateo wasn't overly bothered—he simply threatened Ace should he break Stefano's heart.

Teddy was seated with my father, whilst Antonio and Mateo discussed some form of alliance since I was a factor in all of their lives. After all, both my families have an agreement of no more conflict.

Honestly, it was time for a friendship.

I was leaning against Aidan, who had his uninjured arm wrapped around my shoulder, listening while I continued to apologise for shooting him.

"Kalina, I've said it's fine." Aidan laughed as he placed a kiss on the top of my head, ignoring the glare he received from Tristan.

Before I could say anything else, Tommaso came and sat down opposite us. He didn't say anything, just glared at Aidan.

"He makes you happy?"

I gave Aidan a confused look, and he just rolled his eyes. "Yes," I answered.

"He keeps you safe?"

"Yes."

"You love him?"

"Yes."

Tommaso nodded, his eyes squinting as he looked between Aidan and me. Then he stood up and held his hand out to Aidan.

"I'm Tommaso, Kalina's twin."

Aidan stood up and shook Tommy's hand with a grin on his face. "Nice to meet you. I'm Aidan."

This was why I loved my Tommy. As long as I was safe and happy, everything was good for him.

I couldn't help the smile on my face as the two of them sat and talked, their conversations ranging from their most intense missions to their favourite chocolate.

* * *

A few months later

I realised how wonderful it could be to have friends. I had the Angels, but they were more family than anything. Besides them, there was really only violence in my life, inflicted by others.

But having genuine friends was something I wasn't used to.

However, as I lay on the beach, watching Jayden chase Lorenzo in the shallow water, I knew this friend thing was something I enjoyed.

After some discussion, and only a small amount of convincing for Christopher, Tommaso and

I had decided to spend our birthday in Italy. It was seen as the perfect time to finally explore my family's home.

And it worked perfectly, as both Mateo and Aidan had business here that needed attending. Our birthday may have been a week ago, but this was the time we were using to celebrate.

"Carter, it's a private beach."

I turned to look behind me, where I was sunbathing, to see Aidan trying to convince his little brother to take off the hoodie.

Carter had recently grown, likely his final growth spurt, and he was now standing at six feet. But while we were here in Italy, the poor guy was going to die of heat exhaustion if he continued to dress like this.

"But there's still people," Carter grumbled, trying to end the conversation.

Aidan sighed, not wanting his brother to suffer the effects of his insecurity. He made eye contact with me and gave me a look that said, "Please help."

"Carter, everyone here but Lorenzo has a scar on display. No one is going to judge you for yours."

Taking note of my words, Carter's eyes darted around the family-owned beach. Christopher had multiple gunshot wounds on his arms and legs; Mateo and Antonio the same, with additional knife wounds here and there. Stefano had a scar where his pinky toe had been chopped off and then reattached, though he still won't tell me why. Tristan had wounds where shards of glass had penetrated his skin after smashing a window mid-fight.

Tommaso had a gunshot wound from Jamie.

Ace and Jamie had gunshot wounds from Tommaso and Tristan.

Aidan had gunshot wounds from Tommaso, Tristan, and me.

We really needed to stop shooting each other.

Jayden had a scar on his back from a microwave explosion when he was trying to do something—no doubt experimental and techy. Maxim had a scar from a blowtorch, its flame extending further than expected in the garage. It happened to be a small flamethrower, and the idiot hadn't notice.

And my bikini-clad body spoke for itself.

Hesitantly, Carter took off the hoodie, eyes downcast. He stood up and moved closer to me, and I just gave him a small hug.

"CARTER! SAVE ME!" Lorenzo screamed from the water, where Jayden was tickling him.

With a grin, Carter jumped up and ran down to the beach. I watched from a distance as Carter and Jayden played with Lorenzo, a joyful smile on his chubby little face.

Feeling arms wrap around my waist from behind, I relaxed into Aidan's hold. I couldn't help but chuckle at the glare Antonio was giving him a few feet away, where he was sunbathing.

"Thank you," he mumbled as he kissed the side of my face.

"He doesn't realise no one here would judge him," I replied, my heart aching for my best friend. "I wish he would be like this all the time."

Aidan sighed as his arms tightened. He rested his chin on my head as he looked out towards the sea. "After the fire, I think the only person who could've helped him was our mother."

I sat in silence for a moment, contemplating whether I should ask or not. After all, it had been a peaceful few weeks, and to bring up this topic again . . .

"What is it?" Aidan said.

Confused, I looked up to him, and he continued. "What do you want to ask me?"

He can read me too well.

"What happened to Gatwick?"

The last I saw him, he was in a pool of his own blood, his teeth scattered around his beaten face. The slashes from my blade littered his skin, and there was little left of the man I once called my boyfriend.

Aidan's clean-up crew and guards had taken his barely conscious body, and I hadn't seen him since. I wish I didn't want to know but I do. After everything that happened because of that delusional monster, I wanted to see him suffer.

"He's currently being held in a warehouse of mine, guarded by the crew of Ben's brother," Aidan answered, referring to his Irish underboss.

"I want to see him."

"Not a fucking chance."

I turned around, feeling Aidan's grip loosen on me so I could do so. Kneeling in front of him, our eyes level, I tried to see if there was any way I could convince him without having to actually discuss it.

"Kalina, no," Aidan said, finality evident in his tone.

"Who do you think you are, telling me no." I glared, annoyed by his blatant refusal.

"I'm the one who knows where he is." Aidan smirked.

Fuck! He's got me there.

"Why not?" I whined, trying to figure out why he was so adamant.

"Because after all he did to you and his infatuation with you . . . the idea of you being near him again infuriates me." His jaw was clenched when he finished speaking. His hands had noticeably tightened on my arm, but once he realised that, he loosened his grip.

I don't know whether that's adorable or concerning.

I didn't know what to say to that, so I did the only thing I could think of. Climbing onto his lap, I wrapped my arms around his neck and hugged him tightly. He wrapped his arms around my lower waist, holding me close as he buried his face in my neck, leaving a subtle kiss there.

"I quite like this position." I could hear the smirk in his voice.

As I felt his hands wander slightly lower, a grin formed on my face because I knew what was about to happen.

"ROSSI! GET THOSE HANDS HIGHER OR I'LL CHOP THEM OFF."

Aidan's hands shot up to the curve of my waist at the sound of Antonio, whose voice echoed from the side of the beach where he, Mateo, and Christopher were.

"Leave the kid alone," Christopher scolded, rolling his eyes as he put on his sunglasses and returned to his newspaper.

"You know, I quite like Christopher," Aidan mumbled as he tucked his head into my neck again.

"Yeah, he's pretty chill." I chuckled, watching Antonio sit there, gobsmacked at our father's words.

As Aidan and I cuddled on the beach, all I could think about was how far my families had come. When I met the biologicals, they were rivals with the Chained Angels, and there had been nothing but borderline war between Aidan and my family. But now, here we were in Italy, celebrating my birthday with my twin and my family.

"Mama!"

The tiny body barrelled towards us, his laughter breaking me from my thoughts. His contagious giggles filled the air as he leapt at me. Thankfully, Aidan caught him.

Having my face smashed by a child's body was not particularly pleasant. "What are you doing, little man!" Aidan grinned, shuffling slightly so Lorenzo fit between the two of us.

"I'm hiding from Uncle Carter," Lorenzo whispered, putting his finger to his lips to be quiet.

"Why's that?" I asked, moving his increasingly dark brown hair from his eyes.

"He's the tickle monster." Lorenzo giggled, tucking himself deeper between the two of us.

Aidan and I looked up at each other, a smile breaking out on our faces at the little man wedged between us.

In the joy of the day, my mind completely forgot about Spencer Gatwick.

But little did I know that he was still going to be causing problems.

CHAPTER THIRTY-EIGHT

KALINA

Luxury was never something I was accustomed to. After all, growing up, having heating was not an everyday thing. Every day had been a struggle to survive, and every night a miracle for making it that far. The clothes on my back had been stolen, and the hygiene products had been paid for with the Daniel's meagre wage.

But one thing I could promise was that Lorenzo would grow up in a world where a heated home was the bare minimum.

Tommaso insisted on a shopping spree in a shopping centre not too far from our villa, so now here we were with Lorenzo and Aidan. When Christopher found out where we were going, he handed me his black card and the PIN number. When I protested that it was too much, Antonio scooped me up, carried me out the front door, and placed me on the doorstep.

It was his way of saying, "Shut up and take the money."

"Mama! Look!"

Lorenzo ran ahead, holding Aidan's hand. It was quite a funny sight: a six-foot-four man's giant palm gripping a four-year-old's chubby little hand, bending down to match his three-foot-nine height.

They stopped outside a clothing store. Lorenzo eyes were wide, his smile huge, as he pointed at a minion onesie in the window.

Come on.

How could I not?!?

"Oh my god! YES!" Tommy agreed. My child-of-a-twin brother turned to me, his eyes pleading. "I know his birthday was last month, but look at it."

Chuckling, I nodded. Within seconds, Tommaso had scooped up Lorenzo, holding him to his side as he ran into the shop. Aidan looked at me, pure amusement in his eyes despite his stoic expression.

Mr Mafia gotta keep up appearances.

Taking his outstretched hand, we followed my brother and nephew, who were already inspecting different sizes. I picked up the biggest one I could find, holding it above my head and looking at Aidan. It took him a second to understand what I meant before he overdramatically sighed and took it from my hand.

"The things I do for you," he muttered as he rolled his eyes.

"Try them on first," I told Lorenzo, who was already making his way to the checkout.

A look of realisation spread across his face, his mouth forming an 'O'. Eventually, he nodded. Taking his hand, I led us all to the changing rooms, down to the multiple-gender area.

"Who do you want to go in with you, *piccolo*?" I stroked his black curls away from his face. *(little one)*

"Mama," he replied with a smile as he stepped into a stall. "Can I be a minion now?"

Tommaso and Aidan chuckled at the adorable child and went to their own changing rooms. I went inside with Lorenzo, who quickly kicked off his shoes. He managed to get changed by himself, pulling the hood over his head with a grin.

"MINION!" he cheered, jumping up and down.

Laughing, I made him turn around whilst I got changed, slipping into the onesie after removing my Jordans, flared green trousers, and black boob tube. I pulled my hood over my head.

I picked up Lorenzo and perched him on my hip, planting a kiss on the top of his head. Pulling out my phone, I snapped a few pictures of us in the changing room mirror. A few seconds later, a knock sounded at the door.

"Where's the baby minion?" came the overly joyful voice of Tommaso from the other side.

"The master minion!" Aidan followed.

Mafia men . . .

Lorenzo unlocked the door and burst into a fit of giggles at seeing Tommaso and Aidan as minions. It was ridiculous to see my mafia boss boyfriend dressed as a *Despicable Me* minion.

Have we actually confirmed that he's my boyfriend???

Aidan's eyes held nothing but adoration as he looked at me, a soft smile on his face. I watched as his gaze raked up and down my body, that smile turning into a smirk.

Is this man seriously getting turned on by me in a onesie?

"Tommy?" Lorenzo shouted the nickname he had learned from me, making grabby hands at my brother. "Can we keep looking for clothes?"

Reaching forward, Tommaso took him from my arms. "Of course we can, little man. Let's get you changed first, though."

He grabbed Lorenzo's clothes before taking him back to his changing room. "Meet you at the front in twenty minutes?"

"Yeah. Just don't break Christopher's bank account," I said, giving my brother a pointed stare, knowing he would do so if I did not warn him.

As Tommaso and Lorenzo left, I was quickly but gently shoved back into the changing room, pressed up against the door with Aidan's hand on my neck and waist.

"Are you seriously having a hard time seeing me in a minions onesie?" I deadpanned.

He pushed his hips to mine, his hard cock pressing against my thigh, and offered me a smirk. "I'm always hard around you."

"Horny bastard," I scoffed with a laugh.

"Only for you," he muttered before dipping his head into my neck, placing firm kisses.

I moaned at the feeling of his hands making their way to my hips. My hand curled around his hair, the other resting on his solid chest. His heart was beating so hard, I felt like my palm was being punched with every thud.

Why not fuck with him a bit?

"Do you prefer me dressed as a minion?" I joked. "I knew you always liked the little things."

Aidan's smirk only grew, showing sharp canines that I wanted to feel digging into my skin. "While I love the way this hugs your figure . . ." His hands ran up the sides of my waist, dipping into my hourglass curve. Leaning down, his teeth caught the zipper of the onesie, dragging it down, hazel eyes staring back at me, which caused my knees to weaken. The unzipping revealed my white lace bra. "I prefer this so much more."

He looked up at me with waiting eyes, not moving an inch. "Can I touch you?"

Could this man get any better???

I couldn't get the words to leave my mouth. A nod was all I could manage. Aidan didn't accept that, so I breathed out, "Yes."

Instead of taking off the onesie and bra, he pulled down the lace, freeing my boobs, which the fabric slightly pushed up. Leaning his head down, he took one nipple into his mouth, sucking and lightly biting until it was painfully hard, whilst kneading and twisting the other with his hand. I bit my lip to keep from moaning too loudly, my hands tangled in Aidan's thick brown hair, a mix of pulling away and drawing him closer—the pain exquisite.

His free hand moved from my hip to the waistband of my lace thong, rubbing it with his thumb before sliding inside my soaked underwear. He groaned against my boob, looking up at me through hooded eyes. "Fuck, you're dripping."

I clenched at his words, desperate for him to go further, to feel his fingers deeper, but he held back. Looking down at him, I saw the sadistic smirk on his face.

"You know what to say, beautiful."

This man wanted begging.

I don't beg for anything.

"Aidan, if you don't do something right now, I'll walk out of this changing room and find someone—"

The loud moan that would have echoed the changing room was stolen by Aidan as his lips smashed against my own in a firm kiss whilst three fingers launched inside me all at once. They moved in and out at the perfect speed, curling so they rubbed against my G-spot with every stroke. His flat palm brushed over my clit with each movement, causing an onslaught of moans to tumbled from my lips.

Aidan groaned into the kiss, my pussy crushing his fingers like a vise. Pulling back just enough so I could have some much-needed oxygen, he wasted no time kissing along my jaw and down my neck. His free hand returned to my boob, squeezing and kneading so harshly the pain was almost unbearable.

Almost.

The knot in my stomach tightened, blood trickling from my bitten lip down my chin. Aidan's lips traveled to my ear, placing a soft kiss at its side. "Let go, beautiful."

I came with a cry, biting Aidan's shoulder as I shuddered against the changing room door.

I just let my boyfriend publicly finger me against a changing room door dressed as a minion . . .

I think it's time to admit I need therapy.

Aidan pulled back, a smirk resting on his face. "All you do is drip for me."

He licked the line of blood from my chin to my lip before leaning down for a soft kiss. I could taste the blood on his tongue.

"And as for me liking the little things . . ." Aidan sucked his finger clean, then cupped my boobs. "These aren't little, beautiful, and I fucking love them."

CHAPTER THIRTY-NINE

KALINA

Since I arrived at Christopher's house, something had always bugged me. I could never place my finger on it, but there was always this nagging feeling in the back of my mind—problems from childhood arising, the past preventing me from growing in the future.

"I'm getting a job."

All heads in the kitchen turned to me, a mixture of expressions on their faces. Tommaso looked shocked, Tristan seemingly confused, Stefano hid a grin behind his mug, Antonio nervous. But the ones who had my attention most were Mateo and Christopher.

Mateo seemed pleased. So did Christopher, despite his curious gaze.

"Why?" Tommaso asked, and Tristan nodded in agreement with the question.

"What do you mean why?" Out of every reaction I expected, that was not at the top of my list.

The boys shared a look, and Tristan answered. "You are aware we are billionaires, right? You don't need a job."

Antonio snapped at the two. "That is not the right way to think."

"Agreed," I commented. "That is family money. I want my money. I want to earn something for myself. I want a career that I can call my own. I refuse to be one of those people sitting on my arse all day, collecting money from the government when I am eligible to work."

The remainder of my brothers and Christopher had proud expressions on their faces. Tristan and Tommaso, however, once again shared a look.

"You don't need government money. The family money is for everyone, including you."

Privileged children are the bane of my existence.

"That's not the point." I sighed. "The job, the money, the experience—it will all be mine. You grew up with access to unlimited credit cards. You know how to live; I know how to survive." Realisation dawned on their faces. "I'm going to learn how to live."

No one said anything for a moment before Mateo proposed, "Do you want a job in the mafia or the legal business?"

"Neither," I replied. "I appreciate the offer, but I want complete independence in my own career."

"I have one condition," Christopher said, a note of no argument in his tone.

"I'm eighteen. I don't need your permission for a job," I said, not wanting to be controlled.

"It won't interfere with your work. I promise." At that, I gave him the go-ahead to continue. "There will be a security car outside the establishment and two guards inside."

Mafia family, gang land adoptive family, mafia don boyfriend, attitude and sarcasm.

"Yeah, I think that's the best idea," I agreed.

"Any idea on what job it is you want?" Antonio asked, passing me a fresh cup of tea to go alongside the toast and fruit Stefano had plated in front of me.

"Something fashion-related," I said, "I'll probably start as retail assistant, something part-time. Then, once I finish school again, I want to do a course in either design or fashion, preferably online so I can still spend time with Enzo and work. From then on, a stylist for a major brand. I'm leaning towards Gucci, but I could be persuaded. Build a career, a name, a platform—maybe a brand or magazine of my own. Retire at forty with a million-dollar name, then spend the rest of my life sunbathing, torturing people. You know, classic retirement stuff."

They all laughed but approved. Mateo smiled fondly at me. "You have this all planned out, don't you?"

"Since I was seven." I grinned.

Lorenzo then came barrelling down the hall, little slippers flapping against the hardwood floors. His arms wrapped around my legs, pulling me into a hug once I lifted him from the ground. I placed a kiss on his head.

"Well, then, the job hunt begins." Antonio chuckled, clinking our mugs together.

L.A. was a large city. I had spent hours scoping out where to apply for jobs on my laptop. Eventually, I made my decision.

Aidan drove with one hand on the steering wheel, the other resting on my thigh, the muscles of his arms flexing as he changed gears or steered the car. His black dress shirt had the sleeves rolled up to his elbows, his matching trousers ironed to a crisp. Sunglasses blocked the hazel eyes that I adored, and his thick brown hair was styled away from his face.

I was wearing cream-coloured trousers, a brown off-the-shoulder top that matched my belt, and brown suede ankle boots. My hair flowed in loose dark brown curls.

Aidan parked the car outside the large building, a smile on his face as he turned to me. "I'm happy you're doing this."

"Why? So I don't have to spend your money?" I joked, taking his inked hand in my own.

He shook his head, chuckling slightly. "Beautiful, if you think a job is going to stop me from paying for anything and everything you want, you don't know me well enough."

Smiling, I leaned over the centre console and placed a kiss on his lips. When I tried to pull away, his hand wove its way into my hair, holding me close. Our tongues fought for control but, as always, he won. Slowly pulling away, he gave me a little peck with a grin.

"I love you, beautiful. Now, go get that job."

He leaned back in his seat.

"Love you too," I said as I got out of the car. "Meet me back here in half an hour?"

"I'm not leaving," Aidan answered, pulling out his phone. "Me and Block Blast will wait here for you."

I laughed, wondering why I would expect him to leave. I looked up at the building in front of me. Written in large, block letters was one word: THREAD

The large double doors opened at my approach, revealing rows and rows of clothes—all hung, and piled, and arranged. All designer, all expensive. The floor was marble tile, the walls painted white, with medium-toned oak lining them as shelves and cabinets.

"Holy shit."

A group of workers giggling caught my attention. They were looking at me as I stared around the store.

Shit! Did I say that out loud.

One managed to stop laughing and approached me. She had fiery red hair, a pale complexion, and soft blue eyes. There was a friendliness in her tone. "Is there anything I can help you with?"

"A manager to speak to about a job?" I gave her a smile.

"Oh, that explains the reaction." She giggled. "Most customers don't react like that."

I laughed with her, knowing I was far from the classy, elegant, pearl-necklaced shoppers that frequented here. She guided me through the store, past the aisles of clothing, boots, makeup, fragrances, and jewellery. We then approached a set of double doors stating, "Staff Only."

"If you could just wait here, I'll go and get the manager," she said and headed through the doors when I nodded.

A few minutes later, the employee returned, a dark-skinned woman following her. She had her hair tied into dreadlocks, the majority of them blonde, bringing out the brown of her eyes. Her smile was warm and genuine. She was dressed in a trouser suit. She held out her hand for me to shake.

"I'm Zoe, the manager of this Thread location. I understand you're here to speak about a job?"

I shook her hand, returning the smile. "Hi, I'm Kalina, and yes I was researching last night and saw you had a job opening."

"We do. Would you like to come to my office."

Half an hour later, I was walking outside of the L.A. Thread building with no expression on my face. Aidan's Audi was parked in the exact same spot, directly opposite the door.

As if sensing my approach, he looked up and unlocked the door for me, an expectant expression on his face.

I sat in the passenger seat, put on my seatbelt, and folded my hands in my lap.

When I didn't speak, Aidan broke the silence. "Well . . ."

Turning to face him with a huge grin, I said, "You are looking at the newly hired retail assistant of Thread's L.A."

CHAPTER FORTY

KALINA

Who in their right mind would choose to start a retail job in December?

Hours on end, I spent my time checking out items, stocking shelves, and dealing with customers who could not tell their trainers from their stilettos.

Ace stood outside in his Subaru, a Chained Angel leather vest resting on his back. He had a dopey grin on his face, arms folded over his chest. "There's our working girl."

"Noise," I mumbled, shaking my head as I walked into his open arms, my head landing on his chest.

Ace laughed as he guided me to the passenger seat before getting in himself. Seeing that I hadn't moved at all, he reached over and fastened my seatbelt. "Having a job isn't easy, Kal."

"How would you know, crime boss?" I grinned, opening one heavy eye to see him glaring back at me.

"My job is twice the effort. Evading the police is difficult," Ace joked, pulling out of his parking spot.

We drove home in silence, Ace understanding that I needed minimal noise. After a twelve-hour shift, with three hours of sleep under my belt, my head was pounding. It took half an hour to get home. Ace pulled into the driveway after the guard let him in, Mateo having ordered them to do so.

Matteo approving of enemy relationships is truly, just, chef's kiss.

Stumbling out of the car while rubbing my tired eyes—mindful of my mascara and eyeliner—I followed Ace inside the house. Lorenzo came running up to me, wrapping his arms around my legs.

"Mama, did you have fun at work?" His big brown eyes stared up at me, chocolate smudged around his mouth.

"Lots of fun, *piccolo.*" I smiled down at him, placing a kiss on the top of his head. *(little one)*

"Enzo! Let me wipe your mouth." A red-faced Mateo came barrelling out of the kitchen, frustration slipping through the plastered smile on his face.

"No!" Lorenzo laughed, hiding behind my legs at the sight of his uncle. "I'm saving it for later."

Despite my pounding head, I laughed at the scene before me. The don of the second-most powerful mafia in the world was fighting with a child who refused to wipe the chocolate from his face.

"Enzo, listen to Mateo," I told him in a stern tone. Then I crouched down to his height, whispering, "We both know Tommy will give you more later."

Mateo managed to grab Lorenzo. He held him in his arms, carrying him back to the kitchen. Ace was still standing by the door, and it was then that I realised exactly how he was dressed. His blond hair was styled, adding to the effect of his white T-shirt and black cargos. It was smart for Ace.

"I told you to dress properly."

At the sound of his voice, I turned to see Stefano standing at the foot of the stairs. He was dressed in a crisp navy suit and black dress shirt, tattoos creeping up his neck. He adjusted his silver cuff links while glaring at his boyfriend.

"This is smart for me," Ace justified, hands in his pockets as he shrugged his shoulders.

"Kalina." Stefano sighed, annoyance on his face. "We're going to Vesuvio's."

Immediately, I snapped into action. "Anthony Vecoli, get your arse up those stairs right now."

At the use of his full name, Ace legged it to the staircase, taking them two at a time. I followed after him into Stefano's bedroom. Thankfully, they were both roughly the same build, so getting an outfit for him shouldn't be too difficult.

"Sit." Before I could finish the word, Ace's arse dropped onto Stefano's bed, uneasiness in his eyes.

Yanking open the wooden doors of Stefano's wardrobe, I instantly began flicking through one suit after another. "What sort of idiot wears cargos and a top to a Michelin-starred restaurant for a date?"

"The kind who rides a motorbike and shoots people for a living."

My stern glare drew a quick "sorry" from him.

A few minutes later, I found a charcoal Gucci suit and a black dress shirt. Passing the outfit to Ace, I looked around and realised there weren't any shoes in his size he could borrow.

Realising where my mind was going, he immediately began to protest. "Kal, I can wear these."

No fucking way am I sending him out in an all-black suit with white Jordans.

"Get changed. I'll be back in a moment."

I knew who had the same shoe size as Ace. Getting him to agree to sharing would be slightly more difficult. Knocking on the door—two doors—I waited patiently.

"Come in."

"Can I borrow—"

"Yes, *tesoro*." *(darling)*

That was easier than I thought.

Getting a set of Italian leather shoes off the rack, I closed the door behind me, ignoring the questioning gaze being sent in my direction.

I opened the door to Stefano's room. Ace had fully changed into the outfit I had given him.

"Here," I said, passing him the shoes.

"Where did you get these from?" he asked, sitting on the well-made bed to change into them.

"Christopher."

Once my idiot of a friend was properly dressed, we went back downstairs to Stefano. At the sight of his boyfriend, my brother's eyes lit up. After walking in on the two of them, they told me they had been together for nearly a year, today being their anniversary.

"Thanks, Kalina," Stefano said, an approving look on his face at the sight of his boyfriend not only wearing a suit that accentuated every one of his features, but also the fact that it was his very own clothes.

"Well, he wasn't going to Vesuvio's like that." I grinned, seeing the eye roll from Ace.

After being hugged goodbye by both, they took off from the front door, heading to their anniversary dinner.

* * *

The kitchen boomed with a noise that echoed throughout the house.

Running quickly, I grabbed the nearest thing—a tea towel—and whipped the culprit with it.

"What the fuck!" Tristan glared through my soul.

Tommaso was cackling at our brother's expense.

"I've just put Enzo to bed. Shut up! I can hear you from his room."

A mumbled "sorry" came from his mouth. He grumbled as he turned back to the pizza he and Tommaso were sharing.

"Where are you going?" Tommaso asked.

"I'm spending the night with Aidan."

Tristan seemed like he wanted to say something. Ultimately, he chose not to.

Probably because Aidan beat his arse in the ring.

"See you at school," Tommaso said, waving with a smile. When his eyes turned back to the counter, his gaze caught sight of the purple wrapper in the corner. "Chocolate!"

CHAPTER FORTY-ONE

STEFANO

The day I realised I like men, as well as women, was interesting, to say the least. Mateo, Antonio, and I had been given the night off while I worked for Dad in the mafia. This was before I found my passion for tattooing.

And what would a rowdy trio of young men do?

We went to a strip club. I remembered it like the back of my hand.

An establishment by the name of Serenity. The walls were a brothel red, and the seating was purple velvet, surrounded by mahogany tables. The stages were black and lined with a sparkling gold, with lights of all different colors and shades throughout the room. There were two entrances to the establishment, one on the left side of the building and one on the right. We took the left door, going straight inside after Matteo slipped the bouncer a hundred-dollar bill.

We just didn't notice the clearly gay men lining the door.

Once inside the building, we realized all the furniture and stages were filled with men wearing an array of sequins, glitter, and very little clothing.

"Let's go," Matteo said, a disappointed look on his face at not seeing boobs.

A gay Antonio, who hadn't wanted to go and see naked women, was bouncing on the balls of his feet.

Glancing around the room, my eyes focused on the men with toned abs and tight boxers dancing on the stage and on top of paying customers. "Let's stay."

Both my brothers stared at me with shocked expressions. Matteo chose to voice his thoughts. "Since when has your taste involved men?"

Flicking my gaze back to a particular blond who was making eyes at me, I said, "Since I saw a man who looked like that." My eyes dragged over his tanned body and the way his abs flexed as he walked toward me.

Antonio let out a laugh before bounding over to sit at one of the stages. The man approached me, squeezed my bicep, snaked his hand down to mine, and guided me to a back room.

"Why did the straight brothers have to be children?" I heard Matteo sigh.

Ace held my hand in his own, our tattoos blending together as they crept out from the cuffs of our suits. The maître d's eyes gleamed at the sight of me.

"Mr. Montessori! How wonderful to see you again." He gestured behind him with a smile. "Please follow me to your table."

He guided us through the seated customers before placing us at a VIP table outside, the empty balcony overlooking the ocean, the stars of the night sky glimmering down on the water.

Ace asked, seeing all the tables that were usually here removed, candles replacing their spots.

"I booked out the balcony," I told him, placing a kiss on his cheek.

I pulled out Ace's chair and waited for him to take a seat. Walking around to my own chair, I noticed the pink blush on his cheeks, forcing me to bite my lip so I didn't laugh at his embarrassment.

"Your whiskey, sirs," a waitress said, pouring the whiskey I had preordered into the two glasses on the table. "I'll be back momentarily to take your order."

"No need," I told her. "I'll have the grilled steak, and he'll have the smoked salmon, both with all the sides."

Nodding with a smile, she walked back inside.

Ace smiled at me. "You remembered how much I loved the steak."

"How could I not? All that moaning you did while eating it gave me a hard-on."

A chuckle fell out of his mouth despite him blushing again. It didn't take long for the food to arrive, the two of us chatting while we waited. The waitress placed the food on the table and refilled the whiskey glasses before heading back inside.

For the most part, we were silent as we ate, just smiling at each other whenever we glanced up from our delicious food.

"I did a spine tattoo on this woman this morning," I said, wiping my mouth. "It was a red dragon to represent her father."

"A memorial tattoo?" Ace said, whiskey in hand as he watched me finish my meal, his salmon and salad already gone.

"No." I grinned. "The man was a bastard. She wanted the dragon to represent all the trauma he caused her, the fire being a burn mark on her back, which he actually inflicted on her. She had it as a spine tattoo so she would be reminded that all the pain was behind her."

Ace had a thoughtful look on his face, as if he was thinking the same as me.

"Kalina got the Chained Angel tattoo for a similar reason, didn't she?" I asked, knowing it wasn't mandatory for members to have the tattoo.

A memorable smile spread across his face. "It's her way of knowing her family always has her back."

The moment I found out that "the kid" my boyfriend was so attached to was my long-lost little sister, it felt as if the universe had always tried to make my family realize there was another one of us. The two of us burst into laughter at the revelation. It was the day after we took Kalina to the mall.

Ace told me he had messaged her a warning about her nutjob older brother, warning her of our underground connections and to see if she was truly afraid of us. It was his way of protecting us both from upsetting each other, and it worked perfectly. Kalina realized that we truly cared for her, and I realized just how much she meant to me in such a short span of time.

The night flew by, the two of us talking about anything and everything, from work to the latest episode of our favorite TV show.

"Mark and Lexi deserved their happy ending!" Ace said, a sadness in his tone. "It's as if Shonda wanted us to die with them."

"I know it hurt you." I tried not to laugh, covering my mouth with my hand.

"Hurt me?" Ace gasped. "It destroyed me! They were the definition of 'right person, wrong time.' If you think it just hurt me, you clearly don't know me at all."

Now's the time.

"I do know you," I began. "I know that your Harley from when you were seventeen was your favorite motorcycle. I know your favorite food is smoked salmon, but any other fish makes you want to puke. I know that you love medical drama shows, and it's all you'll watch. I know that you love to fuck with your Chained Angels cut on." He blushed again at this. "And I know that you're the most important thing in the world to me.

We weren't meant to be together after all. We were enemies in every way. But you're mine and I'm yours, and I want nothing more than for the world to know it."

I got out of my chair, pulled out the black velvet box, and opened it to reveal a silver band with a black gemstone engraved onto the metal. Going on one knee, I watched as the tears formed in his eyes,

So, Anthony Vecoli, will you marry me?"

CHAPTER FORTY-TWO

AIDAN

The guards of the mansion glared at me as I leaned against the door of my Audi R8, to which I simply smirked. They knew I was technically still an enemy to their organisation, but the princess of their mafia was mine.

Probably time to sign an alliance with Matteo.

Kalina exited the gates moments later, waving bye to the guards, whose glares softened as they smiled back at her. Her outfit consisted of a black turtleneck, a red-and-black tartan skirt, tights, and knee-high black boots. Her dark curls fell down her shoulders, ending just below her boobs.

Don't get a boner. Don't get a boner.

I swear, anything Kalina wears makes her look mouthwatering: her tight curves, large boobs, and the swell of her ass.

There goes the no-boner.

My grey joggers didn't hide what my mind was thinking.

"Nice to see you too." She chuckled.

Walking into my arms, her eyes focused on the way the black T-shirt I was wearing tightened as my bicep flexed. I held her close, placing a kiss on her forehead and smiling down at her.

"You know I can't help it." I fake-pouted. "You're just too sexy."

A laugh escaped her lips, and I opened the passenger door for her, making sure she was fully settled before closing it. Getting into the driver's seat, I started up the car, then placed my hand on her partially exposed thigh.

"How was work today?" I asked, my thumb rubbing the area just below her skirt.

"As if you don't already know." She turned to me with a pointed stare, a smirk on her face.

"Whatever do you mean?" I questioned, feigning innocence.

"Oh, so the three Irish men I served today who bought a pair of socks, a packet of underwear, and a gift card but still spent five hours in the store weren't there to watch me?"

Fucking idiots.

Who goes to a store full of designer clothes and buys socks???

"Maybe."

Kalina took my hand off her thigh, lifting it to her lips and placing kisses on my knuckles. "I love that you watch out for me. But you are aware my brothers have men sitting in a car outside."

Turning to face her momentarily, I said, "They report to your brothers, not me." I faced the road again. "My men inform me of your safety. I can't run a mafia and watch the store security cameras at the same time, so I have some men there who I trust to protect you."

"Paranoid much?" Kalina smiles. "You know I can take care of myself."

Swiftly pulling the car over to the side of the road, I unclipped her seatbelt and pulled Kalina onto my lap.

"All I do is think about you," I told her, my hand gently grasping her jaw. "When you're not with me, I wonder if you're safe. We live in a world where my paranoia is warranted."

"And when I'm with you?" she questioned, leaning into my chest.

With my free hand on her hip, I pressed her down onto my hard cock. I grinned at the gasp she let out. "This is what happens when I'm with you."

"I guess I can live with the security guards," she whispered before crashing her lips onto mine.

Our lips synchronised their movements. A moan escaped her as I cupped her boob with my hand. My tongue prodded at her mouth, which she firmly denied with a smirk. Smirking back, I harshly squeezed her boob, causing her mouth to open in a gasp. My tongue met hers, the two fighting for control until mine won.

As always.

Kissing at a pace where I was taking what I wanted and Kalina was just accepting the loss of control, she ground her hips on my cock, causing a groan to escape from the back of my throat.

"I want you," she mumbled confidently, hands tugging at the waistband of my joggers.

Despite it being a sports car, there was enough room for me to lift my hips and pull down my joggers and boxers. I leaned back in the seat after reclining it. "Glove compartment."

Knowing what I meant, Kalina reached over and pulled out a condom I had stored in there. She rolled it on me as I simply palmed her ass, grinning as she gulped at the sight of my hard cock, precum leaking from the tip.

Reaching down, I pulled her tight skirt up to her waist and ripped her black tights at the crotch. I pushed her thong to the side before she slowly lowered herself onto me.

We both moaned at the feeling, my cock stretching her to the point that she shook on top of me. My teeth gritted as she held me in a vise-like grip.

"Fuck! You're tight, beautiful."

"You're too big," she moaned, resting her forehead against my left shoulder and still shaking.

"Take it," I groaned, grabbing her hips and making her ride me slowly.

The sensation caused a strangled moan to escape her lips. She braced her hands on my chest. My hands on her hips helped her move until she managed a rhythm, her clit dragging across my pelvis.

Wanting to feel her boobs, I considered lifting her turtleneck before deciding otherwise. Grabbing the neck of the sweater, I ripped it in two to expose her black lace bra.

"Aidan, what the fuck!" she shouted, still grinding on my dick despite her glare.

"I'll buy you more," I groaned, unclipping her strapless bra, which fell down between us.

Chucking it into her seat, I lowered my mouth to her left boob, sucking and biting on the nipple. Her moans swarmed the car as she went down harder on me, hands raking and pulling through my hair.

"Aidan." She clenched down on me, teetering on the edge of an orgasm.

"I know, beautiful," I groaned, switching to biting down on her right nipple, tugging it with my teeth. One hand moved to her left boob, twisting that nipple. The other rested on her crotch, my thumb rubbing her clit harshly. "Just let go."

Kalina came with a scream, strangling my cock as I came with her. My lips sucked on her boob as her teeth bit down on the spot where my neck and shoulder met.

I resurfaced before she did, still rubbing her clit through her orgasm as she shook in my arms for the second time tonight. Her ragged breathing pounded in my ear while her teeth were still biting into the skin of my neck. Coming down from her high, she licked the spot where her teeth were, wiping the blood I felt trickling down my chest.

"Since when have you had a biting kink?" I questioned, pushing a loose strand of hair behind her ear.

A blush coated her cheeks, her inner walls clenching on me at my words. A laugh tumbled from my lips, and I placed a kiss on her forehead.

"I love you," she whispered against my lips.

"I love you too."

She lifted herself from my still-hard dick, wincing as she did so. Taking off the condom, I tied it off and put it on the passenger seat floor.

"How are you still hard?"

"I'm always hard around you." I grinned. "Now close your mouth before we end up here all night."

Tucking my dick away, I pulled my boxers back up and looked at Kalina, who was glaring at me. "What's that look for?"

Kalina gestured to her destroyed turtleneck, but my attention went back to her boobs. "Look what you did."

I reached forward, palmed both of her boobs, and pinched her nipples, causing a gasp to tumble from her lips.

"You owe me a sweater."

"I'll buy you the company." I smirked, placing a kiss on her lips.

Reaching over, I grabbed her bra and helped her put it back on. "I can't have anyone else seeing your tits," I mumbled against her lips. "They're mine."

Once her bra was on, I pulled off my black top and placed it over Kalina, the bottom pooling on her lap as it was so big on her.

"All yours," she murmured, placing a final kiss on my lips before settling back into the passenger seat.

"Let's go home so I can fuck you properly."

CHAPTER FORTY-THREE

KALINA

The sun warmed my body as it penetrated the windows of Aidan's bedroom. The black sheets on his bed were bunched down to my waist. Looking down, I saw Aidan asleep beneath me. He had both arms wrapped around my waist, his face smooshed between my boobs.

This man has an obsession with my boobs.

Sighing, I rested my head back on the pillows just above Aidan's head. It was the reason I hadn't spent the night hunched over. Running my fingers through his hair, I gazed out of the window to see the waves of the Pacific lapping against the shore.

My hand stilled at the sound of a car door slamming in the driveway. Then I felt teeth nip at my nipple, causing a loud "Ouch!" to escape my lips.

Aidan stared up at me with hooded eyes, a sloppy smile on his face.

I returned his smile. "Good morning, baby."

"Morning," he mumbled, his lips enclosing around my boob once again, causing a moan to tumble from my lips.

Aidan rolled us over, causing me to lie on the mattress as his massive frame covered my own. His lips moved to my neck, kissing and sucking on the skin as his hand massaged my boob, the other bracing himself above me.

A loud banging on the bedroom door snapped my attention away from Aidan.

"Ignore it," he mumbled against my lips before kissing me again.

"AIDAN! GET YOUR ASS OUT HERE!"

The two of us shared a look, wondering why Ace was here so early in the morning.

"It won't be important," Aidan said, hand grasping my face as he pulled me in for another kiss.

The door burst open, and Ace ran inside. A scream momentarily left his lips at the sight of Aidan on top of me. Aidan pulled the covers over us, rolled off me, and he glared at his best friend.

"Get the fuck out."

Ace didn't listen and instead went to the bottom of the bed. Aidan went to shout at him again, but Ace held up his left hand, silencing him at the sight of a silver band on his ring finger.

"Stefano proposed!"

A scream of excitement left my lips as I jumped off the bed, holding the covers still as I wrapped my arms around Ace. "Congratulations!"

Aidan quickly pulled on a pair of boxers before hugging Ace himself, patting him on the back and engulfing him in a universal bro hug. "I'm happy for you, man."

"I want all the details!" I squealed, practically bouncing at the idea of Ace getting married. To my brother, at that.

"Come meet me in the kitchen, and I'll tell you all about it," Ace said, leaving the room with the brightest smile I had ever seen plastered across his face.

Aidan turned back to me, a lustfulness in his eyes. "Quickie before you go and have girl talk?"

Rolling my eyes, I made my way to the bathroom, walking away from him. I heard him sigh sadly before I dropped the bedsheets and turned to face him. "You coming for a shower?"

A laugh escaped my lips as I ran into the bathroom, Aidan practically sprinting after me.

Half an hour later, I was fully dressed and ready for school. Ace finished Stefano's proposal story up to the point where they went back to Ace's house. He ended it there for both of our sanities. He left not long after, needing to go to the clubhouse.

Carter wandered into the kitchen, hoodie in hand, wearing a grey top and joggers. "Morning, shortass." He grinned at me, which tugged his scar. He then poured himself a bowl of Cheerios.

"Good morning." I smiled, ecstatic at the news I had received this morning. "Leave for school in fifteen?"

Carter nodded before looking behind me and offering a wave, his mouth full of cereal. Feeling large calloused hands on my waist, I tilted my head back to see Aidan looking down at me lovingly.

"I've got to go to work. Will you be alright, beautiful?" he asked, a concerned expression on his face.

"I'll be fine." I smiled up at him. "Carter's taking me, then I'm going home."

Aidan nodded, then leaned down to give me a kiss goodbye. Pulling away, he looked into my eyes with something I couldn't name.

"I'll see you tonight?" Aidan asked Carter, who nodded in reply. Aidan patted him on the shoulder in farewell as well. "Drive safe with her."

Carter and I left for school not long after, arriving at the same time as my brothers. Tommaso ran out of the car towards me, excitement evident on his face. They were here early today, likely to discuss our brother's engagement. "Do you know about Stefano?"

"Yes." The two of us squealed in happiness. Carter was also grinning, having been filled in by me on the way to school.

Tristan approached, a rare public smile on his face. "Ace told you?" he asked, wrapping his arm around my shoulder in a hug.

"Yeah, he came over this morning," I replied, smiling at my brothers.

"I'm glad they're together." Carter smiled, having had a few good interactions with my brothers over the month. They were friendly with each other now. "They're good for each other."

Just as I was about to reply, a loud, overwhelming boom rang through my ears as I was knocked to the ground. It was accompanied by a bright flash. I felt hands shielding my head and a set of arms wrapping around my body.

"Is everyone alright?" Tristan said as my vision started clearing.

Carter held my head to his chest. We were all crouched down as Tommaso's body covered mine. Tristan was shielding Tommaso, arms around both him and Carter as a protective barrier.

"What the fuck happened?" Carter said, standing up and offering me his hand.

Pulling myself up with Carter's help, Tommaso and Tristan stood again. We turned to look past Tristan, who had blocked us all collectively from the blast.

Metal was flung all around, chunks of green scattered across the car park. Fire blazed in the space, hot flames licking the previously cool air.

"Holy shit!" Tommaso murmured.

"My car," Tristan said, astonishment in his voice.

All that was left of Tristan's green Lamborghini was a pile of flaming rubble—and the realisation of what had just happened. Students from the school ran towards the commotion, and I was thankful Tristan had parked far enough away from Carter that we were safe from the blast.

Pulling my phone of out of my pocket, I saw the time: eight-thirty.

The time we usually parked the car. The car we always took to school.

The car we should have been in when that bomb exploded . . .

CHAPTER FORTY-FOUR

KALINA

Darkness consumed me. The only light came from the small crack between the cabinet doors. The cold nipped at my skin, forcing me into a tighter ball to stay as warm as possible. The pipes beside me were icy, pressing against the goosebumps of my arms.

The bottle of bleach beside me and the packet of sponges behind it were the only other things inside the cabinet. Shivers racked my body as the loud banging from the living room echoed through the walls.

The scream of agony and the shouts of anger forced me further into my sanctuary, knowing this was where I was safe. The lock Daniel had installed inside the cabinet door was on, providing extra protection.

A loud bang echoed through the room, telling me something—or someone—was had been likely shot, followed by the thudding sound of impact. Hours passed, but I heard nothing.

Deciding it was safe, I unlocked the cabinet door from under the sink and crawled out. Stumbling on weak legs into the living room, I saw my mother's latest boyfriend dead on the floor, blood seeping from the bullet wound in his head.

Sighing, I went back and grabbed the bleach and sponge, also filling one of the leak buckets with water and cleaning solution. Dragging the bucket back into the living room, I saw my mother passed out on the furthest couch, the needle on the floor as the crack coursed through her system.

I rolled the body up in the large living room rug, taking more time than necessary due to my smaller and weaker frame. When he was fully wrapped, I began cleaning the bloodstain on the hardwood floor.

That was the first body I had ever cleaned up.

And even at the age of nine, I knew it would not be the last.

* * *

All my brothers surrounded the living room. Some were seated on the couches; others stood around the room. Carter was seated beside me on one of the couches, arms resting on his thighs as Matteo spoke in angry Italian down the phone.

"*Voglio le loro teste! Voglio che le loro teste mi portino dopo che li abbiamo picchiati tutto! Hanno attaccato la mia famiglia! Questo significa guerra! Come cazzo hanno fatto a superare i cancelli per piazzare la bomba? Se non trovi il topo, ti scuoierò vivo io stesso!*" *(I want their heads! I want their heads brought to me after we've beaten everything out of them! They attacked my family! This means war! How the fuck did they get past the gates to plant the bomb? If you don't find the rat, I'll skin you alive myself!)*

The front door slammed open.

Antonio, Christopher, Tristan, Stefano, and Carter all stood with their guns raised.

"WHERE THE FUCK ARE THEY?"

The Irish-Italian tone of his voice instantly identified him to everyone, and a moment later, Aidan stormed into the living room. The veins of his neck bulged, his face red with anger as his eyes frantically searched the room.

Once they landed on me, his worried expression visibly relaxed, and he approached me in long strides. Picking me up from the couch, he held me in a tight hug, and I wrapped my arms around him.

"I was so worried." He sighed, placing multiple kisses on the side of my head. He looked down at Carter. "Are you okay?"

I assumed Carter nodded in reply, as neither said anything. Holding me close as he sat down on the couch, Aidan placed me on his lap, his grip on my waist unwavering.

"What the fuck happened?" he asked, finally acknowledging everyone else in the room.

Christopher decided to be the one to answer. "A bomb was planted on Tristan's car."

"Who was it?" Tommaso asked, all playfulness gone from his tone.

Ever since that bomb went off, I had seen the mafia in the soft, cheerful twin of mine. His expression was harsh, his words aggravated.

"We're still searching." Matteo sighed. "Security didn't pick up on anything."

I thought over the ways that the bomb could have been planted on Tristan's car. Enemies breaking into the property, a traitor sneaking it in, someone slipping it on while Tristan was out—there were so many possibilities.

"Tristan, where have you been in the last twenty-four-hours?" I turned to my brother, still in a state of semi-shock and anger.

"I picked up the pizza with Tom last night, then went out to a girl's house, then . . . then I picked up some daggers from the warehouse and came home," Tristan said, recounting his steps from the night before.

I considered his words, trying to figure out what had left him vulnerable. As realisation hit me, it did the same to Stefano.

"What girl?"

"The waitress from the restaurant when we signed the alliance to get rid of Gatwick," Tristan replied. "Her name's Naomi."

"Was there a time when you were with her long enough for someone to plant the bomb?" I pressed.

Tristan thought for a moment and nodded. "She went for a shower. She lives in a bungalow, so she could have climbed out the window."

"Looks like it's time we paid this Naomi a visit," Aidan grumbled, grip tightening on my waist.

* * *

The drive to Naomi's house was silent. I sat in the passenger seat of Aidan's Range Rover, while Tristan, Carter, and Stefano were in the back, pistols resting on their laps.

"That one there," Tristan said, pointing at the bungalow.

Aidan pulled up outside the house. "Stay in the car," he said to me.

I rolled my eyes, then grabbed the pistol from the glove compartment and stepped out.

"Did you really expect her to listen?" Tristan chuckled as he got out behind Carter.

Aidan sighed, stepping out and standing next to me, gun at his side. We headed to the front door with Carter. I gave Aidan a nod, and he kicked it open, and I stormed in first, gun raised. The others followed closely behind, and we cleared the house, meeting back in the living room.

"Start searching for anything that can give us a lead," Aidan ordered, moving to open the drawer by the fireplace.

* * *

AIDAN

Kalina stayed in the room with me, knowing I wanted her close. Since the explosion that morning, the thought of not having her near me sent my mind racing with images of her being injured—or worse, dead.

Today, I truly realised how much I worried about her. I had always known she was my world, but not knowing if she had been hurt in that explosion made me feel like I was drowning. It was as if the world was swallowing me whole, and I had no way of escaping the pits of hell that waited for me.

"This must be her," Kalina commented, holding a photo frame in her hand.

I walked up to her and took the frame, wanting to see what the woman we were searching for looked like.

My breath got caught in my throat at the sight before me. Blonde, waist-length hair, crystal-blue eyes that I would recognise anywhere. She was older than when I last saw her, about nineteen, with a sad smile—nothing like the genuine one I was used to seeing all those years ago.

"Aidan? What's wrong?" Kalina's hand rested on my cheek, worry swirling in her eyes.

"That girl . . . She's not called Naomi," I muttered.

"What are you on about?" Tristan asked.

My eyes landed on Carter, who looked utterly confused, having only seen me tear up like this on three occasions in my life: when the doctors declared our parents dead, when Carter woke up after the fire and broke down at the sight of his new appearance, and when they declared the woman in the picture dead.

"Aidan, what's going on?" Kalina asked more firmly, turning my face back to hers.

"It's Bianca. Our sister."

* * *

KALINA

No one said anything on the car ride back to Christopher's house, silence consuming us all at the information we had just learned.

It's his sister.

For the second time today, my entire family—Aidan and Carter included—sat in the living room. All attention was on the two men beside me. I held Aidan's hand as we waited for him to explain.

"Six months before Spencer Gatwick set fire to our house and killed our parents, our sister Bianca was in a car accident when she was being driven home from school by one of our Irish members," Aidan said. "The car was incinerated, and all that was left of her was a skeleton. She was thirteen."

Christopher leaned forward from his seat. "Are you sure it was your sister?"

Carter nodded. "She looks exactly like my father."

My thumb stroked the back of Aidan's hand as his ran through his hair. "So your sister planted the bomb?"

"She must have." Aidan sighed. "Those types of bombs only have a twelve-hour timer, max, and the security cameras show nothing to indicate it was planted during the night."

It's his sister.

CHAPTER FORTY-FIVE

AIDAN

Matteo had instructed his men to hunt down Bianca but to not harm her. Carter passed on the same order to Alonzo and Ben, my underbosses.

My mind was spinning, unable to comprehend that my little sister was alive. After all these years—after all the grief, after the funeral—she was alive.

Antonio insisted that Carter and I stay at Christopher's house, saying we were in no state of mind to drive home. Despite Antonio's protests, Christopher let me stay in Kalina's room.

Kalina filled the bathtub with semi-hot water while I sat on the edge, holding me in her arms as we waited for it to fill. She didn't say anything. She simply held my head to her chest as she stood between my parted legs.

A short while later, Kalina turned off the taps and removed my T-shirt. Standing up, I let her unbuckle my belt and pull down my work trousers. I climbed into the bath silently. Stripping herself, Kalina sat down beside me, the bathtub curved around us in a circular shape. She ran her hand through my hair as she used her other hand to hold mine on her lap.

"Do you want to talk about it?" she whispered, placing a kiss just below my ear.

Replying at the same volume, I rested my head on her shoulder, sinking further into the water. "I wanted her back. I wanted my little sister. And she's been alive all this time."

With her wet hand still running through my hair, she asked, "What do you want to do when we find her?"

"I want to help her. God knows what happened to her while they faked her death." I sighed, then a thought hit me. "Who the fuck faked her death?"

Kalina sighed, lifting our joined hands to her lips and placing a kiss on mine. "Think about it, baby."

I turned to her, trying to read exactly what she was thinking. It was as if she knew something I didn't.

Bianca was supposedly killed in a car accident so severe that we never had her body properly identified. She had likely been kidnapped, and God only knew what happened to her after that. Who would fake the death of a thirteen-year-old girl? Six months later, my parents were murdered. Our mafia had grown slightly weaker from the grief their deaths caused.

Spencer Gatwick was the one who murdered my parents.

"Gatwick kidnapped her, didn't he?" I sighed, wishing the truth wasn't what I had just realised.

"It's more than likely," she whispered, placing a gentle kiss on my head.

"What the fuck has he done to her?" A wretched sob left my throat, my body curling into the comfort Kalina offered as best she could with her smaller frame.

"You don't want to know." The broken whisper that left her voice told me she wasn't just thinking of Bianca.

* * *

A few weeks later

This was a monumental occasion. Leaders of the two largest mafias in the world and the president of the California charter of the Chained Angels were seated in the same room. The contract lay on the table before us, each party with a copy to read and sign.

"Is there anything anyone wants to change?" Matteo, whose lawyer had drafted the contract, sat at the head of the table.

The contract was for a three-way alliance.

The Italian Montessori mafia agreed to peace with the Irish-Italian mob and the Chained Angels. Each party would aid the other when called upon in times of conflict. The Irish-Italian mob would supply the guns that the Chained Angels would ship to the Montessoris. The Chained Angels would share in the drug profits as they were distributed by both mafias as well. The legal businesses of Montessori Enterprises and O'Farrell Construction would work together—Matteo's side handling design and planning, while my own would manage building and construction. Carter had signed off on my ownership of his father's legal company years ago, having no interest in the legal side of our business.

"I say we're all set." Ace nodded, signing the contract. He then slid it across the table to me.

I signed my copy, then passed it to Ace, and then I also signed Ace's and Matteo's copies, ensuring that every party had a fully executed agreement.

"Agreed."

Matteo was the last to sign. He then stood up and poured a glass of whiskey for each of us. Matteo raised his glass, Ace and I followed suit, clinking our glasses together.

"To peace and partnership," Matteo toasted.

Ace and I nodded, knowing this would be the strongest alliance in decades. After the drinks, we all sat back down, ready to discuss the matter at hand.

"We have a lead on Bianca," Ace said, folding his hands on the table. "The Nevada charter reported a woman of her description heading back up to California."

"So she's back," I concluded, unsure of how I felt about that information. After all, I had believed her dead for years. I had mourned her. But the first thing she did to gain our attention was plant a bomb on the car that Tristan used every day.

And it was the car Kalina took practically every morning, and the bomb went off during the time they usually arrived at school.

Did my sister try to kill my girlfriend?

"Is that all?" Matteo sighed, clearly wishing there was more to go on.

Honestly, I understood his frustration, and he wasn't even bothered about finding Bianca. His little brothers and sister had been targeted and nearly killed. The fear and anger he must have felt when Tristan called him was the same as when Carter called me.

My heart was in my throat. All I could do was stand and listen as I tried to breathe. I would never forget the words he spoke to me: *"Someone planted a bomb on Tristan's car. It blew up. Don't panic. Kalina and I are safe. We're heading to her house."*

"We've got nothing on her." Ace sighed. "Anything from either of your ends?"

"The bomb planted on Tristan's car was military-grade. That's all we know. It's not something you can make in your kitchen," Matteo said. "A chemist must have made it."

I ran my hand along my jaw, stubble creeping through for not having shaved the past few days, my priorities having been on security for Kalina and Carter. "I'll have Ben do some searching. The bomb-making circles of the underworld are predominantly controlled by my mafia. We might be able to find something."

The meeting concluded not long after. The three of us left the Cove Hotel, part of Matteo's legal hotel chain. Ace didn't stick around, getting on his bike and heading straight for the clubhouse.

The sky had turned dark. Spring was just beginning, meaning the sunset still came relatively early. These past few months had been weird, to say the least.

After all, Kalina had spent her first Christmas with her family, then came down to the clubhouse to spend the afternoon with the Chained Angels, Carter, and me. For Christmas, I had booked her a weekend getaway to Australia with me for the summer. And, in return, Kalina gave me a ring with her name engraved on the band—which the possessive part of me loved—and a preview of her lingerie for our trip.

Best Christmas ever.

"What do you want to do when we find Bianca?" Matteo asked, the two of us standing by the revolving doors of the hotel.

"I want my little sister back," I told him, sighing at the thought of everything she had been through.

"It won't be easy," Matteo commented. "Kalina struggles, and she had less than a year with Gatwick."

"I'll do whatever it takes," I replied, determined.

"I understand that it's difficult having a little sister in this industry, even though we've only known Kalina for less than a year. We'll do whatever we can to help you with Bianca."

"I appreciate that, man." I looked at him. "You know, Kalina really does love you guys. I remember when she decided to tell you everything about her childhood, and you know what her biggest fear was?"

Matteo shook his head, so I continued, "She was worried you'd all hate her, but mainly, she was worried you'd be angry with her, Matteo. She lied when you asked if there was anything else when she told you the minimal details. All she wanted was to feel safe."

Matteo smiled softly. "I'd do anything to keep her safe and happy."

Pulling a pack of cigarettes out of my blazer pocket, I lifted one to my lips. "Want a smoke?"

Matteo nodded, reaching for a cigarette from my hand and lifting it to his lips. Looking up to pass him the lighter, a flash caught my attention just past his head.

Shots rang out, lighting up the previously dark sky. Before I could even think about the pure stupidity of my actions, my hand was on Matteo's head, pushing him down to the floor.

I felt the bullets pierce my flesh. A choked cough escaped my lips. The pain that ran through my body didn't compare to anything I had ever experienced.

"Aidan!" The distant voice of Matteo rang through my ears. "Shit, shit, shit, shit!"

My body landed on the floor with a thud, my hands protecting my head from the concrete beneath me. I couldn't move. I was simply just there.

I felt hands pressing down on the wounds of my body.

"Kalina . . ." I managed to cough, a metallic taste coating my lips.

But the pain didn't compare . . .

"Aidan, hold on," Matteo shouted above my head. "Tell that fucking ambulance to hurry up! He's losing too much blood!"

"Kalina . . . I love her," I whispered, my voice growing hoarse.

"I know you do." Matteo's voice cracked. "So you've gotta hold on for her."

"Tell Carter . . ." Blood pooled in my mouth, the ground around me turning cold. "I want her to have it."

"*Aidan*!"

Matteo's voice grew fainter and fainter until all I could hear were my own laboured breaths.

The pain did not compare to the thought that I might never see Kalina again.

That she would never know what I truly wanted.

CHAPTER FORTY-SIX

TOMMASO

Kalina and I had decided to have a *Barbie* movie marathon; the living room was a fortress of blankets and pillows. She had gone to the kitchen to grab a bowl of popcorn for us.

As I paused the start of the first *Barbie* movie, my phone rang. I grabbed it from the front pouch of my hoodie and answered, seeing it was Matteo.

"Tom, Aidan's been shot." Matteo's panicked voice blared through my ears.

"What?" I shot up from the chair and pulled on my shoes. "What the fuck happened?"

"There was a shooter. They hit—Look it's not important. Just get Kalina down here now," Matteo said, sirens wailing in the background.

"Matteo, slow down—"

"There isn't time to slow down," he snapped, then paused and sighed. "We're at St. Marks. Get Kalina here quick. He doesn't . . . The doctors say he has a twenty percent chance at best."

"We're on our way."

I rushed into the kitchen as I hung up the phone. Kalina was standing by the microwave, wearing a pair of shorts and one of Aidan's hoodies, tied up at her hips.

"Kalina." My voice shook as I spoke.

How do I tell someone the love of their life is about to die?

She turned at the sound of my voice, emptiness in her eyes. "Who is dead?"

"What?" Out of everything I expected her to say, that wasn't it.

"In our line of work, everyone is at risk. I've seen that look on people's faces multiple times before, so I know what it means. Who is dead?"

"He's not dead," I replied, seeing the relief wash over her face. "But he . . . ugh . . . The doctors give him a twenty percent chance."

"Who?"

"Aidan."

Kalina nodded, her face blank. Then, a second later, she clutched her chest, hunched over on the counter as she gasped for breath. Large sobs wracked through her body, and, instantly, I wrapped her in my arms.

She collapsed to the floor in my hold, screams of heart-wrenching agony tearing from her lips. Tears gathered in my eyes as I held my twin, the pieces of her broken heart falling on the floor with her. I pressed her head to my chest, trying to keep my breathing steady so she could mimic it, to stop herself from hyperventilating.

I've never seen anyone so broken.

*　　*　　*

KALINA

"Daniel." I sobbed, trying to apply pressure to the wound in his chest.

"Don't cry, piccolo." (little one)

"I should've listened to you when you said he was trouble," I admitted, still trying to stem the bleeding.

Gently—or weakly—Daniel removed my hands from his chest and held them in his. A soft smile touched his face as blood coated his teeth.

"You're worth so much more than you've been given. Never give up. Don't mourn me, Kalina. I'm dying a peaceful death."

I wept at his words but nodded, letting him continue.

"I got to see my baby sister one last time, and I know my little boy will be safe with her."

I watched as the life drained from his eyes as he took his final breath—the brown eyes that had comforted me all my life closing for the last time.

Daniel was the first person I had truly lost, and I thought that pain was something that would kill me. I watched the life drain from the eyes of the man who had kept me safe my entire life.

But this was so much worse.

His hand was warm. That was all I had to tell me he was alive, aside from the steady beep of the heart monitor. His skin was pale, almost translucent, his eyes closed to the world.

I miss those eyes.

The tube down his throat was connected to a ventilator, the machine that breathed for him. His hair was brushed away from his face, stubble growing along his jaw. I chose to let it grow, not allowing the nurses to shave him.

"What happened?" My voice was scratchy and raw.

Matteo was sitting beside me, wearing joggers and a T-shirt—no more indication that he had been soaked in Aidan's blood hours ago.

"A shooter on a motorcycle came up alongside the hotel while we were standing outside. Aidan saw them before I did and shoved me out the way. They shot him seven times."

All I could do was nod in response, not trusting myself to speak.

"Kalina, what—"

"Can you leave me alone with him?" I asked, my eyes still fixed on his body.

I saw Matteo stand up from the corner of my eye. He placed a kiss on top of my head before leaving the room, the door closing with a click.

This was his second day in the ICU, and the doctors said he was stable but still critical. I watched the rise and fall of his chest, trying to remind myself he was still here.

Holding his hand in mine, I rested my head on the bed. Tears flowed freely from my eyes, soaking the sheets beneath me. Since the moment Matteo first told me what had happened, I had him repeat it to me at least three times a day.

I just could not comprehend the fact that Aidan was in a hospital bed. Aidan—the man I love, the mafia boss everyone feared—was only alive because there was a tube down his throat breathing for him.

The lead surgeon came in moments later, an intern following behind him. "Good evening, Mrs Rossi."

I kinda like the sound of that.

"Is he alright?" I asked, fear seeping into my words.

The doctor did a quick examination, then smiled at me. "He's more than alright. Dr Allison, if you could remove the intubation tube."

"Wait. He needs that." I was about to yank her away from the ventilator, but the doctor gently pulled me back.

"Mrs Rossi, this is a good thing." He smiled down at me. "Mr Rossi is breathing over the tube."

"So . . . he's going to be okay?"

"The worst has passed." The doctor smiled at me. "He should still rest for a few weeks, but once he's awake, you should be able to take him home."

I watched as the intern remove the intubation tube from Aidan's throat. He coughed as it was pulled out.

"He should be awake shortly," the doctor told me before they both left the room.

He's going to be okay.

But I'm going to kill the bastard who put him in here.

CHAPTER FORTY-SEVEN

AIDAN

A month later

I tried opening my eyes, but they felt heavy, as if I were lifting my entire body weight with just the muscles of my eyelids. There was a warmth surrounded me, though, and I knew exactly what—or who—it was.

"Ka—" A cough escaped my dry throat. "Kalina."

"Aidan?" I heard the panic in her tone. A small soft hand landed on my aching bicep.

"Kalina," I mumbled, finally prying my eyes open.

The bright light blinded me for a moment, but it was soon blocked by a shadow. As my vision cleared, I saw the beautiful face of Kalina staring down at me. There were tears in her eyes.

"Aidan?" she whispered, her hand stroking the stubble that was slowly forming into a beard.

"Hey, beautiful." I grinned, placing my hand on her cheek and stroking it with my thumb.

"You're alive." Tears began to stream down her cheeks, and I wiped them away.

"What? Did you think I'd leave you?" I joked. I chuckled, but instantly regretted it as a sharp pain racked my chest. I winced.

Kalina leaned over the bed and placed a kiss on my head, tears still running down her face. "I thought I'd lost you."

Despite the pain, I pulled Kalina onto the hospital bed beside me, holding her with my good arm. "You'll never lose me, beautiful."

I held Kalina as she cried, thanking whatever higher power that I had survived this mess so I could spend the rest of my life with my girl.

"Where was I shot?"

"The shooter got you seven times," Kalina said, her head resting on my bicep. "Your left shoulder, one through-and-through your back, your appendix, three in your intestines, and one on your thigh. The one in your thigh hit the femoral artery, which was why the doctors thought you might not make it."

Her voice cracked towards the end, so I placed a kiss on her forehead, smiling down at her. "I did live, and I don't plan on going anywhere."

The two of us lay comfortably on the hospital bed, resting in each other's embrace. I felt the tension gradually leave Kalina's body, all the stress finally dissipating.

Hours passed, and every so often, a nurse would come in to check my blood pressure and wounds. At first, she protested Kalina being on my bed but eventually let her stay.

Either they knew I would snap at them, or Kalina had been a blubbering mess, and they were just relieved to see her calm down.

"Mr Rossi." A man in a lab coat entered the room, sparing a small smile at the sleeping Kalina in my arms. "I'm here to let you know you're being discharged in the morning. I was your surgeon, and I think you're progressing well enough for you to finish your recovery at home."

"Thanks, Doc." I shook his hand. The second I let go, it returned to Kalina's waist.

Just before he left the room, he gave me a knowing look. "You're lucky to have her. Mrs Rossi never left the room while you were here."

Mrs Rossi . . .

* * *

TRISTAN

"Slowly. Slowly. SLOWLY!"

"Kal, if we go any slower, we'll be standing still." I sighed, my sister's voice scraping at my nerves like a chalkboard.

"Ease up, beautiful. They won't break me." Aidan chuckled from his position above me, one arm slung over my shoulder.

"But if they hurt you, I'll kill them," Kalina shot back, her glare the harshest I had ever seen.

"Move before she skins me," I whispered to Aidan, who nodded and began hobbling again.

Aidan refused a wheelchair, mainly because he was too long for it, so I was helping him limp into his house. Tommaso was carrying his hospital bag. Stefano and Ace were already upstairs cooking with Carter's help. Matteo was still hunting down Bianca, while Antonio handled the front with the legal businesses. Christopher would be bringing Lorenzo over later.

Lorenzo had been crying for Kalina and Aidan all night, but we hadn't tol them—not wanting them to feel guilty. Then Aidan told us to bring him after Kalina declared she wasn't leaving him until he could look after himself.

"Use the elevator. It's behind the stairs," Aidan said while limping.

I did as he said and got us both to the second floor. Kalina and Tommaso had taken the stairs and were already making space for Aidan on the sofa. I helped him lower himself down before collapsing next to him.

"You're one heavy fuck, you know that?" I grumbled, wiping the sweat from my forehead.

"Weak bitch," Aidan scoffed, rolling his eyes.

I was about to punch him, but a glance at Kalina, busy in the kitchen helping chop the vegetables with an impressively sharp knife, made me think better of it.

Stefano and Carter made dinner with help from Tommaso and Kalina, who, by some miracle, didn't burn the house down. We had just finished eating when Christopher wandered in, Lorenzo running ahead of him.

"MAMA! AIDAN!" the child yelled, launching himself at Aidan.

Thankfully, Aidan caught him with his good hand, covering his stomach. I could only imagine what it would feel like to have a child land on seven fresh bullet wounds.

"Hey, *piccolo*," Kalina cooed, taking Lorenzo in her arms and sitting him on her lap. *(little one)*

"Aidan? Grandpa said you were hurt." The sadness in the little boy's tone broke my heart.

When the fuck did I become such a softie?

"I was, buddy, but I'm alright now," Aidan said, brushing Lorenzo's curls away from his face.

"I'm spending the night here with you and Mama?" Lorenzo asked, a smile spreading across his face when Kalina nodded in response.

CHAPTER FORTY-EIGHT

STEFANO

They always say the phone call in the middle of the night can't be good news. I lay in bed, Ace curled on my chest, sleeping peacefully.

These past few weeks had been a lot for him—from a bomb nearly killing Kalina to Aidan being shot down in the middle of the street. He nearly lost his two best friends, and in all our time together, I had never seen him so scared.

His hand rested on my chest, the silver of the ring catching the light from my phone screen. I answered the call with a whisper, my spare hand rubbed the same silver band that claimed Ace as mine.

"Stefano, I need you in my office," Matteo said, exhaustion evident in his tone.

He hung up before I could reply, so I slid out bed without waking Ace. Pulling on a pair of boxers, I left the room and began the five-minute walk to Matteo's office.

I walked in without knocking, since he was the one who called me. He was sitting at his desk, looking a mess—white shirt creased, hair disheveled, purple bags under his eyes.

"I know you're out," Matteo began, referencing the mafia. "But I need help, *fratello*." *(brother)*

I sat down in the leather armchair opposite his desk. "What can I do?"

"Ace's guys reported seeing Bianca in a black Toyota in Nevada. I need you to track the license plate from there and find out where she went next. It was over a week ago, but at this point, it's the only lead we have."

I took the laptop from Matteo's desk and rested it on my lap as I began typing. I grabbed the piece of paper with the license plate on it and started tracking.

"So . . . you and Ace."

I lifted my eyes from the computer to glance at Matteo, who was grinning. "What about it?"

"I'm getting a new brother. Why did you hide your relationship from me for so long?" Matteo's tone was hurt, as if he couldn't believe I had kept it a secret from him.

Sighing, I multitasked—tracking Bianca while speaking to my older brother. "I left the mafia, but you're still my brother, the Don. Ace was the enemy—not just for being an Angel, but also for being Aidan's underboss also. I didn't want to jeopardise anything until I knew it was worth my relationship."

"So you didn't trust me?"

"It's not that. I know what the mafia means to you," I told him. "I wasn't going to put you in a situation where you had to choose between the family and me."

"Stefano." Matteo sighed, rubbing his hand along his well-trimmed beard. "There'd be no question about it. You're my little brother, and whoever makes you happy is good enough for me."

A rare smile broke across my face at his words. Most mafia men would have shot me on sight at the news that their member had been fraternizing with the enemy.

But not Matteo.

When Dad stepped down and Matteo took over, he made us all a promise: the Montessori Family (mafia) would come second, and our family would come first.

We saw what the mafia had done to our mother. All the drugs and danger surrounding her drove her away. Her frustration was usually taken out on me. There was the occasional slap or kick that silenced me from telling my father of her affair. There was fear that one day she would hurt me so badly that even if the truth came out, I would still be the one to suffer most, as Dad loved her so much.

But when I finally told him the truth, I realized his sons came first.

Matteo had followed in our father's footsteps, and I was an idiot not to see it sooner.

"I'm sorry I hid my relationship from you," I told him, realizing I had worried over nothing.

"I'm sorry I made you feel like that was your only choice."

The two of us shared a brief hug, something we hadn't had in years. Then we got back to work.

Hours passed in Matteo's office. He was making phone calls from his desk, regularly checking in for updates on tracking Bianca and managing the daily ins and outs. Everyone had been on high alert due to the attacks, so things hadn't been running as smoothly as usual.

I was still typing on the computer when I discovered that Bianca had ditched the Toyota for a black 2017 Ducati that she had stolen outside a nightclub two weeks ago.

"Hey, Matt? What was the shooter driving?" I asked my brother, who had just hung up the phone.

"They were on a bike," Matteo said, rubbing his temple. The exhaustion was obvious on his face, even more now. "A Ducati. 2017 plate, I think."

I sat stunned in my chair, unable to believe what I was hearing. Catching the expression on my face, Matteo immediately stood up. "Stef? What is it?"

"The shooter . . . it was Bianca."

Neither of us said anything, trying to wrap our minds around the fact that the girl we had been tracking was the one who had tried to kill her own brother.

As much as I hated my brothers on occassion, the number of times I had considered shooting them was zero.

Like when Tommaso gave himself a tattoo in my studio without informing me beforehand. I ended up using the tattoo gun on myself and got an infection because the little shit had fleas.

Or when Tristan "borrowed" my Porsche at fifteen and crashed it into a tree.

Or when Antonio walked in on me fucking a girl without realizing it, and stayed talking to me while I repeatedly told him to leave.

But I never thought about killing them.

"Why would she try to kill Aidan?"

Matteo didn't say anything for a moment before realization dawned over his face. "She wasn't aiming for Aidan. He saw the gun and shoved me out of the way, which left him exposed."

"So Bianca was trying to kill you?" I concluded. "First, she put a bomb in Tristan's car, knowing he, Tom, and Kal used it regularly. Then she took a shot at you . . ."

"This girl is trying to kill us," Matteo confirmed, confusion written across his face.

"But . . . why?"

"I don't know, but I want to find out," Matteo declared. "Keep tracking her."

Half an hour later, I discovered she was now driving a white Ford Focus RS. Using both public and private security cameras, I traced the vehicle, hacking into each system.

"She was in Santa Monica this morning, and now she's . . ."

"Where is she?" Matteo raised his voice at my sudden silence.

"Call Kalina," I told him, horror thick in my tone. "You need to call her now."

"What? Why?" Matteo's voice mirrored my own panic.

"Because Bianca is at Aidan's house right now," I said. "And it looks like she has a pistol with her."

CHAPTER FORTY-NINE

KALINA

The silence of the night was beautiful. I could see the stars in the sky from Aidan's bed, the curtains having been left open. Lorenzo had gone to bed hours ago, sleeping in the room next door, delighted that his bed was massive.

Aidan slept peacefully beside me, his long dark lashes resting against his cheeks, his breathing calm and even. The bandages still covered his abdomen and shoulder, the one on his thigh being a simple gauze. I cleaned and changed the dressings before forcing him into bed, to which he had weakly protested.

Feeling hungry, I decided it was only fitting to eat the chocolate bar from the kitchen cabinet because . . . well, I wanted to.

Slipping out of the bed was easy; I only had one of Aidan's arms to manoeuvre past. I had forbidden him from using his left arm for anything, as it was still healing. Pulling on a pair of Aidan's boxers and one of his hoodies, I quietly opened the bedroom door and slipped out.

I wandered into the kitchen, stifling a yawn with my hand as my bare feet touched the wooden floor. Opening the fridge, I thought I saw something in the corner of my eye.

"Carter?" I asked, wondering if I had actually saw him or if it was just my imagination.

When there was no response, I concluded the latter. Grabbing the carton of milk, I filled a glass and retrieved a chocolate bar from the cabinet.

Carrying it to the kitchen island, I quietly ate my midnight snack and drank my milk. It wasn't until I heard the sound of footsteps that I realised it hadn't been my imagination earlier.

Reaching under the kitchen island, I pulled out the pistol I knew Aidan kept there. But before I could turn around, I was slammed headfirst against the counter, sending the glass flying and shattering on the floor.

The person smashed the butt of their gun into my wrist, causing an agonised shout to leave my lips and the pistol to fly from my grip.

"Shut up." A feminine Irish voice, with a lick of Italian, came from behind me. The weight pressing down on me eased slightly. "Turn around."

Doing as she said, I spun on the spot, hands in the air. In front of me stood Bianca, a gun held tightly in her grasp, pointed at my head.

"Bianca," I said, my tone soft. "What are you doing?"

"You ruined it. You ruined everything!" Her icy eyes were empty, her blonde hair slightly matted, and her skin a ghostly pale.

"What are you talking about?" I asked, noting the slight tremor in her hands, which made me all the more wary of the gun.

"Spencer!" she cried. "He loved you."

Please tell me someone heard that glass smash.

"And . . . that ruined things for you?" I clarified in an understanding tone, trying not to provoke her.

"For years, he loved me. He wouldn't let anyone touch me, and he'd punish me if they did! We were perfect!"

Fucking hell! This girl has had her sense and logic beaten out of her.

I'd be sympathetic if she wasn't about to shoot me.

Bitch.

"And I got in the way of that?" I continued, trying to reason with her whilst also plotting my escape.

"Yes!" she screamed. "The second he met you, I was nothing! All he did was fuck me when you weren't around, and when you were, he let his men do it too. I was the most important thing in the world to him, and YOU RUINED IT!"

I've gotta calm this bitch down before Aidan and I have matching bullet wounds.

Aww! Crippled couple goals.

"Bianca, I'm so sorry. I had no idea what you and Spencer had was so . . . special," I told her, taking a hesitant step towards her. "Let me help you fix your love with him."

"YOU CAN'T! YOUR FAMILY RUINED MY LIFE! THEY TOOK HIM FROM ME WHEN HE CAME

LOOKING FOR YOU! WHEN YOU WENT TO PRISON, I HAD HIM BACK! BUT THEN YOUR FAMILY MOVED YOU HERE, AND HE FOLLOWED YOU! HE LEFT ME BEHIND!"

My god! This girl needs some shock therapy.

"Bianca!"

Both our heads snapped to the archway leading to the bedrooms, where Aidan stood in a pair of joggers. "What are you doing, little sister?"

I could see the terror in his eyes. His little sister holding a gun to his girlfriend was not something anyone wants to witness.

"She needs to die, Aidan!" Bianca's tears streamed down her cheeks. "Spencer won't come back to me as long as she's alive!"

For fuck's sake.

"Bianca, Spencer isn't after Kalina anymore," Aidan said in a soothing tone. He stepped forwards, but she cocked the pistol, forcing him to halt.

Now we were all in the kitchen.

"He loves her more than me. I need to kill her so I can have him back!"

Her icy eyes were crazed, dark bags beneath them betraying years without proper sleep. One wrong move and I was dead.

"Bianca, Spencer's gone," Aidan told her, his hand slowly reaching behind him. "He's dead."

A choked sob escaped her mouth as she raked her free hand through her hair, tears streaming down her cheeks.

"Put the gun down, little sister. He's not coming back. He's not after Kalina. He's dead. Don't shoot Kalina, please. Don't shoot the woman I love,"

Aidan pleaded, his tone soothing, as if trying to calm a wild animal.

Bianca lowered the pistol, glancing between Aidan and me.

"She's the reason he's dead."

"Bianca, no!" I shouted as she raised the gun again, aiming at me—but a shot rang out.

The shot, however, was not from her gun.

Confused, I looked around, then zeroed in on her once again. The bloodstain on her chest slowly spread. A choked sob escaped her lips as she fell to her knees. I watched in astonishment as her body collapsed onto the floor.

Looking up, I saw Aidan rushing towards me, wrapping me tightly in his arms. The barrel of the gun in his hand was still warm, the heat from the discharged bullet radiating from it. He dropped the gun to the floor and cupped my head in his hands, pressing a kiss to my lips as he held me close.

He had just shot his sister for me.

"Are you okay, beautiful?" he whispered against my lips, worry flooding the hazel of his eyes.

"Aidan . . ." I managed to say, still in shock at what I had just witnessed. "You shot her."

"I told you," he murmured against my lips. "You're my world, and I'd do anything to keep you safe."

I responded the only way I knew how in that moment. Pressing my lips to his, I kissed him with every ounce of love I could muster. His lips moved against mine, heat searing through the kiss, telling me exactly how much I meant to him.

"SHE HAS TO DIE!"

Bianca suddenly lunged to her feet once more, gun in hand, blood dripping from her mouth. Completely defenceless, Aidan placed his body in front of mine as two shots rang out again.

Her body thumped to the ground, blood pooling from the fresh wounds.

Both Aidan and I turned towards the kitchen island to see the gun that had been torn from my hand earlier now in the grasp of another. We stared, speechless.

Bianca's cold, dying eyes flickered from the ceiling and then to the one who had killed her.

"Mama, was she a bad lady?"

I think it's time for family therapy.

A few moments later, Carter stumbled out of the archway leading to the bedrooms. He took one look at the scene, shook his head, and turned around.

"Nope. I am not drunk enough for this."

CHAPTER FIFTY

KALINA

Six months later

Whenever I pictured myself getting married, I always had a basic layout of the wedding venue. It would be somewhere meaningful to us, somewhere significant. For imagination's sake, I envisioned a beach, with a large gazebo above the seating and the sunset as the backdrop.

The tablecloths would be white with blue lace stitching. The cake would have three tiers. The crystal-blue waves of the ocean would act as the ladder across the white fondant, leading up to those cute little figurines on top.

The figurines would be sixty-nining, but that's not the point.

Either way, for my wedding day, I had a basic layout.

Ace, on the other hand . . .

"I SAID THE GOLDEN CHERNIMO CHAIRS WITH THE WHITE CUSHIONS AND BIG BOWS SHOULD BE AT THE BACK!"

Stefano and I stood silently in the corner of the country club ballroom, the venue for his and Ace's wedding. It was safe to say Ace had been a bit of a bridezilla these past few weeks.

"THAT IS CASHMERE, NOT GOLD! AND DO YOU SEE ANY BOWS? BECAUSE I FUCKING DON'T!"

"Do you see a bathroom? I don't . . ."

No, now is not the time to compare Ace to Eminem's sarcasm.

"It's not too late to run for it, you know?" I said to Stefano, who stood wide-eyed as he looked at his fiancé.

"I'm too scared to move, let alone run," he whispered back to me.

"WHERE THE FUCK ARE MY SPEAKERS?!? HOW AM I SUPPOSED TO DANCE TO ABBA ON MY WEDDING DAY WITHOUT ANY SPEAKERS?!?"

Aidan wandered into the room with his hands in his cargo pockets, a lit cigarette dangling from his lips. "I can hear that drama queen from outside."

"Don't provoke it," I said, not wanting Ace to have any more reason to shout.

"What's going on?" Maddie asked, having just returned from the bathroom to find everything had gone to shit in just five minutes.

With all the drama surrounding Bianca, I hadn't seen my Chained Angels family in over a month. We had had a big family hug when I arrived at the venue with Aidan an hour ago. Ace, on the other hand, scolded everyone for being sidetracked.

Killian and Luke were coordinating with the bartenders; Jamie and Oliver were taking care of the booze and the bar; and the remaining members were unloading furniture—the same furniture Ace was now bitching about.

The same furniture Ace was now bitching about.

"Maddie, go help him before he has a stroke," I said, not wanting to approach that monster again.

Maddie whipped everyone into shape, making sure the delivery guys took back all the incorrect chairs and returned by the end of the morning with the right ones.

"Are you excited to be married to Ace?" Aidan chuckled, nodding his towards that *thing.*

"Yeah, I am." Stefano grinned. "You haven't seen him, have you?"

* * *

Hours later, the country club ballroom was fully set up for Ace's big day—the one he had invited Stefano to partake in.

Now, Aidan and I were in our hotel room at the country club, both of us staying overnight so we could help prepare Mr Bridezilla in the morning.

I was sprawled out on the bed, wearing beige silk booty shorts and a cami top with black lace fringing. Aidan was seated on the sofa, typing away on his laptop.

Since the death of Bianca, he had been surprisingly doing okay. He had been upset for about a day, but that had been it. When I asked him about it, his response had been simple: *"I chose you over her when I shot her. I thought she was dead. My sister died years ago, beautiful."*

"What are you thinking?" I asked, noticing the contemplative look on his face.

Aidan was quiet for a moment before meeting my gaze with a worried expression. "Do you think Enzo is okay? After shooting Bianca."

When I realised it was my little baby who shot Bianca, I felt like throwing up. I never wanted him to see something so violent at such a young age, let alone participate in it. I spoke to him afterwards, telling him he was never to touch a gun again unless I personally gave him one. But his response had melted my heart:

"I didn't want her to hurt you or Aidan."

That night, I held him as he slept and prayed that my baby would never again have to kill someone to protect me. Until he was old enough to decide his place in our world, I would give him the normal childhood that every child deserved.

"I think that he's good," I told Aidan, who nodded in—what looked to be—relief. "You really do love him, don't you?"

Aidan didn't say anything straight away, his weariness returning. "I'm sorry if it makes you uncomfortable, beautiful, but I do."

Laughing softly, I got out of the bed and walked over to him. He moved his laptop aside and pulled me onto his lap instead.

"Baby, I'm happy that you love him."

"Good." Aidan sighed. "Because I know he comes with you. And I wouldn't have it any other way."

I pressed a kiss to Aidan's lips, intending it to be a simple little "I love you" kiss. But as I was about to pull away, he grabbed a fistful of my hair and pulled me back down.

"Aidan," I said against his lips.

"Mmhm. Just like that, beautiful," he groaned, hands falling down to my arse.

"Aidan." I pushed against his chest, and he pouted. "We need to go to sleep. It's gonna be a long day tomorrow."

"But—"

"No buts," I declared, getting off his lap and climbing back into bed.

"They couldn't have fucking eloped," he grumbled, shutting his laptop and climbing onto the bed with me. He pulled me close, my head resting against his chest.

CHAPTER FIFTY-ONE

KALINA

When we were younger, I always thought Ace was relatively calm and collected. He was never the type to overreact or panic. He was quite level-headed.

But Ace wasn't here today; Anthony Vecoli was.

And Anthony Vecoli was a drama queen.

"This tie doesn't match my eyes. Oh my! Holy fuck, the wedding is ruined! How can the tie not match my eyes!"

Breathe . . . Breathe . . .

"Kalina, my life is over!" Ace, rather, Anthony cried as he dramatically collapsed into my arms.

Breathe . . . Don't take Ace's ability to do it either . . .

"Ace, the lighting is different in here compared to the boutique," I said, soothingly running my fingers through his hair as his head lay on my lap.

"How is the lighting different, Kalina?" he snapped. "I bought the bulbs specially to replicate the boutique."

Stefano loves him . . . Stefano loves him.

"Ace, the curtains are closed." I sighed, shuffling from beneath him and opening the floor-to-ceiling curtains, revealing the bright morning sun.

"Oh." Ace breathed, standing back in front of the mirror with the tie next to his face. "Oh, thank the lord! Crisis averted, people! GET BACK INTO ACTION."

Aidan was manspreading on the sofa, beer in hand, giving a deadpan expression towards Ace. His tie was undone, as were the top two buttons of his shirt. Whilst he was one of the groomsmen, he made no effort to help.

However, as a bridesmaid myself, I had calmed Ace through two panic attacks, made him sit down in the middle of a fit of rage, and wiped his eyes as he cried. All that, and it was just morning.

May I point out it's just 09:30.

The wedding planner, Patricia, who Ace had been coordinating with for the past six months, was in full swing. She was a short, plump woman with grey hair cut into a bob. She had a headset on as she scurried out of the room, clearly used to dealing with overdramatic brides as part of her job.

"Ace!" I shouted as he kept holding his tie up to his face. "Go and get your suit on."

"Oh, my suit!" Ace started, realising he was still wearing his Alien from *Toy Story* onesie. The little alien antenna wobbled as he ran inside the dressing area of his part of the wedding suite.

I turned back to Aidan to saw a sight that melted my heart. Lorenzo was sitting on his leg, having his little navy tie done by Aidan. The love in Aidan's eyes as he looked down at the little boy made me realise that, no matter what, Lorenzo would have someone like Aidan.

Feeling my eyes on him, Aidan looked up over Lorenzo's head, a grin on his face.

Lorenzo turned around, smiling brightly at me and pointing at his tie. "Mama, I look like Aidan!"

A laugh left my lips as I saw show proud he seemed to be, looking like someone he admired.

Ace, having returned for help fastening his cufflinks, stood beside me, a knowing smile on his face.

Leaning into my ear, he whispered, "I call godfather for when you two have kids."

Patricia ran through the doors of the room, the classic "no wedding planner's schedule goes to plan" expression on her face. "They forgot the ribbons for the vases!"

"Nooo!" Ace sank to the floor, horror stricken.

"Oh, for fuck's sake," Aidan grumbled, rolling his eyes.

"Fuck's sake," Lorenzo copied in his little voice.

Aidan stared wide-eyed at me, fearful of the murderous glare on my face. Quickly, he grabbed Lorenzo in his arms and held him against him as a shield.

"Enzo, we don't say that word," I said, crouching down in front of my child.

"But Aidan said it." Lorenzo pouted, wanting to know why he was in trouble.

"And Aidan is in trouble," I said softly, though my eyes were shooting bullets at him. In response, Aidan gave me a sheepish smile.

Walking around the back of the sofa, my manicured hands grabbed Aidan by the jaw, tilting his head back. From this angle, he could see a considerable amount of cleavage from my robe, causing his eyes to drop to it. He instantly became lust-filled, a smirk on his lips.

"No sex for you tonight."

I laughed as the smirk fell from his face, replaced by disappointment. Straightening up, I went behind the curtain in Ace's room, where Patricia stood waiting with my dress. It seemed she and Ace had solved the vase-ribbons catastrophe while I wasn't paying attention. Ace was now adjusting his cufflinks, his suit a specially made grey Gucci with the Chained Angels logo on the back.

Stefano wanted Ace to wear his cut for the wedding, but Ace refused, even though all members tended to get married in it. This was the compromise. Stefano whispered something into Ace's ear, causing him to blush.

I'd rather be sold again than hear what Stefano said.

I took the dress from Patricia and went behind the curtain again. Ace had gone with a blue theme for the wedding, in varying shades, and Stefano agreed—what Ace wanted, Ace got.

The dress was a halter-neck baby blue. The neck was connected with a silver ring, with a band around the waist of the same colour. The dress was tight at the waist but flowed beneath the band, ending around my feet. I slipped into my silver Louis Vuitton heels, adding another five inches to my height.

My hair and makeup had already been done by me, after I refused to let Stefano hire a makeup artist for just me when it was not my wedding day. My dark brown hair flowed in big curls, perfect for a slight touch of concealer, mascara, and eyeliner on my face.

I emerged from behind the curtain to the shocked faces of Aidan, Ace, and Lorenzo. Ace and Lorenzo looked at me in awe. Aidan . . . well, he looked at me as if I were the only person in the room.

"You look beautiful."

"That's my line," Aidan grumbled to Lorenzo, who only smiled in response.

Leaning down, I placed a kiss on Lorenzo's head, who pressed his own kiss to my cheek. Aidan wrapped his arm around my waist, the simple act meaning more than words could ever convey.

I was his.

"Are you ready to get married?" I asked Ace, now dressed in his grey suit with the navy tie.

"I've been ready for over a year. I was just waiting for a ring," Ace joked.

Where the fuck has bridezilla gone???

Leaning down, Ace gave Lorenzo the rings, secured on a baby-blue velvet cushion. Ruffling Lorenzo's hair as he always did, Ace stood upright and turned to face Aidan and me.

"Come on. I'd like to get married before another catastrophe strikes."

"Having a Pegasus ice sculpture instead of a unicorn ice sculpture is not a catastrophe," Aidan said, ignoring the glare he received in return.

We stood at the altar. Aidan was beside me. My brothers were on the other side, all of us facing the aisle and the people who had come to witness the union.

Holding inked hands, Stefano and Ace walked down the aisle together. Smiles lit their faces as they walked past the rows and rows of guests. The side closest to me held Angels. Teddy and Maddie were seated beside each other. Carter, Killian, Luke, and Jamie occupied one row. Behind them were members from the L.A. charter, as well as the those from Manchester. Members of the mafia were seated on the other side, along with other people I recognised from Stefano's tattoo shop. Christopher was in the seat closest to the altar. He wrapped both men in a hug before moving out of their way.

The officiant carried out the service beautifully. Ace and Stefano recited their vows to each other, love radiating through every word.

The entire time, Aidan held my hand in his from behind, giving it the occasional squeeze. Everyone was captivated as Lorenzo presented the rings.

As I stood watching two people I loved get married, all I could think was . . . *I want this.*

CHAPTER FIFTY-TWO

KALINA

Ace demanded that ABBA be blasted throughout the ballroom. He and Stefano danced away, the latter looking distinctly uncomfortable. I watched as my families celebrated together, something I never thought I would see. Keeping an eye on Lorenzo, who was being entertained by Carter and Maxim with the balloons, I stood with Aidan at the bar.

His arm was wrapped around my waist, a glass of champagne in his hand. I admired the way his hair was slicked back from his face. His tattoos crawled up his neck towards his freshly shaved jaw. Aidan's eyes met mine before he glanced to the side, narrowing them significantly.

"Endrizzi," he stated, no welcome in his tone or his face.

Following his gaze, I saw Aidan glaring at an approaching man. He was tall, with a lean but muscular build, eyes a pale blue, and hair an inky black. His suit was a navy Tom Ford, his shoes an Italian black leather. Yet he seemed even younger than me—seventeen at the most. There was an aura of cheek and mischief surrounding him.

"Rossi, how nice to see you," the man, Endrizzi, said upon approach, offering me a dazzling white smile. "I don't believe we have met. I am Domenico Endrizzi."

He reached for my hand, which I hesitantly allowed him to kiss. Aidan's grip on my waist tightened significantly.

"Kalina."

"Kalina . . ." Domenico pressed for a last name, and I hesitated.

Legal or biological?

"Kalina Ross," Aidan supplied, glaring daggers at Domenico.

"Oh, so you're this sister I've heard so much about," Domenico concluded, an intrigued smile on his face.

"And yet I've heard nothing about you," I said, leaning into Aidan's hold to a noticeable point.

Domenico chuckled as his hand slid into his pocket while the other reached behind me for the glass of whiskey on the bar. "I am heir to the Endrizzi Family, an ally of your brother. I'm here representing the family for Stefano's wedding."

Baby mob boss then.

Feeling the anger radiating from Aidan grow, I decided to get rid of this baby mobster. "Well, in that case, Stefano is over there."

Getting the idea, Domenico gave me another one of his charming smiles and walked away. I felt the tension disappear from the man whose arms I was enveloped in.

Standing in front of Aidan, I placed a manicured hand on his face to drag his attention fully to myself. Those mesmerising emerald eyes met my own, protectiveness evident in his gaze.

"Why do you hate him?"

There was no question of Aidan's feelings on the man I had just met, but there was the question of why. I was not naïve. I knew Aidan had many enemies. Everyone in this line of business does. After all, it was a miracle a war didn't break out with my connection to Aidan, Ace, and Stefano.

Matteo and Christopher be slaying . . .

"His family is at war with a prominent mob family in Ireland. We're all connected, themselves and my mafia, but the war is predominately with them. However, the tension between my mafia and his father's still runs thick. My cousin, Daniella, has lost most of her family due to the war."

If there was one thing I had learned in this world, it was that war was inevitable. There was a constant battle for power and control, whether it be for something as meaningful as drugs or as petty as a poker game gone wrong.

And everyone took a side when there was conflict, which would cause the need for alliances. The fact that Aidan's cousin had lost the majority of her family—Aidan's family—from the war makes me believe this will be a long and difficult experience for both sides.

"I have no place in the war." Aidan confirmed when he saw the apprehension on my face. "It's mainly the IRA and the Irish Family who are against the Endrizzi family. The Rossi Family doesn't participate."

I sighed in relief at that news, knowing that we weren't about to deal with a whole other problem. Because, to be perfectly honest, until I get a well-deserved sleep and holiday, I was not doing anything.

"Enough war talk," Aidan declared, placing a kiss on my lips. "May I have this dance, Mrs Rossi?"

"You are aware we're not married, right?" I said, taking his hand nonetheless.

"Yet."

Nah. This man is not teasing me like that.

CHAPTER FIFTY-THREE

I really need to get my own place.

After working a double shift at the store yesterday, I conked out the second I got home.

Grumbling, I raised my face from the mattress to see my door rattling from the pounding coming from the other side.

Rolling out of the bed, I stumbled to the door, unlocking and opening it to reveal Tommaso, who was standing with a bright smile on his eager face.

"No."

"What?" His smile dropped into a confused expression.

"Whatever you want, whatever it is, it can wait," I told him, checking the time on my phone. 6:23. "It can wait another three hours."

"No, it cannot," Tommaso declared, walking past me and into my bedroom, headed straight for the wardrobe. "Today, we are having a spa day," he said with jazz hands.

Yk that friend who isn't gay but everyone believes they are . . .

Ladies and gentlemen, Tommaso Montessori.

"You're paying," I told him, taking the beige sweatshirt and joggers from his hand.

"Well yeah. You're broke cause you refuse money from everyone now that you have a job." Tommaso rolled his eyes, but I saw the proud glint in them. "Plus, I invited you, so it's customary that I pay."

I kicked Tommaso back into the bedroom while I went into the en-suite, closing the door behind me and turning on the shower. Throwing my hair up into a bun, I had a quick shower before getting dressed. Leaving my hair to flow in its natural thick curls, I pulled on the beige sweats.

Tommaso was waiting on the edge of my bed when I returned, eating some of the M&Ms that were on the bedside table. "Took your time."

"Sorry, Tommy but some people value hygiene." I smirked, knowing those M&Ms had been sitting in Carter's gym bag for two months.

Spilled out the packet.

"Whatever." He rolled his eyes. "Let's go."

Tommaso drove us to the beachside spa in his Lamborghini, blasting white girl music the entire way. Now, we were getting a foot massage and our nails done.

"What colour are you thinking?" the nail technician asked as she painted the base of the acrylics.

"Green."

Glaring at Tommaso for answering for me, he gave me a sheepish grin. "Why green?"

"Because . . ." He paused for a moment. "Aidan's eyes are green."

Suspicious . . . but true

I looked back to the waiting nail tech, who had a knowing smirk on her face. "Forrest green with a touch of emerald."

"Imagine being so in love." Tommaso chuckled as a face mask was being smothered on his face.

"Imagine being so lonely, your standing date is your right hand," I countered.

Green's my favourite colour anyway.

At the end of the day, Tommaso and I had underwent full-body massages, mani-pedis, facials, and hot stone massages, and we were granted full access to the swimming pool, hot tub, sauna, and steam room.

I lay on the sofa of Aidan's living room, unable to move. When Tommaso pulled up to his house, Aidan carried me inside from the car.

The smell of seasoned steak fluttered in from the kitchen, where he was now making our dinner. Carter was seated at the other end of the sofa, beer in hand as he munched away on a packet of crisps.

"Are you all packed?" he asked, nodding to the suitcase in the corner of the room.

Aidan and I were taking our trip to Australia tomorrow; hence the dinner at three o'clock. I had packed my suitcase yesterday before work and made sure to adhere to Aidan's checklist: green, bikinis, and lace.

"Yeah, but I'm dreading the flight," I replied. "A seventeen-hour journey is hell."

"But it's seventeen hours with me." Aidan pouted, appearing from the kitchen with two plates of steaks and salad.

"Yay." I took the plate from his hand, grinning as his pout deepened at my sarcasm.

"You'll love it, Kal," Carter told me, smiling at the two of us. "After all, you can always drown him in the sea."

"Why didn't I let you burn to death?" Aidan sighed, glaring at his little brother.

"Because I'm that amazing." Carter laughed. "And, plus, you know I'd haunt you if you let me die."

"So, basically, what you're doing to me now?"

* * *

AIDAN

Mario drove in the dead of the early morning, the streets practically empty. Ben, my Irish mafia underboss was seated on the other side of the limousine, eating a strawberry lace. Alonzo, the Italian underboss was beside him, a stoic expression on his face as he sat with folded arms.

"The shipment of drugs is on its way from Colombia," Alonzo confirmed.

"And our guys are waiting in Florence to have them shipped back to Ireland. The Kings have paid for their cut in advance and are expecting their shipment in two weeks," Ben added.

The Kings are the leaders of the IRA and use drugs and guns to fund their operations. We supply the majority of their drugs, and they do the same for our weapons and The Family, Ireland's main mafia in the country.

Kalina was asleep on my lap. On my first attempt at waking her up, I had her sit up on the bed, but the second I turned around to grab her coffee, she was back to lying down again.

"Make sure the Angels pick up their part of the shipment when the truck passes through Germany," I reminded Alonzo, who nodded in acknowledgment.

Forever the silent one.

"Don, siamo qui," Mario said from the front seat. *(Don, we are here.)*

A moment later, he entered the hangar, the jet ready and waiting to fly to the Gold Coast. Ben and Alonzo were out of the limousine first, grabbing our luggage from the boot. Placing one hand on the back of her head and the other under her ass, I lifted Kalina from the car. The cold air nipped at my exposed skin, causing me to hold Kalina's body closer to me.

I knew I should've put more layers on her.

I yanked the unzipped parka tighter around her body, also checking that the bottoms of her joggers hadn't rolled up past her ankles and fluffy socks.

"Isn't the parka a bit overboard?" Alonzo questioned, raising an eyebrow.

Omfg. His face moves.

"Fuck off," I retorted, goosebumps forming on my arms as my T-shirt clung to my bicep.

"Leave him Al. He's pussy-whipped." Ben chuckled, ignoring the harsh glare I was sending him.

I didn't pay attention to the idiots I called my friends as I carried Kalina onto the jet and placed her down in one of the leather seats, gently tucking a blanket around her. She snuggled into the cushion without making a sound, the fur of the parka hood covering her face.

Ben and Alonzo were handing the luggage to the flight attendant, who was putting the suitcases away in storage. The two of them turned to me, Alonzo emotionless and Ben grinning like a madman.

"Good luck," Ben said, opening his arms for a hug.

Reluctantly, I returned it. Alonzo and I simply nodded at one another. The man couldn't handle humans like an ordinary person.

"I don't need luck."

It was ten o'clock, L.A. time, when Kalina finally woke up, and we were nine hours into our seventeen-hour flight. I was making a glass of whiskey at the bar when she began stirring in her seat, the blanket having already been thrown on the floor in her sleep.

"A parka? Really, Aidan?" Kalina deadpanned once she gained awareness of her surroundings.

"It was cold outside when we left," I replied, pouring her vodka with coke. "I don't want you to get ill, beautiful."

"As much as I appreciate that," —she smiled at me as she unzipped the coat, "—a parka is still a bit excessive."

She removed the coat, revealing the silk pyjama top she still had on from last night. When I got Kalina ready to leave, I just pulled clothes over what she was already wearing. I considered changing her completely, but I didn't want to trigger anything for her while she was sleeping.

"I've left you some clothes over there." I nodded to the table at the other side of the jet, just before the bathroom.

Offering me a quick thank you, Kalina grabbed the clothes and started stripping. I couldn't tear my eyes away from her smooth tan skin, watching as she glided the lace thong up her thick thighs. As she was changing her bra, the door to the kitchen opened near the cockpit.

"Mr Rossi—"

"VATTENE DAL CAZZO!" I angled my body to block Kalina from the flight attendant's view, doing everything I could to not throw the glass in my hand at him. *(Get the fuck out!)*

The boy ran away at lightning speed, spilling the plate of food all over himself.

"Aidan, it wasn't his fault he saw me." Kalina sighed, still standing in her pink lace underwear.

"I don't care. He should know better," I grumbled, walking to her and passing the vodka coke to her.

Yes, it's a communal space but I don't care.

"Thank you." She smiled, taking the glass and placing a kiss on my cheek. "How far away are we?"

"Eight hours," I answered, placing my hands on her waist, one of my thumbs rubbing against her perfect skin.

"That's a long time." Kalina laced her arms around my neck, tilting her head to look up at me. "What should we do?"

"I'm sure we can find something." I placed a kiss on the jagged skin of her collarbone, where the faded scar rested.

The skin may not be soft and smooth there, but it was perfect nonetheless.

Her hands pulled down the waistband of my sweats as my own lifted her off the floor. I sat on the closest seat and placed her on my lap.

"What if someone walks in?" Kalina moaned into my ear as I ran kisses along her neck, my hand pushing her underwear to the side.

"Then they're gonna get a hell of a show."

And their eyeballs for popcorn.

CHAPTER FIFTY-FOUR

KALINA

We landed in the Gold Coast in the evening. The pilot managed to land despite the shaking in his hands. After Aidan and I fucked in the majority of the spaces in his jet, we lay on the sofa completely naked.

That was when the pilot made his way in from the cockpit to inform us that we would be landing shortly. The flight attendant was still traumatised for sure. Aidan grabbed the nearest blanket and threw it over me, not bothering to cover himself.

Which I think is also another reason for the pilot's fear.

He proceeded to verbally attack the man until I grabbed his hand and told the pilot to return to the cockpit.

Now, Aidan and I were lying on the beach. I demanded we spend at least one day away from the private beach Aidan owned.

I was wearing a red bikini; Aidan in a matching pair of swimming trunks. One of the terms of our beach area compromise was that I couldn't tan topless on the public beach, so now I was building a sandcastle while wearing my red bikini.

"Here you go, beautiful." Aidan placed another bucket of water beside me, having just fetched it so I can fill my moat.

I gave him a quick kiss in thanks and went back to engraving the designs of the castle towers.

"You know, you're really not helping the nonce allegations." Aidan sighed as he lay on his beach towel.

A laugh escaped my lips, not expecting that to come from his mouth. Turning, I couldn't help but admire the sight of my boyfriend. His tanned skin glistened with water droplets, which fell into the groove of his abs. His brown hair remained dry and fluffy, making me want to run my hands through it. He had his arms behind his head as he watched me, causing the biceps to bulge.

"You're a criminal. It can't be the worst allegation against you."

I filled the moat of my sandcastle while he laughed, watching as the water slowly stopped sinking into the sand and actually formed a puddle.

"Our dinner reservation is at seven." Aidan had moved to sit beside me, brushing a strand of hair away from my face. "I was thinking we could go for a drink on our beach afterwards?"

"And what time is it now?" I asked, carving the grooves of the roof tiles.

"Four o'clock," Aidan said after checking his Rolex.

Why he was wearing a Rolex at the beach, I'll never understand.

"FOUR!? You're just giving me three hours to get ready!" I shouted, wiping my hands of sand.

"Is that not enough?"

"Aidan! Look at my hair," I said, springing up from the ground and packing our beach bag.

"It's gorgeous." The skepticism in his tone said he didn't know what he was supposed to say at the moment.

"It's curly! And in this humidity, I need at least an hour-and-a-half to tame it!" I flung everything into the bag in record time and started my journey to the black pickup truck. "Let's go!"

Aidan laughed behind me but followed nonetheless. I took the keys out of the bag and got into the driver's seat. Aidan beat me to it, however. "Sorry, beautiful, but you're not driving."

"And why not?" I snapped, not wanting to be flung into the stereotype of women being terrible drivers.

"Because you're a passenger princess." Aidan smiled, lowering his voice once I turned. "And I'd like to return home in one piece."

"I am a safe driver!" I argued, getting in the passenger seat.

Aidan turned to me, a soft smile on his face. He kissed my lips before answering, "Good? Yes. Safe? Not a chance in hell would I associate that word with your driving."

"And what makes my driving so unsafe?" I demanded.

"You drive at least thirty over the speed limit," Aidan deadpanned. "And that's on country roads."

Grumbling, I turned my knees to the door. "I don't see your point."

* * *

I locked Aidan out of the master bathroom when we returned to the beach house, not needing him to distract me while I tried to tame my mop of curls. Once my hair was washed, I meticulously went through my curly hair routine, not allowing the humidity to win this war.

By some miracle, it only took a grand total of one hundred and twelve minutes to get the curls into beautiful thick ringlets. With that, I decided to let Aidan into the room.

"You can come in now," I called as I opened the bathroom door.

"Finally." Aidan groaned as he marched through, instantly wrapping his arms around me from behind. "I've missed you," he muttered into my neck before placing a kiss there.

"Simp." I laughed as I ran my fingers through his hair.

"Only for you." He grinned.

"Proving my point." I laughed as we stood in front of the mirror.

His face was shielded by his hair, which tickled my jaw as he kept his face in my neck. His giant hands rested on my hips, the bathrobe showing the narrowness of my waist and a generous amount of cleavage.

It's giving power couple.

"You know, we still have an hour," Aidan proposed, his hands rising towards my chest.

"Later," I told him. "I didn't spend an hour-and-a-half on my hair just for you to ruin it while we fuck."

He placed a kiss on the top of my head, one of his hands caressing the curls. "You look amazing."

"I'm in a bathrobe." The chuckle that escaped my lips was silenced by him placing another kiss on my head.

"Go put on that dress you've been raving about then," Aidan said. "Because while I think this bathrobe is enough to make you the most beautiful woman in the world, the restaurant has a black-tie policy."

Aidan waited by the sink while I went to the door, which held my dress. It had a scoop neckline with a strapless corset. It was a soft emerald green. The rest of the dress was forest silk that ended by the knees at the front and was floor-length at the back. I paired it with black strappy heels.

I felt Aidan's eyes on me as I changed. "Can you tie me up?" When I felt the smirk on his face from across the room, I continued, "The corset, you dirty bastard."

Chuckling, Aidan grabbed the corset strings and tightened them, tying them off so I could still breathe whilst also being secure.

Aidan's hands on my waist prevented me from turning around. "One second."

It wasn't until I felt the coldness of the chain around my neck did I realise he was putting a necklace on me. It was a Tiffany chain with a small heart pendant.

"Now you're ready."

I turned to face him, seeing that he must have changed clothes when I did. Aidan had brushed his hair away from his face, and his charcoal suit was paired with a black dress shirt and a dark green tie.

Guess green is the theme of the week.

"You look handsome."

"I know."

CHAPTER FIFTY-FIVE

Aidan drove us to the restaurant, having hired no drivers for our holiday. Shamelessly, I admired him the entire drive. He ditched his blazer the second we got to the car, rolling the sleeves of his dark shirt to reveal his tatted arms.

The restaurant was on a cliff just outside the city centre, overlooking the beach and the water below. There were fairy lights lining the soft blue carpet over the marble tiles to the front door. Through the white-paneled double doors was the maître d', who was dressed in a crisp white suit.

"Mr Rossi, your table is right this way."

Aidan didn't even have to introduce himself before we were guided to the balcony, where numerous other couples were seated at their tables. As we walked past, I scanned the food, deciding what I wanted to eat.

There was a waiter already by our table, and he pulled out the chair for me to sit on. Before I could even get to the chair, Aidan had silently made the waiter move.

"Here's your menus." The waiter placed a leather-covered booklet in front of us, offering a polite smile.

"I'll have whatever that is." I nodded at the woman's dish on the table next to us.

The waiter looked taken aback, unsure of what to say.

"And a glass of red," I added.

"So that's the truffle roasted duck." The waiter wrote on his notepad. "And for you, sir?"

"The steak, with extra chili flakes." Aidan didn't even open his menu, his eyes never leaving me. "And the 1984 Old Forester whiskey."

The waiter gave us a smile before collecting our menus and heading back inside the restaurant. I took in the scenery, loving the sound of lapping water.

For years, I was scared of the water, and I still am. Memories of the water filling my lungs, of me drowning, were horrific. I didn't plan on going in the water while we were here, but as I sat opposite the man I loved, I had never felt safer.

"I want to go in the water."

Aidan, whose gaze hadn't left me, offered a smile. He knew of my fears but didn't comment on them. "We can go down later tonight?"

"But I need you to do it with me," I added, feeling the sweat of anxiety beading from my chest at the thought of entering the water alone.

Aidan was all the security I needed.

"Always."

Fuck America.

I never want to return to a country where I was not a fifteen-minute drive away from this exquisite restaurant. The duck was cooked to such a degree that it melted on my tongue. All the spices combined to form a mouthwatering mixture.

"We need to leave," I told Aidan, feeling the corset hindering my exhales.

"What?" Aidan's eyes immediately searched the area around us, his steak knife tightly in his grasp. "What do you see?"

Forgot Mr Mafia has, like, a million enemies . . . Oops.

"I envision my dress bursting if I don't get out of it anytime soon."

Laughing, Aidan called the waiter over for the bill, which he swiftly paid. Waddling outside the restaurant, Aidan had his hand on my waist as he guided me to the truck.

The second I was in the passenger seat, I reached for the strings of my corset and pulled them loose. Sighing, I felt the strings loosen, making my bloated stomach move properly as I breathed. "That's better."

"Do you want to change before we go to the beach?" Aidan asked.

By the tone of his voice, I could tell that was not what he wanted.

"No but I'm taking my heels off," I said, reaching down to undo the straps.

"I'll carry you to the sand." Aidan grinned as he took a glance at me and putting his attention back on the road a second later.

"You just want an excuse to touch me." I laughed, throwing my heels into the backseat.

"Are you complaining?" Aidan countered, a cheeky smirk on his face.

I chose not to reply.

CHAPTER FIFTY-SIX

Drowning was one of the more peaceful ways to die.

Is it? Fuck.

The inability to breathe. Having to accept what one fought so hard to prevent. The forceful way something consumes your entire being. The momentary relief before the impending doom.

"Do you think we'll ever have a normal life?"

Aidan's question stunned me to a stop, the sand sinking its way through my toes as my weight bore down on it.

"I mean, a life where we're not constantly looking over our shoulders. A life where we don't have to deal with guns and drugs and mafia wars."

Looking at him, I stared into those emerald eyes that held so much love and protection for me. "Is that what you want?"

Aidan raised our joined hands to his lips, placing a kiss on the back of mine. "Sometimes, I feel like you've been sucked into a life you never asked for."

"And what about you?" I pressed, my other hand rising up to his face, feeling the fresh stubble beneath my palm.

He sighed, looking up at the sky before meeting my gaze. "It's all so much . . ." Aidan paused for a moment. "But it's not something I think I could give up unless . . ."

"Unless?" My thumb rubbed his cheek, giving him a soft smile.

"Unless you want out."

My breathing momentarily froze before a soft smile broke out on my face. "You'd leave the life for me even though it's the only life you know and I am the only reason for you to depart it?"

Aidan didn't say anything, simply leaned down and placed a kiss on my forehead. "Don't you know it yet, beautiful? I'd give up everything for you—my money, my work, my mafia. I'd destroy anyone who ever laid a hand on you. One word and I'd have my men bursting into all the houses of Manchester to kill every single one of those bastards just so you could feel safe."

What did I do to deserve such a man?

"Aidan, I don't need any of that to feel safe." My voice was little more than a whisper. "You're all I need."

Leaning up, I pulled Aidan down into a kiss. His lips moulded against my own perfectly, searing heat developing as his hands worked their way into my curls and on the curve of my waist. My own were on his chest and the back of his neck, Aidan being the only thing grounding me to the world.

Eventually, I had to pull away, taking in much-needed air. Aidan brushed one of my stray curls out my face, a content smile on his own.

"If you feel it's so much, why don't we make a plan?" I offered, one of my hands running through his thick brown hair in a ghost of a touch.

"Anything you want, beautiful."

"Every year, we take two weeks," I said. "Two weeks where we go away and have a normal, domestic life."

Aidan's smile grew so large, I thought his face would split in half. He wrapped his solid arms around me in a tight hug, placing a kiss on my cheek. "That's perfect, beautiful."

Not long after our agreement, Aidan and I continued our walk across the beach. We were around the corner from Aidan's house, the edge of a cliff blocking our view.

We just walked quietly, hand in hand. It wasn't until we passed the cliff did my eyes widen and my heart beat a hundred times faster.

Candles lined the beach in a walkway that led to the porch. A six-foot heart made of green flowers was standing where the candles ended, the water serving as a background.

"What the fuck?"

"Not the reaction I was expecting, but I'll take it." Aidan laughed, guiding me down the walkway of candles.

Gobsmacked, I walked with him, my eyes taking in the beauty and love around us. We stopped at the heart, and that was when it hit me.

"Kalina, I don't even know where to begin."

Omg, omg, omg, omg, omg, omg.

"From the moment I laid my eyes on you, I knew you were the most beautiful girl I've ever seen."

Why does he have to do this when I need to shit?!?!

"When you stared up at me, it was like my heart was pounding its way out of my chest so it could be closer to you. But then you opened your mouth—"

I couldn't help but laugh at the change from loving tone to faux monotone.

"And I realised it wasn't just your appearance that was beautiful, but your personality as well. The fierceness of your attitude, the kindness you showered over those you cared for, and how could I forget your sarcasm." He playfully rolled his eyes. "I thought I was falling hard when I got to know you. And then we got Enzo back, and, in that moment, when you had him back, I knew you were perfect."

A tear slipped from my eyes, which he was quick to wipe away with the pad of his thumb.

"Despite everything, you turned into such an amazing, kind, loving, and beautiful human being. The fact that I've been able to call you mine has been my greatest achievement in life. But I want to permanently call you mine."

Aidan reached into his back pocket and sank down on one knee. He extended his arm to reveal the most stunning ring I had ever seen. It was silver with diamonds decorating the band. In the centre, there was an almond-shaped emerald with a touch of forest green in the centre.

He got a ring to look like his eyes.

"Kalina, will you marry—"

Aidan didn't get the chance to reply before I was jumping into his arms. "YES!"

His laughter boomed in my ear, and he wrapped one of his arms underneath my bottom to hold me up as I wrapped my legs around his torso. I leaned back in his hold and let him slip the ring on my finger.

"I love you so much."

"I know." Aidan rolled his eyes before bringing me back down for another passion-filled kiss.

I had spent a lot of time feeling like I was drowning in my life. But after so many years, I was drowning once again.

Drowning in the realisation that love has healed all the scars I had without even realising it.

* * *

AIDAN

The heart was right next to me. I rested one arm on it as I waited for Kalina. The smile hadn't fallen from my face since the moment she said yes.

For months, I had been planning this proposal, and I had prepped it to the last detail. I even had someone I trusted light the candles.

"I'm happy for you."

Glancing to my side, I saw Stefano, his arms folded over his chest. Ace was a few feet away, blowing up a life vest till he turned blue in the face.

"Thanks, man." I grinned. "Did you get the photos?"

When I told Kalina's family I intended to marry her, they were ecstatic. And I told them, not asked, as she didn't believe in asking for her father's permission. However, each and every one of them gave me their blessing.

Tommaso demanded that there be photos of the proposal, insisting that Kalina would want to look back on the moment. Ace and Stefano decided to honeymoon in Fiji and sailed over to witness this. Ace had taken a photography course at college when he moved to America and insisted on being the one to capture the moment.

"Ace had about fifty different angles, and we got the water in the background like you asked," Stefano confirmed, a smile on his face.

I'd noticed his smiling had become more regular since he and Ace came out with their relationship.

"Thanks, man," I said once again. "Now, do one before she gets back."

Stefano nodded before offering Ace his hand, causing the latter to drop his life vest for Kalina. The two walked away hand in hand, Ace carrying the camera as they left.

Kalina returned not long after, wearing a black strapless bikini, her hair thrown up into a messy bun. My eyes instantly zeroed in on her hand, which was missing the engagement ring. Red-hot anger burned in my chest.

She fucking took it off.

It wasn't until I ran my eyes over her figure did I see the ring on her necklace.

"I didn't want to risk losing it in the water." Kalina instantly knew why my smile had momentarily dropped.

"Are you ready?" I asked, offering her my hand.

Whilst she spent thirty minutes picking and choosing her swimwear, I had only spent five changing into my black trunks. So, now, I was standing shirtless on the beach.

"Nope." Kalina took my hand in hers, the size comparison almost laughable. "Let's go."

We walked together to the water, and it wasn't until it was pooling at our ankles did Kalina's steps falter.

"Take your time," I said, rubbing my thumb against the back of her hand.

Kalina moved forward but at a slower pace. She took deep breaths, eyes staring straight into mine with nothing but trust.

We moved forward and eventually got to a spot where the water reached her knees and above my ankles. That was when she slowed even more.

"Aidan . . ."

"You're alright," I told her, running a hand through her hair. "Just focus on me."

Doing as I said, Kalina took further steps into the water. I held her hand the entire time, and we didn't stop till the water was at her shoulders.

She was shaking the entire time, so I wrapped my arms around her. Placing a soft kiss on her forehead, I tilted her face up to look at me. "How are you feeling?"

"Weird." Kalina smiled a cautious smile. "But there's no nausea or feeling of impending doom."

I tightened my grip on her. "Do you want to try going underneath?"

Kalina wrapped herself around me, her legs at the bottom of my back and her arms around my neck. I waited until she gave me a response. Once she nodded, I took a few steps further into the water.

Once the water reached her chin, the two of us sank underneath. She clung tighter to me as our heads submerged under the water, but not once did she indicate that it was too much.

A few moments later, I stood back up to my full height, causing both of us to resurface. Droplets rolled down her face. Her hair was soaked, and a few wet strands fell from her bun. A bright smile lit up her face, causing one of my own to form.

"I'm not scared."

Despite all the water, I could see the tears rolling down her cheek. "Why are you crying?"

A choked laugh/sob left her lips. "Because I'm not scared."

When Kalina told me all the abuse she suffered, my heart shattered. Someone so strong could only come from abuse, but I had no idea just how bad she had it. I waited until she fell asleep before I tasked Ben and Alonzo to find every single person that had hurt her. I would have all their information ready, and I would just be waiting for her to ask me to kill them.

With just one word from her, I would give Kalina the world. If it was a world of gore and death and revenge, I would hand her the knife. If it was a world of love, candle-lit dinners, and children, I would give her all of it with the highest level of protection I can conjure. And if it was a world of business meetings, drug deals, and FBI investigations, I would have a copy of the keys and passwords to all areas of legal and illegal businesses available to her.

"You're not scared," I repeated, bringing her into a tight hug.

As the waves splashed against our bodies, all I could focus on was the girl in my arms. The way her body fit perfectly with my own, how her eyes had a hint of darkness in that light blue.

Kalina's eyes were the reason I wanted to do the proposal at the beach. The blue of her eyes matched the water, and the emerald of her ring matched mine.

As sad as it sounded, it was my reasoning.

Kalina looked back at the beach house, a soft smile on her face. "I know where to go for our two weeks away."

Instantly, I knew what she meant. "You want the beach house for our getaway?"

"This is our place."

EPILOGUE

Three years later

Everyone had scars of their own, demons that haunted them in their times of peace, and enemies that lingered and slithered around.

The privacy of the bathroom allowed me a moment to reflect. I traced the scar from my eye, which had faded into a soft pink line. The memories flashed before me. I could feel the chill of the blade as it destroyed what was once perfect skin. Hearing the cry rip from the back of my throat as red coated my face and trickled into my mouth. The way I felt my sight being ripped from me to a point where it would be years later when I would fully understand the damage that was inflicted.

The scar invaded what was once a perfect smoothness, leaving behind the physical imprint of a rough, horrid past.

This scar was the equivalent of my name on a tombstone, the rock being the face it was imprinted on.

People always say mental scars are far worse, playing away like a piano in an orchestra for years nonstop. It had taken years for me to realise that, eventually, the pianist would take a break.

A knock at the bathroom door caught my attention. Picking my glasses up from the marble sink, I placed them back on my face. Taking a final glance in the mirror, I looked over my reflection. My hair was thrown into a clip, a few strands falling down the front of my face. I was wearing a white off-the-shoulder skintight top with beige pants and a brown Gucci belt. My engagement and wedding rings glistened in the light of the room, bringing a small smile to my lips.

When I opened the door, my assistant, Michelle, waited with folders in hand. "Miss Rossi, you have a conference with Mr Karlson and Mrs Rogers at 11—"

"Cancel it. I have court in an hour," I ordered, taking a seat at the head table in the meeting room. "Where are we?"

The entirety of the room had their attention on me, all waiting for my input. Sally, the fashion coordinator, was the one to answer.

"We have narrowed it down to either runway or street fashion. The colour theme being blues, greens, and purples."

I nodded while contemplating the options. "Go with street fashion. Our aim is to up the department sales of streetwear."

"And the photoshoots are to take place in London and New York," said Julian, the shoot manager.

"Make that happen in early November and April. I want summer and winter fashion to be out early," I said, taking a glance at my watch. "Right. Finish up the final details and have them on my desk for tomorrow morning."

With that, I left the room and went to the elevator. Taking it forty-six floors down, I exited the building of Thread Industries and saw my driver waiting by the car.

"Martin, take me to my court hearing, please."

"Yes, Mrs Rossi. Your bag of clothes is in the back seat."

Aidan hired Martin to be my personal driver and bodyguard, the man who was trained in multiple martial art style and who happened to be ex-special forces. I have a beeper in my purse to press should there be an emergency, which would send a signal to Martin's phone. This was the compromise when I refused to allow him to follow me around constantly at work and while shopping.

In the last three years, I had climbed the corporate ladder at Thread Industries, from working as a sales assistant to director of sales and marketing. I had the ability to choose photoshoots: what was worn, who was wearing it, when and where they would take place. Then I also got to decide on what brands to buy for the coming year. I was also in charge of analysing data for the most buys and what would likely be profitable.

"All rise for Judge MacDonald."

The courtroom rose to their feet. I myself was standing on the left side of the courtroom, my lawyer beside me.

I took his advice and wore my favourite summer dress. It was teal-coloured fabric that had a tie-up at the side and reached the knees. I also added the necklace Aidan gifted me in Australia, adding to the ensemble of a respectable woman.

Aidan was standing in the front row directly behind me. Lorenzo was sitting on his lap. Both were wearing plain T-shirt and jeans, anxious smiles on their faces.

Tommaso and Tristan were next to each other, on their best behaviour after multiple threats of death from Mateo should they misbehave. Stefano and Ace were in the row behind, the latter visibly sweating and the former stoic as usual. Mateo, Antonio, and Christopher were wearing worry as they stood beside the happy couple.

We're all shitting it.

We were all invited to sit as the judge did so, and I was careful to not let my nerves show.

"After looking over the case files, I have come to a decision." Judge MacDonald spoke from his seat, gavel in hand. "Kalina Rossi, please stand."

I stood up on my white Louis Vuittons, hands behind my back so the judge would not see me fiddling with my fingers.

"Kalina Rossi, I can see your devotion to the child," the judge began. "I have never seen such a tight-knit family, and I have no intention of separating you."

HOLY SHIT!

"So, Kalina Rossi, I hereby grant you the official adoption and custody of Lorenzo Montessori."

The courtroom erupted into cheers as the judge slammed the gavel down, and I felt the relief in my chest. It was as if all my worries vanished in that moment.

"Mama!" Lorenzo was fighting Aidan's hold, his arms reaching out to me over the wooden barrier of the courtroom.

Gently, I grabbed his face, placing multiple kisses all over his cheeks. Aidan wrapped his spare arm around me, bringing us into one tight hug.

"I love you so much, baby," I told the little boy, his smile growing as he wrapped his arms around my neck.

"I love you too, Mama." Even though he was now seven, Lorenzo still insisted on calling me mama. He said it was keeping in touch with his Italian side, which I found adorable with his little British accent.

"Let's go celebrate," Aidan said, placing a kiss on the top of both of our heads.

Love was what scared me most in this world. Always at risk of being ruined and leaving you to suffer at the actions of someone else.

That used to be my mindset.

I always thought that love was a liability; that, one day, it would be the thing to destroy me. I never realised how wrong I was till I moved to America with my new family.

Daniel was wrong. Christopher was an amazing father, with a never-ending source of love for each and every one of his children.

Mateo showed me that being scared was alright, and all I had to do was ask for help.

Antonio was the mother I never had, fussing and nurturing all of his siblings despite their protests.

Stefano gave me alternative ways of expressing emotions. After all, his body was a canvas of unsaid words.

Tristan gave me the big brother that I lost. While he could never replace Daniel, he was exactly what I needed. I could trust him with my life and my secrets, and that was everything I needed when I met him.

Tommaso showed me how to have fun again. After years of fear and uncertainty, I managed to let loose and enjoy myself without the stress and anxiety that came with the responsibility my previous life held.

Ace held me together when I was falling apart and was always there for me when I needed him.

Lorenzo made me the woman I was today. He made me the mother I always needed. Without doing anything, he showed me how fucked up my mother was and motivated me to give him the best childhood I could muster.

And Aidan . . . he put the broken pieces of me back together. He gave me the encouragement that I needed to start mending what others broke. While everyone else had a contribution, Aidan was the one that inspired me to use what others gifted me.

Love used to terrify me because it made me vulnerable to others. But now I knew that love wasn't what made you vulnerable.

Love made you stronger and gave you a purpose.

And I would never let go of it again.

- The End -

AUTHOR'S NOTE

Thank you so much for reading Life In The Underworld! I'd love to hear your thoughts. Please leave a review on Amazon or Goodreads!

Grab the free bonus chapters for the book at savannaho.awesomeauthors.org!

Savannah O.

If you enjoyed this book, here are samples of other stories you might enjoy!

COLECIA ANN
THE Sergeant AND THE Billionaire
BETWEEN LOVE AND DUTY . . .

CHAPTER ONE

My hands do this weird thing when I'm nervous, and it sometimes takes a while for me to realize I'm doing it. Those who know me well can tell that I'm freaking out when my right hand starts to squeeze the four fingers of my left hand. I hate that I have this obvious tell. A true warrior wouldn't give anything away about herself. But here I am, sitting rigidly in this uncomfortable chair. My right hand squeezes my left fingers as my heart hammers against my rib cage, almost as if it's trying to break free from the confines of my chest cavity. I'm beyond nervous, but I should've seen this day coming.

When the assignment came, I was the only one in our squad of four who wasn't briefed. I was indifferent to it all in that very moment, just as how I've been indifferent to everything and everyone else around me for the past year. So here I am, seated in a brightly lit room that resembles a civilian courthouse. I hide the sneer on my face as I realize that I'm about to be dismissed in a similar manner as any regular, normal soldier. I want to convince myself that this so-called hearing makes sense; that in order for the powers-that-be to truly hide what it is that I've been doing all these years, I need to be dismissed in accordance with the law—it's either this, or death. Honestly, I'd rather face a firing squad.

The flipping of pages followed by someone clearing his throat pulls me from the dark, damp place in my mind that I've trapped myself in. I try to maintain eye contact at all costs, but I'm failing miserably as I sit here and wonder whether life as I know it is about to go up in flames.

The Star-Spangled Banner hanging over the heads of the four men before me suddenly catches my attention. How many lives have I taken in the name of that flag? How many fragile states did I help bring down for the sake of freedom? This is it for me. Now that it's over, was all of it worth it?

I turn my attention back to the four men before me to pull my mind away from those thoughts. None of their faces or names look or sound familiar. I want to chuckle at the setup, but that would be seen as too disrespectful. They sure as hell didn't recruit me, didn't train me, and didn't have my back in the field, but somehow, they get to decide my fate. I want to dig into them. I want to swear, shout—anything to have them not look at me like I'm some kind of broken warrior, yet the only thing I can do is play a guessing game in my head. It's not as funny, but it's the only entertainment I have.

In the middle sits the chair of whatever the hell this committee is called. He's a general, and by the looks of him, I can tell he definitely has a trophy wife. His hair and nails are too properly groomed for him not to have someone at home who manages his personal grooming appointments. When he addressed me earlier, I picked up a Southern drawl, which tells me he's from some part of Texas.

General Texas has two daughters—I can bet my semi-damaged liver on that. The elder is definitely in university, Texas A&M to be exact. It was probably where General Texas met his wife, so his first-born decided to follow in her parents' footsteps. And what's her major?

It has to be sociology. Kids from families like General Texas' never take up anything too heavy at the university level because they're just a little bit dumb, but that doesn't mean they aren't driven. And that brings me to the other daughter. Her older sister got all the attention, the showers of love and praises from both parents, so she has never felt if her parents truly loved her.

Daughter number two started smoking cigarettes in high school and used to bum them off the seniors who took a liking to her because of her massive tits. When she realized that she could get the right amount of attention if she flashed a smile here and a bit of her midriff there, a whole new world opened up to her. And that's why she lives in the Bay Area, where she works as a stripper. She's definitely good at it. The gymnastics she did as a kid seems to have come in handy.

What am I even thinking about? I sigh softly.

I've been in Washington for two days now, kicking myself for taking this dismissal so easily, furious with my decision to not put up a fight for the only life I've ever known. That stupid game doesn't do enough to pull me away from reality. What am I supposed to do once I return to being a civilian? Being normal sounds dreadful enough. I knew that normalcy wasn't my thing when I first arrived at the base in the early days. I was no longer Samantha Wellington, an heiress from the Upper East Side.

I turned myself into a soldier to fight for my country, and I got deeper into it. When I moved away from the general military life and got into the bigger shit, I bore zero resemblance to the pampered girl I used to be. I became a woman who knew how to fight her own battles, a woman who would slit a man's throat without batting an eyelid.

"Sergeant Wellington."

I look at General Texas as he utters my name, and I almost open my mouth to say that I'm only a sergeant on paper. I'm ready to tell him that the title was only given to me in the event that someone in the military began to dig a hole they shouldn't have. Sergeant Samantha Wellington exists just in case my dossier ends up in the hands of those without the proper clearance.

"Yes, sir." I acknowledge him nonchalantly.

I already know what he's going to say, but that doesn't mean I still won't be crushed by the committee's decision.

"After an extensive review of your case, we've determined that it would be best for you to be discharged. This decision doesn't take away from the work you've . . ."

A chill immediately spreads around the room. I shiver uncontrollably as General Texas explains the terms of my discharge. I knew this was going to happen. I'd tried my damnedest to prepare myself for when I heard those words. But it's one thing to imagine it and a completely other thing to actually hear it in reality. I was too preoccupied with steeling myself for what would be the worst news I'll ever receive to make plans for my future sans the military.

"With a general discharge under honorable conditions, there is always the option to reenlist—"

"Reenlist?" My interjection doesn't go over well with them, but I couldn't care less right now. "Somehow that doesn't sound comforting." I glance at the committee menacingly. I know that my outburst is probably making things worse for me, but what other options do I have?

My mind starts pulling memories from random years, of those hardships I had to face. As if being a woman wasn't hard enough, I had to endure ridicule simply because I was a woman trying to make my way in a big man's world. I had to be cautious of the people who were to be my brothers. I had to stand and listen to men above my station make comments about my body, without being able to say jack shit to defend myself. I remember being called a half-breed for the first six weeks of training, and there was not a single damn thing I could do about it.

After going through all of that, I'm being discharged with nothing to show for all that I've done.

A scoff leaves my lips as I sink even lower in my seat. My rigid posture slowly vanishes along with my manners.

"In the event that you do decide to reenlist, we feel it is prudent for you to receive frequent counseling."

I shake my head in disagreement. Shrinks have never been my thing. But then, if I do become desperate enough to reenlist . . .

"Will I at least get to choose my own therapist?"

"I'm afraid not."

I slightly tug at the end of my skirt, trying to suppress the anger brimming beneath my skin.

"You're a fine warrior. You're young, and you are good at what you do. Everyone in this room went through an ordeal similar to yours. We just want you to take some time so you can handle all of this."

My eyes brim with angry tears as I listen to General Texas' last remarks: "Reenlistment gives you the option to reclaim your place within the military, but should you decide not to return, just know that you've served your country well, and the United States of America thanks you for your service."

I watch as dossiers close, and the last bit of water is drained from the cups before the committee members stand. I don't know how I did it, but I managed to remove myself from the chair and gave a salute to my superiors. I stood in that position long after they'd left the room.

The sudden realization that it would be my last salute as a sergeant is too much for me. Hot, heavy tears start rolling down my cheeks. My feet finally give out, and I fall to my knees as I mourn my loss—a loss that comes a year after losing someone close to me. And now it seems that my life is filled with nothing but loss and death.

I don't know how I managed to pick myself up off the floor. I just know I would be too embarrassed to have anyone see me in such a state.

I muster up all the courage. My movements are sluggish and clumsy as I gather my small belongings from the base, my vision still clouded by tears. A mixture of disappointment and pain courses through my veins as it sinks in that I am going home.

For any soldier, the thought of home brings smiles to their faces and a twinkle to their eyes. I should be feeling the same, but under the circumstances, I only feel as if I've failed.

***

On the flight back home, General Texas' words played over and over in my head. I was tired but restless, angry at the situation I've found myself in. This isn't how I imagined my return home.

Home hasn't been the same since my mother died. Heck, I've really never been the same since then. If I think about all the choices I've made since senior high school, some would even say that that was when I began to do things quite unexpected of me. If I were to be honest with myself, I guess being discharged has shown me that I don't have the capacity to handle death well. It's a bit ironic, the more I think about it. Or maybe it's just karma. With so much blood on my hands, I guess my discharge is well-deserved.

With a heavy sigh, I grab my bag from the carousel and make a beeline for the exit. My pace slows when I realize that there are no time constraints. No one is expecting me to be on time, and I'm not racing into a life-and-death matter though in LaGuardia people are always rushing. The city I was born and raised in is one that never sleeps.

How will I ever adjust?

"Sammy girl!"

I turn quickly. Standing a few feet away is the man who's been driving me around this godforsaken city since I was young. For the first time in three days, I've managed to crack a smile. Raji waves excitedly at me, and I chuckle at the sight of him. His thick dark hair hangs just above his shoulders, and as I get closer to him, I can see some streaks of gray in it. Despite this, he still looks as fit as a fiddle. It doesn't take long for me to notice that he's fitted with his sidearm. I don't think he's ever used that thing, and I wonder if it's even real.

"Raji!"

I fight the tears as we embrace. I breathe in, and my body relaxes.

Raji has been with me throughout the many stages of my life. He's more than my driver, more than my bodyguard—not that I need one. He's like a second father, like an uncle that I've never had.

"Oh, Samantha, I've missed you." His voice cracks.

I roll my eyes dramatically, but my smile remains even when he takes my bag.

"But why didn't you come in your uniform?" His thick eyebrows furrow as he notices my attire.

"I don't need it anymore." I loop my arm with his, dragging him toward the automatic doors. “I missed you too, Raji. Who else would be willing to drive me around Manhattan at 2:00 in the morning?”

He chuckles lightly at my question but doesn’t give a response.

I sigh softly. I manage to distract him from his original line of questioning. I wind the window all the way up as I get comfortable in the luxury sedan. The car pulls away smoothly from the airport, and I close my eyes, trying to relax. I need to get used to the fact that no one will be shooting bullets at my moving vehicle. I take a deep breath, forcing myself into believing that being home will be good for me.

“Should I head straight home?”

Home—there’s that word again. At this point, I wouldn’t classify that penthouse overlooking the Upper East Side as my home. My home is wherever my assignment is, whether that be in the Middle East or some mansion of a crazed dictator. The more dangerous it is, the more comfortable and welcome I feel. Home is where I get to pretend to be someone I’m not. It’s a place where I show up when needed and disappear from once the mission is complete. It’s a place of certainty and reward, a place where nothing else matters but the mission.

Damn, I miss home already.

"Uh, could you take me to Wellington Consolidated, please?"

Raji raises an eyebrow at me but refrains from saying anything. I could only imagine the look on my father's face when I show up out of the blue.

MELISSA BENDER
LIES,
BETRAYAL
&
LOVE

Chapter 1

Sage

I groaned as I tried to cover my eyes, shielding the burning sunlight that came into the bedroom. I didn't want to get up. I felt like utter hell. My pounding head didn't make me feel any better either. I yawned as I grabbed a pillow and rolled over, covering my head with it, trying to pass back out.

The sleep I was trying to get back into was short-lived when I heard a loud knock on the door.

"Sage, it's almost two in the afternoon. Please tell me you're up."

I yawned, groaning with annoyance. "I'm up, Mum," I said back to her. "Just wait."

My feet hit the wooden flooring, and I rubbed my eyes, looking around for my underwear. I grabbed what I could and slid on some sweats and a shirt. Walking past a mirror, I glanced at myself. My hair was nothing short of a hairy scarecrow. I didn't look that hung over though, but I knew Mum would be able to tell I had a late one. Hell, it was more than late.

"Sage!" she called out again, her voice hurting my head more than I liked. She was enjoying this. I could tell.

I opened the door of the guesthouse, which was now my living space while I was home from school. "I'm up." I yawned, covering my mouth yet again.

Mum gave me a disapproving look as she made her way in. "Late night? What time did you get in?" she asked, sitting on the large sofa.

Obviously, she wasn't going to be making me breakfast or coffee anytime soon.

"Around four, I think it was." I sat across from her, lying sideways and resting my head on the fluffy cushions.

She shook her head. "Your father won't be happy if he finds out. I told him you got home around eleven. Stick to that story please."

Mum was more laid back than Dad. To him, I was his innocent little girl. I was innocent most of the time, but there were days where I liked to go and have some fun.

I sighed. "Cassie was meant to pick me up, but I didn't see her, and my phone died. I'm sorry."

"How did you get home?" she asked, eyeing me cautiously.

"A taxi," I said.

It was the truth.

She nodded, straightening the stack of books on my coffee table. "Your sister will be married in a couple of months. Please tell me you're going to make it."

"I'm the maid of honor. Of course, I'm going to make it." I laughed. "She needs to chill out and stop stressing."

"You know what your sister is like. Everything needs to be perfect for her day." She laughed, sitting back and smiling. Her wrinkles were showing more—laughter lines as she called them. "How's school been? Any boys you like?"

I blushed, fighting the smile. "Good and nope. No boys."

She hated when I gave her short replies like that. Mum liked to know what was going on and how I was doing, especially when it came to my love life.

"Sage," she said again, this time, a playfulness in her voice. "Why are you smiling?"

If only she knew why I was smiling. I wasn't dating anyone, nor did I want to. I was smiling about last night or this morning. Heck, I couldn't remember. All I remembered was shagging in a club and getting carpet burn on my ass and knees.

The guy was definitely a hottie. At least, I thought he was. My mind was still a little blurry. I went to bed deliciously sore and woke up the same. My lower half was aching. I just couldn't believe we had done that in a club when anyone could have walked in. I had no idea who he was, and it didn't bother me. I never had one-night stands or went to clubs, but I was glad I did.

It was definitely a great end to a bad day.

I realized Mum was still waiting for my answer. "There was a guy, but we didn't work out, so we're just friends." It didn't work out because he was gay.

"Oh, well. I'm sorry to hear that," she said softly.

"It's fine. He is actually coming to the wedding. He's my date." I smiled.

She looked very confused. "I'm sorry. What? You dated, and now he's your date?"

"He's gay. We're more brothers and sisters than anything."

"Gay? You dated a gay man?" she asked, obviously amused by this.

I shook my head. "No. He didn't tell me he was at the time. Then he did, and now we're just close friends."

"Okay. Well, I need to head back to your father. Please stay out of trouble. If you need anything, just let us know, okay?" she asked, standing and walking over to me, placing a kiss against my cheek.

"Thanks, Mum." I got up behind her and locked the door when she left.

I desperately needed a shower. I went into the bathroom and stripped off. As I went to step into the shower, I noticed it: the bruises and marks over my body. I turned around and gasped. There were teeth marks on my ass. God, he did bite hard. I had small bruises on my hips from his fingers and even love bites over my breasts. Damn, this guy went to town with marking my body all over.

As I washed, I wondered if I left any marks on him or if he was thinking about what happened as much as I was. Probably not. It was just a one-night stand. I was sure he had plenty.

He did offer to pay for my ride home after we had finished, and I realized my sister had already left. It was a little weird when we fixed ourselves up. He was very quiet once we both finished, and I felt completely embarrassed that I had done all that to him.

I mean sucking him off and swallowing was something I would only do in a serious relationship and not for a guy in a club. Then when he asked me to bend over so he could eat me from behind, God, I had almost died of embarrassment.

Until his tongue hit me, then I lost it.

When I stepped out of the shower, I went to my room and slid into some silk summer pajamas, climbing back into bed and wanting to sleep the day away.

My thoughts slowly drifted back to the man who touched me last night.

~

Oliver

I stood in the shower, arms out in front of me as I kept my head down, spitting out saliva as guilt consumed my whole body. I couldn't think straight. My head was filled with flashbacks of what happened at the club. The way she felt and her mouth on mine. Remembering how she sounded when she came started to stir my insides enough for my cock to grow.

Then just like that, my hard cock was gone with a single thought. I cheated on my wife.

I cheated on her with some random girl, and I never stopped it. I let it go on even though I knew it was wrong at the time. I felt sick. I wanted to throw up at the thought of what I had done. I went out and let a gorgeous woman suck me off and then I fucked her.

My heart was pounding. My tears were too hard to stop as they ran down from my eyes, mixing in with the water. It was salty, and I sniffled hard, running my hands over my face, wiping them. I had no idea what the fuck I was going to do. Guilt was eating away at me.

"Oliver." I heard Amy call out.

Fuck. She couldn't come in here. She'd know instantly. Just one look at my guilt-ridden face and she'd know I cheated on her. I hated myself more than anything right now.

"Just a minute," I yelled out to her. I ran my hands through my wet hair and took in a deep breath, trying to calm my nerves down.

"Hurry. We need to talk," she called back.

I could tell by her tone that she was annoyed.

I sighed and turned the water off. I dried off quickly, noticing in the mirror that my back had red fingernail marks scratched down it. Even my ass had two bruises from her heels digging in. There was no explaining those without some ridiculous lie about falling into a rose bush naked.

I couldn't get her eyes out of my mind, her smile…I shook my head. I needed to stop thinking about her.

What I needed to do was to tell Amy, but I didn't even know how to do that.

How would I begin to tell my wife that I sunk my dick inside another woman? More than once.

Once was a mistake. Three times wasn't. Three fucking times I blew in her, not counting the blow job she gave me. God, those lips. Fucking hell.

I splashed some cold water over my face to cool myself, pulled on a shirt, and then I opened the door. I walked out. My eyes glassed over, which hopefully, she would assume was mostly from being so hung over.

Amy gave me a smile, and I felt sick.

"What's up?"

"You were out late last night? Where did you go?" she asked, her eyes on mine.

I hadn't spoken to her all day. I slept in the spare room to avoid her. Yeah, I was a fucking coward.

"Just around, few different bars and clubs." I shrugged, trying to keep my voice normal.

She just looked at me. "You didn't come to bed either. Why?"

Fuck. "I, uh, didn't want to wake you up. You say I snore when I drink, and I'd had a few."

"Okay. Well, Cassie called. Something about a lunch today that I knew nothing about?" She crossed her arms. "You know I don't like to be put on the spot, Oliver. You should have asked if I minded before you go making promises to people. I don't know her, and you're lucky you were asleep. I used that as an excuse to say no."

I frowned. Even though I was completely in the wrong, I was pissed. "You what? No. I asked Tony over for lunch, which will now be dinner."

I walked away, but I heard the low hiss of a "Fuck you, asshole" being spat at me.

I spun around and shook my head. It was moments like this when I didn't regret fucking someone else. It was easy for me to think, well, she deserved it. I felt like utter shit over it, but now I didn't know if I did entirely regret it.

"What did you just say?" I asked her, standing closer to her now. "You need to show me a little more respect, Amy. The things I do for you around here."

"Oh, here we go. Blah, Blah. I put a roof over your head. I provide the food and all the nice things you have." She was mocking me; talking like me in a sarcastic, childish voice; and throwing everything I did for her in my face. "I don't give a fuck if you're the only one working, Oliver. I do a lot around here. Who cooks the food you eat? Washes all your clothing? Me. I do it all, so don't start your rant about me being ungrateful. I was working until—"

I cut her off sharply. "No. You were working until you quit your job without talking to me about it first. Your excuse was that work and all the baby talk had you too stressed to focus on your job. We meant to focus on children, but it's not happening. Don't think I don't know about you spending your days shopping with friends. You don't do it all. I cook and clean as well, so don't you dare throw that at me."

"Fuck you, Oliver. Get out!" She snapped angrily.

"You're acting like a spoilt child," I growled, feeling my blood rising at the anger I felt, mostly for myself, but she was making it so much easier to be mad at her right now.

Amy scoffed. "Whatever."

A smile grew over my lips. I was mad but somehow amused by her tantrum. "Well, I guess you're right. I won't have kids when you speak to me like shit. You call Cassie and Tony back and ask them over for dinner."

"No. I don't want them here! Why can't you understand it! You're not the one who doesn't get pregnant each month. You have no idea what it feels like!" She gave my chest a hard push, and I didn't budge.

I was really getting sick of her pushing, shoving, and slapping me.

"I'll be sleeping in the spare room. Good thing I'm used to the no sex around here because I'd be fucked if I'm going to make an effort for it. Not that I turn you on or anything because you told me it doesn't do anything for you." I shook my head angrily at her. "I mean it, Amy. The baby is off the table, and for your information, I do know what it feels like because I'm the one who can't get my wife pregnant. That goes through my head each fucking month."

She had really pissed me off. I walked out and slammed the bedroom door shut.

I called up Tony and invited them over, knowing she wouldn't do it. He sounded as bad as I felt on the phone. His fiancé was at her parent's place, something about her younger sister visiting and she needed to talk wedding stuff. I laid down on the bed in the spare room and stared at the door. I should go and work things out. Hell, calling me a fucking asshole was the least she would call me when she knew what really happened last night.

Amy never came out when Tony came over for dinner. He and I sat on the back deck with a couple of beers and steaks. I wanted to tell him what I had done last night, just to get it off my chest.

But I couldn't. Instead, I just sat there and thought about her.

If you enjoyed this sample, check out Lies, Betrayal, and Love on Amazon

ABOUT THE AUTHOR

I've always loved reading about different experiences of people, good or bad, because it is what shapes us into who we are. Exploring the perspectives of others is a way of gaining a deeper understanding of society. Everyone has their own story.

www.ingramcontent.com/pod-product-compliance
Lightning Source LLC
LaVergne TN
LVHW041056080826
845145LV00007B/1590

* 9 7 8 1 6 4 4 3 4 4 1 9 4 *